Sweet Burden

of

Crossing

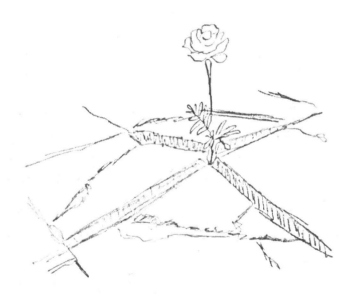

Kate Towle

This book was printed in the United States of America.
Copyright © 2020 Kate Towle
ISBN: 9798564456159
Imprint: Independently published

To my mother Alma Denyse Hughes
For the sweet burdens you have carried in the name of love

Rosemarie,

Let's keep watch for the
miracles that rise through
life's cracks — with every
heart lesson, a gift springs
forth!
                Kate Fowle

"In a country still separated by the stubborn barrier of race, it is inspiring to read a realistic story about two women who take up the challenge of navigating a friendship across the color line. A brave work that makes the case for racial healing, one friendship at a time."

> **--Jonathan Odell**, author of *Miss Hazel and the Rosa Parks League* (Maiden Lane Press) and *The Healing* (Nan A. Talese, First Edition)

"Each page of Kate Towle's story cleverly reveals another reality check on racial trauma and how none of us are immune to the ugly scars inflicted by generations of subtle or overt acts of white supremacy."

> **--Rose McGee**, author of *Story Circle Stories, Kumbayah: The Juneteenth Story* and creator of Sweet Potato Comfort Pie®

"Kate Towle has written a book about struggle, race, and ultimately, about hope. This novel models what can be done with story: how we can communicate with each other across borders and differences by telling a tale. She weaves together the lives of two young women, one white, one Black, into an important,portrayal of what it takes to truly confront our prejudices and become an activist for racial justice. By presenting Chris as a complex character who makes mistakes and keeps on working to change and understand, as well as wrestle with her own personal tragedy, Towle has given us a work of nuance and force. She also gives us, her readers, encouragement, in our own journeys toward activism and advocacy in eliminating white supremacy in all its guises.

> **--Julie Landsman**, author of *A White Teacher Talks About Race* and *Growing Up White*

"The race relations in our country today are more volatile than ever. As a Black man who has experienced the injustice in the criminal system firsthand, the trial scene in this book was especially personal for me. I understood. With the help of people who stand up and share their stories, we have hope of moving forward for a better future."

> **--Dorsey Howard,**
> author of *One Way, No Left Turn*

"Author and community activist Kate Towle takes us on an inspiring journey across the racial divide and into a world where healing is possible and inclusiveness, harmony and love can take root and flourish. A soulful exploration into the timely question of what continues to separate America into 'us' and 'them.'"

> **--Mark Ristau**, author of the award-winning novel,
> *A Hero Dreams*

"This novel provides important insights into the internal and interpersonal dialogues that many aspiring white allies have with themselves and with others. It will prompt reflection for its readers who are white and of color at a time in our nation's history when such introspection and dialogue are needed as much as ever in recent decades. Such reflection is crucial to counter persistent systemic racism that manifests itself in both the micro- and macro-aggressions people of color and indigenous people encounter on a daily basis that too many whites exercise our privilege to ignore."

> **--Paul Spies, PhD**, Professor, School of Urban Education, Metropolitan State University, St. Paul, MN

"At this time, when our nation and much of the world are struggling with and suffering from fear, tribalism and recurring prejudice, the novel *Sweet Burden of Crossing* makes these challenges personal and inspires us to believe individuals can address them. Kate Towle weaves reality and fiction into an engaging story of generational friendship, love and suffering, converted into wise living experiences. The story is emotionally engaging and teaches vital lessons we all can learn and apply within our area of influence."

--Hector E. Garcia, author of *Clash or Complement of Cultures: Peace and Productivity in the New Global Reality*

"I love the richness of the language in this book. I feel like I "know" each character as if I could walk in a room and there they are. An exquisite navigation of the soul with race, father-loss and inherited DNA for connecting human to human."

--Rebecca Janke, Montessori Adjunct Professor, University of Wisconsin River Falls

"Sweet Burden of Crossing is a deep dive into a friendship colored by race, perceptions, misconceptions and cultural precepts. Towle takes us on a journey through the rapids Chris and Rikki must navigate, the risks they must take to cross over the boundaries that the color of one's skin manifested in 1980's America and are still true today."

--- Fay Connors, President and Co-Founder of Twin Cities Prison Ministry

"The book is so deep and rare, with the power to change our society. There's a deep compassion and caring with the book, a spirit of allowing another person's history to impact yours."

--Katie Sample, Among the first African American Social Workers, Minneapolis Public Schools

"I started out pretty much from the beginning with a lump in my throat and it stayed for the entirety of the text. The book is as times emotionally raw and intense and I sometimes had to stop reading and simply process. Which is a good thing. This book stays with the reader. Particularly striking are the themes of justice and trust and reconciliation. I am quite taken by the simple portrayal of the author's very profound faith. I don't personally experience that kind of faith and I am always fascinated when I see others carry it so elegantly."

--Gwekidjiwan (Jeanne Boutang-Croud),
Anishinaabe Historical Researcher and Geneologist

"Kate Towle takes the reader on a journey of cultural interpretation and discovery of both personal and family histories. The story of friendship in the White and Black cultures finds intersections and points of distinctions. The journey to understand another's culture is illuminated through the process of growing self-awareness in the context of what is done, what has been told and what story is believed. Discerning each character's "truth" is revealed in the twists & turns of seemingly fateful revelations and in the celebration of friendship."

--Laurie Fitz, am950 Connections Radio Show Host

"A story that will ignite much-needed conversation and discussion on bridging the divide of race, especially in a classroom setting. This story is a long journey to justice and understanding for two families and the courtroom drama is a compelling way to expose the tremendous cost of racism to families of color."

--Dee Sweeney, Mother, active community member, and career-long public defender with extensive trial experience

"This book touched my heart in a way that I never expected. It is so deeply true. I recommend it highly."

--Pam Winthrop-Lauer, Spiritual Director and Compassionate Communications Coach

"Have you ever been with a friend as they told you a story from their past? Maybe it was on a walk or over a cup of coffee. As your friend told you the events that occurred, you could see they were beginning to understand the deeper meaning behind their experience. As as you listened, you too began to catch a glimpse of the deeper truths their experience was now going to teach you.

That's how I felt reading Kate Towle's book, *Sweet Burden of Crossing*. The calm and insightful storytelling of an interracial friendship between two young women held me completely. The two main characters, Chris and Rikki, grew and developed both individually and as friends in a patient and uncontrived manner. A book hits its mark when it leads me to reflect not only on the actions and decisions of the main characters, but on my actions and life decisions as well. The book has a kindness and truth in it that's never heard and that engages you right in the present moment."

> **--Trish Beckett**, Curriculum Developer, Peace Literacy National Committee

"*Sweet Burden of Crossing* brought me back to another place and time, and that is exactly what I want from a novel. I savored memories of my first years in college and making new and close friends from casual encounters. It was pleasant to remember those days while reading about Chris and Rikki. "Sweet Burden" brought home to me the feeling of love, devotion, confusion and to some extent bewilderment in my early married life."

> **--Frank Beiser**, retiree

"Kate Towle's book *Sweet Burden of Crossing* chronicles interracial friendship in a time and place when this was less common than it is today. Although we now live with much greater intersectionality—at least in urban areas—the complexity of developing deep interracial friendships remains a challenge for many.

"Why make the effort?" asks the character Chris, the protagonist of the novel. Readers may wonder the same as they go through the ups and downs of a tumultuous college friendship. But for all the turmoil these young women experience, their continued engagement allows them to grow in trust and understanding of each other, of themselves, and of the world around them.

"The journey took patience, commitment, an open heart, and a willingness to sit with the discomfort of not-understanding and not-being-understood. Not everyone will be able to bridge the divide caused by centuries of trauma, but for these two women, the reward is a lifetime of expanded understanding and a friendship that lasts through the ages."

> **--Leslie Mackenzie**, Leader of a Transition Movement for environmental sustainability

"This story honors truth; puts recognition of truth and acting upon truth foremost. It is a very contemporary story, a story needed in our time. This story encouraged more talk and thought than most I have read. It's the privilege of a writer to create a story that speaks to many people because it shares the writer's humanity and emphasizes shared humanity. This author has done both."

> **--Bill Smith,** Nuclear Engineer and Soap Maker

Prologue

Minneapolis is burning, and it started just blocks from our children's high school. Following my father's legacy as a community leader in the 60's, I've joined many marches with my children. The 2014 protest to honor Michael Brown's death in Ferguson took place right in front of the Precinct 3 police station that went down this week in bright red flames, torched by anarchists, with no police presence.

"What's happening?" say my white friends. "Where are the police?" Little do they know how that would exacerbate the crisis at hand, the police being the symbol of brutality for Black and Brown people.

The stores being vandalized are where I shop. The day before George Floyd was suffocated by a police officer's fit of rage, with three other officers standing idly by, I was admiring my Beloved Community for the ways we've lifted each other up through the COVID-19 crisis, with food drives, fundraisers, solidarity, brightly-colored murals and utility boxes. Our anchor restaurant, Gandhi Mahal—a generous donor to radio programs that raise the voices of Dakota people on whose land we stand— has burned to the ground. So has our Walgreens, just down the street and a mile from our home.

I haven't shaken like this since I was rushed to the hospital when my children were small—a threshold in my life that surfaced my father's deep imprint in me. This is yet another sacred moment in time. I feel the weight of my father's work viscerally. I want to tell him what I'm learning—how we *all* carry the toxins in our bodies from a culture that gives every advantage to white people. How as white *first responders* to the work—because we've had trauma of our own—we'll take hits from every direction. How relieving our friends of color from their fatigue, without expecting gratitude, is a necessary form of reparation.

1

Today, I came home to a note on the door that said, *Your neighbors are sick of riots and your SJW (social justice warrior) bullshit. Signs down or we burn you in your sleep! You MF want a war you will get one.* They're referring to the Black Lives Matter sign in my lawn.

When I told my neighbors about the sign, they thought I made it up. They wanted PROOF. The only sympathetic neighbor called early the next morning and roused me out of bed. "Groups of white young men are stalking our neighborhoods…getting ahead of the police…they have backpacks with accelerants and they're systematically setting fire to properties!" she said, out-of-breath. She coached me to stay up late and watch videos of a young Black activist, a self-described "Blacktivist," who was staying up late to risk taping the white arsonists. "This is how we can help," she said. "We keep bringing attention to these underground operations." We did just that, but few of our white friends believed us until it was reported in the media.

We'd each been in close touch with our friends of color who were training one another to find—and stop—the perpetrators of violence. In fact, the young President of the NAACP, Leslie Redmond, caught two young men in action and got the Police Chief to join her on her rounds. If anyone tells us they don't believe us, we have a pact to ask them what they've heard from their Black friends. When we say that, most of our white friends tell us they haven't known how to nurture relationships with people of color. When I call my most beloved Black friend of all, she reminds me that *it's gonna get done, because we have good hearts, and we can't help but serve where we are needed.* Here's our story—and why I will always do my all to live by her words.

2

Part One: Abbott Hospital, Minneapolis, 2004

● *Looking at Life from Room 322*

The only thing I can remember before the ambulance came to get me is my husband Chuck calling 911 from our bedroom, then handing me Dad's autograph card from my dresser. I once told him it's the one thing I'd want if there was ever an emergency. After sudden and increased swelling in my face, legs and feet this morning, I finally collapsed. Now, after an interminable wait in the ER, they moved me up to this room. Chuck, coming off the flu, is taking our kids over to friends to relieve our kind neighbors from watching them. He said he'd be right back. I'm smack in the middle of my deepest fear with no clue yet of what's wrong except that I overheard the doctors say *"serious"* to Chuck. I'm all alone, on an IV for fluids, and I don't know what else is being pumped into me. So much for my fear of needles and tendency to faint at the sight of blood. Dear God. Am I fighting for my life here?

Pain is rippling through my body. I can't stop shaking. I'm thirsty and afraid. I repeat the word "healing" over and over in my mind, because it's what I need to do. I also want to talk with someone—anyone—so I press the call button.

With my other hand, I clutch the card my father wrote for me a few short months before he was killed. He and I had been sorting through his box of keepsakes from the U.S. Navy's aircraft carrier 41 together when he found photos of himself standing before stunning vistas in Europe. He also pulled out a stack of cards with his name centered on them: Ryan Fitzgerald.

"What are those for, Daddy?" I'd asked.

"When we were graduating from high school, we wrote each other a message on the back so our friends would have something to remember us by." Then, Dad made one for me. He pulled his fountain pen out of his shirt pocket, eased himself

3

against the back of the couch, and in his finest script—nearly calligraphy in its smooth, pleasing loops—he wrote, "To my beloved baby, who has the wisdom of Solomon."

In the Bible's Song of Solomon, it is written that "wisdom is more precious than jewels, and nothing you desire can compare with her." What did my father see in me that I didn't see? I'd give anything to know that now, but it's one of my big questions to him that will be left a mystery.

As I'm holding the laminated card for dear life—my eyes fixed on my father's beautiful cursive writing—in walks the spitting image of my dad's dear friend, Clarence. I understand then that I've crossed some type of threshold. With Clarence's unique gift of showing up right where he's needed, it seems natural he'd visit me now—except Clarence died a few months ago. A respected Black leader in Michigan City, Indiana, Clarence Sage worked side by side with my father to start a community center to lift families out of poverty in the early days of the Civil Rights Movement when it was a rare and daring act for men to work together across racial lines by choice. I grew up in Michigan City's "twin," LaPorte, and the Community Center still serves both cities.

"Are you my nurse?" I ask him, wondering if Clarence has been reincarnated, or if I've crossed to the other side. My pain assures me I'm still here. Besides, this man is younger, a bit taller —and sure enough, he's wearing a nurse's uniform. The resemblance to Clarence is so strong it brings tears to my eyes.

"I sure am! My name is Marcus," he tells me. "You're Christine, right?"

I nod. "You can call me Chris." He's already scored by knowing my name. An earlier nurse referred to me as Room 322 right outside the door.

He sees me wipe my eyes, then squint at him. "You OK? I'm used to people being surprised when they see me come in the room, but I didn't mean to scare you. Guess I'm not your typical nurse. Now, what can I do for you?"

"Sorry, you look like someone I know…someone I knew." I struggle to catch my breath. "I really feel horrible." I can't stop trembling, one for the cold—and two for the odd feeling I have that Clarence's spirit is with us in this room.

"You might have to tell me more about who I look like. First, let's see if we can make you a little more comfortable." Unlike Clarence, he's fast on his feet, which are supported by white orthopedic, leather clogs. By the time I've taken a breath, he's already closed my blinds slightly for the evening, tucked my blanket around me for warmth and given me a sip of water. "I'm glad you buzzed me. It's time to check your temp and blood pressure anyway." He secures the cuff around my right arm, listens quietly, then gives me the numbers, *"125 over 88."*

"What does that mean?" I ask him.

"It's much better. A bit higher than we want. The doctor's coming in soon to talk with you. Your potassium is low, which explains why your heartbeat's somewhat erratic. Your heart's strong, but we want a good rhythm." He then takes my temp, which is 101 and not exactly perfect either.

He sees I'm clutching Dad's card. "If that's trash, I'll toss it for ya."

"It's not trash. It's important—a keepsake. Thanks, though."

"My, it's a tiny little thing. One of us might accidently throw it away. Where's a place we can keep it so it doesn't get lost?" Marcus's looks, his deep voice and warm expression make me feel more alive, as they remind me of sweet Clarence and my times with him and Dad.

"I'd like to hold it for now."

"Absolutely! But I'm going to go get you a big envelope with your name on it, so we can keep it safe when you need to put it down."

"That'd be awesome. By the way, I really like your shoes."

5

"I thought you might." He winks at me as though he's wearing them just to impress me. "They're so much like slippers that I bought two pairs! They're not cheap, but I'll write down what kind they are before you leave this room, so you can get yourself a pair." Wow. He's the sort of can-do, encouraging guy we need for Carol Moseley Brown's campaign, I think, as I take a mental reprieve from my shivers and unknown plight. Also, if Marcus can envision me leaving this room for a pair of white clogs, then surely I can do that.

"Well, I gotta go see a man about a horse," he says. "But Chris, promise me you're gonna take a drink of water. You came in really dehydrated, and the more water we can get in you, the better you'll feel."

"I promise," I tell him as he leaves the room. And the promise is for me and for Marcus…*and for Clarence and for Dad.*

☻ *The Community Center*

Clarence and my father gave me the example of a truly great friendship. Clarence was a little older than Dad, and their interracial friendship was a direct threat to business as usual. So was Dad's work mandate—to open a regional Social Security office to make benefits more available to vulnerable people: retirees, *minorities,* people with disabilities, immigrants and even the incarcerated. As I was learning the colors of the rainbow, Dad was challenging others to care about people made invisible by society, including African Americans. The race riots of the 60's loomed large in the background of my life, and on a day that Dad luckily wasn't at work, a young man threw a Molotov cocktail right through his office window. That's when we started to receive the threats to Dad's life—and to ours.

I'd overhear Mom and Dad talking quietly about *the threats* and it felt like some poison was finding its way into our home. When the threats picked up, so did Dad's visits, with me no longer in tow, to visit Clarence at the Community Center where he served as Director. Dad was Chairman of the Board.

On Christmas Eve when I was nine, Mom and Dad finally relented to my begging to visit the Community Center again with Dad. I marched in with him smiling, bearing as many food gifts as I could possibly carry. A month before the Christmas holiday, we'd begun filling a tithing bowl, adding a quarter each time one of us left a light on when we sat down to eat dinner. We used whatever we collected to buy non-perishables—and a grand turkey, even bigger than the one we roasted at home, for the Community Center's dinner.

Groups of people were always in the building, adults and children my father knew by name. One mother, who held her coat without buttons around her to stay warm, stared at me until I smiled at her. She narrowed her eyes at me, called me *white trash* and spit at me. My eyes welled with tears, and I began to shake. Dad put his arms around me and steered me to Clarence's office. "Don't worry, Chris Bliss. She doesn't mean to hurt you," he said. "She's been treated badly by some people and she's just afraid."

"Afraid of me, Daddy?"

"No, not so much you, Sweet Pea. Just sick and tired of people who try to hurt her."

"But I'm not gonna hurt her."

"Of course not, Sweet Pea, but she doesn't know that."

Clarence's office was filled with piles of books, boxes and papers. We sat on a soft sofa upholstered with faded stars and moons as Clarence, with his brown skin and tight gray curls, entered in a flurry. He moved more quickly than my father, but once he hopped into the chair behind the desk, he was still and rapt as an owl.

Holding my hand, Dad pulled me up and led me over to him. "Clarence," he said, "Look how my baby girl Chris has grown." Then, he said to me, "Sweetie, you remember Mr. Sage?"

Clarence stood up, smiling, took my other hand and patted it. "My goodness, but how proud your father is of you," he said.

7

Sandwiched there between Dad and this kind man, holding their hands, I felt protected.

I looked at Dad to check his reaction. He was nodding his head, looking at me, then at Clarence over the rim of his black glasses. Clarence asked me if I'd been a good girl, if I thought Santa would come.

Still unsettled by the woman who'd just spit on me, I'd believed I'd been good, but if so, why did she not like me? In my quiet voice, I said, "Well, I've tried to be. But I guess not everyone thinks so."

Clarence raised his eyebrows at me and wrinkled his brow. "What's that? Not everyone?! Oh, honey, I find that hard to believe!"

Dad explained what happened when we were out in the lobby. Then he cupped my face in his hands and held his eyes steady on me. "Now, Sweetie, I want you to listen to what I'm gonna say. You are not the problem or the reason for that woman's anger. She is having a really hard time and is hurting, and she took it out on you. It wasn't right, but you did nothing wrong. Not one thing."

Clarence closed his eyes, lifted his chin high in the air and shook his head. "Oh, my, my, that's too bad," he said, not just to Dad and me, but to the heavens as well. To me he said I was a very good little girl and surely Santa would find me.

I wanted to believe him. Through Dad's whole conversation with Clarence, I looked for things about him I liked and could trust. For one thing, he had a snow globe with the Gateway Arch of St. Louis in it. Once, I rode to the top of that thing with Dad and Uncle Mitch in a traveling capsule shaped just like the globe itself. For another, Dad really liked him. They talked seriously and laughed together. They laughed until Dad's eyes were wet and Clarence was holding on to his stomach. I don't even remember what they were talking about, but I started laughing too. The best thing about Clarence, though, was that he was very kind and he treated me like I mattered, the way that Marcus did just now.

⚫ *Cece*

I follow Marcus's advice and sip more water. I just want to be home with Chuck and the kids. Pain meds are making me woozy and my mind wavers from present to past as the card from Dad spurs more memories. Marcus, being so like Clarence, reminds me of another of Dad's friends.

I'm seven and we're having dinner with the family of Daddy's colleague from the Community Center in Michigan City, Indiana. We've invited them to our house, because the tendency of restaurants to practice de facto segregation makes my parents uncomfortable. The family has a girl my age named Cece. I am struck by her beautiful dark skin. I can't stop staring. Daddy tells me to stop, that staring is not polite. Still, she's different from me. Her hair is braided in close rows, as tidy and neat as Mom's garden. I love it when she smiles and her face lights up. Her teeth are so white compared to mine.

She's holding a pen in her long, slim fingers and practicing writing. She can write her name, and her mom's and dad's. I can only write my name, Christina. My parents call me Chris, but they want me to learn to write my full name.

My dad wants us to be friends too. He's showing me things about Cece he likes. "See, Chrissy, look how Cece holds her pen with her thumb and pointer right by the tip. See how she sits so still in her chair?" Cece is also in a dress, something I've given up on, since the boys started peeking underneath my skirt when I climbed the monkey bars. But Dad asks me if I might like a dress like Cece's. She makes the dress work for her. Dad clearly wants me to see how special she is.

So I test her and see how brave she is. I tell her all about bats, at the top of my list of fears at the time. She's terrified of

9

them, just like me. Of course, I'm telling her all of the awful things, that they suck blood, hang in caves, fly around in the thick of night. Dad is not happy I'm scaring her. He pulls me aside and tells me in his angriest voice that what I'm doing is wrong.

"But Dad," I protest, "I'm only telling her the real things about bats."

Then, my beloved Dad persuades me to do something I would only do for him: give Cece my fabric Batman doll. I absolutely love my Batman doll. Batman saves me from the ugly bats—the sticky, fanged, hanging ones. Without Batman, I'll have no protector, no hero to help me conquer the world.

Because I love my father, I turn my beloved doll over to Cece. Then I feel horrible—about scaring her in the first place and about giving her my doll. I'm upset that Daddy made me give Batman away to protect her instead of me.

Now I'm a Mom. I know what it means to give a doll away. If done freely, it's a sweet expression of generosity. I was forced into it though—an act as unfortunate as that of me scaring my young friend. I had liked Cece so much and was jealous, too.

If I could go back and do it all again, I'd be nice to Cece and wouldn't even bring up the bats. Then we could have still been friends, and Batman would still sit proudly on my shelf, threadbare from the love I'd given him.

☺ *Rikki's Call*

After my lunch of Jello and crackers, the phone rings as I'm drifting off to sleep. I maneuver through my IV tube to answer it. A familiar and enthusiastic voice on the other line says, "I'm callin' for you, Chris. How you doin'? When I called your home, Chuck said you were in the hospital!"

"Rikki?!" "Is it *you*?" *Rikki*—there's no one else I'd rather talk to in this very moment! Rikki's my dearest friend from college, who is Black like my father's friend Clarence. Our relationship reminds me often of my father's with Clarence. After all, it was *their* commitment to one another—and their shared dream of the Community Center—that allowed me interaction with children who weren't white. And I met them on their turf, not mine—which made *me* the one who had to fit in.

"Sure is," she says. "I called your house, and Chuck told me you're having the weekend from hell. He didn't sound so hot either. You two fallin' apart on me?"

"I've missed you, Rikki! How did you know I needed a call?" I whisper it into the phone, because I'm about to start crying. That's our friendship for you. It shows up just in time.

"Well, actually, Chris, I needed to hear your voice, too! What's up with you? How ARE you?"

"They brought me here in an ambulance, Rikki." I sob into the phone.

"You're not yourself, Chris! What's coming down? Tell me!"

"Well, the other day I was just being a mom. Gracie and Max were making capes out of my old scarves, leaping all around the living room. Then Mavis our dog started to vomit a yellowish paste the whole length of the carpet. While I was cleaning that up, Gracie stuck her head in the toilet to blow bubbles."

"Oh my Lord! That would land me in the hospital too. Good thing she didn't jump all the way in!" Rikki laughs heartily on the other end, and my sad tears are now spilling from laughter, like Dad's did with Clarence.

"That's not half of it, Rikki! Max tripped on the carpet with his hot chocolate and spilled it all over himself! I wanted to be anywhere but home. My feet had been swelling earlier, but when I bent down to clean everything up, I noticed my ankles and calves had nearly doubled in size. I cleaned the whole mess, made an appointment at the clinic for the next day and finally put my feet up. By morning, I was running a fever and collapsed. Chuck called an ambulance because I was so weak, I could barely hear him—or move."

11

"Chris, that's awful. Seriously, what do you think is going on?"

"Well, there's a lot of protein in my urine, and my blood pressure shot up. Something's up with my kidney function. Whatever it is, I'm waiting to hear if they can reverse it. They have me on an IV for fluids."

"It's a good thing you're where you are! Sounds like you have some type of nephritis." Of all the things Rikki would have excelled at, she chose to become a medical doctor. She would know.

"What's that?"

"Inflammation of the kidneys, and it can get serious. I'm glad you're under observation."

"Good Lord. Just what I need. When I know more, I'll get back to you. I don't think I'm dying today. Enough about me! Where are you calling from, Rikki?" My heart leaps, thinking she might actually be in town. It'd be like her to give no warning and just appear on my doorstep. Every now and again, she visits Minneapolis for a health convention or conference.

"Still here in Ann Arbor. I don't suppose you got the news from the campaign that Carol's gonna pull out of the race and endorse Howard Dean?" Rikki's pulled me into work on Carol Moseley Braun's presidential campaign—Rikki in Michigan and me in Minnesota. First off, we're both proud to support a Black woman who stood up for women's rights after Clarence Thomas was nominated to the Supreme Court—after Anita Hill's allegations of sexual harassment. Second, Moseley-Braun is the first Black woman to become Senator—*and* to get the Democratic nomination for President.

"Howard Dean, are you kidding me? When did you find that out?"

"Eddie, of course. He knows all the political developments with his Chicago network." Eddie, who was Rikki's foster dad, serves on the City Council in Gary, Indiana.

"So now what do we do?" The disappointment of yet another defeat echoes my body's physical pain.

"Not all that much we can do. No Black candidate for President this time around. You have to wonder if we'll ever get one in the *White* House." She emphasizes *white*.

"I'm tired of bad news, aren't you?"

"Well, I do have some good news. I'd like to come visit you. Is it alright if I come over Easter—in a few months?"

Easter reminds me of *Jesus Christ Superstar*, the last album my father purchased before he died. And of Rikki in a glittering, feathered white midriff like those worn by Judas' back-up singers in the movie, and it makes me smile. What fun we had in college dressing up for Halloween! "I'd love for you to come, Rikki," I say. "Max and Gracie are so cute right now. Chuck's taken them over to some friends we know from their pre-school, so he can stay with me. But Rikki, here's something you should know. Clarence—I mean my nurse looks just like Clarence! It's like he's right here in the hospital with me!" Just saying that feels as though I've breathed in oxygen. And now I have something to look forward to!

"Wow, Clarence, huh?" Rikki says quietly.

"When he walked in the room, I swear to God I didn't know if I'd crossed to the other side or was still on Earth. I mean, I'm lying here in bed, cursing my plight, unsure if I'm taking my last breath. Then Clarence—I mean his younger look-alike—walks in, and it's like traveling back in time."

"That's remarkable, Chris! What are the chances that we both knew Clarence back then, anyway?" Rikki's doctor's voice has transformed back into the youthful, passionate voice of my old college friend.

"Not just *knew* him. He was my father's *best* friend." The more I think about Dad and Clarence, I realize I had no idea—in all those years they worked together while I was growing up—

how much risk each of them was taking to heal our country's racial divide.

"And how much Clarence meant to *us*! OK, Girl. You'd better get some rest and we can talk later." Rikki's permission to rest sounds good and my shoulder is throbbing from bending into the phone to avoid pulling at the IV. I yawn directly into the phone and Rikki teases me about her being too much of a bore.

That wakes me momentarily. "Rikki, you're anything but. It's so good to talk with you. Can't wait to see you!" Part of me listens, and part of me wonders whether I should visit her in Michigan or have her stay in our chaotic home. Another yawn and the rest of me succumbs to the pain meds and exhaustion.

I later wake with a start, trying to recall Rikki's signoff. I can't. And damn, I forgot to ask about her father. I must have already been dozing when she said goodbye. As I drift off more, I remember I never did start the washing machine after throwing in the towels from cleaning yesterday's messes. I used to think Rikki was obsessed with washing her clothes. Now I make it a priority too. Sometimes the only evidence that I've been a good mother are the piles of clothes, fresh and tucked neatly in everyone's drawers. The washer is my biggest ally—it helps me create order where none exists. My thoughts fall back to the first time Rikki and I were in the dorm laundry room together.

Part Two: Leon College, September 1980

● *The Laundry Room*

The dryers clank rhythmically with buttons and straps hitting their drums as I walk in, my arms full, and I stumble upon a student in a sorting frenzy, tossing her clothes into piles. The coin washers and dryers are in Gray Hall's basement, and only two of us are there. She looks up at me once but doesn't say anything. She then mutters something to herself as she fills a washer with whites, detergent, and softener, then closes the lid. She drops a couple quarters in the slots of the dispenser and gives it a push. The coins jam. She curses under her breath and hits the metal slide again. When that doesn't work, she jiggles the dispenser, then pushes the coin return. Unable to make anything work, she steps back, gives the whole machine a hard kick and hisses at it.

"Need some help?" I ask her.

"What would *you* do with the god-awful thing?" she asks back.

"Well, let me see," I say, and I make a humble attempt to jimmy the dispenser myself, surprised that I have a paper clip in my pocket to poke the coins.

I recognize the student as Rikki Daniels, the swim team's champion, a distinction that allows her the freedom to move between social groups, unlike the dozen other minority women on campus. She has a mysterious elegance about her, even in jeans and hiking boots, with hair as thick and natural as spun raffia.

Rikki watches me, crosses her arms over her stomach and sticks out her left hip.

I smile at her and humbly say, "The coins have to sit just right in their slots to work. I had trouble with this machine last week." The more closely she watches me, the more my fingers are sweating and slippery. I end up flipping the mangled clip up into

15

the air so that it flies right in her face and lands at her feet.

"I'm SO sorry!" I stoop down to get it, but she holds her arm out to block me and says, "Forget it! I'm usin' another machine!"

Red-faced, I want to just disappear, but I have quite a lot of my own laundry. I'm suddenly aware of the time and the sickening sweet, floral smells of detergent mixed with fabric softener. My economics class starts in ten minutes and I don't dare get there late. I'm already struggling with some of the concepts and want to show the professor I'm committed.

Rikki grumbles a litany of expletives as she unloads laundry from the first machine and carries it to a second, while detergent flours her shirt. The hard heels of her boots pound the cement floor and echo through the room. That dispenser works. As the water rushes into the machine. she yells, "Hallelujah!" Then she drops the washer lid, so one last bang reverberates around us.

I look right at her again, ready with a congratulatory smile. She must know I'm watching yet doesn't turn back to look at me as she heads out.

Still, I'd smiled at her and tried to be nice. I've learned from my mother that smiles are a gift. In this world of hardships and borrowed time, the one thing that costs no time or money to give is a smile. Mom never told me how awful it feels to smile at someone repeatedly and be ignored.

The click of Rikki's heels fades as she makes her way down the hallway. I'll be late to class and it's all my own doing. I imagine telling my prof why I'm late. "Well, you see Dr. Warner, I was doing laundry and helped someone whose machine jammed." "You see, Dr. Warner, there's this Black student on campus, I'm sure you know her. I was just trying to help and get her to smile at me. My father said you should act with respect and be mindful when you're with a person with brown skin so that they don't feel invisible." But somehow, I was the one to feel invisible.

I try to imagine how Dad would respond in this situation. I can hear his answer: *Just keep trying, my girl. Try to respect and be kind to everybody whether you understand them or not.*

Late as I am, it's good I'm alone now. I pick up my clothes, throw them in a machine, and as if Rikki herself gave me permission, I kick my own plastic yellow laundry basket so hard it slides on the smooth cement and lands right smack in front of her washer. The washer is churning, getting its job done, mocking me for standing still. I stick my tongue out at it, push coins into my own machine and pour in detergent.

At first, I wonder how Rikki could get so upset over a stupid washing machine. That is, until I realize how good it feels to release some of my own frustration. In my family, anger's an emotion only expressed with those closest to you and even then, it's not viewed as a healthy thing. It's a sign that things are unraveling—scary and unstable. What's more, the only way you can ever express it in public is if you're decrying our country's lack of justice for the underserved and poor.

Campus, March 1981
● *The Ride Board*

For spring break, Mom persuades me to scope out other students that might need rides home from campus, so I put a note on the Student Center bulletin board that I have room for someone heading to Indiana.

Within the week, I learn from Marilyn in the Admissions Office that there's only one other student from Indiana—Rikki Daniels. I think twice, unable to imagine the two of us driving together for nine hours, but ultimately, suspend judgment and dial Rikki's number. To my surprise, she picks up.

"Hi, this is Chris Fitzgerald. Is this Rikki?"

"This is Rikki. Who'd you say this is?"

"Chris Fitzgerald. I'm from Indiana—LaPorte. I found out

17

from Admissions that you're from Gary. Would you like to ride home with me...I mean share a ride...for spring break."

"You're from *LaPorte!?*"

"I am. And I saw on the ride board you're from Gary, right?"

"I *am* from Gary." *Silence.* Gary—the part of our drive where we'd plug our noses to avoid the foul, rotten smell of the steel mills.

I continue, feeling oddly solicitous, as though I'm trying to get her to buy something from me. "Well, Gary's right on my way, of course, if you could use a ride."

Another awkward silence. Maybe she's hung up. But then, I hear her clear her throat and say, "That's real nice of you and everything, but uh, well...I'm not sure yet...if I'm actually going home. I appreciate you callin,' though. What'd you say your name was?"

"Chris Fitzgerald. As in F. Scott—no relation though. I was in the laundry room with you a few weeks ago when you couldn't get the machine to work."

"Oh, that was *you.* Named after St. Paul's glory boy-- Fitzgerald."

I wonder what she really thinks of Fitzgerald. He had a huge impact on me. After I wrote my high school senior paper on the resemblance of Fitzgerald's women characters to his wife Zelda, I wanted to come here for college. "What brought you here to Minnesota?" I ask quickly, so I don't lose her interest.

"I was recruited to come here. My science grades and being a swimmer didn't hurt. If you want the honest-to-God truth, it's because I'm Black. They've been trying to draw in minority students from the five-state area. They better stay at it—the place is far too white at the moment."

Her candor gives me pause, but I like it. "I noticed that too," I say. "There are fewer Blacks here, in fact, than at my high school. The school has its work to do," I say. "Still, the reason I'm calling is that we're both Hoosiers." *Hoosiers*—the word sounds so funny now while I use it with Rikki. "We're the token messiahs from Indiana," I add, which I believe could sound better.

"Excuse me?" asks Rikki.

"Messiahs…I'm sorry. It's from Richard Bach's bestseller, *Illusions*. It's about a modern savior who lands in Indiana as a biplane pilot. I love it when things and people from Indiana have a national impact—like Michael Jackson."

"Michael Jackson's my hometown boy! As for the New Age stuff, I don't give it much attention." Rikki speaks her mind.

At least I appealed to her with Michael Jackson. "Let me know if you'd like to ride home with me," I say.

"Sounds good," Rikki tells me. "I'll call you back soon. Thanks for asking me."

I give her my number, then hang up the phone, stare at it for a minute, wondering what the heck might follow with her call back. I throw myself on the bed and close my eyes. Little did I know that the demands of academics would be but the iceberg's tip of my college learning experience.

● *Presidential Scholars*

On a Friday evening, I choose a Presidential Scholar article review over a kegger hosted by the boys at the ATO frat house. We discuss an article that suggests guilt is over-rated and risky. It is not a feeling, but more an anesthetic, masking deeper feelings (fear, sadness and anger) that signal what we really need.

Chuck, a Scholar I've grown fond of for his clean, lopsided smile, jumps right in. With the clear voice of a narrator, he says, "I don't know why people write articles like this. They've got it all wrong. A guilt feeling is a healthy incentive to look deeper. It links our emotions to our conscience…ties the two together." He says this with all seriousness, his eyes alert to our reactions. For the first time since I met him, I notice that his eyes have an added glimmer in them that he directs right at me.

19

Is it his brain synapses firing—or is he flirting?

Being invited to play with the ideas makes me wiggle in my seat, and I'm right there. "I agree with the article," I tell him. "Getting down to our natural feelings, whether sadness about what we've done, or anger at ourselves, is our best hope. When we know the source of our feelings, we can move through them. They instruct our minds what we need to do so we can let the feeling pass through our body. Guilt is a cover that adds layers of confusion. It hangs on and disrupts any sense of resolution. The author gets it!"

"Wait a minute," Chuck counters. "Guilt's not an anesthetic though—it's really just our conscience. That's what makes us human, and we need to live in the guilt until we understand our lesson. Guilt gives us moral discretion...distinguishes us from other animals. Allows us emotional sophistication. It holds our actions in check when we're headed for danger."

"I was the little Catholic girl who behaved like I was supposed to, and the nuns still wanted me to feel guilty," I argue. "Moral authority can be oppressive to our soul. It can get in the way of authentic sadness, fear or even happiness! Even when I was a tiny baby, my religion saw me as having a stained soul— and needing to be baptized for my redemption! I can't buy this crazy notion that I've been flawed to begin with. I *can* jive with your notion of our human gift of moral awareness." I wrap my white pullover around my head like a habit and push my glasses down my nose, pretending to be the omnipresent Sister Clare, my 6th grade teacher, scrutinizing one's every move, from the careful loops in our cursive writing to the length of our shoelaces.

"My dear," I say with my own precise, but nagging voice, staring right into Chuck's curious eyes, "God is watching you at all times, *at all times,* and when you chew your pencil, or throw away your food from lunch, or pick flowers outside the refectory that don't belong to you, God knows your sins. Now, don't get into bad habits." I pull my sweater off my head and shake it playfully at Chuck. I realize I've made a pun, and I also realize that I really, really like this guy. The two of us have just put on a show, and as everyone laughs, we laugh too, at ourselves and our performance together. It's whole-body laughter, not just the silly and repressed smiles we pass off to each other on campus.

I feel a tinge of the guilt Chuck is defending for pre-empting his good insights with clowning around. But it ends up being our best Presidential Scholar meeting yet. Even our advisors, Dr. Watson and Dr. Perry, join in and share stories of their youth—times when they got in trouble and had to rely on a combination of wit, instincts and ethics to correct their own course. Much of that led to their own interests in psychology and spirituality. Their confessions ease my inhibitions more than any fraternity night could. When we wrap up our meeting, I have a new love interest *and* a new resolve to keep my grades up—to remain one of the Scholars.

I realize that Chuck and I could probably spend hours talking. His comments throughout the review are refreshing, a shift from the extremes on campus—the cynical, hardened professors on the one hand—and the partiers relying on alcohol and drugs to either access their own deep thinking or keep it at bay.

As we walk out, Chuck invites me to go shopping with him for tennis shoes. So we hop on a bus to the closest mall and traipse from store to store. Chuck doesn't just try on shoes. He glides around in them, pretends to kick balls and shoot baskets. He tries on about twenty pairs before he decides on one, testing the poor clerk's patience along with the shoes. He asks questions as though his very life will depend on which pair he buys. This is the first time I've ever shopped seriously with a guy. I marvel at the way he quickly laces the try-ons all the way up. Then he presses his finger over his big toe, flexes his ankle while sitting and walks

21

around.

When we get back to campus, I invite Chuck in to my dorm room. We make small talk about my photographs on the wall and the imitation Gobelin unicorn tapestry I bought in Paris that now hangs by my bed. Chuck takes my hand as he prepares to leave, setting off a wave of tingles in me, my skin rising to his touch. He tells me I'm a lot of fun. No guy has ever told me that before.

Right when he's brushing my face gently during our good-bye hug, the phone rings. I let it ring until it stops. Then it starts up again. The distraction breaks our trance, and I excuse myself to answer it.

It's Rikki. There I am, Chuck's hand in mine, relishing it as he runs his fingers up and down from the top of my middle finger to my wrist. He's kissing my cheek as I speak to her, and I have this great opportunity to put into play all my musings about guilt. But I freeze and blow it. I pull away from Chuck and gesture "stop" with my palm so I can absorb the shock of what Rikki is saying. She'd like to drive with me to Gary.

"That's great, Rikki," I tell her, happy that I won't have to make the trip alone, but already questioning if I'm doing the right thing. I tell her I'll call her back in the next day or two so we can make a plan.

"Was that Rikki Daniels you were talking to?" Chuck asks after I hang up. After all, there's only one Rikki.

"Yep, you know her?"

"I do. She's an amazing athlete and she doesn't even *need* shoes to do *her* magic," he says, pulling me close to him again.

"That is true," I say. "I promise I won't pick up the phone if it rings again." Chuck's ability to concentrate is remarkable, and now that the focus is on me, I decide to take full advantage.

Spring Break, Sophomore Year, 1981
  ☻ *Going Back to Indiana*

When the day comes to drive 500 miles with a Black girl I don't know, I'm guided by a queer and compelling obedience. There's something about Rikki that draws me to her. When she enters a space, it becomes more alive, as a room does when drapes are pulled open and morning light pours in. I want to both impress her and win her trust, so I'm filled with anticipation. I don't want to say or do something that might offend her.

I pull up to Umoja House, our campus residence for Black students, where Rikki lives. She's outside, talking with two of her friends while she waits for me. When I pull up, one of her housemates points at me and raises her eyebrows. Rikki leans in close to her and says something. All three of them turn at once to stare at me and my red Pinto wagon. I open my car door and get out, take a deep breath and walk towards them. They draw back in, and I can't hear what they say.

"Good morning, Rikki. Hi everyone. I'm Chris."

Rikki's the only one to turn toward me. "This is all I'm bringing," she says, and points at an old green duffel bag with a windbreaker thrown over it.

"We've got the whole car to ourselves," I say, my attempt to be light-hearted. "Would you like to put your bag on the floor or in the back?"

"The back's fine," she says. Her friends continue to look away from me, and I see Rikki's not going to help with an introduction.

"Hope you all have a great spring break," I say. "Looks like it's gonna be a beautiful day here in Minnesota." It feels so small, but in my awkwardness of being the outsider, it's what comes to mind.

Rikki's friend who didn't look up at all when I approached turns to me now and says, "You too." The friend who raised her eyebrow looks down at her feet, waiting for me to leave.

23

I walk back to lift the hatch, and as I wait uncomfortably for Rikki to say her good-byes, I sweep sand from the area where Rikki's bag will fit.

Rikki turns towards her friends and says, "I'll see you in a week. Hope you have fun without me!" They both hug her tight and walk back toward the house.

Rikki sticks the coat under her arm and throws her bag in the back. I slam the hatchback, then we settle next to each other in the front seats and hit the road. I look at her intermittently and smile, trying to break the ice, absorbing her fragrance, an earthy blend of patchouli and musk. It reminds me of an import boutique near campus that carries oils, beads and fabrics from India. Her hair is braided into elegant, twisted coils, a sign of her life and artistic spirit beyond the pool.

For the first half hour, we say very little. I muse to myself that our silence is, in part, a complex maze of cultural assumptions not easily navigated, and I let that be okay. At our first pit stop, Rikki needs a tampon, and it's odd that I have one because I don't have my period. Giving it to her eases things. Not long after, we both see a billboard of dancing cigarettes, look at each other at the same time and laugh. Rikki doesn't smoke, thank God. She's a much easier passenger than I'd imagined, and it turns out we're on the same restroom schedule.

After we stop in Eau Claire to grab coffee at a truck stop, Rikki sees my eyes are drooping. "Mind if I read you some of my book *Catcher in the Rye* to help keep you awake?"

"Go ahead," I say. "It'll make the time go faster, too. Are you reading that for a class?"

"Hell no! Not during spring break. I'm readin' it on my own time. You know Mark Chapman, the guy who murdered John Lennon last December?" She looks at me to see if I know anything about him.

"What about him?"

"Chapman read the book when he was 16, the age of the

24

character Holden Caulfield in the book. He identified so much with Caulfield that he thought he would finally *become* him once he killed Lennon."

"Are you kidding me?! That's horrible. Why'd he choose John Lennon?"

"He saw Lennon as a symbol of a generation of adults creating an ugly and miserable world, filled with hypocrites."

"That's interesting. Lennon was anything but a hypocrite. I mean here's a guy who invites us all to imagine a world where we can live as one." The thought of some killer thinking Lennon is other than authentic upsets me. I ask Rikki to unwrap one of the butterscotch candies we just bought for me, and she does.

"That's not the point, really. The point's that Caulfield is on the threshold of becoming an adult and that scares the hell out of him. He can't accept the death of his brother or playing by adult rules that are disingenuous. He romanticizes childhood, but he wants the privileges of being adult…you know, the sex, drinking, and cigarettes. He's like most of us on the threshold of growing up, right?"

I shake my head yes and start to notice darker clouds assemble in the sky. Bad storms are one of the things that scare *the hell out of me,* I think to myself.

"Somehow," she continues, "Chapman identified with Caulfield's paranoia that he had all the answers and the world was out to get him. Chapman didn't have anything against Lennon except that he was a symbol of his adult generation."

"Reminds me a bit of *The Outsiders,*" I say. "Both boys rode the ragged edge of sanity to cope with the loss of someone they loved. It's one of my favorite books, both riveting and hard to read because of all the trauma. And the author was only 18 when she published it! What draws you to Salinger?"

"My Uncle Nate. He's my foster mom's brother who lives in Indianapolis. When I started school, Nate gave me a whole list of books, and this one's at the top, though anything he recommends generally works for me. If you'd like, I can read the exact part where the title comes from."

"Go for it," I say.

"Anyway, I keep picturing all these little kids playing some game in this big field of rye and all," Rikki reads to me. *"Thousands of little kids, and nobody's around—nobody big, I mean—except me. And I'm standing on the edge of some crazy cliff. What I have to do, I have to catch everybody if they start to go over the cliff—I mean if they're running and they don't look where they're going I have to come out from somewhere and catch them. That's all I'd do all day. I'd just be the catcher in the rye and all. I know it's crazy, but that's the only thing I'd really like to be."*

As I tell Rikki why that's part of why I'd like to become a teacher, I drive us through long stretches of Wisconsin, keeping the speedometer at a steady 60 mph. It's unseasonably hot for spring in the north, and I'm hoping that the impending rain can cool things off. My Ford Pinto is a miserable car in the heat, and even the gusts of wind can't cool the sweat trickling down my chest. Yet, I feel wakeful and even jazzed to be talking with Rikki like this.

I know she's sizing me up, yet I don't want her to feel strange around me. When I was five, my best friend Margaret and I had a ritual to get through the weirdness of becoming friends. We would hold our hands together, palm against palm, and rub our fingers over each other's skin at the same time. Then we would shiver together for the odd feeling—*the willies*—that our friendship pact gave us. Driving next to Rikki for this trip, each aware of the other's every move, reminds me of Margaret—of being in our own skin while testing out the other's at the same time. I'd never realized how driving in a car with someone you don't know makes you feel vulnerable. Every little movement, breath or word is magnified, because you can't move away when any discomfort hits.

As the miles pass, I notice the intervals between Rikki's

nervous coughs, how she holds her breath when I pass other cars. I see that she picks her cuticles and that she stretches her hamstrings first thing when she gets out of the car.

Sometimes I'll look over at Rikki and she'll have her eyes half open, as if she's going to drift off to sleep. At one point, she catches me looking at her and says, "You know, Chris, it must be nice to have your own car. I rely so much on public transport I can barely remember the last time I was in a car. I can actually relax…no noise, no side conversations, no worry about getting off at the right bus stop." As she says it, she scoots down into her seat, propping her feet on my glove compartment.

"You don't mind, do you?" she asks, and I shake my head no, even as I note to myself that I would have asked first.

Something about my expression inadvertently put Rikki on her guard, and she pulls her feet down and pulls herself back up in her seat. "No, really it's OK," I say. But she stays that way, and it's some time before she even turns a page.

"Should we listen to some music?" I ask to break the silence. "I have a shoebox in the back—on the floor—that has cassettes. Find one you like."

She gives me a thumbs-up and asks, "Do you have any of the old Spinners hits?"

"I can't believe you asked me that! I was just thinking that myself! Let's play *Could It Be I'm Falling in Love.*" What are the chances that Rikki would read my mind, I wonder?

Rikki reaches back behind me, pulls up my collection and spots the cassette right away. "You've got a lot of these things," she says, as she pulls it out and hands it to me.

"That's pretty much what I spend my money on, besides books." I pop the cassette in, fast forward a little to find the song. But it's the song *Ghetto Child* that plays. I move to fast forward some more, but Rikki reaches over to stop me and says, "Let's listen to this." She knows it by heart and sings it at the top of her lungs. Interesting. It's the first time I really hear the lyrics.

27

"Life ain't so easy..."

I forget the time, forget the worries, even forget where we're headed. Despite the difficult story behind the lyrics, I feel grateful that we both love this music and that Rikki's more herself with me.

I, on the other hand, sense that it might be some time before I can really let Rikki know the songs I like. God knows any number of my musical selections might turn her off. I sing loudly to Broadway soundtracks, buy every Barbra Streisand album that comes out, and am inspired by the Carpenters *and* Earth, Wind and Fire. My musical taste is as much about re-living memories as it is musical appreciation. When I find myself gasping for air beneath the undertow of my father loss, my favorite songs stir what's best in me and get me back on track.

Rikki clearly has her secrets too. When I ask her where her parents live, she hesitates. I ask her if she has much family in Gary, and a wall goes up.

She crosses her arms and says, "You know, Chris, my family's small. It's not something I talk about much. They're pretty private, and besides there's so much going on, I don't know where to begin."

Yet, when I pop in a cassette with Van McCoy's hit *The Hustle,* Rikki says, "This reminds me of dancing the hustle with my girlfriends," and she starts to move rhythmically in her seat. "I need something with just the right beat—something that can bring us all together. When we gather over a pot of Grandma Walker's stew, we all get in the groove."

"So, is that before or after you eat the stew?" I ask, winking at her.

"Whenever we feel it!" she says. "Grandma keeps a big vat of stew on the stove on Sunday afternoon, with salad, homemade bread and sweet potato pie. We all come over and serve ourselves when we have time. After we all eat, Grandma puts an album on her turntable, and we all start the hustle, twisting each other around to the music. It's the BEST!"

"Is *Grandma* your mom's mom?" I ask. Rikki sways back and forth as the song comes to an end, then closes her eyes to reflect on her response.

"Grandma Walker's my *foster* mom's mom. Not my real grandma. But not only can she cook, she can COOK!" Rikki beams at me as she says it, and I can see that she's relieved to be truthful with me that she was raised in a *foster home.*

"She sounds like a lot of fun." I want to ask more questions, but I hold back when I see she has something she wants to tell me.

"Grandma always wants to tell me how charmed my life is and wonders when I'll figure it out." She watches me until I turn to look at her. "I wonder when I'll figure it out, too, sometimes." She belts out a hearty laugh. "Grandma goes on and on about how the Good Lord has been so good to her." I notice that Rikki says "Lard," not "Lord," like my own grandma from St. Louis.

"Gotta love grandmas, huh?" I say. "My own grandma, my dad's mom, keeps telling us she birthed him with a rosary in her hands. She had a love of the drink. With all the Irish in her, she would have a few, persuade someone to drive her, and they would go all over the city cheering up people who were poor or sick. One day I went with her on her rounds and watched in awe as she lifted people's spirits with her stories and mischief!"

"That's it, Chris! Our grandmas know how to make people come alive with their love. Grandma Walker wears her full apron, and she stirs not just spices and stew, but *memories.* Her face beams with delight when she moves her head, her hips and spoon like a gyroscope rotating in all directions!"

Rikki's excitement for the vitality and faith of our grandmothers thrills me, too, sending a wave of energy through my body. "That gives me goosebumps," I say, lifting my arm up to show them to her. I wonder why it is that Rikki's not visiting her real parents. But the moment's too sweet to pry.

29

● *Ice Cream Break*

The heat continues to hang heavy. We've traveled almost two hours with no AC. As I drive, I entertain myself with the mirages in the dips of the highway asphalt—imaginary puddles that disappear as we approach them. Thankfully, there's a Dairy Queen in Osseo, Wisconsin that starts its season early, so Rikki and I stop for ice cream. Rikki orders a Dilly Bar, just as my mom would do.

I spring for a hot fudge sundae with all kinds of toppings and eat one bite right after another until I can feel the waist of my jeans tighten. Knowing I'll enjoy my new love interest better if I stay trim, I throw half my sundae away. I notice that Rikki's eating her smaller bar slowly and thoroughly—and by the way, has plenty of room in her jeans to spare. I adjust my waist so I'm in a comfortable position for driving, and we start off again. It's still about 300 miles to Chicago. Next to me, Rikki's licking all the chocolate off the popsicle stick.

Dreaming of the sundae I left behind, I switch on the radio to the classical station. When I was four and too afraid to sleep alone, Dad used to play classical music for me. He'd point out his favorite parts, telling me which instruments were playing. When I got older, he'd tell me stories about the composers' lives. *You'll never be bored as long as there's classical music in the world, my child. I'd play for hours by the square-box stereo console that appeared to float on thin legs, listening to soundtracks from The Singing Nun, The Sound of Music and West Side Story.*

The music comforts me, but obviously not Rikki, who rolls her eyes and crosses her arms. "There's body language for you," I say, and we laugh as I move the radio dial to find a rhythm and blues station. "Better, right?"

"Absolutely." She smiles.

"Who are you visiting in Gary?" I ask, wanting again to ease things. But she pulls back.

Nothing but quiet.

"My parents, that's all," she finally says softly. "I have another Dad, too—in Michigan City."

I look up at the entrance to the Interstate and decide impromptu to pull over to a Mobil to fill up for gas in the same town. "My dad helped his friend start a community center in Michigan City. I wouldn't be surprised if our dads knew each other," I tell her. "By the way, maybe we'd better use the restroom before we leave town."

"Good idea. I don't see my *real* Dad all that much. I don't feel very close to him," is all she says, sighing deeply, as she grabs her purse to go inside the convenience store, leaving me frustrated that I can't figure out how to keep the conversation going.

🙂 *A Storm is Brewing*
Rikki's stretching inside the store when I come in to pay for our gas, and we both jump when the storm sirens start to blare. It's getting dark fast, even though it's just late afternoon. We buy pop and a small bag of popcorn for the drive from a young mechanic whose hands and face are blackened by oil.

It starts to sprinkle, and a strong breeze comes up, mixing the smell of fresh dirt and fertilizer from the field across the road with the fumes from the garage. "Where ya headed?" the mechanic asks.

"LaPorte, Indiana," I tell him.

"There's a big storm blowin' in," he says with concern. "You better pay attention and seek shelter before it gets too bad out there." Outside everything has taken on an olive-green tint, including the tree leaves as they twist in the wind and bare their silver backsides.

"Thanks. It's only a half hour to Madison. We can stop there." My head is knotted in pain as we head to the car—I've had to be more alert than usual to what I do and say. My legs ache from keeping the gas pedal at a steady speed, and my stomach's churning at the thought of a storm.

Rikki watches me move more slowly, sees my discomfort and offers to drive. Much as I want to rely on her, I know she isn't used to being in cars and I don't know her driving ability. "I'll be fine," I tell Rikki, so I jump in the driver's seat again and take the wheel.

Within ten minutes of driving, a downpour and hail belt at my old Pinto with such force that we have no choice but to pull over into another rest stop. The forecaster on the crackling radio advises against unnecessary travel and suggests we take shelter. Storms are moving north from Iowa, and funnel clouds have been sighted. I saw one evaporate in the distance with my father as a child and was at once fascinated and terrified. Until I was in high school, I'd pray regularly for safety from tornadoes.

When we're able to get back on the road again, the radio isn't any clearer than the road, so we leave it off. The windshield wipers wave furiously at us as we watch the cars idle slowly through the downpour, their taillights blinking on and off like lightning bugs.

I grip the steering wheel from the edge of my seat, braking abruptly a few times as the drivers adjust to the iffy visibility. We cheer at every road sign, our beacons of progress. "It's gonna take more than an hour to get to Madison now," I say. "We should spend the night somewhere."

Rikki agrees. "We're not getting very far. I don't think we'd be the only ones to stop somewhere. Which means there may not be any places open."

That thought raises my anxiety, and I start saying Hail Mary's in my mind, doing my best to concentrate on the words. The actual words, *Blessed art thou among women, and blessed is the fruit of thy womb, Jesus,* don't help me so much as the rhythm and repetition. Rikki looks at me gripping the wheel with both hands and sees I'm afraid. "You alright?" she asks.

"I'm OK," I lie. "Just never cared for storms." *Never*

cared for them—that's an understatement.

"I've never driven through anything like this," she says. "But I kind of like the challenge." I can see she does. Where before she seemed rather bored, the rain and commotion have roused her energy. She starts humming, then singing, *"Good times, these are THE good times! Leave your cares behind, these are THE good times."* Those words go down much easier than my Hail Mary's, and Rikki's spunk lifts me from my fear. It also seems to make the rain fall more gently, and as we head south on Interstate 90 towards Madison, there's a clearing.

"If we take the Highway 12 exit, we'll end up in Lake Geneva," I tell Rikki. "They call it the Riviera of the Midwest—a whole resort area around a lake, with catamarans and mansions hidden behind Wisconsin farms and cornfields. When I was ten, the summer before Dad died, I had a reunion there with Mom's family.

"Are you serious?" Rikki asks. "I never knew there was a Riviera in Wisconsin."

"I hadn't either," I say. "I grew up around lakes, but this was my first real exposure to people with lots of money. What I remember, though, is what my dad did with Mom's big family. Everyone was wound-up tight about getting to Catholic mass that Sunday morning. Some of the family wanted to go, but others wanted to stay and talk. On one side were the elders, the patriarchs who took pride in finding a church each Sunday no matter where they were. Then there were younger relatives who wanted to dodge mass, like my mother's younger brothers-in-law, including Uncle Mitch, who had a twinkle in his eye."

"So, you had fights in your family about going to church, too, huh?"

"This time in particular! Right in the middle of an all-out verbal battle, Dad stood up, cleared his throat and said with a loving half-grin, 'You know, I've heard that if there's a conflict between you and your brother, you'd better clear it up before you

33

take communion. I've also heard it said that when two or more are gathered in His name, God's already in our midst. Let's remind ourselves for a minute why we go to mass. If God is with us, and we need to make some peace between us to take communion anyway, why not have a little prayer and breaking of the bread right this very moment?'"

"Your dad did that?"

Rikki's need to stay alert while we drive through the rain has her genuinely engaged, so I keep going. "Uncle Mitch and others started to yell, 'Amen, Ryan!' I looked over at Uncle Mitch who was beaming, while Dad made the sign of the cross in Latin. Can you believe that nearly all my relatives were making the sign right with him?!'"

"Seriously? Wow! If your dad hadn't been Catholic, sounds like he could have been a preacher."

"He definitely had it in him. He found a bag of pretzels on the picnic table next to him, held them up, blessed them and passed the bag around. All the while he was telling us in his deep, resonant voice that God is love and that we're only as good at mass as we are at caring for each other in the here and now. Somehow he brought everybody together that day and taught us all a lesson—even the elders."

"Wow, Chris," Rikki says, "You have a really cool dad. I hope I can meet him."

She glances at me—and I go quiet. How I wish I *could* take her to meet him. Didn't I just tell her that he died? I say it again, that painful revelation: "My dad died that September."

"That's rough. You didn't grow up with your father either. WOW." Then the next question: "How did he die?"

"His car—our family station wagon—was hit by a train. It all happened just a few weeks after I started 5th grade. I forgot to bring my eyeglasses to school, and it happened right after he brought them to me." Knowing things are getting more intense, I change the subject to better news. It's a technique I've learned to soften the blow of my story. "Anyway, that family reunion was a defining moment for me to understand my dad. He had that type of command and mixed it with love. He could get people to do things that made us all better, making it seem we'd thought of it ourselves."

Rikki sighs. There's a silence between us, as though she wants me to keep going. The thing is, once I bring up the tragedy, it tends to shut things down. Still, she looks over at me a few times—to see my expression, to see how I am. That calms me, and it seems to calm her too.

When we hit Madison, Rikki says that maybe it'd be wise to keep driving. But we're getting severe weather alerts on the radio. We drive around Madison's lakes looking for a place to eat and end up finding a Best Western two blocks from Lake Monona. We agree we could probably afford to stay in Madison by splitting the cost, so I drive the car near the entrance so I can run in and check on the price. When we learn it's affordable, we decide to skip eating out all together and just invest in our safety. I love staying in hotels, and this is the first time I've ever paid for a room with my own money. Even with rotten weather and barely knowing Rikki—this feels like an adventurous start to spring break. The room has two double beds, and Rikki throws her bag on the one by the window. She quickly changes into her athletic gear, realizing that she has an opening for a jog if she can beat the storm.

Outside, the wind is starting to blow. Our window looks out on uninviting office buildings, a convenience store and a couple of family restaurants.

A billboard advertising cigarettes looms in the distance. Its model smiles at us with her flawless complexion, her sleek legs drawn up to her body in the style of the famous Farrah Fawcett pose. "Isn't she just gorgeous?" I comment to Rikki, as I point her out. "But she reeks of tobacco if you get close up," I tease.

"Want nothing to do with her!" Rikki says. "You smoke?"

she then asks more seriously.

"I've tried it," I say. "I used to go to dinner with my friend Jane, and we'd smoke through dinner to act cool and grown-up. Then we'd drink coffee and light up some more. Glad I'm over that." I ask her back.

"I grew up around it. It was in the first breath I took. When I was little, my mom and dad smoked so much that I couldn't wait to get to the clean smell of chlorine at the pool."

"When did you start swimming?"

"I took my first jump in the water at the beach, and no one could get me out. My mom said I'd swim in mud if given the chance. But I hardly got to a beach or pool 'til I joined up with my foster parents, Liza and Eddie Cooper. That's when I became obsessed about the water. When the lifeguards would swim, I'd watch 'em. Then I'd dive in and try to do exactly what they were doin.'"

I still wonder what happened to Rikki's birth parents. Instead, I ask Rikki how often she practices.

"Every single day I can." she says. "And since we don't have a pool here, I'd better get out for a run."

"You sure? It's going to get bad again out there," I say, as I head to the Coke machine in the hallway.

"It's alright."

I'm walking back to the room and Rikki jogs past me in her shorts and Nikes. "I'll be back in a flash," Rikki says over her shoulder and bolts out the door and down the stairs.

My heart sinks. I can't believe it. We came here to be safe, but there she goes.

My empty stomach pleads for food, so I pull out snacks from my cooler and nibble anxiously as I throw on pajama pants with my Celtic t-shirt with its green and white shamrocks for luck. I plop on the bed, read a little and nod off. Tornado sirens blare, and I'm bolted upright as the rain pounds at our hotel window. I take deep breaths and switch on the TV. The meteorologist is urging listeners to take shelter at once. My heart starts pounding. Where the hell is Rikki? I look at the clock, and it's been half an hour since she dashed out of here.

● *The Center of the Storm*

My adrenaline ramps even higher, and I want to hide in the bathroom with my book. But I've got to find Rikki! I release my breaths as though I'm blowing out candles, try to tell myself that everything's going to be all right—to let go. But an inner panicky voice that visits, ever since my father's tragedy, overrides the other—reminds me that sometimes things simply *aren't* all right. Horrible things happen to other people just like they happened to my father—and *to me.*

I run to the closest exit and open it, yelling "Rikki!!!!" in a high, shrill voice. Some tree limbs are coming down and objects are flying like darts.

One of the men from the hotel comes to pull me back inside. "Come inside right now, Miss," he yells over my own calls. "Your screams are upsetting everyone." His arm at my back, he guides me back in the door, where I see lodgers clustering for safety halfway down the hall, near the interior stairwell, away from the windows. It's late evening now, and some other residents are also in their pajamas—or robes. A father is holding his daughter who's about five years old. She's sound asleep and snoring softly, even with all the chaos.

I'm drawn to him because he's a father but turn to a young man whose golf shirt has the hotel logo and who's acting like huddling in a storm is a natural thing to do. As he tells his co-worker they need to use the intercom, I butt in and say, "I need help. My friend's out in the storm!" I stare at him, trembling, until he looks me in the eye.

"There are people caught in the storm, I know," he says, "but I've gotta focus on helping our guests."

37

I interrupt him. "But my friend!" I say. "She IS a guest—we need to find her!" My voice is shaking and my whole body's trembling. I'm convinced that Rikki's gotten lost, smashed by a tree, or thrown against a building.

"Calm down!" an older woman wearing a rose-scented fragrance cries in my ear.

"Daddy...Daddy, the storm's gonna get us, Daddy!" another child is screaming. She's about ten, the age I was when my father was killed, looking as I did in her pink shorts, anklets and Keds.

The manager grabs his co-worker's arm and pulls her over to me. "Jen, this woman says her friend—one of our guests—is out in the storm. Take her to the front desk with you. Hurry. Get someone there to help her while you announce the storm."

The winds turn violent now, howling and whistling, slamming debris against our building. The electricity goes out, and the voices around me rise, then muffle, while the hotel man turns on his big flashlight and says loudly, "Quiet folks. Let's keep it calm. Everybody's okay here." Everyone huddles closer, shaking along with the walls around us.

The young woman instructed to help me, who's summoned her own courage to move, gently touches my forearm and whispers loudly in my ear, "C'mon, let's go call the police to find your friend. My name's Amy, by the way," she says. "Can you describe your friend to me?"

Having to describe Rikki in an emergency gives me pause. "She's Black," I say, "with her hair in thick, shoulder-length braids. She's wearing athletic clothes. She went out jogging." Now that they'll know she's Black, will they still prioritize finding her? Should I have just told her Rikki was wearing a bright orange tank top and black bike pants? Amy dials 911, and even though she repeats what I told her nearly verbatim, the operator wants to file the report directly with me. Amy hands me the phone.

"What's her relationship to you?" the woman asks.

38

"She's my friend," I say. *A friend is a present you give yourself,* says a poster in my childhood bedroom. *It'd be a present if we could find her*!

By the time I'm done filing the report, the storm is dying down and the lights flicker, then come back on. Thank God. And with the hush of the wind, there's a relieved chatter as people go back to their rooms.

I want to go outside and look for Rikki, but the manager tells me to stay—that the police are out looking and will come by. I'm exhausted and shuffle to our room, grateful this building stayed in one piece, while dread increases because Rikki hasn't returned. Maybe she's in our room.

I open the door and there's no Rikki, just her green bag to remind me this is real—and a *real emergency*. The parking lot is flooded, but no Rikki out there either. A few people are walking across the lot, with water up past their ankles. Debris is scattered all over: plastic bottles, electronics, a bicycle wheel. The wind's still whipping up from time to time, but the worst is over.

Our hotel is located right between Madison's lakes, but that doesn't give me a clue where to start. Rikki could be anywhere. My head's throbbing, and I realize that I will be of little help to Rikki if I find her and she's injured. I'm overcome by fatigue and throw myself on the bed to pray that she finds her way back. My body's trembling in waves. I'm hitting my limit, where I don't even care what happens.

Deep somewhere in my mind, I'm in the basement trying to escape the tornado again. I'm not sure whose basement it is, but it smells of cat urine. I'm crouching against a wall to be safe from the approaching storm, holding a dim flashlight. I feel trapped. I see the approaching tornado through a small window near me. It's a twirling cylinder of Velcro, with random objects stuck to its periphery. Captured by the spin is my childhood doll named "Chrissy" like me. She has long red hair that grows if you pull it out, then snaps back into her head if you press a button on her stomach. I'm grasping to free Chrissy from the storm's centrifugal force. Her hair is pulled out as far as it will go, waving about in the violent winds. The tornado has other spinning vortexes within it that extend out into infinity.

The winds calm and I go outside to check my belongings. I'm outside a farmhouse in the country surrounded by a few sheds, tall maple trees and rolling meadows. There's nothing left of my things. I walk toward the meadow, which turns into a magnificent beach with gentle waves lapping against the sand and aqua waters that stretch far into the horizon. Clusters of thick, tall dune grass appear around me. The sound of the waves pulls my fears out into the water, dissolving them. I alternately hold my breath, then take in deep, full breaths of the salt air. Gulls fly over me, then swoop down to retrieve their meals, and I'm at peace.

A man appears in the vast lake, walking out of it as though he's climbing a stairway from within the water. His face is not discernible, but I focus less on that than on the feeling he gives me. I'm not frightened. Instead of running, I stay and wait as he comes closer to me.

He approaches me lovingly, gently. Still, I do not see his face. Once he enfolds me in his arms, I know it's my father. I try to stay close, but as I reach to touch him, my hand slips through the mirage of his body. I try again, and again, and finally I feel him—solid and strong. He's here to assure me that his love for me is still very much alive.

I wake with a deep sigh and remember where I am. No Rikki in the room, or sign that she's been here, but with the dream of Dad still fresh I'm not diving into a panic. In the bathroom I toss cool water on my face and as I look at myself in the mirror, I see a curious thing: the eyes smiling at me seem to be my father's and not my own. *He's in me, I realize, for the first time since he*

40

died. I hold exactly one-half of his genes.

● *Calm after the Storm*

With that realization, a couple tears and a calmer version of myself surface, and I locate the number of the office where I filed the report. Just as I start to dial, in walks Rikki, drenched. She's limping a little.

I drop the phone and run to hug her. "Rikki, my God, where've you been? I've been worried sick. The police are looking for you."

"Ha! Like they would be any help! Quite a storm, wasn't it?" She avoids my comment about looking for her and just smiles. "I waited in the Stadium when the storm got bad—and then came back out when it let up."

"It was a real tornado, Rikki! We did the drill here, and the electricity went out for a while. People were seriously concerned…I mean, I was too. . . especially about *you*!"

She pulls in, becomes quiet and self-contained. I offer her some snacks, but she tells me she's already grabbed a bite. I wonder where, as she closes the bathroom door and turns on the shower. I call the front desk, let them know Rikki's here, and ask them to call off the search. I call Mom, too, and let her know I'm alright. I wonder if Rikki will call her foster parents.

As if she's read my mind, Rikki says, "I have to call Liza," right as she comes out of the bathroom. She's already dressed in her pajamas, a pair of cotton black drawstring pants and a plain white t-shirt.

"Your foster mom, right?" I ask, not holding back now. I'll find out tomorrow anyway.

"Liza? Yes, Liza's my mom…," Rikki starts, looking at me quizzically to see if that's enough. I must look puzzled, because she adds, "She is my *foster* Mom."

It seems like Rikki has never had to explain this to anyone. I know how it is to fight to keep the painful details at bay. Still,

41

I'm left wondering how a child feels when they're *fostered,* but not *adopted.* My little friend Jenny from grade school was adopted, and I always knew it, because she was the only Korean child in my Catholic School. That couldn't have been easy either. There were no other brown or Black children at St. Joe's. The only noticeable disparities other than that were between the smart children and the slow learners.

All of a sudden, I smell root beer, and I see that Rikki's brewed herself some Sassafras tea while I was on the phone with my own mother. She asks if I want some.

"Sure," I say. "Used to drink sassafras tea with my daddy. We had roots behind our house in Indiana."

Rikki's got more important things on her mind. "What time you think I'll be home tomorrow?" she asks.

"Barring any more tornadoes, earthquakes or floods, we'll get there by late morning."

"That's good," she says. "You know—I have a favor to ask you." I imagine she'll want to talk about how we pay for the gas and room. "I'm gonna call Liza now, and I'm used to having private phone conversations with her. Would you mind leaving the room?"

The bathroom won't work—the walls are paper thin. That leaves the hallway, with which I'm all too familiar.

"Uh...sure…" I respond. "Just give me a minute. I'll throw on some clothes." Not knowing what else to do, I dress in front of her, leaving the Celtic top on but throwing a zip-up jacket over it. I always dress in front of my roommate Annie. I've never thought twice about it. But now, I want to hide my white, Germanic legs as I change into my jeans. I wonder if she's looking at my ample thighs or the small marks where I've cut myself shaving. Even as we're sharing this room, I have the feeling of being in an athletic equipment store, or any place where I add little value. I don't want to be white in this moment.

Rikki lies on her bed, pretends to be reading, and as I open the door to leave, I ask if she'll come get me once she's done on the phone. "I will," she asserts. There's no humility, no attempt to make my displacement comfortable. I realize again how little I know Rikki, nor can I guess how long she'll be on the phone. Irritated, with my sassafras tea memory as comfort, I grab my journal and head out the door.

● *The No English Rule*
Out in the lobby, a man with ripped jeans, a black t-shirt and bandana is watching J.R. Ewing glorify narcissism on TV. I've never watched an episode of *Dallas*, but now that I'm with Rikki, I consider the show from her perspective. What it's like to see the popularity of shows filled with white people who make the accumulation of power and wealth a sport? It seems the opposite direction of where we need to go.

I journal a little, but I'm so sleepy and my eyes burn as if I'm cutting onions. I can only put my notebook and pen on the table next to me and nod off.

When Rikki finds me at God knows what night hour, I'm fast asleep on the lobby sofa. The TV's been turned off, and Rikki's the only one in the lobby besides the reservation clerk. "Uh, Chris, it's really late. Took me a while to get hold of Liza and Eddie. You can come back to the room now". No smile or anything, but she did keep her promise.

I rise up, alarmed, like a kid who's overslept and missed the school bus. "I...uh...oh. . .I fell asleep. What time is it?"

"It's around midnight," Rikki tells me. "C'mon, let's go get some sleep."

She holds her arm out to pull me up, and when I grab it, she pulls me along as though I'm in my golden years. I let her. My eyes have a film over them, and everything seems a blur. Then I think of what to say. "Rikki, I'm so glad you came with me. I can't imagine going through all this just by myself."

She's silent, but nods. After an eternity, she says, "I'm glad I came with, too. If you hadn't offered the ride, I'd have stayed on campus. And Liza and Eddie would...I mean I miss those two. They're my family, you know."

Back in our room, we both climb in our beds. I ask Rikki what time she plans to get up. Rikki coughs loudly and ends up passing gas too. I give her a serious look and ask, "What time was that?" And then I smile. We both start howling with laughter.

When we're through being slap-happy, she tells me that we can head out early, but not as early as swim practice. She's often at the pool with the team at 6:00am, so she lets me set the time at 7:30am.

We say our goodnights, and she dozes off. I expect to, but I'm at that beyond-tired state where I lie uneasy with my mind churning, wishing that Rikki and I could naturally share more laughter, *wishing I wasn't white so I could understand her better.* Being able to really say what's on my mind will take some time. As I doze, my mind takes me back to my first experience of cultural humility:

Through the Indiana University Honors Program in Foreign Language, I traveled with a group of high school students under a "no English" rule. Most of the other kids were French students well beyond my socioeconomic level who'd been groomed to master the language. Most of them had two parents who trained them to read the newspaper and engaged them in discussions of current events. Not me. Mom's a photographer, not a newspaper-savvy intellectual. So, there I was with a group of people I didn't know whose social status intimidated me, and many of them knew each other. Being the only student from my high school, I was even more the odd one out. It didn't help that it was my first trip overseas—far from home without Mom— triggering unresolved grief and homesickness. Couple that with the French who cursed each time I mispronounced one of their words, and you can get a sense of the angst I held. To this day, I hesitate when I have to decide to "tutois" or "vousvois" someone. I don't like to offend people, and just making errors in conjugation is an insult to the French. Doesn't matter how well-intended I am!

Now I have the same feelings about being white and learning to respect Rikki's experience of being Black. Before he died, my dad talked with me about how chattel slavery in the U.S. was wrong and relatively recent—how we owe something to Black Americans for the way we've treated them. While my mother agreed with my father about civil rights, Dad crossed the color line early on. He made friends with Black boys in his neighborhood and they played football together. If he were still alive, what would he tell me about his friendship with Mr. Sage and others from the Community Center? There's so much I want to ask him now, but it's too late.

"You know," he'd say, "I've got folks working under me whose grandparents were slaves just a few generations ago. They've passed down stories that white men like me aren't to be trusted. So, I ask myself how I might earn their trust. What do I need to do? When I ask a Black person to do something for me, I feel differently than when I ask a white person. I want to come across respectful, you know. Not like they're the only one providing a service. I mean, as their boss, I'm a servant too."

Mom so often told him not to think too much. "It's your problem," she'd say, "You think of things no one else would." "Keep it simple," she'd say, "It's not as hard as you're making it." And she would say the same things to me. Perhaps she was right. But it was precisely my dad's good, hard thinking that earned him respect from so many people and allowed him to produce a radio program about government services to the poor.

Rikki's snoring intermittently in the bed right next to mine. When I first started rooming with Annie, I would stay awake listening to her quiet breathing, because I wasn't used to sleeping so close to someone else outside of high school sleepovers. I listen to Rikki as her breathing changes to little puffs as she exhales. I pull my pillow over my head, and I pray a few *Our Fathers*, giving particular focus to *deliver us from evil and forgive us our trespasses*.

☻ *The Coopers*

Shortly before noon the next day, we finally pull up to Rikki's home, the Cooper's, a brick house, three stories high. Rikki points me to a parking space down the block. As I open the hatchback, I watch the faces of passersby with more caution than I'm used to. I want to ask Rikki how safe the neighborhood is, but I don't want to be honest about my fear.

"C'mon!" Rikki picks up the pace and bounds up the freshly painted stairs ahead of me. The porch is lovely and inviting. There's a thick, lush asparagus fern on one side and a swing on the other with a young Black girl about eight years old stringing a necklace with bright, plastic beads as she rocks. She sees us both and shyly looks down.

Rikki smiles. "You must be Regina. I've heard so many good things about you."

"You have?" The girl, whose hairdo juts out wide and in all directions like the fern, looks surprised and respectfully stops the beading, waiting for more information. She's a younger version of Rikki, sure of herself, focused. There's something else about her, a hint of caution. I keep my eyes on her, but she's not quite ready to look at me.

"Who's the necklace for?" Rikki asks, genuinely curious. Rikki's calmer, more cheerful than I've seen her. The child seems to shine a new light on her, making her gentler, softer.

Rikki sits on the swing next to Regina and asks if Liza is there. She looks up at me, then at Regina. "Regina," she starts, "this is my friend Chris."

Regina looks at me for the first time, her eyes looking

more through me than at me. I'm not able to capture her interest as much as I want to. Still, I smile and tell her it's nice to meet her. Regina looks back down at her work and holds it tight. Her hands are noticeably shaking.

"Chris and I go to college together. She's my friend." Rikki and I exchange a look of understanding. My being white makes this child afraid of me. Rikki reads my mind, acts on it, then nods at me to see if I get it. Regina's poor reception of me is unexpected, but to be respected, and Rikki doesn't waste time on it. Rikki asks what she's been up to with Liza. No sooner does she mention her name, then a resonant voice from the door answers, "I'm right here, sweetheart!"

Liza opens the screen door, and Rikki jumps up from the swing with the biggest smile I've ever seen, and the two embrace in a long, laughing, tight squeeze. Liza's a radiant woman, with her hair styled in small, soft curls and regal in a lemon-yellow, cotton sheath dress. She's wearing a lapis blue half-apron and has a practical elegance and versatile beauty that Rikki's imprinted. She whispers something in Rikki's ears. Is it about me?

I attempt intermittent looks at Regina, even as part of me wants to slip out of the scene through a trap door so she's not so frightened. Regina clutches her beads and nylon cord in her lap and simply wants nothing to do with me.

Liza extends her hand and shakes mine, smiling. "You must be Chris. Thank you for getting our Rikki home safe. And please pardon the apron! I'm just finishing lunch," she says warmly.

I like Liza. She has a boundless, welcoming energy, reminding me of my favorite middle school teacher who knew how to put everyone at ease, keep us engaged and have us know we'd all do well with her. The same hands that greeted me reach down and help Regina gather her beads into an empty margarine tub. "See you been showin' Rikki and Chris your lovely work, my girl," she says. "Who's this one for?"

"It's for YOU!" Regina beams her full smile and confidence at Liza.

"Well, lucky me," Liza says, holding the unfinished strand up to her neck and posing like a model bedecked with diamonds.

While Rikki and Regina get acquainted, Liza gives me a few directions on getting back on I-90 East. She mentions signs for Portage, Valparaiso, West Joliet Rd., and I'm hit with how close I am to home. I'll be there with Mom in an hour! As I wave good-bye, my excitement rises.

I tune in to WLS, my favorite high school station, and "Hold Your Head Up" comes on. On a cellular level, my body returns to adolescence, and I feel myself wearing hip huggers, bell bottom jeans and feeling proud in a bikini. That peculiar yearning infuses my spirit, flooding me with memories of moving into our house with my father and mother, riding my bicycle with my father, sledding on the magnificent hills behind our home; and then, after Dad died: my confusion, my body growing into a woman's while I held on tightly to my innocence, my first kiss down by our neighbor's pond, my kitty Laurel with whom I shared all my sorrows, and the children I babysat, pretending they were my own.

☻ *Mom's Spell*

When I pull up the driveway to my own home, Mom pops out before I can open the door. "Hi, Sweetie! It's about time you got home!" she says, greeting me with a big glowing smile and a favorite sky-blue V-neck that accentuates her eyes. She's wearing the jade butterfly pin, her jewelry for special occasions. It's like I'm a child again, like I've just arrived home from Girl Scout camp. Hugging Mom sparks more memories: playing the piano next to her, my dress with striped pastels and buttons the size of half dollars, writing letters together at the dining room table, cross-stitching as we watched Sonny & Cher, being tucked in at night until I went to high school. Secretly sampling her perfume

48

and red lipstick for my first date.

"It's good to be home, Mom," I say. "It's been quite a trip."

"It's been a long wait!" she admits. I know it's been. Much as Mom is never one to be bored, my moving to college has left a void in her life. It's not a void she talks about, but I sense it in her frequent mention of me coming home and the way she closely observes everything I do. She moves a little more slowly than I remember. As a child, she buzzed around me doing endless chores, and I had to work to hold her attention.

Mom's taken an interest in black and white photography, which she places in light wood or black frames. She's also adopted a white and black decorating scheme and many of the vibrant colors I've known are missing. She's replaced her Delft Blue pottery from Holland, her dried flower wreaths and my homemade ceramics with sleek black vases and iron candlestick holders, a black clock and lamps. It gives the house a polished look, but there's something spiritless about it. I miss the piles of my clothes, my bright childhood artwork hung in simple plastic, my découpage vases with rough glue on the edges. Our home was once my art gallery. It's Mom's gallery now, sleeker, but less inviting.

"C'mon in and have a bite to eat with me," she says, taking one of my bags. Mom's still in the middle of making a salad. Carrot shavings are on the cutting board and in the sink. Grilled chicken slices are on another cutting board by the stove. She has vinegar and olive oil in a soup bowl with a whole clove of garlic next to it. Mom knows just what she's doing and pays attention to every detail. She assembles the salads onto our plates, first the romaine with chicken slices on top, then peppers, carrots, purple onion and sunflower seeds. On one side are cantaloupe slices and a mini croissant. She's also made a whipped vanilla mousse with her mixer she bought with Green Stamps. We'll be drinking iced tea from glasses, each with a small lemon slice on its rim.

49

"Grab your plate and let's sit down," Mom says, leading me to the table.

When I see the teak wood is exposed with no tablecloth, I open my eyes wide and say, "Mom, you're not using a tablecloth!" It's a big risk for Mom to let go of that protection, a sign she's breaking old patterns that blocked her bold spirit.

"The wood's beautiful," she says, "It's a shame to hide it. We have to be careful not to spill though." Mom's purchased lovely cream-colored, woven cotton placemats and in the center of the table, there's a simple glass vase with pink Peruvian lilies.

"You're very quiet, my dear. It's not like you. What's on your mind?"

"It's nice to see you make changes, Mom...I mean decorating the house the way you like it," I lie. In my mind, I wonder how far she'll go to indulge her taste for precision.

"How are your classes?" Mom asks. "Are you still committed to teaching?"

"I really am. I've even taken some time to visit classrooms at local schools. I'm eager to student teach, but I'm waiting to hear when I'll start."

"You're more patient than I am," she says, sitting quietly, not even taking a bite and looking closely at me for my reaction.

"What makes you say that?" Her full attention warms me like a sweater.

"You've always been able to connect with people better than me. I can imagine you'll be a very good teacher."

"I actually got my connecting skills from you, Mom. You're always winning people over. You're the only one I know who becomes a lifelong friend to someone you sit next to on an airplane." I have visions of her sitting on her towel with me at the beach, with her long, slim legs and rhinestone cat-eye glasses, striking up a conversation with the women next to us.

"I *used* to be that way, but since your dad died, I just don't feel like being around people." Mom spears a piece of cantaloupe with her fork and takes a hearty bite.

"Wow, Mom, that could explain why you get frustrated with people now even before you're with them. While you're running around ironing and finding what shoes you're gonna wear, you're almost mad at them for getting you out!"

She nods. "I guess I am—it's more being frustrated about facing other people's expectations of me."

"Well, can't we all relate to that?"

Ever since I was little, I've always had to have myself ready and waiting to go before social outings with Mom. When Mom's ready to leave our house, she wants me right on her heels. She'll emerge from the bathroom, her short, black hair perfectly tucked behind her ears, her small curls framing her ears from the back. She accents her wide, blue eyes with black eyeliner, giving her a perky, dignified Audrey Hepburn look. Her trademark is creamy red lipstick, not a line out of place. My mother, when she feels up to it, is the height of elegance.

When Dad was still alive, I'd ask her why she didn't become a model or a movie star, and every time she'd answer, "Because I have a better life than they do. I have the *real* romance and the *real* good life those women only dream of." She was right. Now, I ask her again, the way I always have: "Do you still believe you've had a better life than the models and the movie stars?" She scoots closer to the table and to me. I know she loves this question, as much as the memory of me asking it over the years.

"Oh yes, Chris, I've told you and will tell you again. The lives they project on camera and on the screen are all an illusion. My life has had its shakeups—and losing your father broke my heart— but I'm richer beyond measure for the love and lessons he gave me, Chrissy, and so are you." Her eyes widen with passion and fill with tears. She reaches across the table to hold my hand. It's as cathartic for me as it is for her.

51

"Mom, seriously, what was it like being married to Dad—I mean in the end?"

"Your father was a brilliant man, Christine," she begins. "He was a committed servant and an inspiration to the community. He received a medal of honor from the Navy for saving a man during the Korean War. You know how proud he was of our American Flag and the Navy Anthem. He believed that you could work within systems to make them better. His role models were Father Flanagan who started Boys Town and John F. Kennedy. Your dad and John Kennedy were both grandchildren of Irish immigrants. Both were impassioned to serve their country and push their limits of achievement. While Kennedy's son John-John and you were learning to crawl, our homes were filled with books, Celtic crosses and Navy medals. But after JFK was assassinated, your father was devastated. We all were."

I was born before Kennedy was assassinated, before the world even knew Dr. Martin Luther King had a dream. A charge of energy courses through me as my own heart remembers what it lost. "He was so busy all the time, Mom. I can count on two hands the times I remember just playing and dreaming alone with him, when you weren't around." Dad's presence was evanescent. Even after he died, my thoughts of him have calmed me more than left me shaken. But how can I possibly remember all my moments with him? I was so little, with no idea I'd someday wished I'd have memorized everything about him for a lifetime.

"He was always too busy—like most people. And I do get frustrated with them," Mom says. "God love them, they get so judgmental. They don't say anything, but I feel it. They nag at me to get out more, to join volunteer committees, to promote their political campaign. They have *no* idea of the burden I'm holding—being true to your father's legacy but finding my own way with it."

She gets up to clear the plates, while I gather the napkins and serving dishes and follow her into the kitchen. "I get it, Mom.

It's kind of a sweet and heavy burden. Dad built a community that loved him, that still needs and expects your support. But you need and deserve to follow your own creative dreams now."

"So true, Chris. I know it's important for me to get out and be with people, though I could never come close to giving them what your father did. I'll always fall short." She shrugs and looks at me, the color drained from her cheeks.

"People can be hard on us, Mom," I say.

"I have to forgive them. It's not their fault. How could they begin to understand what I've been through?"

The fresh rustle of a breeze floats in through the dining room windows. One minute, the tree branches are still. The next, prompted by the wind, they move in waves, bowing to each other like seasoned dancers, knowing when to lead and follow, with a silent understanding, an instinct. The coolness refreshes me. I may always have some confusion in figuring out the more intricate dance steps with Mom, but I trust our rhythms as much as I trust nature itself.

"It's good to be home," I say, and I step into Mom's tight embrace.

After helping Mom clean up and thanking her, I stop at the bathroom, bury my face in a clean towel just to smell her laundry detergent. I have the same at college, but it smells better at home. When I went to my first overnight camp as a child, I used my towel for a whole week without washing it just to have the fragrance of home when I needed it.

I look at myself in the same mirror in which I'd primp and preen for high school dates, the same mirror in which I watched myself cry after Dad died. My eyes are a bit swollen, my mascara smudged under my eyes. In spite of lack of sleep from finals and yesterday's storm drama, I don't look too much the worse for wear. My skin is clear. I'm wearing my hair short these days, like Mom's, and I pride myself in slightly resembling her. She has finer features than me. I have the wider nose and thick, pouting lips of my father. I also have a small vertical line between my eyebrows as my father did. It's the one groove on my face. Mom's noticed it and has tried to smooth it away with her fingertips. She tells me often not to squint. Even so, I can't erase that line any more than I can help talking with a deep voice (not Mom's voice, but Dad's).

Thinking of Dad and his work, I think of Rikki in Gary and imagine myself in her world, separated from her real parents. Surely her extended family was separated during slavery. And her ancestors shipped as chattel from Africa. How much separation and pain can humans bear?

I go to my room. It's exactly as I left it. I look in my closet, pull out my treasure box. In it, I have coins from France and Italy, my infant ID bracelet with tiny beads that spell "Fitzgerald," a few seashells, a brown rock with joined white crosses imprinted by nature on each side, and a black and white skunk I'd crafted of pipe cleaners. My father loved it, and so when he died, I placed a duplicate of it with him so that he could take it with him to the other side.

The skunk was a symbol to Dad of racial unity, and he'd kept it on his desk by a photograph of our family.

"Why do you love him?" I'd asked Dad a few months before he died.

"Two reasons," he'd said. "One, because he's from you. Two, he's bi-racial."

"What's bi-racial?" I'd asked.

"Bi-racial means he's made from two different colors, black and white, so naturally just by being himself, he brings the two together. He's integrated. He can get along with everyone." For that reason, Dad had named him Number Two.

"Does that mean I need some black skin in me to get along with everyone, Daddy?"

He'd smiled, hugged me, patted my back. But then he assumed his pensive look. He stared past me, as if he didn't see

54

me, as if his eyes were fixed on something across the room. I hated when he did that. The look scared me, made me wonder if someone else had slipped inside my father when I wasn't paying attention.

"Dad?" I'd ask. I'd get mad at him when he did that. It was the only time I did.

But then he'd smile at me and his eyes would click right on mine.

Mom told me that Dad had been on an antidepressant that muted the sparkle in his eyes and the animating force within him. Like an owl, he had seemed to look both at me and beyond me at the same time.

"Sweetie, anybody with any color of skin can get along. I just like 'Number Two,' because he's very sweet and appealing."

Before leaving for college, I met with friends at a coffee shop on the main strip in LaPorte, Indiana. I'd had my skunk in my pocket for good luck. As I reached for my car keys, I pulled out the little skunk instead, and just then the jukebox played my dad's favorite song "Secret Love." After that, the skunk took on mystical properties and stayed with my valuables at home.

I sometimes wish my skin was part black like Number Two's. The lowliest of animals to most people, *my* skunk was a saintly redeemer. My father had me look beyond the common perception of skunks to the possibility that they might hold a key to reconciling two different worlds in conflict with one another. To Dad, my humble skunk embodied the reconciled black and white divisions that swirled around us, their own kind of putrid.

When I told Rikki about Dad's tragedy, I realized that I haven't ever seen his obituary. Perhaps now it's time to get a record of it, see it for myself. For some reason I want to find this out for myself, instead of asking Mom. I don't think she needs to remember that right now. It's time for me to find out for myself what other eyes saw at the time of his death.

Kate Towle

● *For the Record*

When I turned five, my father moved us from his civil service work in Moline, Illinois to live in the town of LaPorte, Indiana. The very name (in French "the door") suggests a threshold. Mostly, I remember LaPorte as a charming Midwestern town with sun-dappled maple trees and a moderate climate built around six thriving lakes. I never had a reason to find the Sheriff's office. Now as a college student, I learn that it's hidden, along with the jail, behind our landmark courthouse with its red sandstone and open-arched clock tower that welcomes visitors to downtown. Since I'm out running errands without Mom, I decide to stop in to locate Dad's accident report. I'm told that the record is open to the public for a fee of $10.00, so I pay a stocky, tall officer who takes my application. He tells me to take a seat. He'll know in about ten minutes if it has to be retrieved from another building.

My father's death was as strange as it was tragic. He was driving our family's baby blue Chrysler station wagon onto the train tracks at the Second Street and Orchard Avenue crossing when the wagon stalled. He was struck and killed by a Penn Central freight train that carried my father and our family wagon nearly a half mile down the tracks. A year after he died, the City Council met to discuss the flasher lights at the Second Street crossing. A councilman said that train engineers tended, at the time, to overrun the switch that activated the crossing's flasher lights. The lights had been flashing constantly. Motorists could never be sure if a train was actually coming.

I sit down and look around me. I've never been so close to our jail. The large bench beneath me resembles a church pew. This is a hallowed space, with innocent and guilty people filtering through its doors like positive and negative charges across a cell membrane, leaving their lives to fate, and hopefully a recalibration. The rest of us doing business here can only feel the

56

echoes of pounding footsteps and the air of foreboding within the walls. Officers walk by, glancing at me quickly. I wonder how many young women like me step foot in here—with jeans and college sweatshirts, hair freshly combed, faces scrubbed clean.

I'm here to learn the truth about my father. My class on historical evidence and analysis has me respecting the way something like a race riot, or my father's tragedy, can be understood differently depending on who is telling the story. To the authorities, my father's death at a railroad crossing was just another casualty. To me and Mom, it was the major catastrophe that forever changed our world. I used to overhear my father talk about his visits with people who were incarcerated. They lived in isolation from their parents, their children and lovers. They loved the best they could. My father's stories of their humor, courage, and resilience were different from anything you'd read in a public record. His accident record won't say anything about who he really was.

Impatient, I walk over to the display case in the corner of the room, trying to quiet the squeak of my tennis shoes on the polished linoleum. The receptionist nods to me from her workstation, elevated like a judge's bench, in the corner of the room. She's dressed in the official blue officer's uniform.

The impressive display of confiscated weapons makes me take a deep breath. "You've got quite the collection," I say, as if she's gathered them herself.

"They're nothing to brag about," she says, sighing as she gives me a look of disgust. Clearly, working across from the weapons day after day has triggered her disdain for the weapons, the work they represent and the people, like me, who constantly interrupt her.

"They're better off here than being put to use," I say, as much to myself as to her. It's an eerie exhibit, these tools of violence that thieves and madmen have used in my hometown.

"Officer Reilly's helping you, right?" the receptionist asks. She knows he is, but it's been about fifteen minutes. I sit again in one of the waiting room's black vinyl chairs and pick up a section of the newspaper. Queen Elizabeth has given her consent to the marriage of Prince Charles to Lady Diana Spencer. Egypt's selling Soviet weapons to Iraq. We're approaching the 2nd anniversary of the Three Mile Island nuclear plant accident. In the local news, an Indiana State Highway Commission mechanic was killed when a tire he was inflating exploded. College hasn't allowed me to read the paper much. It's important, I tell myself, to know what's going on in the world.

The ticking of the wall clock and the intermittent typing of the receptionist echo in the room's silence. I startle when the phone rings. The receptionist, wide-eyed, looks right at me, as if she wants me to hear what she's saying.

"Oh, my God. I can't believe it…just now?" She turns on a little transistor radio next to her, and the two of us hear that our 40th President, Ronald Wilson Reagan, has just been shot. Not only the president, but a Secret Service agent, a police officer and Press Secretary James Brady were all critically wounded but have miraculously survived.

I can't believe it either. Reagan's been President for only two months. The campaign process that elected him was the first time I seriously followed an election—and the first time I voted. I attended a few rallies for the Independent candidate, John Anderson, and nearly voted for him. When I heard that Reagan was elected, I joined a couple dozen students on campus to wear black all day in protest. In the end, I believed that Carter had not been given nearly enough time to fulfill his agenda for peace and the release of the hostages in Iran. How is it that the hostages were finally released during the month of Reagan's inauguration? Reagan wasn't the President I wanted, but I'm stunned that someone tried to kill him.

Officer Reilly opens the swinging door to the lobby. He's holding a few papers.

"I've got your report, Miss. Must be your lucky day." He winks at me. "Give me a minute to make some notes for Cassie here so she can make you a copy."

"Reilly, have you heard the news?" she asks as she removes the staple and begins copying.

"You mean the assassination attempt?"

"Some idiot named Hinckley shot our president! The news says it's the first assassination attempt since some lady pulled the trigger on Gerald Ford, but the gun didn't fire. And the first since the Kennedy's were shot." She pulls out a clipboard from her desk that holds a thick stack of papers. The pen, attached by a metal cord, falls to the desk with a zipping sound.

Reilly looks over at me to see if I'm hearing the conversation. "Thankfully, he didn't kill anyone. Now, they're saying that there were three others injured besides the president, and that it's a good thing he was shot on the left, not the center, of his chest. He's in stable condition. One of the guys shot was a D.C. police officer just doing his job. And the damn press secretary was shot in the head, so he can't tell us what's happening."

With all the guns and knives from other crimes before me, and the news that our president was shot, I remember the life lesson that forever stole my innocence—*tragedies happen to real people.* One happened to me. Even when Dad warned me that we shouldn't bring any valuables with us when we went to his office and the Community Center because of the threats, I thought his protection was all I needed.

Cassie pulls up the report, staples both copies and brings it to me. "Here you go, Miss Fitzgerald," she says.

"Thanks so much!" I say. Not always able to find the papers I need even in my dorm room, I'm stunned that the officer

59

located it in short order. I thank Officer Reilly and Cassie, head out the big double doors and sit on the cement steps to read the report of my father's death which isn't even a page long.

Most disturbing is a black and white photograph of our station wagon with its hood and driver's seat so crumpled and smashed it is barely recognizable. The driver's side tire is detached and hanging from what remains of the front chassis. My heart feels as crushed as the car. I sink on the stairs; a wave of nausea pours through my body. I read on. "The County Deputy coroner listed a cervical spinal fracture as the cause of death. The engineer of the train said it had been traveling about 35 miles per hour at the time of the collision. Damage to the train was estimated at $1500."

Photocopied at the back of the report is the obituary from our town newspaper, the LaPorte Herald-Argus. In addition to listing me and my mother as "survivors," the piece tells me some things about my father that I would otherwise not have known: that he served on the parish council of our church, that he was an officer of the Lions Club, *the president of* the Michigan City Community Center Board and even a committee member of the Center Township 4-H Club. The article also says that "police were unable to determine what may have caused the car to stall but indicated the auto went onto the crossing slowly, as if it were coasting." My father looks official and solemn in the photograph of him that accompanies the article. This is *not* the father I remember. I catch myself in a daze, my mind trying to settle on any thought it can, but unable to focus. I fold my hands together as if I'm in praying in church.

A soft wind swirls around me, and my discoveries make me tremble. I attempt to calm myself, pulling out old adages from Mom and Dad, long ago memorized and taken to heart. *This too shall pass...when one door closes, another opens...time heals all wounds...look to your dreams...*

As tears slip down my cheeks, I close my eyes to remember all the miracles that I've known, the spelling bees I've won, the friends I've made at just the right time, Mom's tendency to write me or call right when I need to hear her voice, the letter inviting me to France, my acceptance to college and presidential scholarship. Clearly, I've been blessed, except for the tragedy of Dad's death. My mother—whose stoicism was bolstered by her exacting German father and the brave, poised examples of Jackie Kennedy and Coretta King—stands strong through all this loss. I know it'll do me no good to bring this report back to her. She's had it with the pain, and will quickly snuff it out, as if it would become a kitchen fire growing out of control threatening to consume the life we've cobbled together since Dad died.

Pain shoots through my neck, and my stomach turns. At the bottom of the report, an Officer Stanley has written in cursive, "Besides the conductor, the only witness we have is a man who was walking his dog on 2nd Street between Weller and Orchard. He claims he saw the car pull slowly onto the tracks and stop. Potential suicide." There's another notation, made in April 1972, only seven months after the incident: *Mechanic of the 1965 light blue Chrysler Rambler wagon claims vehicle had a history of stalling. Ruled an accident.* The report is stamped "CLOSED" with a large black stamp.

Potential suicide. Stunned, my mind reels. Dad staring at the walls, tracing things with his eyes. Dad's squinted eyes, the deep groove in his forehead. Long hours sleeping over the weekend. Always on the move and rarely just relaxing, even at dinner. Few of the things other dads do with their children: helping me with my science fair project, taking me to ball games, or to get ice cream. Instead, when he took walks with me, he talked about The Pentagon Papers, the U.S. government lying to the American people, the war in Vietnam, Tricky Dick, working for the federal government. "I'm taking on a whole, rotten, immoral civil service system," he told me on a walk. "The rules are OK, but the referees are lousy!"

"What does *taking on* mean?" I asked him.

"It means that you're taking responsibility when all the people around you are being lazy," he told me. "Promise me, Chris, that whatever you do, your actions will meet your intentions."

"What are *intentions,* Daddy?" I asked him.

"Intentions are the things you want to do, that are important for you to do," he said.

What did Daddy see in his office, in the civil servant system, that made him so sick? And what about the Molotov cocktail thrown through the field office window, intended to kill him? Dad was under threat in a way I never realized.

Clearly, it's in Mom's best interest to leave this behind her. Even if she believed that Dad was somehow being played by an immoral system before the crash, she wouldn't want me to know. She's managed to hide the obituary from me for years. I'm hit with a pounding truth: all that's left me from my dad's final moments is a mystery.

What would Rikki say about all this? *Rikki, do you know that I got the accident report from my father's death and there's some question that he may have parked his car on the tracks?* No, it's not an option. It's too much to share at once.

Now what?

Thunder claps as I dash to the car. The rain starts pouring, with more questions pouring into my mind and heart, along with more longing to cull whatever meaning from them I can.

● *The YWCA*

On the way back to school, I stop to pick up Rikki at her YWCA, a three-story building at the end of a block with restaurants, a hardware store, post office and dental practice. The building is so new that as you walk in you catch a heady whiff of fresh lumber and virgin cement. The Y was one of the organizations for which my father raised money. Unlike some fathers, who would teach about the maples, elms and sumac, or teach about the wildlife in nature, my father talked about his work with the poor, our need to conserve electricity and water so that other people had resources, and about a new social program he was developing with policy makers called "Medicare." I loved him so—the way he could gather a crowd and then speak to them of sharing our belongings, and the way he'd persuade me and Mom to put a dime in our tithing bowl each time we left a light on before dinner. How many families like ours sacrificed so that centers like this could be built?

There's a palpable buzz, an undercurrent, when I walk in the building to meet Rikki and Regina. Except for a young woman wearing sunglasses atop her thick, black hair and speaking with a slight Spanish accent, my skin is the whitest in the room. All eyes are on me. How many times does Rikki enter my world and feel she's the only African American there? It can never be easy.

The receptionist sits behind a semi-circle desk. A group of restless children wait with a teenager in a tie-dyed, Grateful Dead t-shirt. She cautions the children to relax and be still, telling them that the bus to the museum will arrive any minute. The children are crazed with anticipation as they pummel their flustered guide with questions and pleas for attention.

The smaller children are most obvious about staring at me, then whispering to their pals and looking at me again. One small girl looks right at me and asks, "What you doin' here?"

"I've come here to meet friends," I answer. As I see Rikki approach, I check her reaction. She winks at me, but acts like all this is old hat, makes her way to the reception desk, and guides Regina by the arm to sign in.

The Grateful Dead teen leader is struggling to contain the little ones in the center, and I wonder how she'll manage them in a museum. Then she begins to put fabric wrist bands with adjustable hand cuffs on each child. She'll do it with a leash that allows her to watch as many children as possible with limited resources. Once they get to the museum, the cuffs will fasten with small straps to a rope she's carrying. I see how few support staff there are as they struggle to meet the children's needs. It seems a fact of our culture that anything to do with the care and development of children doesn't attract a lot of money. I may be crazy but knowing the need has fueled my commitment to becoming a teacher.

Thoughts of school obligations and the long drive there make me check my watch. "We'd better get on the road," I say quietly to Rikki. Before long, we're waving good-bye to sweet Regina whose face is pressed against the window of the front entrance as we head back to Minnesota.

Fall Semester, 1981
☻ *Drinking from Many Fountains*
With school starting up again, my budding friendship with Rikki is under the pressure of each of us trying to honor our separate friendship circles. Our friends come from two different worlds. It's an ongoing test to see how much each of us can override our insular zones of safety and deliberately move beyond what feels most familiar.

Rikki's school friends are hip, savvy, headstrong and tough. They are street smart and resilient, resigned to the ills of the world, yet willing to press through to get where they want to go. If they have an air of entitlement, it's more about our country and institutions giving them the respect they're due, rather than being coddled and soothed on their way to adulthood. They expect nothing from no one, but they demand all they can get. They grow weary of white people deciding what they need.

A few of Rikki's friends don't hide their suspicion of me being her white friend. They don't smile easily, and when they do talk with me around, our moments of eye contact are few and far between. I try to be mindful of what I say and how I say it so as to earn their trust. I try hard to not to be invasive, to smile at them warmly, so their time with Rikki stays protected. Rikki doesn't seem to notice that some of her friends ignore me. Yet as reluctant as they are to let me in, they still nod when they see me on campus.

Listening to Rikki speak with her friends reminds me of the "argot," or slang that youth my age spoke when I was in France. Just like that scenario where I was always the foreigner, it feels taboo for me to adopt any of the vernacular of Rikki and her friends. The dialogue becomes curiously slow and different when it comes time for me to speak. When Rikki's in flow with her friends, I look on respectfully, trusting that time and serendipity will guide me where my limited perspective of their world does not. They move into their own cultural and linguistic groove, where the word "ask" becomes "aks." Anita's from Mississippi, so the way she says she's alright is to say that she's "skrait." When the girls talk around me, they choose whether or not to use the –s in the present tense or to use the –ed in the past tense. So instead of saying, "She dances," they say, "She dance." Unlike French, this is a language mostly off-limits to me, though Rikki allows me to call her "Girl" and I've even taken to calling Annie and my other friends that when I'm feeling bold.

I know for a fact that Rikki feels no more comfortable in my circle. My other college friends don't even think to consider how their lot in life makes everything easier. They're used to seeing their own skin color represented in ads and media, used to feeling in control of their lives. They walk into groups with the comfort of knowing they're in the majority and they walk through campus with little fear of being distrusted or the victim of aggression. Pampered and sometimes prissy, they tend to put their needs first. They believe, for the most part, that the work of civil rights has been largely completed. From Rikki and my dad, I've learned that, in fact, our American legacy of racism is old and deep, complex and intergenerational. Of course, most of my friends don't want to hear that. Nor are they comfortable with the amount of time I spend with Rikki, even though she and I have nothing to hide as we practice speaking the truth about race with one another. They think Rikki and her friends are overly sensitive.

I've never been one to stay in just one circle, or to drink from just one fountain. That can confuse people, and put them off, because they can't easily categorize me, or understand the passion I harbor for the big issues of poverty and racism, or how I've inherited this work from my father. I bet Dad confused people too. I'm seeing now how others' misinterpretation of his huge-hearted acceptance of everyone may have contributed to his early death.

Sometimes, when Rikki and I cross over into each other's circles, I wonder how much she really trusts me. I call her more than she calls me. She's back in the groove of her pre-med studies and the rigors of swim practice. Her schedule leaves little time for friends. Mine has its own demands. I'm completing coursework for an education major, volunteering in schools part-time and doing my best to attend campus events. I'm impressed when I make it to the cafeteria for dinner. Rikki's never easy for me to read, and I wonder at times how deep our bond is since our trip to Indiana. I scan my memory for what stays real from our exchanges.

☻ *Making Peace with the Night*

One evening, Rikki comes over to me in the cafeteria at dinnertime as I'm eating with my friend Beth, an attractive Scandinavian with bouncy, blond curls that fall to her shoulders and turn heads. Beth looks on in surprise as Rikki approaches and pats my back.

"We gotta talk, Girl," she says. "When's a good time?" She has glasses on, meaning she's been studying hard, and she peers at me over the rim with the whites of her eyes.

"After dinner, Rik," I say, surprising myself by shortening her name, pulled in by an unusual warmth she's exuding and genuine joy to see her. She doesn't seem to mind my playing with her name and invites me to walk with her after dinner. She's going to run an errand, then come back for me. I can tell that something's up.

I finish my dinner, say farewell to Beth, and head over to wait for Rikki. My father is the only person I know who's really risked making friends across the color line. I don't know a single student here that's good at it, or who is really committed. I value what I have with Rikki.

The difference between Rikki and me is that Rikki doesn't seem to puzzle over her life while I think about mine all the time. She buzzes through her days, meets the tasks at hand. She slips through air and water as though she's made of both and commands them. You've seen that kind of girl: pure energy, arms and legs toned with muscles that stand out and draw attention. Her slender curves rising up to a fine head crowned by a cascade of braids.

Rikki interrupts my thoughts, walks through the lobby to meet me. "Hey, Chris. How's it goin'?"

"I'm doing well," I say. "Do you have time to take a little walk and get off campus?"

"As much time as it takes," she says, in a rare surrender to slowed pace.

Much as I want to jump in and tell Rikki about my day, I wait and stay silent, unusual for me. Rikki clears her throat, raises her thumb to her mouth and chews on her nail. Then she stretches her arms out in front of her before relaxing them.

When the silence between us gets to be too much, she looks at me and I smile. I can't help but say, "I'm glad you wanted to talk. What's up?"

She looks down, watches her toes stepping forward as if she's relearning how to walk. "Chris," she says, still focused on each step, "There's something I haven't told you."

"What is it, Rik?" I ask, looking at her. She looks up and gives me eye contact, but quickly looks down again.

"Well, here's the thing," she begins, "there's a reason why I don't see my dad much." She pauses again, and even though she's taken her glasses off, she looks at me as though she's still peering over the rim.

"Why's that?" I ask, not knowing what else to say.

"He's in prison, Chris. In prison."

"Oh, Rikki, no," I say. I didn't expect this. Not at all.

"It's true. There's always been a chance that he might be released, but he's been put away for some time." Rikki releases a sigh, then sits down against a decorative rock in front of one of the neighborhood homes. Her face turns colorless and her thick, brown lips are ashen. I put my hand on her arm to steady her and wait for her to continue. "Liza's chosen, for better or worse, to keep my whereabouts unknown to my father. She wants me to tell him what I want him to know. He has no idea I've ended up in college here in St. Paul. I do write to him, though, about being a student, so he knows I'm in college."

"You do?" I try to offer more, but the words wad up on my lips and don't go any farther.

"How…" I pause, "did that happen?" I want to know, and yet I don't. Already my heart feels as though there's a fist in it, and I fear Rikki telling me her father's a mass murderer or something.

"Chris, I can't get into the details right now, but my daddy's been in prison since I was seven. Daddy and Mama…had something happen...and my Mama didn't survive." Though I've suspected Rikki was hiding something from me, learning this only twists my heart. She continues. "My father was charged with her death. Liza and Eddie came forth to be my foster parents."

She's fidgeting, her movements sudden and jerky, as though her whole body is a twitching muscle.

"It must be impossible to write to your father," I say. She

nods. My mind begins to imagine wicked violence. Then I remember the time I was a witness to a five-year-old immigrant boy run over by a car in France—how all of us had to piece together the story from our different vantage points. Is Rikki's father still dangerous? Did she watch her father murder her mother? How does she keep up with her studies and swimming with all this in her past?

"Even though Liza and Eddie are my foster parents, they've raised me as their own. Before then, things were iffy. My parents loved me the best they could, but they were poor. They lived with a lot of tension. There was very little money in either of their families and relations were strained. My mom's brother, James, was on kidney dialysis, and it would have been a financial hardship for him to raise me. Uncle James grew up with Eddie and they were close friends. When he contacted Eddie about the tragedy, he and Liza offered right away for me to live with them. Dad was estranged from his relatives in Alabama, and Uncle James wanted me to stay within driving distance of my school, friends, and educators for emotional support. It turned out to be a good decision. Liza and Eddie have treated me as their own—and even supported me with a few visits with my dad's family. Dad's case has had a lot of publicity. It was a good thing that Liza and Eddie are a power couple and can shield me."

Rikki backs up against the rock to ground herself. Her body's drenched in sweat. When our eyes meet, she starts sobbing. The tears roll down her cheeks, onto her shirt. Not having a Kleenex, I reach up and gently dab her eyes. Skin to skin. She pulls away.

"Don't touch me, Chris. Wipe someone else's tears." She scolds me. "You have no right, no fuckin' right to take away my tears. You have no idea." And she's right. I don't.

I'm stunned. "Rik," I raise my voice to say, "I'm on your side. I'm on your side, Girl. I have no right to stop your tears."

"No one's on my side," she says, seething now,

enunciating each word.

"Not true," I say, looking right at the pain within Rikki's eyes. When others look away, I tend to look deeper, sometimes to the point of confrontation, sometimes clarity and honesty. Part of it is my curiosity—and part of it's a longing to move beyond illusions. "Look Rikki, I'm really humbled that you would share what's happening in your life with me this way. If there's a way I can help, I want to be there for you. Really. I do."

She watches me, with the same wary expression the woman at the Community Center had when she called me *white trash* as a child. I start to feel an ancient burden of divide. It hits me that I can't expect anything of her in the state she's in. I'm thinking, *Damn it, Rikki. Cut me slack, will you?* She's taking her anger out on me, asking me to hold it *for* her, rather than hold it *with* her. I don't deserve this, but my being white doesn't help. I may be her friend, but I can't quickly peel away the layers of racial mistrust always swirling around us.

If Rikki's father really did kill her mother, what did he do to her that I don't know of? Could she ever feel safe after that?

"Girl, you're one of the bravest people I know. You'll be alright through this," I say. "I know you'll be." Really, I have no idea how, but Rikki has come to matter to me, and so I make a commitment to her to ride this one out.

Rikki's face is wet, both from crying and sweat. We're both edgy and vulnerable from our strong feelings and the hammer of our differences. A chilling evening wind cuts right through us. We start walking again to stay warm.

Rikki looks at me and says calmly, "There are flurries in the forecast. A frost. All these lovely flowers are gonna die."

"I don't know what to freak out about more," I say, "frost in the forecast or Ronald Reagan's popularity in the polls."

Rikki shakes her head, exhales with a short laugh. "You got that right. There's no shortage of things to be freakin' about."

"No, there's not, and I probably do it more than you."

"What d'you mean?" she quizzes me. "You're one of the calmest people I know. I can't stand it about you."

"Me—calm?" I've fooled her—clearly. She has no idea of the anxiety I carry around—I'm a fatherless daughter too. My dad's not even alive. One of my teachers once told me that I've even shouldered my mom's grief, because Dad's death was such a shock.

"No, Rikki, I'm not calm. I just appear that way. For one thing, I'm not in an organized sport like you are. All I have to do is make my classes, do my homework and some community work with kids. And I'm still up at 3:00am fretting. I never had insomnia until I came to this place. Now unless I study till midnight and crash, I can't get a good night's sleep. So, how do you do it all?"

"The minute I slow down, it scares the wits outta me," Rikki admits then, staring out into the distance, as the sun dips behind the buildings and the sky's bright colors gradually dim, turning over its remaining light to streetlamps and neon signs. Rikki's in no hurry to leave, but I'm increasingly antsy as the sun goes down. I no longer question the source of my body's trembling. I just resign myself to endure the discomfort and to make peace with the night.

Rikki doesn't seem to give the dark another thought. Unlike me, she can't just jump in a car anytime she needs something. She relies on public transport and the driving records of people like me she trusts to drive her. As she finds her way around the cities, she keeps company with folks who are used to sharing public spaces and don't enjoy the moments alone—that I have when I'm driving.

I ask Rikki if she's ever afraid of the dark.

"Not out here," she says. "Sometimes, I almost feel safer among strangers. They don't know me, so they don't know all the ways to hurt me."

"You know, Rikki, a lot of people think you've got the

perfect life. You brought the swim team to the best season it's had in twenty years. You make any old rag look good on you. But people have no idea, do they?"

She stops again at a half-fence bordering a parking lot and stares at her cuticles again. Her nose is running, there's a scar above her eyebrow, a mole on her left cheek that's not a beauty mark. No, she isn't perfect. And mingling with her trademark patchouli is the scent of sweat and anger.

Sometimes when you really like someone and find you're linked to them by forces of circumstance and the heart, you're in a new world with no guideposts. What doesn't work one minute makes sense the next, and your intuition takes you where social graces and intellect can't go.

Rikki and I look at each other with tears in our eyes—the kind that come when you can see clear to the other side of things and everything in front of you starts to glisten—as if cleansed by rain.

● *The Beasts and the Children*

In the fall of my sophomore year, I immerse myself as a teacher's aide in a second-grade classroom, and this becomes my sport: to hold the children's interest in learning and to have my actions meet my intentions so they'll listen to me.

Ms. Hunter, the classroom teacher, is part cheerleader and part entertainer. She's admitted that it's always a leap of faith for her to share the class with volunteers and student teachers. With the holidays approaching, she's invited me to engage the children in a series of folktales about the harvest. We've been painting corn shocks and pumpkins, talking about the importance of food. Half the students in the class live below the poverty line and getting the students to count their blessings is more challenging than I'd hoped. One of the children, Jesse, is an easy sell. He has five siblings and tells us that he'd like our class to have a food shelf. That way, children can get a coupon for each item they bring in and then use it when they need something. Students whose families have what they need can privately give their coupons to the teacher for other students to use. Jesse tells the class that his mother takes care of people's gardens and has planted a vegetable garden outside their apartment. He tells us he'd really like to give his harvest to the rabbits. I make a little nervous laugh and make a fuss over Jesse being sweet to the animals.

The gold and orange hues woven through the tree branches reflect into the classroom, restoring my sense of awe. The colors are equally bright within the class: leaves we've pressed and laminated; rubbings of the leaves, bark and stems. I've strung some twinkling orange lights near our reading corner, and we've decorated our poems with light brown sparkles. I like to bask in the cozy space we've created. The materials are plentiful and organized, and the children can access them as they wish. The designs we've made are electric. Splashes of the boys' and girls' natural creativity are everywhere in the room. Even the rowdiest group, who has stayed focused in smaller spurts—and whose members buzz around the classroom distracting the others—has contributed to the vibrancy in many ways. Leroy, who sulks with each new activity, is happily engaged drawing a Halloween picture with elaborate jack-o-lanterns and ghouls. As for me, I don't pause very often. There's always something to clean up, always a child to guide or comfort. I'm in a rare, delicious moment of stillness, where the children are fending for themselves. At such moments, I believe that I am not crazy after all for having this dream of becoming a teacher.

A teacher's aide breezes in, places a few message slips on Ms. Hunter's desk, and nods hello. With someone else in the room, the children immediately begin jostling for the aide's attention. I try to keep them in their places to finish their work, then feel a pang of guilt for thinking that I'll be glad to say good-bye to them at the end of the school day. The more they ask for adult attention, the more our natural impulse is to pull away. Just how much attention can I give them before it will have diminished returns? I can guess the few who get their parents undivided attention. The rest keep tapping me on the shoulder to tell me things or they go off in their own corners and tend to secretive matters, like showing their friends toys—some stolen objects—they've sneaked to school. I love these kids, even when they cause my neck muscles to tighten and sometimes make me take deep breaths to stay calm.

Ms. Hunter sees that I'm struggling with the transition and encourages me to read *Wind in the Willows* to the children. We laugh at the images of the small animals chatting with each other as they scramble about with their chores. I keep one eye on Michael, who provides most of the humor for the class, till it goes overboard. He's just returned from the Principal's office. He keeps his head down, won't look me in the eye. It's an expression I saw recently on the face of a man in the post office mopping the floor, when he seemed capable of so much more. Michael frowns when the rest of us laugh. I hear him whisper, "I don't want to learn" to his friend Lars. I try to let it go. The other children deserve attention now, but sometimes Michael will escalate his antics if he thinks I'm ignoring him.

I keep reading until the words seem suspended in time—as they cast their own spell on the group seated around me. I catch myself going through the motions, holding my back erect, focusing harder on being present. Before long, Ms. Hunter signals the end of class. She leads the children in singing a song about harvesting plants that had grown from seeds. We form a friendship circle as we end the song, holding hands with each other, our arms crossed in front of us so that when we spin around, arms over our heads, we remain in a circle faced out to the world in a beautiful moment of solidarity.

It only lasts a second. All goodwill is disrupted when Michael drops Jenna's hand, calls her the n-word and says he'll kick her if she doesn't stop looking at him. He might as well have kicked us all because his anger has just flooded the room, taking all good feelings with it. First Ms. Hunter informs the group that what Michael said was not OK. She dismisses the other students. Then she grabs Michael's hand and pulls him to one side of her. With her other hand, she squeezes Jenna's shoulder and tells her she'll be with her in a minute. Ms. Hunter walks with Michael to the reading corner with its sparkling string of lights. With her hands on both his shoulders, she motions for him to sit on the reading bench. She kneels in front of him and looks him squarely in the eyes. "Michael," she says, "Name calling and threats of violence are not OK."

Michael stares at her through vacant eyes, as if her speech is too garbled and he can't make any sense of it.

"Michael, I'm going to have to call Dan and have you spend a few moments with him," she continues. Dan is the school's behavior specialist who deals with the kids who disrupt their classrooms.

The pain in Michael's expression alarms me. In one of my recent education class discussions about urban schools, I remember thinking that one thing most of us students in education (and most of us *are white*) are concerned about is appealing to children with racial heritages different than ours. But here's Michael, every bit as white as I am. Then, I remember that without one person to believe in him, acting out will be a way of life. "I want to see you do well," Ms. Hunter says, as though she's reading my mind. "Calling Jenna names and threatening to hurt her is not taking care of yourself."

A parent volunteer and her daughter, a student in the class, are sitting with Jenna. The mom tells Jenna that Michael won't be allowed to kick her. Since I was able to observe Ms. Hunter's approach with Michael, I move toward Jenna. When the parent sees I'm coming, she motions for her daughter to leave with her.

Jenna's still crying at her worktable. I bend down to her and say, "Jenna, I really liked how you talked during our reading time about how hard it was for the animals to be Toad's friend when he's making poor choices. That happens in our class too. What Michael said to you must have really hurt."

She nods yes with her sad, glistening eyes, then scrunches her face in pain.

"Listen to me, Jenna," I tell her. "We're going to teach Michael, through our example, how to be nice. If he's mean to you again, tell him that won't work for you and move away."

The whole thing gives me an awful feeling. It's unnerving to see a child so bitter and wounded at such a young age, so filled with hurt.

Then it strikes me that Michael and Jenna are so much alike. They both have single mothers striving to raise them well with limited resources, both are at the same reading level, both sometimes hyper-sensitive to the actions of those around them. Each of them scribbles O's all over their spelling tests. They even talk the same way: hesitant, deliberate. I can't get either of them to hang their backpacks on their hooks.

Ms. Hunter comes over to have a word with Jenna, and I hug Jenna good-bye. I grab my purse and jacket from behind the teacher's desk—and notice that Michael is gathering his things too. I sidle beside him and whisper, "What next, Batman?" subscribing to the cultural cop-out of using superheroes to appeal to little boys. I'm desperate, and my compassion for parents increases.

"I ain't no Bat-Man," Michael whines.

"What hero are you then?" I ask.

"I don't believe in heroes," he says. "I'm the villain."

"Not if I have anything to say about it," I say.

"I can just shoot people out of my way!" Michael says, triumphantly.

"But Michael, that's not gonna get you the friends you want," I say quickly, not giving him time to respond. I look him right in his angry eyes and tell him I think he could use a good friend. Michael looks at me, pulls a frog clicker out of his pocket, starts clicking it ad infinitum.

"Cool frog," I say. "Can I see him?" He clicks the thing a couple dozen times, then holds it out for me. I put my hand out to take it, and he pulls it back and puts his head down.

"You actually like my frog?" he asks, genuinely curious. I shake my head yes. He doesn't expect me to care. He puts his frog back in his pocket, kicks the floor a few times and reluctantly studies my face to see if I have green skin.

"You're cool, Michael. You have angry feelings inside you, but they're not all of you. I love your curiosity."

"What's curiosity?"

"Well, you know, the part of you that likes to find out why things work the way they do."

"Want to see my clicker now?" He holds it out again, and I feel like Charlie Brown being tricked to kick the football for the umpteenth time.

"Well wait a minute, Michael," I say. "I would like you to just be yourself and try to get along with everyone."

"I can't," he says. "I hate Jenna. I hate Black people." My heart sinks. Jenna's bright, talented and one of the classes' best huggers, and all Michael can see is her race.

"Michael," I say—and I quietly plead with my father and the Holy Spirit to help me out here—"what you hate is being different from Jenna. But what if...you and Jenna could play math bingo together? I can ask her tomorrow. "

He gives me a skeptical look, right as Dan enters the room. Michael flings his backpack over his shoulder and leaves with Dan to discuss his consequences. Young Michael already has so many demons in his young life that I find myself frightened for him and for our world. I want to help Ms. Hunter tidy up the classroom, but first I catch my breath with a long stare at the brightly colored dragonflies made by the children hung like mobiles from the ceiling. I wish on each single dragonfly that

Michael will let down his defenses and play bingo with Jenna. And that once he's ready, Jenna will join him.

As Ms. Hunter and I walk out of the classroom, it's not Michael and Jenna that she has on her mind. Instead, she confides in me that Jesse was forced to eat his pet rabbits to survive during the Bosnian War and that, with these children, we have to keep ourselves quietly open to their experiences—often their trauma.

I look at the explosion of beauty before me, the colors of honey and sienna against the blue sky—and relish the visual bounty of my favorite season. Yet it's also colored by the world I now see through the eyes of Jesse, Michael, and Jenna. Why must they live with such pain in their young hearts? I want them to know that as adults, we have our own struggles—but every time two people overcome our differences, it's still every bit as miraculous as an autumn day's breathtaking splendor.

☻ *No Playbook for This*

I've begun to share so much with Rikki that I never would have imagined I would, about our fathers, today's children, our challenges and our dreams. She lets me more into her world each day. I borrow her hair gel when my own hair is kinked. I loan her towels for swimming. I'm more candid with her. I make sure she's ready before I give her a hug. When she walks in a room, I sit a little straighter, clear my head for the engagement. After we're together, I reflect on what we've said.

I stay alert to the subtle ways in which our lives are different. Rikki brings me to places I've never been, and I feel more alive around her. She makes me want to be a better person.

We know we're being tested—that the racial cards are stacked against us—but we both want to share who we are authentically and be *real* friends. There's no playbook for this— few living examples of how it works *except Dad and Clarence.* Rikki doesn't shame me for not always understanding the Black experience. She tells it like it is. Before we met, I didn't have to pay much attention to the fact that our lunch tables were segregated. Even as Rikki and I have become friends, we still obey a gravitational pull to sit with our cultural peers.

That's what I'm doing, as an unexpected lunchroom fire drill unmoors us from our comfort zones. Once it's over, and we move through the disruption back into the dining hall, I stay by Rikki and sit by her Black friends as if it's the most natural thing in the world. I know that my presence changes the conversation in a significant way and feel a tug at my heart, knowing that my being white changes everything.

Two women, Debra and Dinah, are sitting with Rikki, and a couple of guys on the basketball team. They don't tell me their names, nor do I ask. Rikki introduces me as one of her best friends and says I'm cool. While it's my ticket into the conversation, I feel awkward, and I don't want to speak too long

"How you know Rikki?" Dinah asks me.

"We've got an Indiana connection," I tell her. "Rikki lives in Gary, and I live about 20 miles from there. We got to know each other when we did a rideshare."

"That's a long drive—past Chicago, right?" she asks. She offers a half-smile. "I'm from St. Louis. It's about ten hours. But my step-dad moved here. I go to his house on holidays."

"Y'all like it here?" I ask, surprising myself to use the Southern English, but saying "you" sounded unreasonably formal. Even so, Debra doesn't look at me the whole time.

"I like it," one of the guys says. He has a deep, rich voice despite his tall, thin build, and I wonder if he's had training as an actor. "I like the International Studies Program. The Director's from Ghana, and she makes sure we attract students in from all over."

"Really?" I ask, making an extra effort to look at Debra and appeal to her, but she keeps her head down. "Do you know how many international students we have?"

79

"I'd say three dozen," he says. "But don't quote me." He smiles at me at that point.

"You like it here, huh?" Dinah asks me.

"I do," I tell her. "I grew up in a small town. The only metro area I've been before this was Chicago—on high school field trips. Or as an exchange student in Paris."

The other guy tells me he that his family moved here from Chicago, since they'd heard that there was more opportunity for work, and it was easier to find a good place to live. He said he likes Minnesota, being from Mississippi originally, but also says that it's not all it's cracked up to be. "Here, there are people who look at you like they've never seen a Black person before, and many of them probably haven't. I just feel the eye on me, like they're expecting me to jump 'em or somethin'." As he says it, Debra watches him carefully and finally looks at me for my reaction.

I'm quiet at first—and a bit flooded, because my experience always seems different. "It is really hard how all this plays out," I say. "My mom told me that she actually *was* robbed on the streets of Chicago. She's never elaborated. My father, on the other hand, thought nothing of making friends with boys from *the projects* that bordered his neighborhood. He bragged to me about how they'd get into their share of mischief together, hopping trains and throwing corn on neighbors' porches on Halloween. My classmates in my small town defied stereotypes. Our President of Student Council at my high school, Spence Lewis, was both Black and exemplary, and Muriel Taylor won all kinds of awards on the debate team." Instinctively, I knew that they constantly had to prove themselves to people who judged them as less accomplished—and more likely to stir trouble.

Debra waits for me to finish, then says, "I get so sick of people watching every single thing I do," she says, "staring at me like I'm on exhibit. Gets old!" I know she especially wants me to hear this.

80

I want to say more, to relate to her. All I can do is to stay silent, as I reflect on the discomfort of being one who watches—and having to confess, at least to myself, that I *must* listen to better understand what it's like to be Black in our country.

Halloween, October 1981
☻ *Politics and Religion*

Rikki has a new love interest, and I meet him for the first time outside the cafeteria. Since she's just had her hair cut very short, I'm torn between giving attention to the man with her and her stunning new cut. She looks regal, with the look bringing out her high cheekbones and almond-shaped eyes. She could easily be featured in one of those oversized glossy hairstyle books at the salon.

She says she did it for swimming—the chlorine and her hair became a bad combination. A good many of her friends have resigned themselves to spending hours in the stylist's chair to wear an eye-catching braid, but Rikki doesn't want to be one of them. Her hair's been cut so close to her head that when you look at her sideways, her head curves into a perfect question mark.

At the cafeteria before our Halloween dinner, she's wearing a black wool coat with black faux fur around the collar. Underneath, she has on black pedal pushers, and a form-fitting lavender sweater that hugs her hips. She's painted her nails dark brown. I rarely see Rikki in anything so snug to her body, but I'm always struck with how solid and muscular she is, whether she's casual or formal. She's wearing her trademark silver earrings, which stay the same no matter what other ways she expresses her individuality. I admire how she builds her style around something so perpetual and distinguished, while I express mine with different earrings every day.

She introduces her new friend, Darrell, and he greets me warmly. His hands are so large that when I shake one of them, I'm aware of stretching my fingers and thumb across his palm. When I look at him, he is looking at me kindly, with genuine interest. Darrell, not Rikki, invites me to sit down and eat with them.

"Rikki's talked to me about you," he says. "She says you're an education major and you like kids."

"She's right. There's a long line of teachers in my family—my uncles, Grandma, my great-uncle in Who's Who for teaching history. When I was only five, I'd gather the neighbor kids to teach them how to write and even turned our backyard shed into a library. It's in my blood. I've always wanted to be a teacher."

"It takes a special inclination, that's for sure," he says, looking me straight in the eye. "I like being with kids one-on-one, but the trick is keepin' 'em busy. They get bored easily if they're not outside. At least that's the kind of kid I was. Seems like you have to civilize 'em, too." He grins at me, sizing me up for my reaction between bites of chili.

"That's definitely the challenge," I tell him. "I mean what gets me is all the abstract theory about teaching, and all the layers to it. People underestimate teachers. There are so many skills that go into it—a broad range of knowledge, getting along with people, strong organization, knowing how to create and deliver curriculum, and perhaps most of all—being willing to surrender to chaos." I can feel my cheeks turning red, because I've kept going without taking a breath and feel like I just blew up a balloon.

"My God, that's a lot. And we all know that teachers don't get paid what they're worth." He seems more intent on our conversation than eating, as though we're practicing a language together.

"It's too bad the profession has that reputation. In cultures like Japan, teachers are much better paid and even receive housing allowances, but they have to work much longer hours. They're highly respected though. I'd like to see our country value teachers more."

82

"Well," he says, "when ya think of the contributions teachers make to a child's life and well-bein', seems we'd invest a little more. Doctors get paid well, and they're mostly lookin' at the body." I'm excited that Darrell gets this and let him continue.

"The thing is," he says, "the ones in our society who don't bring in the money...babies and children, seniors, nursin' the sick, the poor...any job on the front lines of servin,' teachin,', nursin,', parentin'...won't pay all that well. I know it, 'cause those are the things my family's women do. All the important stuff." He sighs, stretches his arms out together.

I scrunch my face into a grimace knowing he's right. *My first awareness of women's issues was playing with Barbie dolls on the shaggy orange living room carpet. They were born in 1959. While they were all the rage, so were books by feminist Betty Friedan. But only in college have I thought about the ways women's bodies—particularly Black bodies—have been used to hold community and culture together.*

"I've upset you, haven't I?" he asks, "I hope I haven't made you think twice about teachin'."

Rikki looks up from a notebook she's been studying and says, "So, you actually think Chris would change her plans because of *you*?" She gives him a look over the rim of her glasses, asking who he thinks he is as pointedly as possible, without words.

"You haven't upset me," I lie, as my neck tightens, and I remember a student teacher in our education advisory telling me how students will do anything to test new authority in the classroom. "I know it won't be easy, but I've always wanted to do it. I have an instinct for being with kids. My uncles who are teachers haven't done too badly for themselves. Enough about me, though. What are you studying, Darrell?"

"Poli-Sci and I may want to get into law. I'm into social policies that counter the full impact of racial isolation and create upward mobility for inner-city youth. There've been so few Black policy makers, and this is an excitin' time to get into it. There's a growin' debate between Black influencers about how to solve the crisis of urban poverty. Right now, I'm doin' a compare and contrast paper between sociologist William J. Wilson and economist Glenn Loury. Loury's a conservative—he believes in limits to what the government can do and that as Blacks, we have to help ourselves out of poverty. Wilson doesn't believe that so much should be put on the individual, but on the social conditions resulting from cultural isolation."

"Wow, that's intense," I say. "My mom says that if you want to make friends, you can talk about anything you want except politics and religion. That was her way, I guess, of saying *she* didn't want to. So, I haven't really had much practice."

"In our house, it's quite the opposite. Everything's about politics and religion. How 'bout you, Ms. Rikki?"

"Well," Rikki begins, "considering my dad *is* a politician, that's pretty much what we talk about. Because of what some of us have lived, we don't have the luxury to *not talk* politics and religion. If the majority of policies have been on your side as a white person, what's in it for ya to talk about this stuff? I learned early on that your beliefs can lead to death threats. My dad's had 'em. What I know is that wherever he goes, he ends up talkin' about policies that impact people's lives." *Which dad?* Again, I notice that Rikki's not revealing that Liza and Eddie are *foster* parents.

"I'd imagine," says Darrell, "that lots of that discussion has to do with education."

"A large part of it," Rikki says. "He talks about it at church, in community and school board meetings, even at sports events. It all takes a lot of his time. He says our lack of attention to education and health could do us all in."

"And whether or not the people who most need those resources can get 'em..." Darrell adds, "...is where political science comes in."

My mind's inundated with complex thoughts, making my

body flush with heat. I wish I hadn't said what I did about my mom. My own father received death threats too, so I really don't have the luxury of avoiding these issues either. Every morning I watched him pack his briefcase, tucking his papers in next to his mace gun. "I want to make something clear," I say, swallowing my angst. "I don't think I have the luxury to not talk about these things. They affected my family too. I think my mom wants to leave it in the past, what happened to us." *I was born in 1961, just a few weeks before the Freedom Riders boarded their first bus from our nation's capital to challenge the laws and practices that enforced racial segregation. As I took my first breaths, Nashville's Reverend James Lawson, a disciple of Dr. Martin Luther King, was mentoring students, Black and white, to sit on city buses side-by-side.*

"Again," Rikki says, "It's because you *can*." She lowers her chin and gives me her look.

Her comment only fuels my defenses. "But see, Rikki, what Darrell doesn't know about me, or my father, is that he was a white man involved in the Civil Rights Movement. He *did* get involved. He *did* expect me to pay attention. He *didn't* survive it."

"You mean your dad was killed? How old were you?" Darrell asks.

"It's a long story," I say, "but race did play a role in my father's death. I'm not sure all the ways, because my mom goes silent on it, but if he'd stayed away from politics *and* religion, he might still be here."

Rikki bears with me, though I know she's impatient with me. "I never know what to think when white people weigh in on race issues."

"I understand," I say. "The issue of race *is* important to all of us. Somehow, we have to figure this out." I realize I have to stop here—and listen.

"Chris," Rikki says, raising her voice, "race played a role

in my mother's death, too. And unlike your mother, my own father *cannot* leave it in the past." *But wait, I thought that Rikki's mom and dad were in a fight...*

Rikki's got me. *How was her mother killed?* For one thing, my mom is still alive. Mom has, in fact, been able to move away from all this and create a new life for herself to heal. Rikki—and her family—are still pounded daily by cultural suggestions that they're inferior. *I have strong feelings about this I don't know how to manage.*

Darrell shrinks his tall body down closer to the conversation, and it's like we're all huddled under an umbrella trying to hear each other in the rain. "Whoa, Ladies," he says. "Wait one minute. You mean to tell me that you both lost parents because of this stuff?"

I look at Rikki and shrug. Rikki nods reluctantly. *This is the first time Rikki's tied her mother's death to racial tension!* Most people believe my own father's death was an *accident. But we both grew up with death threats.* And if it wasn't for that, Rikki's mother and my father *might* still be alive.

"Well, that's somethin', isn't it? I mean, isn't that *somethin'*?! How long'd it take for you two to figure that out?" Darrell looks back and forth between us, not wanting to miss anything. *But we never did figure it out before this moment.*

Rikki pulls herself up from the table to shift the focus, reminding me in the most ironic way of my mother who would do the same. She doesn't answer Darrell. Nor do I, leaving him to ask again, "C'mon now, Ladies. Seriously—how long?"

As I follow Rikki to clear our food trays, she whispers to me to call her after dinner, because for a little while now, we've planned to hang together at the campus Halloween dance.

Darrell trails behind me confused, and I finally share my own response. "It's taken until *this moment*, Darrell—and you can take some credit for that. I've really liked talking to you."

Darrell puts his hand on my shoulder, leans close to me and gently whispers, "Thanks for lettin' me know."

On that particular night, I realize that there are places Rikki goes (the pool, the science lab and the streets of Gary) that carry stories I don't hear—and yet other places where we share the narrative, even when it takes us to ugly realities. And even as we piece the narratives together, they keep changing depending on who is doing the telling and who is listening. I'm more reserved than Rikki in some ways, yet I've been the first to share the source of my deepest grief. In other ways, it's Rikki who inspires *me* to stretch. It's a gift that seems to come from us both being survivors—a code we share that pulls us into each other's energy field, defying our expectations and sometimes landing us on entirely new ground.

● *Dancing with the Rope Bridge*

As Rikki and I prepare for the Halloween dance, we decide to channel our alter-egos—with me dressed as the devil and Rikki as a Catholic nun. She has the full habit, with a crisp white collar we put together out of white cardboard, a black dress, stockings, black orthopedic shoes, and a rosary at her waist. Her habit is wrapped tightly over her ears. No silver hoops or make-up. Nor does she mention our talk at dinner, and we're having too much fun to bring it up.

"Gonna go about my bidness of bearing Blackness," she enunciates teasingly, hands on her rosary-clad waist. I laugh so hard that my cheeks get sore. My red face actually fits right in with my devil outfit. I'm wearing a wig, fishnet stockings under a cherry red dress, the kind that wraps into a V over the chest. I have poison-apple earrings, and the words "Falling Angel" which I stitched myself over the college insignia of my red baseball cap. I've also printed the words "Live backwards spells *evil*," and irony of all ironies, pasted them over a "Your Vote Counts" Jimmy

87

Carter campaign button.

There's an intimacy about prepping together to be a Halloween couple, as we stand close to each other looking in the mirror. To be mindful of the attention I bring to my ample lips, I've literally amassed a collection of light-colored lipsticks. Now, I have to decide if I'll risk a darker color to carry the costume. As I watch Rikki admire her own full lips in the mirror, I see value in my own. They're a beauty asset, not the nuisance I've made them.

Rikki and I head out together to the old dining room in Gray Hall. We pay for the dance together, and get our hands stamped at the entrance. I feel comfortable in my skin, and even though I'll never know what it's like to be Black, I'm beginning to feel a sense of belonging with Rikki and her friends. When the music starts, the beat channels its way through my veins—people *are meant* to dance. Folks who sway together stay together. Rikki's friends filter into the room, clustering around both of us. Cheryl is with them. She is Rikki's chum and lived in Umoja House before Geneva. Cheryl's shaved her hair close to her scalp like Rikki's and wears small silver posts in her ears. She has the tattoo of a bright purple cluster of grapes on the nape of her neck. Rikki calls her "Queenie," a name off-limits for me as befitting as it may be. I even tell Rikki it sounds like a slam, but Rikki assures me that it has to do with Cheryl's being a goddess amongst her friends. Rikki adds that Cheryl wants nothing to do with men and prefers to hang with women. "She hurls her opinions at folks like javelins," Rikki warned me. "You have to be ready to deflect them or you'll play the fool." Not wanting that, I listen to the two of them and get into the rhythm and the dance to excuse myself from conversation.

But Cheryl wants to know why I'm here, and Rikki senses it. "Queenie," Rikki says, "this is Chris." Cheryl mumbles hello to me. She whispers something to Rikki, who responds quietly, "You can trust her." I check Queenie's reaction, but she steps to Rikki's side and looks away as if to shield herself from me. She makes a few more comments to Rikki, but Rikki changes the subject and gives her hell: "Did you beat the shit out of Jake on the test, Queenie?"

"Sure did," Queenie tells her and smiles wide, telling Rikki all about the stats test she aced. Rikki turns to me and tells me that Queenie would like to be a sociologist, and if her stats results are any indication, she'll lick the research aspect of the field. She's confused as to why Rikki would bother to bring me to the dance, and I realize this isn't easy for Rikki. She's acting as the rope bridge over which the two of us can cross. I remember Clarence playing that role so that visitors to the Community Center could size Daddy up and see if he had anything to offer. That was the first time I'd seen a person not warm to Daddy instantly. Neither his sweet humor, nor his ease with crossing the color line as a youth in the ethnically-mixed Midtown area of Alton, Illinois in the 50's, could change the fact that he was a white man—and the face of the oppressor.

And here I am now. Rikki's my only bridge to stand on, a foundation that shifts underfoot as we both sway and lurch into unknown territory.

Trying to find that sweet spot for crossing, I comment to Cheryl that it must be frustrating that there aren't more people in the room who look like her.

"What on earth?" she asks, in disbelief. "I don't want anyone to look like me. I am my own person and have my own unique costume. Thank you very much." She looks away and shakes her head.

It forces me to correct myself. "What I meant," I say, "is that most of the students here are white."

"Oh, you noticed that, huh?" she responds, hands on her hips, beneath which her thick legs are filling out her black leotards and a snugly-fit black and yellow tunic.

"Impossible not to," I say. "It's something Rikki tells me about—what it's like to be a minority here on campus."

Cheryl shrugs, glances at my face. "I don't consider myself a MIN-ORA-TEE," she says. "I'm BLACK and proud of it!" I notice a few of the hockey and football players look at Cheryl and wince. If Cheryl stretches my social graces, she must explode theirs, as she moves confidently in her Blackness and her plucky bee get-up.

Perhaps Rikki would have had a similar response to me had the Coopers not adopted her and taught her, through their example, how to deal with folks from the white community like me. A lot of us don't mean any harm, but it takes us some time to *get it*—to understand the legacy of hatred and violence my own ancestors perpetrated, and the vast distance between our experiences.

I know Rikki tells Cheryl things. Cheryl knows, for instance, that Rikki's real Dad is in prison for murder. I remember that Rikki was happy with Cheryl for having her back when Rikki missed a barbecue at Umoja House. According to Rikki, Cheryl told the other women to leave Rikki alone, that she has her trials and hasn't had it easy. For that reason, I respect Cheryl, but I have a way to go to win her over.

As we move into the night, Rikki's friends form a dancing spiral around me and her, and Cheryl stays right in with the rest of them. I stay put, feeling awkward with the attention Rikki and I are getting, but I have no need to back out of the ring—no impulse to leave and or to socialize with girls from my own hall or guys from my classes. I stay with the dance, knowing campus friends are watching me closely and judging, and for once, it doesn't matter. I dance proudly and with abandon, knowing the same glorious red blood flows through all our veins. At first, I keep looking at them all, at Cheryl and at Rikki, trusting the rhythm. I watch groups of fellow students circling around each other, oblivious to other groups. It's as though we're in some big mechanical system that operates as a whole with a million tiny parts rotating around each other. Sweat trickles down my face, back and neck. Usually it bothers me, but if there's one thing I love to do, it's to dance. The sweat comes easy and without strain.

Rikki doesn't always dance right next to me through the evening, but she's never far away either. There's a moment, though, where a flash of the band's spotlights catches me and stirs my adrenaline. I look over to see Queenie looking right in my eyes, grinning from ear to ear as if she's won some type of lottery. "I ain't never seen the likes of you," is all she says at first. But then, she comes right up, squeezes my shoulder with her broad, strong hand and says, "Girl, you're alright. Somethin' 'bout you is alright." Like going from the formal "vousvoie" to the informal "tutoie" in French, I've been let in a hair and I don't take it lightly.

I tell Rikki that—that I've been let in by Queenie, and she tilts her head at me as if trying to hear me better. Then she looks at me straight in the eye and says, "I'm only going to tell you this once. Don't be anybody but yourself. Just be yourself. You'll be *fine*."

November 1981

☻ *Mozart's Sonata*

My roommate Annie's out doing photo-shoots for the yearbook in early November and won't be back until later in the evening. It gives me some privacy to invite Chuck, the guy I've been seeing since before I met Rikki, to our room. While I tidy up, I reflect on my life with Annie. We have trundle beds that form an "L" shape, a cozy arrangement that works great when Annie and I stay up into the night talking about our classes, our professors, and the guys we like. On cold days, when the heat pops on, we laugh hysterically about the "goblins" who drum and hiss within the dorm's old steam vents. Annie and I are cheery and respectful in the morning, and sometimes we'll throw *My Sharona* by *The Knack* or our favorite songs from *Grease* on the turntable.

With Chuck, I default to classical music on the radio, as if to make the room my own. When he gets to our room, I show him photos from home and my high school to break the ice. "Check out my friend Pam and how we both styled our hair the exact same way."

"So, you went for conformity over individuality," he says. "How about your senior photo?"

I find it and hold the book in front of us both so that I can study the photo myself—and his reaction to it—at the same time. Wish I hadn't tried so hard for the camera. "Look at you with your pearls," he says to me. "Pretty classy for a high school senior." He winks at me.

Chuck spots a book of poetry on my bookshelf, pulls it off and opens to a limerick that he reads to me:

> *There once was a scholar named Troy*
> *Who studied too hard to have joy*
> *He worked day and night*
> *With no rest in sight*
> *Then he knew he was no longer a boy.*

The limerick and music are mesmerizing, and I feel heat rise through my body to my face. Chuck puts one arm behind my back and quietly walks me over to my bed, nudging me to sit down. With his other hand, he lifts my chin to his kiss, and my small dreamcatcher hanging nearby is fluttering.

Chuck's eyes are closed and when he opens them I'm taken aback by the intensity of his gaze. I close mine tightly.

He reaches up under my shirt to unsnap the back of my bra. This is my time to stop the conquest, but I want it, and the longing makes me lose all sense of time. I allow Chuck to fumble with my bra's hook. The fumbling first calms me, then doubles my arousal.

A gentle rain begins that mists the window near us. It caresses my soul, and I snuggle in closer to Chuck as though I've known him forever. He stops his work on the bra hooks and we lose ourselves in kissing, exploring each other's tongues and then sprinkling brief, passionate kisses on different parts of our lips. He knows how to stoke the fires. Mozart helps with the movement, rhythm—an element of surprise.

Just as I stop expecting it, Chuck succeeds in his unlatching, and my breasts spring free, stirring the deepest sense of ecstasy I've known. Chuck lifts me up with one arm and lays me back gently on the bed, lifts my shirt and begins to kiss my breasts with the same short, teasing kisses. Mozart's sonata is interrupted by the melodious voice of the radio announcer, telling us that showers will continue into the evening.

Beethoven's Pastoral Symphony plays as Chuck kisses my lips, then softly blows in my ear. I'm thankful for the music. The classical pieces are sublime, an invitation to the eternal, unlike transient popular tunes. I put my arms up under Chuck's shirt and stroke his soft strong contours to return his favors. Teasing and anticipating, we slowly and reverently discover one another. I match his movements gently, wholeheartedly. I lift his shirt, stroke his chest, nestle my head in the fur of his chest.

"You're beautiful," Chuck says. "I love being with you." The intensity and precocity of our longing is unexpected, but it casts its invigorating spell, and we both surrender to passion.

"You're good at this," I say after our heartbeats finally calm down. "Had a lot of practice?" It's a question every girl wants answered.

"Not as much as you'd think. I respond well to good input." He smiles and winks.

I settle in against him and know that I could sleep like this for hours. The sweetness of his warmth, a clean fragrance about him, soothes me. It's a tenderness I've been missing from my life and I like it. I want it. I'm comforted, strangely, too, by the conviction that at the heart of all this, we are friends.

I look up at the wall clock, ticking softly, moving onward whether or not we want it to. I'm one who curses clocks, especially since my father's death. It is nearing 8:00 p.m. and I remind Chuck Annie will be coming back soon to break our spell.

"What'll she do if she sees us together smooching on your bed?"

"She'll probably give me a standing ovation."

"Oh, she's been trying to set you up?"

"Well, not exactly. She just thinks I need to live a more normal life."

"What's normal?"

I grin. "Doing more of what we just did—my opinion, by the way, not necessarily Annie's."

"I can help with that." I'm inexplicably drawn to Chuck and I silence myself to study why. The thick bottom lip, the cleft in his chin. Then there's the hair cut short and tidy near his forehead and sideburns, yet left long, wavy and a bit defiant in back. Youthful eyes, ready to crack a smile or to be serious, depending on what the situation requires. All of this could derail me completely.

Chuck takes my hand and strokes it. He traces my fingers with his index fingers, then strokes each finger separately between his thumb and index finger. "That's divine," I tell him. "Don't ever stop." He's captured my attention and my heart.

"There's so much I don't know about you, so much to learn," I say, thudding back to reality quicker than I'd like.

"How do you like me so far?" Chuck asks, winking at me, making me feel again as though I've known him forever.

"I like you a lot," I say, matter-of-factly, comforted as I am by his strange ability to put me at ease. He's lured me into his world on a weekday evening. No parties, no mind-altering substances to take the edge off. Is it something I can trust?

He continues to caress my hand, gathering his fingers in the center of my palm, then moving them out. My whole body's tingling again, but the clock says almost 8:00, and I point to it and sigh. Then he asks me, out of the blue, "How well do you know

Rikki?"

I sit up straight, look him in square in the eye. "Rikki? You mean Rikki Daniels?" (As if there could be another.) I'm stunned, the way you're stunned when you find out someone's been watching you undress in front of your window and you'd thought you were protected, shielded from view.

For reasons I can't explain, Rikki's been a more private and sacred part of my world. Yet, her spirit is ubiquitous, occupying my thoughts more frequently. As if she is somehow watching the two of us, I motion for Chuck to relatch my bra, and we begin adjusting our clothes.

All the while, I tell Chuck I've known Rikki since the end of first semester, and that we got to know each other from our drive to our childhood homes in Indiana over spring break.

"That must have been fun," he says with a grin.

"What makes you say that?" I inquire. "What do you know about Rikki?"

"I've seen you with her a lot, and it's surprised me." he says. "She's a wizard in the water, really. I've not seen anything like it."

"So, what surprises you about that—us being friends?"

"A few things," Chuck says. "For one, you're not a swimmer and Rikki clearly invests most her time there and…well, it's a bit segregated here on campus, and you're breaking that trend by hanging with her."

"You talk as though you know her pretty well yourself, Chuck. I didn't even realize you knew her."

"*Everybody* knows Rikki," he says. "She's sort of a campus phenom, right?"

I'm ready to hear him say how beautiful she is too. He stops at the athletic. Chuck has an athletic build himself, so he knows. I feel his strength mingled with the lightness of his touch. Will it disappoint him that I'm not the athletic type? Chuck's comments about Rikki feel like a betrayal of our privacy. They're thoughts that belong to my "other" world—the one where I'm supposed to be writing about Maria Montessori's view that children must be able to choose their activities and get to know them through the process of play.

I ask him again, "Why'd you bring up Rikki?" I smile at him, as sincerely as I can under the circumstances. I'm going through all the cycles of a relationship in a day's time, and admittedly I don't want to think too much about where all this is leading.

"It seems you're close—that's all. I'm curious," he says, and I put a halt to the chaotic story lines in my head. Chuck stands up, crosses over to the chair by my desk, spins it around a few times, then sits with his elbow on his knee, propping up his chin.

Annie's key turns in the door. She opens it with a vengeance, sees the two of us and it startles her. I haven't had a man in the room since we've been roommates, and I'm sure I look like we've been making out. Then there's the very real fact that Chuck's looks can stun a woman even if there's nothing else going on. Annie's response is to smooth her hair behind her ears, which she does when she's feeling nervous. She gives a quick glance down at what she's wearing.

"Annie, I'd like you to meet Chuck," I say. "We're both in the Presidential Scholars Program and just ran into each other in the cafeteria." I wink at Chuck.

"Annie," Chuck says, standing up to shake her hand. I catch a glimpse of myself in the mirror over our dorm-room sink. My cheeks are flushed, my thick hair is going every which way. I'm not the kind who looks presentable when I rise out of bed. I look suspiciously unkempt, yet part of me feels quietly ravishing, invincible, touched by the messiness of deep attraction.

"I need to get going," Chuck then says to us both, as he winks at me and motions me out the door with him.

Annie gives me a hesitant smile. "I'm gonna lock up," she says. "I've got to get ready for bed. It's a big day for me tomorrow." Annie's blond hair is pulled up high in back into a perfect ponytail. Sweaty wisps of hair frame her face. With no make-up today and her lips pursed, she doesn't have her usual glow. Or maybe it's just because I'm glowing more right now.

"I won't be long," I tell her. "Just going for a short walk." We close the door behind us, and Chuck tells me he's had fun with me. He kisses me on the cheek as though he's been doing it for years. I wonder how I'd feel right now if Rikki's name hadn't come up. So much around me seems to get back to her. Yet it's the crack in the cup that makes it all real.

I see Chuck doesn't leave pebbles unturned, and that's how he's getting me under his skin. He pulls my arm with one hand, then slides his hand down to catch mine. He squeezes it two times, then shakes it as though we've been business partners, honoring some primitive contract. Without a word, as the rain turns to flurries, he turns and walks into the darkness. I stand watching his commanding figure grow smaller and smaller.

☻ *Dr. Greer's Dilemma*

Rikki's the most valued swimmer on our college team. She brings the team its fastest times and has carried the team to top standing in the Minnesota Intercollegiate Athletic Conference (MIAC) Division III circuit. She's doing it right along with achieving high grades in rigorous pre-med classes. Our walks and outings are often interrupted by her need to squeeze in another sequence of laps or to tend a project she's begun in the lab. If she's developing a stunning gift in all of this, it's that she's stopped worrying about what other people think. "I'm an anomaly," she tells me. "I might as well name it." I attribute a lot of this to Liza's influence. She's there when she needs to be, listens when it counts, feeds Rikki with a steady diet of encouragement, and negotiates the financial backing with Eddie.

Rikki's life is steady and enviable more often than not, but I'm learning about the secret world she navigates to get there. The sore spot in her campus experience—a coach who seems to cater to a group of elite, white swimmers—can't hold her back from beating her own times and those of most girls in Division III competition, even as they sometimes treat her more as a nuisance than the star she is. Rikki has been keeping her hair short and textured, easier for swimming.

After Rikki's swim practice one night, we go out for Chinese food at the corner restaurant on the periphery of campus. Rikki confides in me that she's really had it with swimming being such an elite sport. Even though the Coopers encouraged her to come here to Minnesota (mostly because one of our new social science profs, Dr. Terrence Greer, went to Morehouse College with Eddie), she still wonders if this is the right place for her. She hates being the only African American girl on the swim team, but that isn't the half of it.

"There's no reason to be here. No reason at all," she tells me. "Look, I'm a token Black. The admissions office is just dying to get my mug on one of their marketing brochures to show off the school's diversity. But I'm sick of all the white think. And I don't exactly fit in with the rich little Black girls either—the ones who go to Harvard, Spelman or Howard. Dr. Greer did heavy marketing to Liza and Eddie."

"Have you spent much time with him?" I ask. It seems like a logical question, given that he knows her parents personally and has been a contact and all.

"I like Dr. Greer, but he's married to a white woman, so what's his commitment to improving the Black cultural experience in the U.S.? He keeps telling me to be patient. That's not the right approach!" Rikki rubs her own worry crease that's developing between her eyebrows. I'm digesting what just slipped out of her. Was it a back-handed compliment—that she's not thinking of *me* as white?

"Wait a minute," I say. "What's wrong with being

married to a white woman?" I can feel my cheeks heating up.

"Everything! I have a thing about brothers marrying white women. How can Dr. Greer affirm his own African-centered heritage—and that of his children—by hanging out in an extended family that's white? Surely, there's enough conforming to sounding and acting white that he has to do already, especially since he's in Academia. And maybe I would have been better off at an HBCU school—the standards are a lot higher. Damn, I mean Spelman has more Black women earning Ph.D.'s than Georgia Tech!" She crosses her arms over her chest, as if to show her physical strength as much as that of her conviction.

"Wow, that's amazing," I say. "But you must have really trusted Dr. Greer to come here, knowing what you do." I feel my head pounding, because I know if I'm not truthful I won't be able to live with myself. "Rikki, isn't it a bit like you hanging out with me, even though I'm white? That doesn't have to mean you're betraying your heritage, does it?" I feel a need to respect not only our cultural backgrounds, but to meet each other halfway, too. Shouldn't those of us who are open to what Black people experience get some credit?

"I'm not having sex with you, Chris, and I'm not spending every day for the rest of my life with you. And I'd rather die in hell or stay single than get it on with a white man." Rikki says this as we stop by my entrance to Gray Hall, where the majority of my dorm-mates are white women. I'm stunned. Wasn't part of Martin Luther King, Jr's dream for little white and Black boys and girls to attend school together a dream for white and Black women and men to cross the boundaries of race together as well? Rikki's statement makes her sound not all that different from segregationists in the 60's who feared interracial marriage!

"Rikki, I'm surprised to hear you say that." It's all I can say. It's really the first time I've ever disagreed with her. Until now, I've always met her halfway, been the one to acquiesce to her point of view—to emphasize how deeply I, too, am concerned about racial inequality. But here I have to draw the line and defend the integrity of bi-racial friendships and marriage. It's what we're doing, for goodness sakes!

"Well, then be surprised," is all she says. "I mean it. Sisters don't take too well to white women going around and stealing our men!"

I ask myself how we got here from Dr. Greer, and I see that to Rikki, he's bought in to the white system, and even if he is Eddie's friend, he's suspect. I get the impression that Rikki doesn't really know Dr. Greer all that well.

"I'm tired. It's not the time to get into all this," I say, and I open the door to my stairwell. "We'd better get back to studying." I tell her good night. Rikki and I have never hugged as I do with my other friends, and yet we've seemed to naturally agree when to call it a day. Tonight, she starts to walk off before I've even moved to step inside my building. I say goodnight again, but she doesn't turn around, and she doesn't say it back. A piece of shingle from the dorm's old building flies off the roof and hits the ground between us, as if to lend a staccato effect to the silence between us. For the first time, I let it go and walk up my stairs to my room with Annie.

☻ *Annie*

When I find Annie, quietly studious in her flannel PJs and headwrap, I have to admit that she has met my pre-college standards for the ideal roommate. Before I came to school, she was the type of girl I'd imagined would be my friend: smart, collegiate, quietly confident, silly and frisky, yet low maintenance. There's no need for me to talk to Annie about our friendship. It's a given. We'll even help each other's children learn to walk one day. I feel good with Annie. Like Rikki, Annie wasn't raised by her birth parents. In this case, she was adopted into a family with a father who is a business entrepreneur and author, and a mother who makes a full-time job of community service. They are the only parents she's ever known.

As I consider why my two friends, Annie and Rikki, were not raised in their families by birth, I realize that at times, each one of us feels like an orphan, especially those of us who had an early exposure to loss. Annie grew up in a luxury home, where hardly a thing was out of place and all the upkeep—from the lush, pretty gardens to the shining glass in expansive windows—had been thoughtfully arranged. Even so, the fact that she's adopted keeps her humble and open to people she doesn't necessarily understand.

For the first time since I've been friends with Rikki, I want to get Annie's take on things. "Annie," I say, "I know you're studying, but I wonder if you can talk."

"What's up, Chris?" Annie asks, sitting on her trundle, back against the wall, holding a yellow marker in her hand like a dart.

"Well, it's about Rikki," I tell her. "I know I haven't introduced you to her, but you've seen us spending a lot of time together. We've been getting to know each other since we drove home during break. I like talking with her, because she gives me a perspective that I wouldn't have otherwise—like what she experienced as a young Black girl in grade school."

Annie's so tired that she's holding her chin up with her fist as her mind deciphers what I'm asking of her. Still, she gives me her full attention.

"Jen and the other girls on our hall have asked me about you," Annie says, "...they wonder what your relationship is like. I haven't been sure what to say."

"What our friendship is like... If I were hanging out with any other white friend on campus, it wouldn't matter. We wouldn't be talked about."

Annie reaches up and twists her blond hair into a spiral. "Well, Chris, I mean your friendship is unique, because she is black and you're white. You seem *close* to each other, and that's

101

uncommon. I'm sure they mean no harm. They're just curious."

"Well, we have gotten close," I admit, as I rub my necklace charm, the Chinese symbol for *love*. "All the same, I'm still learning about Rikki's beliefs, and tonight's the first night we've really disagreed. Rikki doesn't believe that white women should date Black men, but not for the reasons you might think. She thinks they betray their culture when they choose white women." I stare ahead for a minute because I'm hurt. I genuinely care about Rikki and I don't really want to badmouth her to Annie.

Annie shifts a bit on the bed, pulls her psychology text off her lap and straightens her nightgown. "Well, I can see how black women might resent having their men take interest in white women instead of them. She might feel that it's a rejection of black women."

"No, I don't think that's it exactly. From what Rikki told me, it's more of a rejection of their cultural heritage."

"You're OK with white men dating black women, right?"

"If they want to, yes." I scan the relationships I know and can only think of one white guy I know in a relationship with a Black woman, and she's from Ghana. She wasn't born and raised here.

"You know, Chris, there's a lot more freedom now, but that doesn't mean people will go beyond their comfort zones. I mean what's funny is that you and Rikki *are* friends, so she's already acknowledging that it's OK to be friends with a white person." She stands up, says she needs to get ready for bed, and pulls the basket filled with her facial cleanser and toothpaste off her dresser.

"Yep, it's OK for us to be friends, but it's whole different ball game in terms of dating," I say, watching Annie wash her face.

"Yes, I think that's it," Annie says, "and that's brave enough. There are a whole lot of black people who want nothing to do with us. How'd the marriage theme come up anyway?"

"One of our new social science profs is married to a white woman. He's friends with Rikki's foster father too. Rikki says he's not as committed to understanding the Black experience in the U.S. if he's trying to get out of it by marrying a white woman." I sit down on my desk chair in a slump, with my head and body tilted back.

"Don't over-think it," Annie says, hanging up her washcloth, then popping into bed. "What does it really matter? He can't walk away from the black experience any more easily than a honeybee can abandon its hive. What keeps me from getting closer to someone who's black…well, the hatred of white people is so strong that it seems like there's nothing I can do right. I keep trying, but it always gets down to having to give myself up to earn their trust. I'm wiped out, Chris, and have a test tomorrow. Sorry, but I'd better call it a day." Annie pulls her covers over her and settles in sideways.

"Annie, we really can't give up. If we're gonna make things better, we have to be willing to feel uncomfortable. It's the only way to get to deeper understanding."

"I hear you, Chris," Annie mumbles, but it needs to be reciprocal."

Reciprocity. It's hard even between white friends. I feel we owe so much to the African American people for what they've suffered. Really, it's on us to rebuild trust. Yet, I know what Annie means. There's such a cohesion between the Black students on campus, because there are so few of them. I might have an in through Rikki, but I can't ever belong really. I know my place.

Still, I respect Annie for saying out loud what others only think. It makes her easier to trust even when we don't agree on everything. She's had her own hardships. When I saw Annie's majestic, beautifully landscaped home, I told her I'd never known anyone who lived in such a place. She told me it wasn't her *real* home. When I asked her what she meant, she told me that her real mother wasn't ready to have her and lives in a one-bedroom

103

apartment. She led me over to one of her shelves, pulled off a baby-food sized jar of dirt and placed it in my hand. "This is dirt from my *real* mother's garden," she said. When I asked her how she got it, she told me it was the only thing her birth mother had left for her.

Reflections: Minneapolis, 1981
☻ *The New Civil Rights Bill*

Dad was always giving rides to people, and once he gave a ride home to a little girl my age. She sat next to me, but I wasn't so comfortable with that. She had a musty odor about her, reminiscent of my Grandma's attic. Her flowered dress was dulled by stains, her long, dark hair limp and pungent from excess oils. I wanted to bring her home with me and let her fill my tub with luscious bubbles and have Dad sing his "Little Fishy" song to her. Instead, I sat quietly, trying out different comments to her in my imagination. By the time we arrived at her home, which looked like a small store with windows painted white for privacy, I'd only managed to ask her how she liked going to school. She didn't like that question much, just shrugged her shoulders and said good-bye. After Dad walked her to the door and her mother let her in, I asked Dad why her mother wouldn't help her take a bath or wash her clothes. He told me that water was a luxury not every family could afford, but she could get her needs met at the Community Center.

I often went along when Dad gave rides—to the Community Center, the Boy Scouts or to church where Dad was a frequent lector. On the way to pick people up, I could talk with him and ask him about things. Otherwise, it seemed that I was waiting for his attention, for those moments when he would take me aside and talk to me about the world, show me how to use the turntable or take photos with his camera. I waited to have his full attention the way you wait for a holiday, but even a holiday came more predictably. He tucked me in at night though. That's when he'd tell me a good many of his thoughts about everything, even the naughty things he did as a boy. He told me that he'd sneak to the ravines in the park at the end of his block so that he and his friend Wade could hang out with two Black boys they liked, Earl and Gordon, without any of their parents knowing.

"Why didn't you want them to find out?' I asked.

I remember his smile fading while he explained to me that Jim Crow was not a person, but very horrible state and local segregation laws enforced in the deep South and practiced in the North that prevented whites and Blacks from being able to spend time together in public. That's how I learned that until the 50's and 60's, Blacks were not allowed into our public libraries or schools, so they had to support each other with reading and education. They were even buried in separate cemeteries! They were leery of whites for good reason, Dad taught me, and they worked hard to be self-sufficient. When I was a toddler, Dad and Mom would invite Black friends to our home for dinner because they couldn't sit comfortably together in a restaurant. I had so many questions at the time and they've only multiplied since. Why did we have to separate people like that because of their skin color and what is it that made my father go against the grain and make time for people that others ignored?

Mom waited, as I did, to have her own personal time with Dad. She waited while he developed one social program after another through President Johnson's *War on Poverty.* When he wasn't at the Community Center or working with young boys in the criminal justice system, he was on the radio talking about the importance of social security for seniors, immigrants, and people with disabilities. Mom was generally quiet about such things. Most days, she didn't want to talk about all the things Dad did when he wasn't with us. I remember one day though, when I was seven years old, that she was very upset after talking to him on the telephone, and I asked her if she liked Dad's work. "Daddy's work is very honorable, Chrissy," she told me. "But there are people who work for him who don't particularly like him."

I just couldn't believe that. I would count the days until Dad and I could take a hike or a bike ride together. It's not just that he was my dad. It's that he was driven by a sense of wonder that would make even the most mundane task—like weeding the garden—a moment of discovery. Once he figured something out—whether fixing a speaker, repairing a bike, or frying an egg—he would rub his hands together in excitement. But it was his ability to make anything he did sacred, even listening to someone, that gave him superpowers. Most people, after being around my father for even a few minutes, left happier than when they found him. By the time he'd listened to anything on their mind, they'd be laughing, smiling, and sometimes talking about ways that they, too, could make a difference.

"It doesn't make any sense that someone wouldn't want to be around Daddy," I insisted to Mom. "It just isn't possible."

"Well, it is," she said, "There's a lady who is supposed to support Daddy, but when he asks her to do something for him, she acts like she doesn't hear him. She ignores Daddy and misses important deadlines."

"What's a deadline?" That sounds like something I'd like to miss too. "Maybe that is a good thing."

My mom's face softened and the light came back into her eyes as though something I said really helped her. "The deadline," she explained, is the time by which a project has to be finished."

"Or you're dead?" I'd asked.

Mom laughed, which I didn't expect because I was feeling very serious. "You're not dead—it's just the time when the project is supposed to come to an end."

"What happens when the lady doesn't finish the projects?" I asked her.

"Then Daddy doesn't look good, and his boss gets frustrated with him," Mom told me.

106

"Can't he just tell her she has to do the work, or she'll be in trouble?"

"No, Chrissy. Daddy can't say that."

"Why, Mom?"

"Because it's sensitive, Chrissy, and the woman is black. And she's had a rough go of it in life."

Now that I'm Rikki's friend, I've thought a lot about that conversation with Mom. For years, it didn't make sense to me. Grandma's housekeeper, Mrs. Noble, was Black, and I liked her best of all Grandma's visitors. She would hide things under her dish towel and make me guess what they were by their shapes. She hid an eraser, a perfume bottle, a bottle opener. Once, she even hid Grandma's denture case, which I wouldn't have guessed in a million years. Most things I'd guess, and when I did, she would break into "Done Found My Lost Sheep," and talk to me about how God finds every one of us no matter what shape we're in or how good a hiding place we've found. At Easter time, Mrs. Noble sang "Were you there when they crucified my Lord?" It was the only time I've seen my father weep. He just kept saying, "Yes, yes, I was there." That time, Mrs. Noble used her dish cloth to wipe his tears and I knew she loved him.

On one of our walks when I had him just to myself, Dad told me all about the new Civil Rights Bill that he and many others had fought for—they'd braved demonstrations, marches and boycotts to stand with Black people so that they would have equal rights at work, school and places like the public library. Dad had become the manager of the Social Security office a few years after the law was passed, when I was five.

Dad didn't march from Selma to Montgomery with Dr. King, but he drove to Chicago for a demonstration for fair housing with the Chicago Freedom Movement with Clarence and some of his family. Dad told me that many whites were involved in the Chicago Freedom Movement, after Dr. King moved his family to a Chicago slum to bring attention to the housing issue and the Civil Rights Movement expanded in the North. Dad said he and his friend who went with him to visit young men in prison were the only two white men to attend the local meetings about the new law. Dad wanted the young men in prison to get their Social Security cards.

When Mom told me about the woman at the federal Social Security office who didn't want to listen to my father, it was the only person I knew who didn't like him.

During the day, my father met with every hurdle imaginable as he created social programs to serve people who were poor and under-served; on evenings and weekends, he worked tirelessly to bring his ideas to his community and youth programs like the Girls and Boy Scouts and 4-H, so that more children could have opportunities to learn about civics and leadership. Then he would go to work with the woman who could see nothing in him but the face of the enemy. She'd been hurt so badly by whites that she could only treat Dad the way she'd been treated. What a loss—she would never get to know my father the way most of us knew him. I often wonder what happened to her after Dad was killed. *How did she feel when he died?*

● *Transformed by Swimming*

One night, I dream that my father is a swimmer. I watch him take his place at the end of the pool, prepared for a race. His body is slim and muscular, all his chest hairs shaved off. His goggles are in place and he's poised to win. Everyone's betting he'll be the winner. I know he's my father, but he's not in his own body. His beer belly, his bald head, his shuffling and depression— all the things that make him my father—are hidden from view. His fear of the water, for one! (He wouldn't even go in the water with me because his eyesight was so poor.) I recognize his thick lower lip, the dimple in his chin (like Chuck's), and the way he rubs his hands together about five times when he's satisfied with his

108

efforts.

Then he's in the water, swimming so fast I can no longer tell which swimmer is him. He's flying through the water, the water rippling and bubbling where he should be. I'm convinced a giant vortex, an undertow, has swallowed him alive. The pool takes on the magnitude and dangers of the ocean. The race, which occurs in fractions of seconds, is in slow motion now. I hold my breath watching for him to emerge from the water. Soon I'm in a panic, telling the coaches they should have never allowed this kind of thing—for a race to finish if one of the swimmers is not visible.

I wake myself up from yelling it out, then go back to sleep exhausted. In the next sequence, the coaches are watching from the pool deck as my father emerges from the water the winner. He's broken a world record. My dream even plays reruns for me so that I can see that yes, he is the winner. He isn't hurt, nor is he out of breath. There are only two changes that I can see—his skin is black now. Two, I call him but he looks right past me. He can't see me there. No amount of yelling or cheering gets his attention. I wake up shaking and crying this time around, convinced the world (not me) is convulsing—that the very world will break into pieces.

☻ *Letting Go of Rikki*

Since I haven't spent time with Rikki since our edgy conversation about interracial marriage, I'm only hearing of Rikki the star through the grapevine. Also, we have a new swim coach, who signs off as Coach D on the team's column in our campus newspaper. Rikki's mentioned often—she's expected to cinch a title in the MIAC sports conference. So far, she's beat our college's records in the 200-yard freestyle relay and in the 200-yard individual medley. Everyone has a renewed interest in swimming because she's that good. She's broken records beyond larger regional colleges that have traditionally earned All-Conference honors and produced several Olympians.

On a day with no classes and with Annie away at home, I heat up some baked beans in my mini-crockpot, brew a pot of coffee for breakfast and muse about my friendship with Rikki.

I look in the mirror. I'm as white as they come. A sheltered girl, whose parents, as much as they cared for civil rights, revered a Christ figure with light skin and blue eyes—and never mentioned that he may have had darker skin or brown eyes. I grew up on beans and weenies served with cornbread in the Catholic-school cafeteria. Wherever I live, I have trinkets that betray my white-bread youth: my rosary with my name that I still pray before bed and let the angels finish when I fall asleep, the angel on my desk with long, golden hair, her skin white as a swan's feathers. I wear ballerina shoes, white t-shirts and gold jewelry with gems probably mined in South Africa. I read pop-psych when I'm in a rut.

I sit at my dorm room desk overlooking the courtyard. An airplane booms overhead and impatient drivers honk at each other on the busy thoroughfare west of campus. Everyone's going about their business, while I sit overwhelmed at the implications of being white. Thinking I may have learned where Rikki's pain is lodged like a buried secret code, I reach for the phone, wondering what lies on the other side of my risk. As I'm dialing her number, it rings and my heart and adrenaline surge in concert.

"Hello, Rikki here," she says. What are the chances of getting her on the first try?

"Hi Rikki," I say and then there's an impossible silence that would drive a radio station to ruin. I have her now, though, and I'm going to listen and give her the room to fill me in.

"I hear you're going out with Chuck."

"Well, we...uh..." I can't say I'm with him. I can say and I do that he's a nice guy. I want to ask why that's her opening question, but I stay quiet.

"Our lives are different...and uh...I just want to say we're not...well...." This isn't like Rikki, not like Rikki at all.

Something's happened. She's one to know exactly, at all times, what's on her mind. "I think…" she continues, "we're just not meant to be…"

"Meant to be what, Rikki?"

"Meant to be friends."

I plant my feet flat on the ground. I read that you're supposed to keep your feet flat for equilibrium in an argument. "What'd I do?" I ask. I'm trembling.

Then it all comes at me. "You think you're on some goddamn mission to fix me, like I'm some charity case." She enunciates the word "charity" with a shaking voice.

Tears form quickly. "Rikki, my God," I say, "You're furious with me." How'd my good intention to call her backfire so badly?

"I am. You make me sick, that's all. You make me sick. You're just like the rest of them, and you know it. This is the problem with be-friending a white person. You have these little moments of trust and then they go and do something stupid and it just exhausts the hell outta ya."

Now I feel about the size of Jenna and Michael. And like them, I don't know what I've done to stir such venom.

"Rikki, what's up? This isn't like you. You…"

"You're full of shit," she yells at me through the phone.

Was it my mere suggestion that it's OK for a Black man to marry a white woman that Rikki can't even give me the time of day? Yet, it's alright for her to ask about Chuck, a *white* man. Damn her!!

Still I don't give up easily. "Rikki, look I know I've disappointed you," I say, trying to calm my own shaky voice and trembling body. "I'm sorry."

"Rikki, I have been in my own world. But," I say while sniffling, "I'd like you in it."

With that, she hangs up. The friendship's over. It's just been too much. My risk backfired and I have to move on, even as

I replay our dialogue. I feel I've failed big time. Maybe Rikki's the kind of friend you keep giving to, keep confiding in, and the more loving and truthful you are, the more she lashes out. She finds your soft spot and blows it to the size of a Macy's Thanksgiving balloon. The whole time you're thinking, "There's not a thing I could do to please this person, so why do I try?" You ask yourself if you've tried hard enough or if there's not one more thing you could do. Then it hits you—*letting go is the most loving thing you can do.*

● *Part of the Problem*

Often after I've been with Rikki, I feel guilty for feeling close to Annie, my white roommate who has always been provided for, whose worries have never been about money and whose only liberal political belief is that women should be allowed to have abortions. Annie and I don't talk politics much—when it comes to the part about taxes, we'll each be on our way. Yet, we agree on many things: we agree, for instance, on how to decorate our room, and that sex before marriage can work if two people love each other. We agree on matters of etiquette. Annie takes responsibility to clean our room and asks permission if she's going to invite a friend. I do the same. I absolutely love this about Annie: she allows her pet hermit crab, Donna, to go on a morning walk. We can listen to old Jackson 5 albums together and know all the lyrics by heart. The clincher about Annie is her sheer comfort with her body. She does gymnastics and yoga in her underwear while I'm studying and it's the most natural thing in the world, no different than brushing her teeth. When I exercise, I don't just slip it in. It's a whole ritual, requiring music, an outfit and privacy.

Annie puts her family first, then her friends and prioritizes from there. I'm Annie's friend because I was assigned to be her roommate. It could last forever, but it may be over as soon as we leave college. Annie is big on reciprocity and birthdays. She bakes

112

me cakes and considers her friends, her lamps, soap bars, record albums and even her pet hermit crab Donna as property we share. Annie doesn't read the paper and obsess about world affairs. Her real talent lies in organizing friends around ballroom dances and free concerts. She likes to invite people, then sit back and watch what happens between them. She'd happily make a mess if it would bring people together for fun.

Rikki would do no such thing. More important to her than how friends down the hall are getting along is how the children in the world are finding food to eat. She'll tell you that and then she'll go swim for an hour. After her swim, she'll say that fair international distribution of health care is why she wants to become a medical doctor.

But both Rikki and Annie, different as they are, have moxie with a conscience. Energetic and not apt to let anything stop them, they care about people when you get right down to it. Rikki's learned that she needs to care for herself first. Rikki looks at me through a few lenses and has always wondered if I'm the real deal. The expectations are always high, but before this last falling out, she's watched out for me, told me things she'd tell no one. I've always challenged her comfort zone, but up to now she's liked me anyway. She'd come upon my naiveté on some issue and frankly show me her gentle side. She got a kick out of me, if not always in the moment, then over time. We are very different (opposites maybe?) which has made our dialogue an exercise in transcendence. Rikki wouldn't understand the first thing about why I love Annie. To her, Annie and my other white friends are all part of the same problem. Just being white, even if I was born this way and can't help my cultural heritage, makes me part of the problem.

● *Absurd Things We Do*
In mid-December, the trees are dancing wildly as I walk from the library to our room in a cold rain. Shivering, I pull on the

113

thick-yarned cable sweater Mom bought me at a craft festival the first week of school. Annie's left me a note that she's spending the night at her friend Marcy's and I'm pleased to have the place to myself. I light a candle, pull out my early childhood ed textbook, settle in at my desk and get to the work of recording age-appropriate behaviors for school children.

A knock at my door startles me. I've lost track of time. It's 11:00pm according to the clock by my bed. I rub my eyes and want to ignore the knocks—my God, it's late! But the rapping becomes rhythmic, like a Morris code, and I know it's Rikki.

"Open the door, Girl. It's time we talk." She's whispering it like a chant—repeating it softly now with a quiet, steady beat. I begin to question the choices I've made.

Still not answering wouldn't be right. She's taking initiative.

Before I do, I whisper, "I'm here." It's the first time I used my voice today. I've been holed up studying. I say it again, louder. It's a game we're playing—cat and mouse. I'm the one testing the waters this time.

"Open sesame, Girl," she repeats.

She has me, and I hate her for it. Somewhere I read that a sign of a healthy friendship is good timing. Her timing sucks and things are strained. I've all but given up on our relationship. God, she's high maintenance.

I open up and absorb her look, as if seeing her for the first time. Her head's wrapped elegantly in a turban and she's wearing her silver hoops. She's dressed in black sweat clothes. She's thrown on a pair of black high-heeled boots. Only Rikki can wear anything and it works. If I'd had a doll of her as a child, I'd have played with it for hours. She's as good for my soul as she is dangerous. Is that the way it's supposed to be with someone we want to love?

"It's you. I wouldn't open the door for anyone else," I say.

"Oh, how about the little sweetie of yours? Is he off

somewhere?"

What's this—is she jealous? "He's around. He's just learning not to bother me when I have studying to do."

"Yeah, the work's picking up. I needed a break."

"Interesting what work avoidance will do," I say, surprising Rikki and myself. She gives me her pissed-off look and I smile. I'm back on track with her. What else do I do? "What's up, Rikki? Why are you here?"

"Stop messing with me, Girl!" she says, the backlash of anger surfacing yet again. Pretty naïve of me to expect reconciliation so soon. Her words sting for the thousandth time, but I start to see through them. I've been taking Rikki's anger personally, but she's only treating me as she's been treated.

"OK, I will," I say, "though I'm still not clear on what set you off in the first place." I feel like a clown and must look like one. I haven't even washed my bed head and forged through this day on the tethers of my own energy.

"God, you look beat," she says, echoing my own thoughts. "World isn't treating you too well, is it?"

"No worse than it's treating you," I respond, sticking my tongue out at her. It's the perfect thing to do. She starts laughing at me, from a place deep within her. It's nearly an involuntary reflex and can't be stopped despite her best efforts to be mad at me.

At some point, I join in, laughing at her, at myself, at the absurd things we do when mirroring gets too intense. We're fools in the pursuit of each other's approval and neither one of us can put a finger on the source of our madness. I watch the candle flame flicker on my desk, my education book open and inviting. We're propelled by a mysterious chemistry, Rikki and me. Maybe I don't need to know the reasons anymore and neither does she.

"Seriously, we can be somewhat of a mess, can't we?" I ask, and she shakes her head and says, "Speak for yourself." I tell her I've missed her, was worried the relationship was over and we hug. Then she tells me she has to go and we leave it alone.

I return to my desk and sit, my hands over my face, my arms propped on my elbows, and stare at the door for about five minutes. My relationship with Rikki is resilient, sacred and fragile all at the same time. I carry it in my heart like a premonition of deep change ahead, even with life's daunting shortness. It's as if by being friends against all odds, Rikki and I are repairing something *sacred*. Would I feel this way if Annie and I had a disagreement and she came back to me?

Still, you don't make a big deal about the past with Rikki. You just keep moving full-speed ahead and mount hurdles in the way as they appear. I keep my mouth shut. I'm the one who loves revisiting the roads I've been on, even if it hurts. Even with Chuck, I can find strength in pulling out pieces of our lives, examining them under the microscope, polishing them, too, as though they're stones found on the beach. We turn them over in our palms, feel them, play with "what if's." Not because we have any regrets. We just wonder what to do next time.

And so, we're moving forward. This is the last we'll talk about our cold war. Rikki's been infused with that old worldview that if you bring anything up about childhood, you're muddying the waters. Yet, every so often, when I least expect it, Rikki will tell me something about her life that stops me in my tracks. She told me, for instance, that her birth father hates whites so much that he wanted her to attend an all-Black college. Though she rarely sees him, he has power as her father and part of him is in Rikki. Sometimes I can feel her father's hatred in Rikki. She wrestles with the part of herself that's drawn to me or my being white.

There aren't loads of rules governing bonds between women and much fewer if the women aren't romantic partners. Add a racial mix to the equation, and there are even less.

I sing with Rikki at church, eat at her tables, shop in her

favorite import stores and the whole time we talk. We talk about cultural idiosyncrasies. I complain that white people never throw anything away. Rikki laments that Black women try to emulate white hairstyles. Sometimes we can laugh about the strange things we do that bother or impress people on our side of the color line. And secretly, with each other, we make promises to just keep learning about one another and keep people guessing. *I still don't know what really happened to Rikki's mother, but it would be cruel to ask anything about it.*

☻ *A Fragile Balance*

Knowing that Rikki likes a good workout, I leave her a note at Umoja House to propose something energizing. She calls me later in the day. "It's been awhile," she says. "About time we get together to hang out, isn't it? Let's be spontaneous."

"Let's go skating," I say. "I haven't skated since I junior high! Should we go?" She's game, and so we set a date—which I approach with a jittery excitement since the last time I skated I came home bruised from falling. I didn't get my skates sharpened, which surely didn't help.

Later in the day, as we prepare for open skating at the Parade Ice Garden in Minneapolis, I waste no time in sharpening my blades. As Rikki and I lace up our skates, I tell her about how once I found my old skates hanging from a nail in Mom's basement filled with birdseed that a busy mouse had stored in them. Rikki assures me that she hasn't skated any more than I have.

When we first move out onto the ice, my ankles feel as though they'll snap off like the tip of a string bean. A few small glides, and I pick up the pace.

The first couple of times around the rink, I feel liberated and let my body flow freely. My skates are gliding beneath me, my arms swaying alternately for balance. The mechanics come back to me, and I pick up my speed and flow effortlessly forward.

117

Hockey players sprint around us, with bent knees, their backs erect and low. They move as fluidly as Rikki does in the water. Squealing children dart in and around us, more concerned with keeping up with friends than with falling. One tall woman wearing a sleeveless white turtleneck and form-fitting black leggings, spins in circles like a ballerina and into a floating arabesque. She practices the moves over and over, making it look easy. Sometimes she skates with her male partner, who is practicing his jumps. Rikki studies the wizard skaters as if she's a mynah bird memorizing sound patterns. It doesn't seem to help her. She glides, cautiously and childlike, around the rink, often grabbing my arm to steady herself.

After a half hour, the rink dims the lights, unleashes the disco balls and Donna Summers' voice. I pick up my pace and watch Rikki, who for the first time since I've known her, is struggling to keep up with me. I slow down, let her catch up and grab me, try to keep my own fragile balance as I absorb the fullness of her weight.

"It's good to see you, Rikki," I tell her, laughing. I'm havin' a good time myself—'cept I'd better practice if I'm gonna do this again."

"This *is* practice," I say.

"I guess it is. But I mean…don't they let the beginners have the rink from time to time?"

"This is it. It's the only way to start." I wink at her.

She looks at me like I'm speaking a foreign language that she's heard but can't quite grasp. "You mean I have to be out here making a fool of myself every time I come?"

"You're doing well," I say, which isn't entirely a lie, because she's nearly keeping up with me and I'm making it around the rink without falling. "C'mon, let's work on technique." I bend over slightly, put my weight first on one skate, then the other, pushing sideways with my skating stroke. I glide on one skate, as long as I can, then switch and glide on the other. Rikki watches

118

me, grinning ear to ear. She's wearing wire-rim glasses that she uses mostly for studying, and they've slipped down to the end of her nose. There's a look of delight in her eyes.

"So…," she says looking at me," when's the last time you skated?"

"I really can't remember," I say, and it's the truth.

"So, where'd you learn how to do this?"

"Our neighbors had a pond they let us use. And I'd go skating sometimes with the Girl Scouts. I had to earn one of the badges."

"Did I hear you right?" she asks. "What'd you have to do to earn that?"

"I can't remember all the things. But I did have to skate backwards."

"Skate backwards?"

"Look at *those* guys." It almost seems as if the hockey players heard me. They skate backwards in droves to Michael Jackson's "Don't Stop Till You Get Enough."

"Amazing," is all Rikki can say.

I start skating backwards, too, choppy and slow, but I stay with it and try to focus on what I'm doing. "Haven't worked this hard the whole semester," I say, smiling at Rikki who's trying to decide if I know what I'm doing. "The fact is, no one observed me for the Girl Scout badge. They took my word for it." We laugh.

I start moving forward again with Rikki so the two of us can talk. She's stopped grabbing for me and is holding her own on the ice, focused on not falling and resigned to the fact that she can't keep up with me. "I still say you earned the badge," she says, in awe that people even do this. "I won't do it again," she says.

"You won't come skating with me again?" I ask, surprised, knowing full well she likes the athletic challenge.

"No, not that. I won't let my ego get in the way of our friendship again."

With the loud music, I'm sure I'm not hearing right. "You

119

what?" I ask again. I look at her to see if her facial expression will inform me.

"I get a kick out of you, Chris. I get a big kick out of you, Girl." She grins widely with her lips closed—while looking at me—then loses her balance and falls right smack on her strong, firm hind end. She doesn't know whether to laugh or cry. She's used to being agile and invincible—screwing up isn't in her repertoire. Skaters whiz by and I offer her a hand. Together, we pull her up. She wobbles into a few forward glides.

"Mind if we just skate together?" she asks, and I realize she means linking arms and me slowing down to go at her pace.

I nod, we link arms and skate ahead as she regains composure from her fall. We skate in tandem for a bit, silently paying attention to our glides.

"Do you notice…" Rikki asks, "that I'm the only Black person in here?"

I scan the rink area and sure enough, she is. Rikki's taught me to pay attention to this when it happens, but I've been so absorbed in getting back into skating that it didn't faze me this time around. "You're right," I acknowledge. "How come Black people don't skate?" I shrug my shoulders. *There are very few Black swimmers too.* It gets down to resources, I know, but I also know that Blacks have had to fight for everything they have. It's not even possible to fight for things you don't even know you're missing.

All too often, I go places with Rikki and she's the only Black person. She believes she never quite fits in. Because this is a defining theme in her life, I've never been able to persuade her that I never quite fit in either, but for different reasons. One, I think too much. Two, I move beyond the cultural mores for friendship. Three, many of our fellow students are upper-class (unlike me) and they've never had to worry a day about money (unlike me). (Even Rikki's foster family has a higher income than Mom and me.)

"I don't know why I met you, Chris," Rikki says, as if my thoughts flowed through our linked arms straight to her limbic system. *She's gonna tell me somehow that I'm not the misfit I think I am.* "You're alright, even if you can skate better than me." It's funny to see Rikki beyond her athletic comfort zone—that she has to slow down and learn things she doesn't know just like the rest of us.

"I'm glad you're doing OK with me, Rikki." I'm referring both to our misunderstanding and to skating. I don't tell her that I'm not comfortable on skates and that my legs hurt so bad I wouldn't mind if I waited a year before doing this again. Unable to focus both on skating and our conversation, I suggest we wrap up. We skate over to the benches near the lockers and sit down.

"I am doing OK," she says, "but there's something I haven't told you." She pulls out a stick of Juicy Fruit gum, my absolute favorite, and offers me a piece. "It's my dad..." she says, "Tyrone...he really wants to see me. Wants me to come to Michigan City."

I don't know how to respond, so I unwrap the gum. "When's the last time you saw him?"

"Liza and I went to see him in the fall before I came to school."

We change into our shoes, then grab our bags and head for my stalwart red Pinto. It's started to snow. The flakes are so big that you can see their lace patterns as they land. "Winter's here," I say. She smiles at me, doesn't say anything.

I slip *Charlie Brown's Christmas* into the cassette player once we're in the car. All my friends who ride with me know I love Charlie Brown music, even in the summertime. "You ever been in a state prison?" Rikki asks me. That's the trick about becoming an adult—you have to segue from catching snowflakes on your tongue, ice skating and the meaning of Christmas to the ugly realities of life.

"Never been—only visited a jail. *I think of the LaPorte County Sheriff's Office and finding my father's "accident" report. And I'm also touched that Rikki is opening up to me.* "How's your dad doing?"

"I really don't know," Rikki says. "I'd like to go see him at Christmas, even though I'll be staying in Gary." *Rikki's father lives in prison. I can't even imagine what that would be like.*

"I'm sure you'll find a way," I say. I'm dying to ask her more questions, but I look over and see that she's comforted by the music, and I leave it at that.

☻ *Kwanzaa*

The first Christmas Eve after my father died, Mom and I were invited to Dad's friend Clarence's house with his wife, Callie, three sons, two daughters and all their grandchildren. The dinner offered many firsts for me. It was the first time I was ever in an African American home. It was also the first time we shared Christmas with a family beyond our own. It was also the first time to eat venison, a gift from Clarence's son, Dexter, who had shot two deer that season.

Though my mother's family was large, rarely did we gather together as a family in one home. At Christmas, it had just been our little family, unless we visited my grandparents. Since Mom had spent so much time with her family after Dad's death in September, she jumped at an invitation by Clarence to spend Christmas Day with him and his family. It was Clarence whose counsel Daddy sought most often before he died. Clarence and Callie graciously welcomed us into their home and treated my mother like royalty.

Mom, still fragile from the tragedy four months prior, was seated by Clarence and Callie, with a placemat of Kente cloth, a small African basket under her glass and silverware with ebony handles placed elegantly on each side of her plate. My own place setting had the silverware with ebony, but I didn't have the special African cloth or basket. The family was excited because it was the first holiday season where they would celebrate a new African American tradition called Kwanzaa.

One of my own favorite holiday rituals is to light candles. In the center of the table, dressed in red, black and green, was a candelabra called a *Kinara,* with one black candle in the middle, three red candles on the left and three green candles on the right, each of which stood for a cultural value, or *principle.* Mom and I lit our own candles for Advent—lighting a candle each week as we prepared for Christmas. Maya Tolchin, a girl I'd met through the Community Center, lit candles on a *menorah* for Hanukkah, to celebrate the triumph of light over darkness.

To explain the Kwanzaa ritual about to begin the day after Christmas, Clarence called his children and his grandchildren, who'd been sitting at smaller, card tables, to assemble around the family table. I asked Mom why Blacks celebrated two holidays, and she told me that Kwanzaa wasn't another holiday like Christmas, but a celebration specifically for African American people.

Clarence's family and grandchildren were very excited to see the Kinara and all the "gifts" around it, including nuts, fruit, gourds, an ear of corn and a wooden goblet called a *unity cup.* With his deep, clear voice, Clarence explained to his children that this new holiday was just created to honor the African people's reverence for community. He also explained that the black candle represents the theme for the first day of Kwanzaa, *Umoja,* which means *unity.* Each day, the children and parents would ask one another "Habari gani?" meaning "What's the news?" in Swahili, to which they would respond with the principle of Kwanzaa for that day.

Then Clarence watered a plant on the table in front of him, saying that he was giving *libations* to thank my father for his work. "We are honored today to have the family of Ryan Fitzgerald with us. Ryan was a man ahead of his time, a man of wisdom and courage. We are blessed to have his wife, Mary, with us today, and his daughter, Chris. We know that Ryan had a heart for the marginalized and saw no one as disposable: the people who were incarcerated that he visited each week and the children who come to our Center hungry with few safe spaces to be children, because they have already had to carry the weight of poverty. Ryan was a man of conviction who lived what he believed, a man who treated kings and paupers with the same level of respect. Let's raise a toast to Ryan and dedicate our Christmas dinner to him!"

The children knew to raise their small paper cups with Kool-Aid and to tap them against one another in celebration. When Clarence said again, "To Ryan!," they followed his example, yelling excitedly "To Ryan!" with their innocent, passionate young voices. I watched on with amazement, my eyes flooding with tears, for the warmth and empathy Clarence inspired in his family—and for all the times I've been approached with suspicion by African Americans who could not see past my being white.

When it came time to eat, I was seated next to Clarence's son Dexter and across from his daughter Marvella. Clarence's grandchildren about my age of ten years old had left for their card table in the living room, and I was the only young person to stay at the adult table. I whispered to Mom that I thought I should go with the other children, but she whispered back, "Chris, you're a guest of honor. Stay here." As we ate, Dexter talked about the day he caught the deer, that he shot it in the leg initially so that it couldn't move, but then shot a bullet into its heart. Marvella was the only one to watch for my reaction. Finally, she interrupted him. "Really, Dexter, this young girl is not going to finish her meal if you go on and on about that." Dexter winked at me and said he knew that I was a big girl and could handle it.

My stomach started churning because I wasn't used to thinking that meat came from killing. Marvella's attention to me was a big relief and a bonding moment for the two of us. Unlike most adults who asked me if I liked my school, she asked me what I did for fun. I told her that I liked to have TV nights with friends and sometimes bake bread and cookies with them. "Bread and cookies!" Marvella repeated excitedly. "Mom, I think we have a young baker here," she said. I nodded and smiled at her. But I didn't bake all that much. After Daddy died, I lost interest in most things. To get my mind off our loss, Mom was taking me to classes where I learned how to paint the type of ceramics that you make with a mold. The skill lies mostly in picking out paint colors, then spending most of your time brushing it on with the right thickness.

Callie listened to Marvella, though, and said, "Chris, since you understand the value of baking, I'd like you to help me cut and serve the pies."

Davonna, tall and slim, with a training bra beneath her sweater, overheard her grandma and complained. "But that's my job, Grandma!"

Grandma responded lovingly, "Of course it is! And Chris here likes to bake, so she'll really appreciate our sweet potato and bourbon walnut pies!" There was a crescendo of "mmm...mmms," a few yells for pie, and Davonna got up to follow her grandma into the kitchen.

"C'mon, Chris." Callie motioned for me to follow her into the kitchen. She gave the bourbon pie to Davonna and the sweet potato pie to me, showed us how big to make each slice and how to move it in one piece to a plate. I was glad to get the sweet potato pie because it was my favorite color—autumn harvest orange, richer and thicker than the traditional pumpkin pie in my family. But when I went to pick up my first piece with the wide blade of the knife, half of the piece fell off onto the linoleum counter.

Davonna laughed nervously. "What are you doing?" she asked. "You can't even move a piece of pie without breaking it."

Heat flooded through my cheeks and I stood there shaking. I didn't know whether to throw the piece away that I'd dropped. "That can be my piece," I quickly said. I scooped it onto the plate and pushed it toward the other half. I didn't know what else to say. Davonna already had four pieces sliced and centered on plates and was proud of her pace. I had to ask her to excuse me to reach past her for a paper towel, then wipe where I had spilled. I kept my eyes on her so that I could shrug or smile, but she stayed focused on her pie slices and her own efficiency.

I took some deep breaths and started to slice again—slowly —because I realized my knife wasn't as wide as Davonna's.

"Why are you here?" she asked.

"I think it's because I mentioned to your Aunt that I like to bake," I said.

"No, that's not what I mean," she said. "I mean why are you at our house?"

My eyes filled with tears, tears for the kindness of the family invitation and tears for not measuring up with Davonna, the one I was really supposed to impress because she's closest to my age. I wanted to go home—I'd lost my appetite.

"My dad was good friends with your Grandpa," I said. "And he just…got killed."

"Got killed? By a gun?" she asked.

"No, he was hit….by a…train," I said quietly. I felt so ashamed, as though I had failed, being one with no father and serving pie I didn't even bake. My eyes had already welled up with tears, and poor Davonna was dumbfounded. She had no idea why I was there. When her Grandpa had given his toast, talking about Daddy in the past tense, it didn't hit her he was no longer alive like the deer we were clearing off our plates.

She was quiet for an eternity, as she finished slicing the pie, then just said, "Wow, may he rest in peace." *What about peace for me*, I thought. Callie came bustling in then to see how we were doing. All of Davonna's pieces of pies were nicely sliced and centered on their plates. As for me, there I was, tears streaming down my face, only three pie slices dropped sadly on plates as I fought to contain my nerves.

Callie was alarmed. "Are you OK, Chris? Did you cut yourself?" she asked.

By then, I was covering my eyes in pain, wiping my tears with the same towel I'd wiped the counter—and speechless.

"Davonna, why aren't you helping her?" Callie asked, troubled that Davonna was focused on her pie slices instead of me.

At that moment, little Lena came running into the kitchen with her book, yelling, "I can read, Grandma! I can READ!" When she saw Grandma pre-occupied with the pies, she turned to me with curiosity, but mostly with trust, and tugged on the sleeve of my cable-knit sweater. "Hey, you sad?" she asked me, "I can read to you." Her act of kindness warmed me, and I followed her to the living room, where the adults had begun to gather in the upholstered chairs. The book cover drawing of two baby squirrels, sitting side-by-side on a branch, the soft plumes of their tales curving up their backs like a Mohawk. Lena walked to the only empty chair and said, "You get in the chair and I'll get on your lap." I sat down and she turned around so I could pull her up on my lap. She nestled her head, braided and accented with red, green and black beads, beneath my chin, slid her back into the curve of my body and opened to the first page. The book *Solomon Saves the Squirrels* was the story of a boy who found baby squirrels who fell from their nest and did not have a mother.

"Solomon…played…in…the…yard…after…the…rain," she read, while her tiny finger pointed to each letter and each word. "By…the…tree…he…saw…two…little…" When she saw the drawing of the fallen babies, she turned around and cupped my chin with her tiny hand so that I would pay attention. "The squirrel babies lost their mommy!" she said. "That's why Solomon got to feed them."

As we sat together, Lena's mom, Natalie, came over to us to check on her. "I see Lena's got your ear," she whispered to me.

"I'm really reading, Mommy. I figgered it out!" Lena shouted, excitedly.

127

"Good for you, Ms. Lena," her mom said, winking at me. I realized then that Lena's mom thought she was just pretending.

"She is *really* reading," I said. "Aren't you, Lena?"

"Yes, Mommy, listen. Furry…aminals…all…alone. Baby…squirrels!" Whether or not Lena knew all the letters, she knew the story and kept at it until her cousin Marcus came by on a firetruck scoot car and nudged her to play with him. While the adults around me ate pie, I played with Lena and Marcus as they took turns sitting on the fire engine while I gently pushed them. Marcus yelled "Ooo-ooh…ooh-ooh" like a siren. Davonna didn't come into the room from the kitchen until it was time for me and Mom to leave. I was embarrassed still by my clumsiness with the pie. But my parents had taught me to be kind, and so I caught her eye and greeted her. She blinked at me, and offered a half smile, but neither of us said good-bye.

College Interim, January 1982
☻ *The Chill of the Night*

For an education paper about self-esteem, I've been reflecting upon the ways that Rikki and I have dealt with our different losses—her loss of both parents, one to death and one to prison; and my own questions about my father's mysterious death. What did our fathers really experience that we can't ever know: her father, as he lost his wife, then somehow ended up incarcerated; my own father, with his car that stopped on the train tracks, whether or not it stalled. Whether we talk openly about it or not, it's something we understand about each other—a quiet longing for truth that sits like a hungry orphan waiting to be fed by whatever scraps are left. It's that hunger that makes me call Rikki's house.

Geneva answers the phone and tells me Rikki just left with a "bizarre white lady." "She's tall, has flowers in her balcony and a Mary Tyler Moore 60's flip cut. Too big for her thin body. Know what I mean? Her hair comes off bigger than the rest of her. Looks like one of them country girls or something. Don't look like a professor or nothing like that. Rikki just grabbed her things and left—said nothing to nobody."

"Wow," I say. "It might have had something to do with her father."

"My god, I hope he wasn't screwing that bitch," Geneva says.

I thought Geneva knew about Tyrone's incarceration. She might, but it's not my place to tell. "Well, she's either bringing bad news—or maybe good. What was Rikki's mood?"

"Rikki's mood…" Geneva was giving it thought. "You know Rikki. She doesn't wear it on her sleeve like some folks. She's always doing something more important than the rest of us. You know what I'm sayin'?" Geneva laughs loudly. "Couldn't tell if she was worried. She was just rushing around as usual."

"Gotcha." I say. "Well, when she comes back, will you have her call me?"

"Sure thing," she says, and though I don't have any more answers, I've learned that Rikki trusts me on a deep level to have told me the truth about her dad. I want to call Liza to see if she knows more, but I know that's not the right move. It's important to trust Rikki now.

I succumb to a moment of keen awareness, where I'm glimpsing Rikki's life in a new way I haven't considered before. What would it be like to be in a home and to lose everything—not only your mother, but your trust in your father. Your home? I internalized the vacant stares from people who couldn't hold the news of my father's death, but what would happen if you had the death of one parent, and your other parent was considered responsible? The questions slap me as hard as the 10-below wind chill I face as I step out into the night.

The arctic gusts sting my face and I gasp to catch my breath. Campus streetlights shine on slabs of ice here and there so I can avoid slipping on them. I pick up my pace and everything feels doubly magnified—the snow crackling beneath my boots, the crisp words riding into the night on the vapor of student breaths. The exaggerated sounds and coldness invigorate me and put the beauty around me in focus: a pinecone preserved in a frozen puddle; branches woven together in an icy web; a sky so lucid that each planet and star seems a flicker of hope.

In the cafeteria, Annie, Beth and Jenny, three girls from my floor, ask me to join them and I decline. I'm in no mood to hold a conversation, so I tell them I have work to do. I hear Annie mutter to Beth as I walk away from them. A nasty imagined voice in me—an amalgam of all the voices of my white female peers— starts to question why I am spending so much time with Rikki. I tell it to shush and look at the clock, curse the sorry state of racism we live in—that we all inherit as our country's original sin.

I don't feel as though I fit anywhere: not in Rikki's world, not in my own. As my head spins, I realize I feel *envy* for Rikki. I envy her athleticism and her intelligence. Her courage in the face of the unknown. But most of all, *I want to be able to see my own father again*, so that I could talk to him about all this. I have a recurring dream that his death was only an illusion, that all I need do is call and he'll come find me, and the problem is I'm not calling. In a whisper that no one can hear as I sit alone at my table, I implore him, "Daddy, come find me. Come help understand all this. I just want to see you one more time."

The fatigue of the last few days rises over me. There's no point in staying here when I'm not hungry and I can barely sit up straight. I take the underground tunnel that passes from the cafeteria to my dorm. I don't like to travel it alone. It's dark and disturbing, painted a mustard yellow with graffiti and a graphic student drawing of a penis. It's the underbelly of the college, nearly un-traveled by staff.

When I get to our room, my stomach feels as though it's being pulled inside-out. I grab a washcloth by the sink, wipe my face, then hold it up again and sob into it. A glance in the mirror betrays my swollen eyes. I lay, for what seems like hours, despondent on my bed, staring at cracks and waves in the ceiling. If Annie returns, I want to be anywhere other than in this roomen, but there's no place to go. I hate the lack of privacy on campus for times like this. But I get up, throw on a thick white cotton sweater, brew myself some tea and pull out Leo Buscaglia's *Love,* a book that someone gave me as a gift for college. I spray on a little *Shalimar*, a graduation gift from one of Mom's wealthier clients. The soft, powdery fragrance calms me, reminds me of visits to the Water Tower Place in Chicago and my first exposure to the trains, crowds and department stores of a large city. While some people would abhor the train station advertisements for perfume and watches we could never afford, I found an odd comfort in them. They got me to dream not of death, but of the immortality of affluence—deceiving us that we can go on forever, because we have the means to buy items of beauty. My premature introduction to death made me a thinker, but the woodsy blend of citrus and vanilla helps turn the filter off and stills my mind. In *Jesus Christ Superstar,* even Jesus didn't mind that Mary Magdalene anointed him with fine oils before he would sweat them off in blood in the Garden of Gethsemane.

● *A Strange Gift*

January interim means less homework, and Annie's been staying out later with Beth and Jenny, doing what college girls do: talking about romantic partners, doing their nails, looking through magazines and just hanging out. There's one thing that I like to do that the rest of them don't. I like to read things by choice, not the things that teachers assign me to read. Give me Hemingway's *The Sun Also Rises*, and I'll be just fine, thank you. Lately, I've taken a liking to the expatriates who lived in London and Paris, where I hope to live one day. I'm a bit of a rebel and like to read about philosophy and art. I miss the long hours I had at home sitting around in my pajamas with a book I can't put down. What I hate most about being in college is the imposition of a professor's syllabus. After that, I hate knowing that Annie will be paying attention to anything I'm reading, and it's no longer my secret. In college, everything you do is subject to outside opinion. I've lost the privacy I had when living alone with Mom. Having a roommate is both the sister I never had and another pressure to conform.

At one point in the early morning, Annie comes softly into our room, washes her face and gets into bed. I don't let on that I'm awake, lying quietly in bed trying different ways to trick my over-functioning mind back into slumber. First I meditate, saying the mantra "Om mani padme hum," which means "enlightenment is within everything," over and over in my mind, wishing to have the body, spirit and mind of the Buddha. But then, I'm distracted by thoughts of my large, unruly Catholic family. Dad was a layperson homilist, a Parish Council volunteer and a regular usher. My cousin Mick, two years my senior, used to say, "Father, Son and Holy Ghost, who does the least will win the most," referring to a vicious rivalry with his little brother. Mick won his parent's favor by church-going, but rarely showed up for his share of family chores. My unconventional Aunt Rose is responsible for my interest in Buddhism.

The mantra's not working so I work specifically on my breathing, "In 2-3-4, Out 2-3-4," imagining that I'm sitting in a warm, pulsating body of water with healing energy flowing through my body. A deep peace stirs in me. If I were a cat, I'd be purring.

I hear the radiators hiss, Annie's soft breaths as she sleeps, the ticking of my desk clock across the room. Then I hear something unexpected—that sounds like a burst of rain showers on the window. Since rain isn't in the equation during January interim, with our below-freezing temps, I open my eyes, and look around the room. It's my cue that Rikki's down at the door wanting to talk—a spray of pebbles at my window. I look over at

Annie still fast asleep. Go, Annie. She sure sleeps more easily and deeply than I do.

I throw on my sweatshirt and step into my slippers, then head down two floors to the side entrance. Sure enough, it's Rikki, looking as tired and confused as I feel.

"Rikki!" I say. She jumps and startles me too.

When I let her in, her eyes are swollen from crying. She smells like tobacco and looks a far cry from the cocky, pulled-together athlete we know her to be.

"Chris," she tells me, trembling. "A lady who knew my real parents and witnessed my mother's death just came all the way from Indiana to talk to me. Her name's Maryl McCullough. She was a teenager when I was little…" Then Rikki just starts bawling.

I watch her, stunned, and tell her it's okay, my voice raspy from fatigue. "Just let it out."

"Maryl," Rikki begins, pacing her words so as not to cry, "saw the whole thing. She used to come by…I called her my *watchover girl,* because she watched me for my parents. On the day the tragedy happened…Maryl heard my parents arguing and watched them from the office window near the staircase landing. She watched my mom lose her balance and fall back—and my dad reach for her but it was too late. *She saw everything, but she was so shocked…she ran from her family's office down the office stairway to the restaurant below to find her mother.* She believes…she says she KNOWS my dad is innocent!" Chris, do you hear me?" she screams. "INNOCENT! Girl…he's…."

"Oh my God," is all I can say. I touch her arm with one hand and move the other to my own heart. She lets me wipe her face with my pajama sleeve. We're shivering, both from the shock of Rikki's news and the freezing cold. I pull Rikki away from the frosted metal door, further into the stairwell. "C'mon, let's go sit in the laundry room," I say, and I lead the way in silence. I breathe a sigh of relief when no one's there.

Rikki and I find a corner and rest our backs against the wall. I pull out a plaid blanket from someone's basket of dried clothes and throw it over our legs. The tart, clean fragrance of detergent helps keep me awake. The two of us tune in to each other as though we've found a clear frequency on a radio dial.

"Tell me more about Maryl," I say. "Why would she come all this way to find you?"

"She's the daughter of my parents' former landlord, Jim Jowers," Rikki tells me. "He ran Jim's Grill, the restaurant on the ground level of the building we lived in, on the same floor of the restaurant's office space, in Michigan City. When my mother was killed.....when she fell...." Rikki replaces the word *killed* with *fell*. It's something I've done myself in describing my own father's death. "Maryl was in shock..." she says. It's a shocking revelation, and I wait for more. "She saw my parents' interaction...saw my mother fall, watched her fall backwards all the way down the stairs. She ran out of the restaurant and was there when the police arrived and charged my father with murder...when they hardly asked him any questions and didn't listen when he tried to tell what happened." Rikki starts sobbing.

I pull the blanket up for her to hold for comfort if she needs to. She pulls it tight around her face, releasing long, rising wails. I wish we were anywhere but in a dorm full of interim students in the middle of the night. But here we are, and despite all our questions and recent crossed signals with each other, we're here, together—understanding each other.

This is a first for me, to witness this type of deep pain in a friend. I've only glimpsed such grief when my mother was overcome by sadness after my father died. As her daughter, I instinctively distanced myself from her sorrow because I didn't know how to deal with my own. I still hide my own eyes when I cry. But somehow, right here and now with Rikki feels like a sacred moment. Our uncommon friendship has created a space for pain to finally surface and be released. My own eyes flood with tears.

Rikki stops crying and I just put my hand on hers. We sit and rock together. I don't know who needs it more, her or me. When Dad died, I began tracing things with my eyes, cracks in the wall, shadows on books, the soothing play of light on the carpet. Now, I'm tracing the cobwebs and grime that have nested in the laundry room corners and ceiling. The tracing has become like a visual mantra that calms my spirit and helps me stay grounded.

"What's amazing," I tell Rikki, "is that the woman—Maryl—has kept this secret all these years, but now wants to help. You wonder what's in it for her. She's come all the way here on her own expense. She must really believe your father is innocent. Look at the time and energy she's investing."

Rikki sits straight up, resolute. "Oh my God, that is so true," Rikki says to me. Her color comes back as she calibrates her new insight to a better read of what really happened. "Maryl told me that she wanted to do this ever since it happened, but she had to wait until her father was no longer a threat. When she'd tried to explain what happened, he told her she was crazy. He coerced and bullied her...told her what she saw was murder. Said my father was dangerous and deserved a harsh sentence."

"It was a wicked lie," I say. "Evil."

Then her whole body shudders. "It was a lie," she repeats, shaking her head.

"Chris, I was watching from behind Mama and Papa. I didn't know what to believe. I watched the whole thing. Mama and Papa were tired...Papa raised his voice because he didn't want Mama to leave the house when she was nine months pregnant. My Mama lost her balance right in the heat of their exchange. But it wasn't...couldn't have been...Papa's fault. Maryl's sure it was an accident all along. I see now—Papa was unjustly accused." She blinks as she speaks, her eyes and heart adjusting to the avalanche of new information.

"I believe that's true," I say. "Maryl couldn't live with

your father being innocent and you not knowing. She could have let this whole thing go. But she didn't—and she can't. It's like she's brought you a strange—overdue—gift."

Rikki twists the blanket tassels in her fingers as she thinks through all this. "You know," she finally says, "Maryl told me she always wondered what happened to me. She said that she believed her father was cruel to mine and that she never felt comfortable with the outcome. She said her father was a bigot and a racist, and that his comments about Black people torment her. He was also an abuser—of Maryl *and* her mother. He died just a year ago. Not long after, Maryl's mother gave her a letter—*that she'd had notarized*— validating that Tyrone was wrongly accused. She'd written it when Maryl was 21, but never actually gave it to her. She stored it in a safety deposit box at the bank. In the letter, she urged Maryl to act on her conscience, to find me to get him exonerated as soon as possible!" Rikki takes a long pause and exchanges her look of sadness for one of resolve—which I've seen when Rikki grabs her swim bag to leave for a competition. "There's no time to waste. I gotta let my dad know what I know."

"I'm blown away," I tell her. "I can't imagine what this is like for you." The adrenaline has flooded me, and my head is pounding with the impact of our shared realization.

"I can't believe how stupid I've been! Here I've stayed distant from my own father all my life because of what some racist white man said that made it too easy to accuse him of being guilty. How could I do that? How could I not have questioned that? This is a hideous culture sometimes, Chris. It's hideous! Everywhere I go, I work my ass off to shine because some folks wanna make all kinds of judgments about me 'cuz I'm Black. Or they just treat me like I'm invisible. And what could be more convenient than making my dad invisible by putting him in prison?! My God, I've played into it."

"But you had no idea. How old were you?" I ask.

"I was seven," Rikki says. "It all happened so fast I

couldn't make sense of it, and I was just a child. But Maryl said she never saw Papa hurt Mama or push her down those stairs. She just saw Mama lose her balance. Mama was nine months pregnant, you know. She just lost her balance. The stairs were steep… I was taken away by a strange man with dark eyes and black glasses. Next thing I knew Papa was in trouble and they wouldn't let me see him, except behind bars. I was moved to my uncle's until the Coopers invited me to stay with them.

"My God," I whisper under my breath. "And this whole time you just didn't know." *Rikki's mother was pregnant. My God. So Rikki lost a sibling too.*

"I was scared—and very confused."

"I was ten when my dad died. I didn't really know what happened either."

"You didn't?"

"Absolutely not," I say. "Some people think it was an accident, some a suicide. I'll never know. But in your situation, you *do* know. And you can do something about it."

"Maryl says we can support my father with a retrial and he can be acquitted after all this time. She's already spoken with one of her attorney friends. She and her mother want to see him freed. They hold the guilt of her father's racism and my own father's imprisonment and can't live with it any longer. She says she'll be a witness. She just wants to know if I want to go through with it. In so many ways, I don't know my Papa. Our whole relationship will be different now." Rikki's Papa lost the love of his life, his unborn child and his daughter all at the same time. Now there's hope for him to seek reparations too.

"Have you told Liza and Eddie?"

Rikki looks at me, lifts her face to the ceiling and lets out a huge sigh. "Not yet. I'll call them first thing in the morning. They've been trying to get him out since the get-go," she says. "I've got a lot of work to do. But first I gotta get some sleep."

The door to the laundry room opens slightly and we're

both startled. It's only a draft of air. "You're right. We need rest. Let's go." Rikki gets up, takes my hand and pulls me up.

As we reach the door, Rikki hugs me tightly, and I hug her back. We stay in our embrace longer than usual. Rikki apologizes for pulling away over the past month. Once we release each other, she steps out boldly into the frozen night. There's an aura and strength around her that seems to light things up. An unfamiliar hope stirs within me, reminding me that every pearl starts out disguised as the foreign matter that sets an oyster towards its true mission.

March 1982
☻ *The Trust Deficit*

Tyrone's retrial is set for May, finals week. The dates are scheduled, chips falling where they may, according to the unrelenting calendars of legal professionals.

Even though Rikki's not competing in the spring, she swims at meets through a private club at the state university and is still beating her own records. The added phone calls and legal counsel for the trial demand a huge amount of her time. She's told me it's like having a hungry kitten on your doorstep—you don't regret the time it takes, even as your best plans can be shot to hell.

For the first time since I arrived at college, I'm beginning to dream of life beyond school. I want to be a professional, earn my paycheck, bring home money I'll spend on a place of my own. But first things first—I'm just learning about classroom management and child psychology for my first student teaching assignment. In the midst of all of this—I'm keeping up with news of the proceedings leading up to the court case and helping wherever I can.

Since I'll be going to Tyrone's trial with Rikki, she feeds me details of new developments over dinner, in the library, in our rooms, even when I'm with Chuck. Beyond Chuck, it's a secret.

It's a struggle that gives us a mission, a window beyond the campus life that can become provincial and predictable. At every turn I feel like my dad is fully present with me on this. I can't not help Rikki. Even with the horrible aspects of the trial—the presumption that her father fatally injured her mother—it calls us both to attend to what really matters in life and to take campus life with a grain of salt. We've been granted permission to take our finals early so Rikki can take the stand in Michigan City, Indiana on May 20th, which would have been my father's birthday. At first we planned to drive. Then Liza offered to buy both Rikki and me plane tickets to Chicago where she'll meet us at the airport. Mom's thrilled about it, but Chuck's not. He doesn't understand why I'm giving Rikki so much of my free time, planning to spend my spring break with her, not him.

Believing that part of the problem is that I haven't kept Chuck up to speed on why it's so important for me to go with her, I invite him to my room.

It's one of these days when I'm feeling terrific. They come every so often. I notice the beauty in the world and I'm absolutely a part of it. Icicles are melting from roofs outside my window, glistening for their last hurrah. Birds are chattering, flitting on and off trees, jostling straggler leaves that hold tight to branches and reflect the morning sun. Blood is coursing through my veins and I feel good about it. I look in the mirror and I'm pleased with what I find there. My own eyes are bright and sparkling. I interact with my own image, smiling back at it and fluttering my eyelashes. "This is the only body you have," I say to myself. "Treat it nicely, will ya?"

And then, "Get ready. Chuck's coming."

I certainly don't have to primp and preen for Chuck. He knows me in all my seasons. He's seen me in my bathrobe, with a heating pad over my stomach to soothe menstrual cramps. He's watched me wash my face a million times—he's seen me wet at the pool, mascara smudged under my eyes like athletic eye black strips to deflect the sun.

I smooth lotion on my face and then cover it with Lançome foundation, which I bought as a rebellion against my student budget. I savor the feeling of it, smooth it up my cheeks and gently under my eyes. Perhaps the promise of the good life can coax me to study harder?

Chuck's rhythmic knock at the door lets me know he's arrived. I listen a minute to his familiar 2/3 beat before answering. He looks spectacularly romantic. He's holding a dozen roses out to me with a full, lopsided grin spread across his face, and I'm utterly charmed. I plant a kiss on his forehead, then breathe in the roses' fragrance.

"You've just caught me by surprise, Chuck. Roses just because, romance in the middle of the school day. It's like you're trying to buy my attention. I'm not used to that!"

"Does it take getting used to?"

Actually…no…no, it doesn't. It's really very wonderful of you. It's just that I'd hoped to talk with you."

"About what, Sweetie?" Chuck looks genuinely concerned.

"I feel bad we haven't seen more of each other. I want to talk with you about things—about my trip."

"Do you want to do that now?" I watch him closely to see if he means it, or if I've upset him. He clearly looks more disappointed than absorbed. "Maybe we better sit down if we're gonna talk," he sighs, and he guides me over to my bed, the lower of our two trundles. I pull the bed out from Annie's for leg room—as our sofa. Chuck asks me if I'm serious about traveling with Rikki to her father's retrial. "I'm not real thrilled about it," he says. "Not just because I want you to stay here—I just don't know where your friendship with Rikki is getting you."

"How can you say that, Chuck? Rikki's a good friend and I'm looking forward to this," I say. "Just because you don't know

140

quite what to do with Rikki doesn't mean she isn't a good friend. These are powerful circumstances for her. It won't be easy. This has turned her world upside down, but she's learning about her real father and how he's been unfairly accused. She could use a friend, and I'm going to be that friend."

Chuck and I are really sandwiched together on the trundle, but we take the room we have to face each other. "But, Chris, really, in many ways you don't know Rikki very well. And it seems that in very little time, you're sacrificing a lot to support her. Lately, you're with Rikki every day and you only plan to see me once or twice a week. I mean…I'm happy you get along so well and you care about each other, but I'm finding it hard to get your attention. That's all."

I'm sacrificing a lot to support her. I don't know her that well. I feel waves of heat dart through me as Chuck says these things. "I'm sorry that you feel left out, Chuck, but you don't have a right to tell me how well I know Rikki."

Chuck is all wide-eyed now. He straightens his back, "Look, Chris, I don't know how to say this. But you almost seem *pre-occupied* with our friend Rikki. I feel you pulling back from *our* relationship. You mean a lot to me, but I've never gone out with anyone who makes a *friend* more important than her relationship with me. I wonder sometimes if it's because Rikki is black, and you're trying too hard to be sympathetic to her because you're white." He clears his throat, as my own mercury keeps rising and the heat settles into my face.

I don't want to give up on Chuck either. I love Chuck. But why does loving Chuck mean that I have to limit the time I spend with Rikki? It feels so judgmental, so competitive. Must everything be a competition? My thoughts bounce against one another like molecules colliding. I can't think straight. I wiggle my turquoise ring up over my knuckle and back.

Chuck watches me intently, waiting for my answer. What does he mean to me? We sit in stone silence while the clock on

141

my desk marks time. How to continue this conversation? Chuck has no idea. And really, I do love him and I don't want to turn him away.

"We've always seemed to connect—you and me," I begin. "Even when I've been nervous about seeing you, it all goes away after we've been together just a few minutes. I'm energized by you—you leave me better than when you find me. It's a good feeling. I wouldn't trade it away for all the world."

"Being with Rikki is like that, too," I continue, "but it has its own demands. I am sensitive about Rikki being Black because we look at the world very differently. And yet, losing our fathers the way we did, and even both coming from Indiana, has a power about it we can't deny. I'm learning things from Rikki I could learn from no one else. Yes, I *am* learning what it means to stay the course in an interracial friendship. The world challenges our friendship far more than it supports it. It's not easy, but it's very important to me, to both of us. And now, even you, Chuck. Even *you* are challenging me. I'm so disappointed. I've thought until now that you understood this. But you have to understand something now, please. *Our* relationship is never questioned by the outside world like my relationship with Rikki is. I *have* to think about that. You *have* to give me room for that!"

"C'mon, Chris," Chuck says. "It's the 80's. We're past that. There are all kinds of bi-racial friendships."

"OK, Chuck—you show me *one*! Tell me of one relationship you know of besides mine with Rikki that's not sexual. Name one! And really, Chuck, you know my white friends give me strange looks, too, when I spend so much time with Rikki. Would we be having this talk if I were planning to travel with a white friend?"

Chuck pulls his palms up together as if in prayer, then rests his head on them. One thing I really like about Chuck is his capacity for reflection. He hears me out, even if he doesn't agree with me in the end.

142

Finally, he just says, "I just don't know. You're right. You are an attentive friend. But it's almost like there's part of you that likes Rikki *because* she's not like us and you want to win her over. Aren't you working twice as hard to get her attention?"

Now, I'm wound up tight as a drum. I cross my legs and fold my arms over my chest. Is Chuck right? Am I giving too much to Rikki to prove something? And if I am, what am I trying to prove—that she can trust a white woman? When Rikki does something I don't like, I tend to let it go…to not talk to her about it. I don't share sadness or express much vulnerability around her, because I believe that would be asking too much. I mean we've come a long way on the matter of race, but it seems like reconciling the past means that whites like me have to do a whole lot more listening than talking.

"Maybe I am," I tell Chuck. "But Chuck, don't you think that whites need to build a whole lot of trust with Blacks, and some of us need to step up, be patient and invest in this? I began this relationship with a trust deficit. So, yes, I do need to take more time to build that trust than I would with a white friend! That's part of the deal, Chuck. I'm OK with that, and I need you to be. In spite of it all, Rikki and I are becoming close friends. This is not a competition."

Chuck stares across the room at a farm painting of Annie's. Chuck knows so many of my secret longings, but he still doesn't fully know who I am.

He shifts to lean more on his side, so he can watch me and not the painting. I feel good about that.

He takes my hand and polishes my nails with his thumb. "You have nice hands," he tells me. I smile and say thank you, then sit with him quietly. We're in a daze. This is our first misunderstanding.

"Look, Chris," he finally says. "This sucks. I didn't mean to upset you. Quite the opposite. I'm surprised myself at how much I want to be with you. This is just an unfamiliar dynamic—

your whole relationship with Rikki. I don't know her that well, and we're all really busy. This is my way of asking for more time with you."

He says it as I study the chipped paint on the door to my room, start to trace it with my eyes, searching there for familiar shapes. I can see the shape of a small bird in the paint—a symbol of freedom? "I don't know if I can give you that right now," I say. "I'm not saying I don't love time with you. I just have so many demands on my time, exams and papers, classroom visits, campus meetings. I don't want the pressure of letting you down if I'm not calling you more often."

"I feel so awful," he says. "This isn't at all what I intended. I've upset you. And here I came by to make you happy." He looks for my reaction, and I give him a look, the kind of look Rikki gives me when she expects more of me. She's definitely rubbing off on me—and with her, as with Chuck, I have to understand what part of me I will not compromise to be loved.

"This isn't about you, Chuck. And it's not about Rikki either. It really is about me getting clear on what I need for myself. You are part of that. We just need to figure it out, that's all. And I need you to trust that I know what's right for me."

"Look, we were fine…I mean things were OK until Rikki's dad's trial came up. I wish you'd give me half the attention you give your friendship with her."

"Chuck, did you hear me?" I answer pointedly with my own question.

"I'm sorry," he says. "You're right. I need to accept what's right for you. But does that mean we're still together?"

"We're good, Chuck," I answer. "If you can indulge me a little on my need for space, and extra time with Rikki, we'll be OK."

He shakes his head yes and leans in to kiss me. It's a simple kiss, and I know it's not what he hoped for. "Thank you so much for the flowers," I say. "They're really beautiful, and you're so kind to me."

When I was still in high school, my friend Bridget, a year older than me, liked to give me advice about guys. "Play hard to get," she said. "That way, you'll keep him interested in you." I abhor the advice now, and any such talk of dating manipulation. I don't want to play games with Chuck. I like him too much. But I see that he's worried about us. How did I not realize that my time with Rikki would challenge him or us?

"You're welcome," he says, kissing me again, then pulling us both up so he can leave. He moves in slow motion to the door, but once there, opens it wide. "I'll see you later then." I nod. He waits a few more seconds for my response, but I'm cloaked in the silence now and I've lost interest in any more words. Chuck kisses me again on the cheek, then turns around and ambles down the long empty hallway. I'm left to watch him as though he's someone I've only just met.

● *Lines and Angles*

When he's finally disappeared, I play a game with myself and pretend I don't have sight. I try to walk backwards to my desk chair without hitting anything or looking. As I take my slow steps, I ask myself: How can I digest my first dozen roses and my first falling out with Chuck all in the same morning? Is this really about Rikki? I've never wanted to be the type who loses touch with her girlfriends and treats them as second-class citizens because I have a man in my life. I know the test is a tough one for Chuck but it's one he has to pass.

I have to pass it too. If I'm really the friend I imagine myself to be, then I have to go about my merry business just for my own sake. Can't let my emotions get the best of me. Gotta take all this in stride.

And what better way than to tackle my geometry assignment? I dread it the most, which means that I have to

145

get to it first. Our professor, Dr. Jenkins, sees it as her moral imperative to teach us the art of resolve. She tells us in her thoughtful, commanding way that whatever we do, we've got to see to it that our actions meet our intentions. This is why we believe her: Jenkins begins her lectures right on time, every Monday, Wednesday and Friday at 10:30am. A few minutes before class starts, she stands, all five feet of her, before her altar, an oak table that holds a few open books and a glass of water. Here's the thing: she keeps her eyes closed until every student is seated and still. If you've ever watched someone stand up in front of a group, eyes closed, it's a bold act.

I think of Jenkins as being in deliberate communion with the gods to determine what our grade will be should we defy her code of silence. Precisely on time, she opens her eyes, void of any emotion, and scans the class. Her silky, black hair is pulled back into a perfectly firm and round bun. Her designer glasses are spotless—she must clean them before each class. Her wool suit coat fits her petite frame impeccably. Each class she wears an intriguing necklace that looks more like an art piece than jewelry. Her "piece," whether a bone or a sterling silver amulet, beams at us from the valley of her throat. Jenkins doesn't miss a beat. Even when you're relaxed and smiling with her, you know she's watching you closely—filing your every move and comment into whatever mental bank she stores her information.

I want to emulate her. I marvel at her clockwork. Descartes, in as much he believed that our bodies and minds are machines, would have used Jenkins as his example. What amazes me is that, polished as she is, and as resolute, she's attractive and engaging. She gets us all, including the rowdy young men, to listen and to go the extra mile. She does this by getting us to laugh.

"I'm a math teacher," she teases. "I'm supposed to get mean." She smiles mischievously at us to make sure we get the double entendre. "Trust me, I'm calculating numbers and the value you bring to this class each moment. What's your number?"

What's my number? I wonder, leaning back into my dorm chair instead of sitting on the edge of my seat where I complete most assignments.

Today's assignment calls for work on the hypotenuse side of a triangle. I look at the word a few times to make sure I'll spell it right. It ends with the word "nuse," and as I look at it, I think of a "noose." I make a joke with myself that this math work is, in fact, choking. (Could be why Jenkins protects her neck with strong jewelry.)

"Math's cumulative," Mom always said. "Each part builds on the last. She who loses attention is lost." Thanks to Jenkins, I'm growing in awareness that the world is full of lines and angles which I can measure and calculate. Still, taking geometry humbles me. It's one of the few classes where I hesitate with my answers, fearing I'm wrong. Rikki thinks math's a piece of cake.

Chuck's a Poli Sci major. He's good at math, but he can take it or leave it. Rikki's facility with math and with swimming are an inspiration. How'd she get to be so good at everything with the ongoing disruption in her early life? After my father died when I was ten, I lost interest in learning. It became harder for me to pay attention. I have ample compassion for children who went through trauma. It's one of the reasons I'm called to becoming a teacher.

Much as geometry's not my forté, I'm obedient to the work so I can become a teacher. As I'm teaching little Zack in Rm. 124 that a quadrilateral is a closed, four-sided figure and that the sum of four angles is 360 degrees, I'm really telling him that there's a whole world out there to discover. That even though his father beats his mother and his children don't sleep well at night when he's out drinking, there exists a reality where opposite sides of a parallelogram are always equal and where all four of its angles are right angles. It's a predictable logic in an unpredictable world, one you can trust, a world of intelligence and "smarts," the likes of which is taught by undaunted spirits like Professor Jenkins. When you tap into that world, you know the right answers to things the way the earth instinctively knows it must circle continuously around the sun.

☻ *The Energy Field of Youth*

Our airplane to Chicago is its own mini-world, with all of the trappings and symbols of being human. Rikki closes her eyes and clutches the armrests as we take off, chewing her gum like there's no tomorrow. She checks all her cuticles, puts her gum in a tissue and pokes it into the armrest ashtray. After take-off, the passengers near me, except Rikki, act as if nothing spectacular just happened. How can they? Once we're up in the air and the plane begins its ascent into the atmosphere, Rikki slowly starts to relax. She stretches her legs out and yawns, then looks at me and says, "We're still going up, aren't we?"

"We should stabilize pretty soon." I'm watching the seatbelt light, so I can get to the bathroom before the flight attendants fill the aisle with their food carts.

"I don't travel much," Rikki answered, "Remember our last trip from hell?"

I nod yes. She's absolutely right. Our first trip together was a test of wits and stamina, but it *is* how we bonded. Now that we're taking a plane together, it feels as though Rikki's a part of my family.

Rikki didn't want to sit by the window, so I get to sit by the window where all my life I've wanted to be. There's a teenager on the other side of Rikki, by the aisle. She has sunglasses atop her head even as we're sitting in the aircraft. She's got a paperback book open on her lap and she's following every word with the long

148

nail, painted lavender, on her pointer finger. Even though her nose is in her book, we have to be careful what we talk about. Absorbed as she is, the girl will hear everything.

The pilot announces that the plane has reached its cruising altitude, that we'll be in Chicago in less than an hour where we can expect clear weather and a temperature of 60 degrees.

The clouds have opened now. Beneath their thin white veil, there's a patchwork of miniscule buildings, fields, and borders. "You can see the ground now," I say to Rikki, and she leans over me, far as she can, looks down and sighs.

"So that's what we look like to the angels," she says. "No wonder it's a bitch for them to answer us when we're hurtin'. When I was little I had a guardian angel named Melinda. Wonder where *she* is now."

The stewardess has her cart right near our row now and she's asking our teenager what she would like to drink.

I tell the stewardess I'll pass on a drink. "You sure?" she asks. She's more dismayed by not being able to serve me than by the plane's shifts and bumps as we hit a pocket of turbulence. Rikki asks for 7Up and soda crackers.

"I bet Melinda's with us," I tell Rikki.

"I seem to remember her when I need to," she says. "She does a number of things for me—helps me find things I lose, win swim meets and ace tests. I think of her when I see the color orange."

Well I just learned something new. Rikki is always wearing something orange, whether it's her clothes or jewelry. She even loves the color in what she eats—carrots, oranges, and sweet potatoes.

Our young seatmate's finished her drink and put her tray back up. She's opened her book, and I sense she's distracted by our conversation. I catch her spying me and I give her a close-lipped smile. "Good book?" I ask her at one point.

"Madeline L'Engle," she says. So, she gives me the name

149

of the author and not the book. If a book's worth its weight in gold, you'll read half of it before memorizing who the author is. Our eavesdropping teen picks favorite authors. I'm sure she does. Then, she reads every single book she can find by that person and goes on to someone else. It's not only the drama she's after. It's the aura of the author, the miraculous soul who has performed the impossible, novel after novel after novel.

As soon as the stewardess finishes serving, I muster the nerve to displace Rikki and the young woman to make my way to the plane's mini toilet. It's my chance to examine the other passengers, to see who would have to die with me if the plane went down. Lovely thoughts, I know, but I never take for granted the people with whom I share planes and elevators.

In the cramped airplane john, I'm insignificant as can be, in my little boat out at sea. I don't hurry up as I usually do, though I know people are waiting. It takes some pluck to sit here and just feel the oddness of it. It's my only private place on the aircraft, and it helps me relax. As the pilot announces our descent into Chicago, the clock ticks faster.

When I get back to our seats, Rikki is talking to Megan, our young seatmate, who will be visiting her older sister who just had a baby. Megan and Rikki smile at me, let me in and resume their conversation. Megan's clutching her book, *A Ring of Endless Light*, as though it's a lucky charm. She asks Rikki who she is visiting.

"A bunch of folks," Rikki says, then looks at me and winks. "The time will go *fast*." She emphasizes the word *fast*, says nothing more.

Out my window, it looks as though someone is slowly moving a magnifying glass over the buildings, houses, and cars. I study the aerial view of Chicago, growing darker as the sun moves closer to the horizon. I love my first view of Lake Michigan.

In her excitement to land in Chicago, Megan describes her sister's baby to Rikki. The baby has the kind of hair that sticks straight up no matter how much you comb it. She smiles easily at two months old and nearly sleeps through the night. Megan's sister really lucked out to have such a calm, happy baby. The teacher in me gets stirred out of remission. I'm thinking there's no such thing as a not-nice baby, that even colicky babies are precious and smile easily when they're loved. Rikki just listens. She's a master at this game and knows how to keep quiet so she needn't say a word about her own family.

Before long, there's the landing plane's bump on the runway, and the plane's slowing down. Rikki is saying her good-byes to Megan. My heart is singing, as much because we've landed safely as it is because I'm not far from the energy field of my own youth.

Part Three: *Tyrone's Retrial, May 1982*

☻ *The Mingling of Light and Dark*

The Court is smaller than I expected. At first blush, it reminds me of a church, with rows of long wooden benches and the judge's stand looking like the high pulpit. There are tables between the rows where we're seated and the witness stand. I'm sitting with Liza and Eddie. We're on the right-hand side of the courtroom audience, facing the court reporter on our left. The stately room gives the smallest of sounds a stereophonic quality, whether they're books closing, people re-arranging their chairs or high heels clicking. Though the ceilings are high, the room feels stuffy. We're closed off from any source of fresh light and air. On the wainscoted walls hang paintings of legal dignitaries who have presided in these chambers before.

Nothing softens the dead echoes, the claps and scrapes of movement on the cold floors. This building is filled with shadows and the maelstrom of emotions that swirl around the determination of justice. If a church is a sanctuary for the quiet spirit of love and compassion, then the courtroom reminds us of other forces that come from civic life—not only the temptation to wrong one another, but also to release or pardon someone from a dark deed or transgression. While the priest interprets the moral lessons of faith, the judge listens and waits for flickers of truth. The jurors interpret the court's mingling of light and dark, deciding the consequences for those, who deliberately or through circumstance, have violated the elusive codes of morality within the confines of law.

Things aren't ever as they seem. Murderers and thieves are in and around us, breathing the same air, inhabiting our same spaces without our knowing. But the opposite is also true. The falsely-accused go about their lives with heroic patience. We cast our shadows on them, then toss them aside too freely. The passage of time is often the only arbiter of justice that can really track innocence. Judges and jurors are human, welding together strands of logic and intuition into their best interpretation. In the end, the jury lives with the nagging possibility that it has falsely mistaken an innocent for an outlaw.

Tyrone enters the room with his public defender. My God, he looks like Rikki! He's thinner but has Rikki's same sturdy build and posture—erect with his head, shoulders, and hips perfectly aligned. His hair is cut close to his scalp, and he's wearing wire-rimmed, aviator glasses. He's clean-shaven, wearing only a short-sleeved, white shirt, and unbelted gray trousers.

When he looks right at me, I realize that Rikki is trusting me to do right by my presence here. With my white skin, I stand out from all the others who are in this room hoping to see justice for Tyrone. I can't know what they experience. I can only observe—and hold with Rikki—the elusive shards of truth so that the light can reveal them and free her father from the insidious lies of racism.

The judge, a woman of Asian descent, enters the courtroom, with all eyes on her commanding black robe. Her short hair is tucked neatly behind her ears—and her stone-cold sober face downplays her femininity and natural beauty. What she lacks in size, she makes up for with taut, dispassionate professionalism, and a strong presence.

The jury of seven men and five women enter stage right, are sworn in and seated. All, except one of the men, are white like me. It feels like the characters in an epic drama have all entered the stage. Rikki was told by Tyrone's attorney that they have just spent the last two days being prepped and assessed for this trial — the process of *voir dire*. Our judge introduces herself as Judge Clara Tan and runs through a list of rules we must all heed to stay in the courtroom. She asks us to remain silent and to keep our voices low during court sessions. We sit placid and expectant, waiting for the scene to unfold. She asserts that this is a retrial for

153

the July 1968 death of Joveda Daniels. "Today," she begins, "We will listen to opening statements."

The prosecuting attorney, Mr. Clyde Olson, is like a machine that's passed inspection. He's starched, reserved, and poised. I have the thought he'd be this way whether on vacation, the golf course, or playing with his grandkids. Everything seems firmly within his control.

My life has given me little exposure to this type of man. My own father didn't hide his warm, human side. Some say that's what did him in. He always had room for the downtrodden and paid less attention to his own needs. You could see it in the slight paunch of his stomach, the horn-rim glasses that never sat straight on his face, his one suitcoat that drooped at the shoulders. Yet, Clyde Olson's tailored precision could never match my father's ability to articulate his passion.

Tyrone's attorney, Mr. Dennis Connelly, is more my father's type—and more casual in his appearance, with the thin hairs he has left uncombed and his pen in his pocket. What he lacks in polish of dress he makes up for in alertness and calm confidence.

Rikki and I haven't spoken a word to each other since we entered the courtroom, holding in our own strong emotions minute to minute. We're focused on what lies ahead. Rikki looks casual, but slick, in her cream-colored blouse that ties at the neck and black pin skirt. Her silver hoops shine beneath the fluorescent lighting. She could easily be an attorney herself, especially with the aloofness she's adopted to stay vigilant.

When she's called to the witness stand, I give her a firm press on her arm to convey I'm fully with her. She stands to the left of Judge Tan's desk, and though I know she's trembling slightly, she appears intelligent and poised. Her spirit of confidence in competition kicks in, as it does when she stands ready to dive off her starting block before the crowd at swim meets. Those in the courtroom study her as she calmly swears to tell the whole truth.

"Ms. Daniels," begins Olson, "how old were you when your mother died?"

"I was seven years old."

"Did you see your mother fall down the stairs the morning of June 12, 1968?" asks Olson.

"Yes, I did," Rikki answers.

"Tell me, Ms. Daniels," Olson proceeds, "what was your father, Tyrone Daniels, doing at the time your mother, Joveda Daniels, fell?

Rikki looks at Tyrone, who stares straight ahead. If he feels the energy of her gaze, he doesn't let on. He's following Olson's questions closely.

"Mama was leaving the house," Rikki begins, "for groceries. She was making banana bread for me, showing me how, when she realized we were out of eggs."

"Ms. Daniels," Olson interrupts," was your father with her at the top of the stairs, close enough to push her?"

"Objection, Your Honor!" barks Connelly, wiping his forehead with a white handkerchief.

Judge Tan asks that the question be re-stated.

Olson regroups and asks Rikki to describe what happened before she witnessed the fall. His voice is steady and commanding, like that of an airline pilot notifying passengers he's initiating the plane's descent to land.

"He was coming home as she was leaving," Rikki answers. "He asked her where she was going and she said to get food."

"Tell me how your parents interacted."

"They were standing together at the top of the stairs. Dad asked Mom to stay home. She said she'd be right back. He reached out for her arm to pull her towards him, and she pulled away and lost her balance."

"Did he touch her, Ms. Daniels?"

"Yes, he had his arm on hers as she was stepping backwards. She slipped." Rikki sits tall, shoulders back and chin up—perfect posture.

I glance at Tyrone for his reaction. He hasn't changed expression, but he's rubbing the back of his neck with his left hand.

Olson asks what Rikki did at that point. "I screamed. My mother was falling down the stairs and Daddy wasn't able to catch her."

"What did your father, Mr. Tyrone Daniels, do right after your mother's fall?"

"He called her name and ran down the stairs to help her. He held her in his arms and tried to resuscitate her. He called for help, but no one came." Rikki looks over at her father. He's looking down, studying his hands.

"What did you do after your mother fell?" Olson inquires, as natural as if the two of them were talking at the breakfast table.

"I kept screaming! I kept trying to touch my mom—and..." Rikki slows down, "she had my sister inside of her. I begged her to wake up."

"Did you at any time hold your father accountable for what had happened?" Olson asks more abruptly.

"I do not believe my father would hurt my mother—or push her," Rikki says. She stops there, staring at Olson with a look of determination.

"Ms. Daniels, you told someone who interviewed you in August of 1968 that you didn't know if your father pushed your mother." Olson hands a document to Judge Tan and Connelly. "Your Honor," Olson says, addressing Judge Tan, "I am pointing to line 3, page 25."

The challenge sets off whispers between a few people behind us.

"I was only a child," Rikki begins. Her eyes are wide, her

pupils dilated. "I had just watched my mother fall to her death. I was too young to understand what had happened. I never blamed my father. I was confused and angry, devastated that it happened."

"No further questions," Olson says, self-satisfied. I shake my head in dismay. It's not a good start.

Rikki closes her eyes to get her bearings, then turns them right on Mr. Olson. "I have one more thing to say."

Judge Tan looks at Rikki and asks her to hold her comments for questioning by Mr. Connelly.

Mr. Connelly stands up, comes forward and tucks his pencil behind his ear. He stands little more than five feet tall, but the lines around his eyes give him a wise expression.

"Ms. Daniels," begins Connelly, "Describe your family life in 1968?"

"I had a good life," Rikki begins. "My parents took care of me the best they could."

"Tell me about your father," says Connelly.

Rikki's in her head. She looks at the jury to gather her thoughts, then looks my way but doesn't establish eye contact. "My father wrote songs that were minor hits on the Black radio circuit. He didn't have the business background to get his songs registered and copyrighted. His profits were taken by the record distribution company. It upset him greatly, but he gave it all he had." She looks over at her father and nods. Tyrone nods back.

"What about your mother, Rikki?" Connelly continues.

"My mother was a very bright woman," Rikki says, straining her voice to get the words out. She looks at me and I smile slightly. "Though my mother didn't ever make it to college, she had a skill for math. She had a network of local people who brought their children to her for math tutoring. People said that she was a good teacher. Degrees didn't seem to matter so much then." Rikki sits back in her chair, takes a deep breath, and looks at Connelly to see if she should continue. He nods at her.

Rikki scans the jury and fixes her eyes on a petite woman

in a black sheath dress, wearing no make-up or jewelry. I look at the woman too. She looks attentive, if haggard, as she absorbs the tension of the court proceedings.

Rikki clears her throat. "My father would sit and play his guitar for me. He liked going to work. It was important to him. We never had lots of money. That was hard on my parents. When my mom found out she was pregnant, Papa got concerned about finding more work."

"What did your father do for work, Ms. Daniels?"

"My father did what he could—odd jobs, cleaning and painting. Sometimes, he'd actually get paid to play his music." Rikki's voice wavers slightly at the end of her statement but she holds it together, taking deep breaths where she needs to and fixing her eyes on Connelly's. There's a deep silence in the room.

Connelly, the red tones of his complexion deepening, asks Rikki if her father ever hit her.

Rikki shifts in her chair, then tells Connelly, "No, no, he did not."

"Did you ever see him hit your mother?"

"No," Rikki says. "Like most couples, my parents would sometimes argue over money. But they were never violent with each other."

Rikki sits up taller and looks over at Tyrone, who's cast his eyes down.

"Tell me about your contact with your father now," Connelly states, fixing his gaze right on Rikki.

"I see him twice a year, more if I can. I'm a premed student and a swimmer, so it's hard for me to get to Michigan City. I write to him."

"You're a premed student? You had to get a high grade-point average, didn't you?"

"Yes, Mr. Connelly," Rikki says. "I was in the top twenty-five in my high school senior class, top ten in math." That alone establishes her intelligence and capacity in my mind. I can't even hold a torch to Rikki's grades, and I could never hold those grades while training for a sport at the same time.

"Anything else you remember or want to tell the jury?" Connelly asks.

"Yes, sir." Rikki sits even taller, bringing all her strength and composure to the next sentence. "I did not see my father push my mother..." Rikki pauses and takes a deep breath. "...down the stairs. I do not believe he killed her."

Judge Tan waits for the silence after Rikki's voice trails off. Then she pounds her gavel, tells us all that the trial will resume in about ten minutes. She excuses the jury, and people in the courtroom get up to stretch. I look around the room to watch the reaction. I recognize the people who are here to support Tyrone's release: Liza and Eddie; Rikki's out-of-town relatives who want her to stay in close proximity to her father; and Dan McKee, a baker and neighbor of Tyrone's who has visited him in prison since his incarceration. I've never seen Dan before, but I've read a few of Rikki's letters from Tyrone in which he described the kind, soulful man.

I scan the somber expressions, then stop at the face of a man whose tight gray curls on dark brown skin give him a dashing, distinguished look. He seems familiar to me in a comforting way, and I rack my brain to remember where I've seen him before. Seeing him puts me in that surreal place where you glimpse a piece of your past, but it comes off more as dream than reality. Then the answer comes: It's *Clarence,* my father's friend! How can it be?! Clarence is from another story entirely. But it *is* Clarence, Clarence Sage—my father's dear friend—here in this room. I haven't seen him in over eight years! *It's the nearest thing I could have to my own father standing with me.* I tremble with an inexplicable awe, the kind that brings you to life when you thought all was lost. Clarence!? My God, why's he here—why's he here at Tyrone's trial?

Bits and pieces of my father's work with Clarence come

back to me. We used to bring turkey and canned goods to the Community Center, where Clarence was the Director—and Daddy, Board President. Clarence, jolly yet patient, made frequent references to the "undying power of God." He wasn't Christian in an overbearing way, but in the best way possible, because he was living the gospel. Clarence was always shaking his head when he wasn't smiling. He spoke often of the need to prevail, to stand steady against the forces of evil. At the time, I could only see evil in terms of the devil—green, daunting, and hideous, defeated by St. Michael in my childhood catechism book. Now the evil he spoke of feels real to me and present in this room. And it's not emanating from Tyrone.

I watch as Clarence stands to greet Liza and Eddie. As Rikki walks over to hug Liza, he approaches her and pats her arm. Clarence has mythic proportions in my memory, so I tremble the closer I get to him. Within seconds, I'm shaking his hand and looking in his eyes again. Does he notice me? Must I say who I am?

"Clarence," Rikki says naturally, "this is my friend Chris Fitzgerald from school," and to me, "Chris, Mr. Sage is a family friend."

Judge Tan pounds her gavel, tells us all that the retrial will now resume and that we must take our seats.

Clarence is studying me. I'm studying him too. He's much older now—there are more lines on his face, and his eyebrows are gray with age. "Fitzgerald," he mutters. "Ryan Fitzgerald…" and then as I start to say that I'm Ryan's daughter, he looks at me and says, "Are you Chris...Chris…?" and then "My God, you're Ryan's daughter! Dear Child," he says, holding my hand tightly with one hand, and holding his heart with his other. I see tears forming in his eyes. "How…where….?"

I promise him that I'll check in with him later. Some people say that when things are at their worst, that's when the greatest breakthroughs occur. As I smile humbly at Clarence, I feel as though I'm indeed looking at a holy man. Here I am with Rikki, within miles of our childhood homes, learning how we grew up near one another and had our lives touched by the same prominent Black leader.

Rikki's breaking a sweat, and I can smell her fragrance along with other scents mingling in this open, institutional space: leather, a faint smell of paint, cheap—and even men's cologne.

When Rikki's called to the stand a final time, Connelly establishes her as a healthy, balanced woman who excels at her studies and swimming. Rikki remains diplomatic and self-assured throughout the questioning. She listens, her face flooded with afternoon light slipping in through the transom windows over the courtroom doors. As if it's cleansing her, Rikki tells the judge and jury that her father is a brave man who has tried not to lose himself in the madness of prison life. He wouldn't hurt anyone, Rikki tells them. He's been the victim of a sick system that failed him in every regard. My love for Rikki swells. I look over at Liza and Eddie and can see they're relaxing in their chairs. Liza looks serene. Her head's tilted and she acknowledges me with a gentle smile.

Rikki told me last night that I may never know what it's like to wake up each day and have to think about my race. She's right. Because of my father, though, I do think about race on *most* days. What you can't tell by looking at me is that my father—who worked alongside Clarence to build the Michigan City Community Center—who taught me about Dr. Martin Luther King Jr.'s work for Civil Rights as much as he taught me about Jesus Christ, and who fought alongside Black friends in the Korean War—worked in a federal office with a few federal employees who hated whites, one of whom had attempted to knife him. My grandparents blamed their neighborhood's decline on Blacks, and Dad spent his life trying to prove them wrong. Now, as I listen to attorneys debate the fate of my friend's father, I have a renewed respect for my own father's work, and how against all odds and logic, he defied the prejudice around him and saw his fate closely tied to others, regardless of race.

● *A Taste for Miracles*

Mom and I agreed that I'll stay with her until the final night of the retrial, before I fly back to the Twin Cities with Rikki. As much as Mom wants to be with me right away, she knows I'm "home" because of the trial at the Michigan City Courthouse. When she pulls in front of the courthouse to pick me up, she pops out of her gold Dodge Dart to give me a hug. Mom looks great in a sky-colored cardigan that draws out her lovely blue eyes. She lights up when she sees me, and I know she lives for these moments we're together. As I look at her closely, I see new lines on her face. She keeps one arm behind me which she uses to nudge me into the front passenger seat.

I have another idea, though, and ask her to park and please come in. I want to surprise her that I've run into Clarence after all this time. Getting Mom to cooperate when she's fixed on her own idea is like getting children to come in off the playground.

"Mom, Dad's friend Clarence is here at the trial."

"What, Christine? Did you mean Clarence Sage?"

"Yes, Mom, it's *Clarence,*" I say calmly.

"Alright, I'll park," Mom says, catching her breath—and *catching on* that there's an element of serendipity in this whole scenario. I point to a space nearby that's open. Mom is more of a scientist than I am. She believes in God without a doubt, but her latent grief from my father's tragedy has dulled her appetite for miracles.

Mom parks and gets out. We reach to one another for a second hug, but there's no time to linger. As we make our way quickly into the building to find Clarence, I thank her for coming to get me and tell her what she wants to hear—that her investment in my education's been worth it. My grades are good, all is well and I'm not risking anything by taking this time to be here.

As we enter the lobby, Mom spots Clarence and wastes no time in walking up to him. I see that he too has recognized her right away. Before I'm able to also introduce her to Liza and Eddie, Mom and Clarence hug, and this time she stays in the embrace until he's good and ready to let her go. "What a pleasure to see you, Mary!" he says. "I saw your lovely daughter Chris earlier today, but I had no idea…"

"I don't know how it happened that Chris became involved…" my mom starts to say, but before she can even finish, Clarence is telling her how very wonderful it is that I am continuing my father's work for justice, and that God brought me in contact with the Cooper family. Mom looks at me and smiles, and I quietly thank Clarence for helping me feel a little less crazy. Clarence introduces her to Liza, then Eddie, and to family members. With her magnificent diplomacy, Liza holds my mom's hand in hers and tells her what a gift I've been to her foster daughter. Rikki walks into the lobby at that moment, as if she's overheard Liza talking about her. I've been thinking so much about the retrial these last few days. Now I'm absorbing how Rikki and her father experienced tragic death in their little family, just like me and Mom.

When I see that Mom has a moment free from introductions, I tap on her shoulder, and say, "Mom, I'd like you to meet Rikki."

"Hello, Ms. Fitzgerald," Rikki says first. "It's great to meet you! Chris has become a good friend. I feel your support through her. You've probably heard what we're going through here. I couldn't do this without her." *A good friend.* It's the first time I hear Rikki acknowledge our friendship out loud in public, and it means the world to me.

"Well, hello, Rikki," Mom says, taking in Rikki's bright, sincere eyes, sturdy body and poise. "It's about time we met, isn't it? I'm really glad you have Chris' support. She speaks so highly of you." *Thanks, Mom, I think to myself.*

"I'm glad we can support *each other.* Turns out we have a fair amount in common—and not just coming from the same area."

"I see that," Mom says, "Just the fact that we all know Clarence! Even though everyone seems to know Clarence, if you know what I mean." Mom winks at Rikki. "Anyway, we'd better get going so you can rest up for tomorrow. What time will things get started?"

"Connelly says to be there by 9:00am."

"I've already talked to Clarence about the morning, Chris," Mom says. "He's asked me if he can pick you up at our house and take you out to breakfast. If it's OK with you, I'll tell Clarence that's all right."

"That'll be wonderful, Mom—thanks," I say, grateful that Mom understands the value of me spending one-on-one time with Clarence. While Rikki only knows *of* Clarence through her foster parents, he and I have had short, *albeit transformative* exchanges with each other.

Rikki whispers to me that she, Liza, and Eddie are going to make the drive back to Gary. Mom and I wish everyone a good night. The powerful community support that surrounds Tyrone's retrial reminds me of the gatherings, dinners, and invitations that pulled us through the fog around my father's funeral. Now, as then, Clarence's presence brings meaning and kindness where little else makes sense. Deep within our psyches, Rikki and I both hold memory of being frightened young children—with lives torn apart by tragedy—who are struggling to make peace with the light of each day. Clarence is the kind of person who keeps us believing it's possible.

As we drive home from the courthouse, Mom tells me that she thinks she remembers the news articles about Rikki when she was orphaned in Michigan City by her father's error, and I correct her immediately. "The media's biased, Mom! The whole reason I'm here is because Rikki's father did *not push her mother—or make a mistake*. Her mother *fell* and her father was *set up!"*

"But Chris," Mom continues, "what I'm getting at is that Tyrone had to be one of the prisoners that your dad used to visit before he died. We talked about the little girl in the paper, you know."

"Mom," I say, about ready to burst, "that little girl is now my friend! Amazing, but true." Mom is quickly coming around.

"How is it even possible?" Mom asks me, truly unable to find words. She stops the car at a stoplight and looks me straight in the eye. "Chris, how is this even possible? I mean, this is more than a coincidence."

"See, Mom, that's what I've been trying to tell you. Rikki's not just any ordinary friend."

"No, she's not. And Honey, you never told me she knew the Sages."

"I didn't know until today!"

"Oh, my."

"It never even occurred to me that Dad would have had anything to do with Tyrone. That didn't cross my mind!"

Mom's driving with her left hand while using her right hand to reach in her purse for her lipstick. If there's anything she can't stand, it's being without her lipstick. It's as though she wants to be looking her best for the full impact of this realization. "Chris," she reflects again, "This is stunning, the fact that you linked up with this girl at your college all the way up in Minnesota. I just don't know how it could have happened. It's almost as if Daddy himself had a part in this plan. It's almost as if…" She puts her lipstick on and looks at me briefly, then back at the road.

She stays quiet, and so I finish her sentence. "It's almost as if you and I can believe in miracles again," I say. "What do you say? Let's have a go of it."

After tossing her lipstick back in her bag, she squeezes

my left hand and tells me that I've always been a godsend to her, that my being there through the toughest times is really what allowed her to get through. "It's hard to believe you've left the nest so quickly," she says, "and yet I've known I couldn't hold onto you forever. It's been important for you to have your own life. But now it's all coming together. I've missed you so much, being so far away, Chris. But if you didn't go to Minnesota you wouldn't have met Rikki or realized Clarence's tie to her." Her eyes are twinkling, and I honestly haven't seen her this way since the Christmas before Dad's depression—before the tragedy that would take his life and our happiness with it. When Mom sparkles all over the way she does now, she exudes the confidence and charisma of a legendary beauty.

● *The Driver's Seat*

When we arrive home, it's so familiar to me at first—like any day I'm just getting home from high school. When I stop to use the bathroom, I see how it's quaint and elegant. Mom's put out a lush hand towel with an embroidered pattern of muguet and a matching pump soap with that fragrance, made in France. Lily of the Valley is Mom's favorite fragrance, but I think of it as the fleeting, tiny white bells that appear for just one week in the spring. I pick up the hand towel and look closely at the decorative stitching, something I liked to do when I was younger, before homework deadlines overtook my idle time.

The more I look around, the more I see that everything in our home looks more vibrant, as if I'm suddenly seeing Mom's photographs, her quilted wall hangings and handsome pottery for the first time. I don't take them for granted as I did when I looked at them every day. Mom brings me a cup of chamomile tea and steers me towards the dining room table, where she's laid out a serving tray with Gouda cheese, gourmet crackers, and red seedless grapes.

"Sit down," she urges me. "There's something I've wanted to give you. I've kept it from you—maybe because I wasn't sure how you would react—but I think you could benefit from it now." She gives me the look that this is a rare instance where she might open up with her feelings, that this is really important. I'm flooded with a mix of curiosity and concern for her.

Mom walks over to bags sitting on the floor near the living room sofa and pulls up a vinyl tote that says *Quilters know how to piece things together* on it. I expect her to show me a quilt she's making. Instead, she pulls out a vintage, faux-leather 3-ring photo album. "We may need a little time with this," she says, and sits right next to me at the table so that we can go through it together. When I open the book, a photograph falls out—it's of my father's high school football team from the year 1947-1948. It's actually a thick photocopy of the original, and the faces are blurred, so it takes me a minute to find my father. He's in the front row, his back straighter than the others, like my back is now. While most of his teammates are either smiling or squinting, some with pained expressions, my father's look is one of quiet confidence. He is only sixteen years old, a sophomore in high school and the team's quarterback. The other loose piece in the album is a laminated ink drawing of Snoopy dancing, arms wide open, with a cartoon bubble that says, "Happiness is a friend who lets you be yourself and still loves you." The drawing was made for my father by my fifth-grade teacher, Sister Francis. It's dated May 1971, just eleven years ago and four short months before he was killed. Sister Francis was a favorite of many at St. Joseph's Parochial School in LaPorte. She'd even play baseball with us, wearing her habit—and kept playing when her veil fell to the ground, ignoring us and her veil as we laughed at her whimsy.

I page through the album, noting that the photographs aren't meticulously organized like the ones for Mom's photography business, but slipped in organically as though she would be the only one to look at them. They're intimate in the way

167

that the cap off the toothpaste and disheveled morning hair are expected when you love someone. In a few of the photos, where Dad is with classmates at the U.S. Naval Supply School or in guard formation at the Tomb of the Unknown Soldier, she has used a ballpoint pen to circle his face so that we can't miss him. Though lacking her professional design, the photos and mementos assembled by Mom were no less important to her. She put together poignant and intimate glimpses of my father's life, despite her pain around our tragedy.

The first photograph in the album is that of my paternal grandmother and grandfather on their wedding day. My grandfather is looking down at his bride, who is lovingly gazing up into his eyes. Their eyes aren't visible to the camera, but what is visible of my grandfather's face, a full bottom lip and a finely shaped nose, would in time be passed on to my father. Grandpa is touching the back and arm of the chair on which Grandma sits, solemnly present to her beauty and leaning towards her with reverence as if he has discovered a rare bloom.

I flip a few pages forward, opening to what has become my favorite photo of my father. He's behind the wheel in a glistening black convertible, his arm on the door and his class ring catching the light. He's sitting tall, in suit and tie, his hair combed back in thick waves, his lips and eyes pulled into a confident and teasing smile, daring the world to take him on, to give him one battle he can't conquer. Unlike the other photographs, this one has no time or place. What made him feel so good that day?

I move on to photos of my father in the Navy, to newspaper photos and articles about his mentoring of boys and his management position for the Social Security Administration. There he is lettering in track, graduating from high school and college, stationed with the Navy in Florence, Italy. Also included are my father's first employment letter offering him $4,080 a year, clippings of inspirational quotes he saved, a *May 22, 1960* article from the *Rockford Morning Star* honoring him for breaking the language barrier to inform Spanish-speaking citizens of their social security rights. In one photograph of him, he's lost his thick, dark hair and is wearing black, G-man glasses and an increasingly disquieted look. It has nothing but the caption *"Helps Folks"* beneath it.

Next, I find the 1965 obituary of my paternal grandfather, whom I don't remember though there's a photo of him holding me as an infant. There are photos of my father shaking hands with elected officials, letters of recognition from his superiors and congressmen. There are photos of Dad and Mom with me as a baby, where the collective joy on our faces is vibrant, lifting off the page to warm my heart.

Mom sits patiently as I marvel at it all. She's uncharacteristically quiet, only to ask, "He had quite a life, didn't he?" I shake my head yes, sigh and turn the page to his college grades, high grades all except for a C in Physics. There's a Father's Day card from me, just having learned to master the letters of D-a-d-d-y to add to those of my own name.

As I study the photos, articles, letters and certificates, I begin to internalize that my father's strong sense of ethics and steady commitment to justice were exemplary. In one letter, a Republican Congressman from Illinois, Tom Railsback, wrote to my father: *I am sure no man ever left behind him a finer record of loyalty and devotion to his work*—and *how fortunate the Social Security Administration is to have a man so eminently fitted to cope with the problems of today and the future.* (On one of the new Post-It notes, Mom wrote: *Railsback formed a bipartisan coalition that led to Nixon's impeachment.*) WOW. Dad earned the respect of influential people!

Excited to read more, I turn the page and immediately see that photo from the paper Mom hid from me, the disfigured, jagged version of our baby-blue, Chrysler Newport station wagon. I gasp for air, and blink tears from my eyes. This was our family car, *the* symbol of our vacations to tour the Gettysburg battlefields and to Québec with Grandma, with a tailgate that could either swing open like a door or swing down like that of a truck. It was the favorite image Dad used in home movies as he learned to make objects vanish with his Kodak movie camera. Its hood and driver's seat are flattened, the rear wheel lodged between railroad tracks. Where my father used to sit and drive so proudly, the door's been ripped off, and the round knobs I'd turn for the lights and radio are exposed—dangling pathetically. Two of the headlights stare down the tracks off the side of the car, hanging next to the front tire. That tire has snapped off the steering rack, resting, defeated, by the second set of tracks. This car felt invincible as it carried us to escapes from life's cares—I've dreamt of it in color! In this photo, it's reduced to a deformed wall of steel with only the prized tailgate intact. In the back of the wagon, there is some unidentifiable object—a floor lamp perhaps—which I look at until my eyes are strained. But I can't make out what it is, any more than I can understand why this tragedy had to happen.

Mom remains still, her arms folded over her stomach, holding her pained gaze steady on the ground. She senses me looking back at her, takes a deep breath and uncrosses her arms, then abruptly clasps her hands together like a child with a new game to play. "Well, so, now you've seen it," she says. "There you have it! We can't spend too much time on this. I'm leaving it with you. It's yours."

I can't shift my emotions so quickly. "My God, Mom," I say, "I never saw the car. How on earth did you get through this?"

"Oh, Honey, I'll never get that damn car out of my head, but life goes on." Mom begins, a hint of irritation at my question. If I didn't know her well, I'd have thought she was angry at me, but I know her voice is a camouflage of deeper pain. "You just move on," she repeats curtly, and I'm reminded that her pride, like asphalt poured over nature to allow for driving, is how she's survived. "I had no choice. I did the next thing. I got up, I showered, I made the bed, I made food for us, ate what I could, went to church, you know. I've kept this from you long enough. And though it's time for you to see it, don't let it overtake you." She sits back, pulls her shoulder blades back against the upholstery, and holds her left pointer finger in her right hand over her stomach as if she's a reporter keeping her poise. In Mom's usual way of wanting closure, she's quickly bequeathing me with both her treasure and her burden. She wants to make the transfer as seamless as possible.

The sacred compilation, perfect in its mingling of life's sweetness with the unthinkable, has me on edge though. Much as I've been trained to respect Mom's need to go forward, I'm focused impossibly on the magnetic pull of the book. I want to shake off the impact of the images, but the harder I try, the more they flood me, with ineffable sweetness and pain.

In the spring of 1971, my father ran out into our street in front of a car that was speeding by. It swerved and Dad was spared, but it led to his admittance to the Michigan City Hospital, confusing ten-year-old me who thought that hospitals were places to treat only physical wounds. After he came home from the hospital, the two of us would listen to Jesus Christ *Superstar* for hours. The soundtrack had just come out and was all the rage. Dad and I would belt out the "What's the buzz?" song together. My father always stopped the album when it came to the track of the Crucifixion. But once, he had fallen asleep while we were listening, and I heard the horrific sounds of the nails being pounded into Jesus' flesh, the sound of ghastly, degrading laughter rising in the background. I woke my father up, frightened, and demanded that he turn it off. I knew how to work the turntable myself, but I wouldn't dare go near the haunted speakers and the wicked sounds within them. I wanted the *Superstar* soundtrack, but I didn't want the Crucifixion.

My new gift from Mom, like the rock opera in its fullness, illuminates the tender and heroic moments of my father's last days, right up until the tragic ending—that part of the recording that deforms and mocks a dignified life. Ever since the accident, part of me has blamed myself because it was on Dad's way home from bringing me my glasses at school that the crash occurred.

"Why'd it happen?" I dare to ask Mom for the millionth time.

"There are things we aren't meant to know, Christine," she tells me as if on script. "The old wagon just happened to stall at the wrong place and time."

"But Mom," I plead. "Why would Daddy pull out onto the tracks when he could clearly see the train coming?" It isn't the first time I've asked these questions. Maybe the answer will change now that Mom has opened this small window to exploration.

Yet, my persistence has an opposite effect. "Chris, enough is enough. You know what happened. It was a horrible *accident*. Now let's move on and be thankful for all the wonderful things in our lives." To protect us both from unnecessary pain, she stands up, closes the album, centers the loose pages within it, and runs her hand across the smooth cover. "It's important to know where we came from, but having all the answers just isn't possible. What matters is what we make of our lives moving forward. I'm going to get a glass of water."

I pull open the book again, this time to the photograph of Dad in the convertible. There, I find his self-assuredness, with a hint of daring, as he sat beaming at the camera from that magnificent car. The photo isn't dated, but I imagine that he's in his early 20's, right before joining the Navy. In the invincibility of his youth, he had the world by the tail. Until his seaplane crashed in the Korean War. Until he fought for civil rights and learned the deep complexities of race and poverty in 1960's America. Until a President of the United States forever tarnished the Executive Branch through corrupt and evil deception. Until, despite being a civic leader, his work with juvenile justice, his visits to the prison, and his work for the Community Center with his dear friend Clarence, he was nonetheless hated by Black separatists working in the Social Security Administration who wanted nothing to do with a white manager's fight for human rights. Until anonymous death threats, from white supremacists and Black separatists, tore him apart. Our terribly mutilated Chrysler—and the wounded spirit of the man who died there—is a far cry from that of the handsome young man's. Oppression, whatever its origin, defaces the promise of shared humanity. Much as I want to understand all the reasons, I defer to Mom's wisdom. What matters now is the work we do to move forward.

☻ *A Wider Lens*

Clarence picks me up in the morning. As we're leaving the driveway, Mom runs out with wet hair, in a sweatshirt, to bring him a full plate of cookies for his family. He knows the streets of Michigan City like the back of his hand. The homes have character, each one very different from the next. There's also something I don't see often—iron bars and boarded windows, whole porches collapsing, shingles pulling from roofs. Clarence pulls back the foil, smiles and offers me a cookie. I shake my head no.

"How do you like school in Minnesota?" he asks me.

"I like it. The winters get cold, but I love the way the community turns it into something fun like the Winter Carnival."

"I sure miss your father," Clarence says. His words soothe me in a way I didn't know I needed. I settle in my seat and begin to really *see* Clarence. Until now, he's only been an image from memory, one that became blurred and chimerical after my father's passing. Now, he's a real, breathing man, tall and steady like a sacred tree, his face and hands wearing the lines and marks of time.

Dad had always talked about Clarence as though he needed our help.

"I remember how you and your dad used to visit the

Center with all your donations," Clarence says. He would greet us at the lobby door, then bring us into his office filled with books, papers and polaroid photos. "When your dad and I got talking, we'd lose track of time. You can't do that with everyone. But we had a vision for the Center's potential. We'd brainstorm for hours about ways to lift people from poverty."

"Yes, I remember that. While you two talked, I'd stare for hours at the photos of the Center's youth—until I'd nearly memorized them. But I never got to play with them as much as I wanted to."

"Your father had many places to take you, dear Chris."

As I ride with Clarence in his Ford Crown Victoria, I see firsthand he isn't poor. He's wearing tailored trousers, a light brown leather jacket and polished black leather shoes. He's clean-shaven with a fragrance that's slightly sweet and aromatic like fine pipe tobacco. He's created a sanctuary in his automobile, that smells like a combination of leather, vanilla and coconut. I take deep breaths and inhale fully. Though the volume's down, I hear the crisp horn solos and mellow rhythms of Herbie Hancock. The simple, pleasant luxuries remind me of Mom's old Ford Maverick with electric windows. I'd marvel that I wouldn't have to strain to roll down the windows—that a tiny button could do so much. Like having a power window for the first time, being with Clarence is smooth and easy.

Clarence brings me to a mom-and-pop diner with a speckled-yellow Formica counter. I'm the only white person in the place, so when I walk in with Clarence, there's a noticeable hush. "Maggie, my Girl, this is my young friend, Chris," Clarence says to the owner, Maggie. Maggie's a sizable woman with her glasses on a lanyard, nearly shelved on her full chest.

"Hi Chris," Maggie says, giving me a quick once-over, then fixing her light brown eyes on my friend. "Whatchu up to, Clarence?"

Clarence sighs. "We're just here for some sustenance,

Maggie. Got to go to court today. There's a brother wrongly accused of murder, of his wife no less."

"Oh shit, what'll it be next time?" Maggie asks. "You know the guy?" Maggie asks me directly, and I nod.

"Friends with his daughter," I respond quickly, doing my best to keep the rhythm of our exchange. The exchange brings a déjà vu of walking into the Center, me and my father being the only white people in the room. As white people, we don't often experience what it's like to be in the minority. Rikki says it's what it's *usually* like for her, even to this day.

Clarence invites me to pick a booth and we settle in. I place my paper napkin across my lap and follow Clarence to look at the menu. He orders a soft-boiled egg with toast, and I go for the breakfast special, eggs, hash browns, and bacon. Maggie brings us each a cup of coffee. I ask Clarence if he travels often between Gary and Michigan City. He tells me he does some business in Gary and has a sister there. After our breakfast, we'll have a 5-minute drive to get to the courthouse, just blocks from Clarence's legendary Community Center.

As caffeine starts to kick in, I realize I have so many questions and so little time. Energized, I ask Clarence what it was like to work with my father. I wait for him to rave, as others have, about my father's sense of humor, his kindness, and their friendship. Instead, he grows solemn, as though ready to bow his head in prayer. His sober face is not the look of someone who will tell me what I want to hear. "I had my worries about your father," Clarence tells me. "He'd call me when he got depressed."

Clarence's tone is matter-of-fact. "When he was *depressed*?" I ask aloud, checking that I'm hearing him right. I feel bad that Clarence is choosing to emphasize *that* part of my father. He clearly has skill as a leader who can deliver the hard truth *and* hold people's trust while doing it—staying both humble and astute. He knows about rising strong—the way a plant pushes

175

itself up between sidewalk cracks.

"Yes, that's when he called, Child," Clarence assures me, as if it's the one thing he must say to me before he never sees me again. To think of my father, with all his gifts, being remembered this way sets my cheeks to burning. It's the last thing I want others to remember. There was so much more to Dad. But Clarence continues. "He'd lost hope in his dreams. That's a perilous thing. He was quick to take on the struggles of people around him. He believed that if he only did this or the other thing, he'd rustle up some justice and he could be responsible for positive change. But as we know, life can throw one curveball after another, and you gotta get clear on which ones you can hit. No one can hit each one. But your father thought he could. He went chasing after every single one."

I'm straining to understand Clarence's feedback. I think of how, at certain times, my father would be deep in thought, and I couldn't get him to smile. I thought I wasn't good enough. The times I'd get my report card, with the highest marks in the classroom, and Dad would tell me all the ways I needed to work harder. The way that Dad would speak with self-assurance and command like Clarence, even as he lay in a hospital bed for reasons I couldn't explain—physically, he looked healthy. If he was so sure of what he was saying, then why was he there? It seemed my father couldn't assimilate the events shaping his future, any more than Tyrone can during his trial.

Clarence, then as now, was the type who could see through a wider lens. I'm trying to stand in that place with him now.

Through Clarence's eyes, I start to internalize that perhaps it was my father who needed help, more than Clarence or the Community Center. My father was no more special—or perhaps every bit as special—as the troubled men and youth Clarence served. Clarence can't help but recall my father's deep sadness *along with* his charisma and the way he won people over. "I was sad to see your father go," Clarence tells me. "It's hard when someone goes before his time."

"When would have been my father's time?" I ask Clarence.

"I can't say, Chris. Your father was always *ahead of his time*, seeing things others couldn't, a prophet in his own land. Perhaps..." he says, reflecting, "he'd have done better had he learned to honor the timing of things...had he known how to wait." I remember now—my father saying "*patience*" to himself repeatedly as if it were a mantra.

As I take a few bites, my senses are focused on Clarence's reflections. Did Daddy not have the patience to overcome the forces against him? Did he give up? Is that what his "accident" was about? "Clarence?" I ask. "Is it possible...do you think that my father's death was not really an *accident*?"

"That's between your father and our Creator," Clarence says as though he's telling me the temperature outside. I can see by his lack of hesitancy that he's thought this through. He looks at his watch and nods at me that it's time to go to the courthouse. Maggie brings the bill and Clarence pays her in cash. I reach into my pocket and find two five-dollar bills. I hand them both to Clarence. He won't accept them. "Please," he says. "I want to do this." We stand to leave, and seeing that a light rain's begun, Clarence helps me slip into my windbreaker, then zips his own jacket.

I thank him. I want to know that my father meant something to Clarence. "My father spoke so highly of you, Clarence. Was the feeling mutual?" I ask now, eager to know.

Clarence sits back down in the booth and looks up at me as I stand waiting. "Honey," Clarence says, looking deep into my eyes, "your father was a *very good* man. There was no one like him. He was a visionary and my dearest friend. You can be proud to be his daughter." His answer works, and I'm relieved.

"Thank you, Clarence. Thanks," I say. "I can't believe this

has brought us back together again. What are the chances?"

"It's the way the Lord works," he says.

Clarence has a slight limp as we make our way back to his car. He's getting on in age as my father would have been. I ask him how he knows Tyrone.

"From the Community Center," is all he says, and he tells me he knows Liza and Eddie from their political work in Gary, Indiana—and that he also knew Jim McCullough, Tyrone's landlord and employer, from the Chamber of Commerce.

"Wow," I say, "You're connected to *all* of this."

Clarence shakes his head yes, says, "I am. And I haven't told you this, but I'm going to testify. Jim McCullough, who owned the building where your friend and her father lived…he was not to be trusted."

"*Really?*" I ask again, surprised both that he'll testify, and to hear Clarence say *anything* negative about another person.

"Yes, he never wanted the Community Center in business, for the mere fact that it supported Black people."

"My God—that's horrible," I say. I'm finally getting it. This community is so small and interwoven that the death threats *to my own father* could have been tied to McCullough. We just don't know.

"Perhaps, if we're fortunate," Clarence says, weighing every word, "there will be justice there's not been in a long time."

☺ *Separate Fountains*

In the courtroom, Judge Tan excuses the jury and sends them to the jury room so that Mr. Olson can select a clerk to read Mr. McCullough's former testimony. Connelly objects to the reading of the transcript as hearsay and states that it violates Tyrone's 6th Amendment right to confront witnesses against him. Tan allows the testimony. She indicates that Mr. McCullough is unavailable and had been subjected to cross-examination in Tyrone's presence in the first trial. When the jury members return to the courtroom, they learn that Mr. McCullough's previous testimony will be read.

Channeled through the clerk's voice, McCullough tells us that Tyrone would often stand downstairs in the bar flirting with the women clientele, and that he often touched the women.

"He's a drinker," said McCullough. "Often, he has bloodshot eyes and slurs his words. He yells in a loud voice at his wife and child from the upstairs apartment. People in the neighborhood don't like him...in fact, business owners pressured me to do something to Daniels, but I would never do anything to hurt someone because he's black. I supported Mr. Daniels," McCullough claimed. "That is until I saw him womanizing while his pregnant wife was stuck with domestic duties. Then I became concerned that he was lazy and didn't hold his share of the bargain. Still, it was his own business. I stayed out of the conflict as much as I could."

After a while I stop listening. I wonder how the jury members can make their decision. I look over at Tyrone, and he's bent over with his head down. I remember Rikki telling me on our walks that there were so many awful things said about her father, she would find herself believing them. Since the admission by McCullough's daughter, Maryl, that she witnessed Joveda's fall, Rikki has no doubt about her father's innocence. Will her perspective about her father mean anything? I wonder if coming here has been a set-up, if Tyrone will just be placed back in prison. If I were a member of the jury at this point, I would have to believe that Rikki has little reliable memory of her mother's fall and that Mr. McCullough's telling of the shadow side of Tyrone carries power, even beyond his grave. My father used to say, "Consider the source, Chrissy. Think about the person who's telling you the story. Do you believe him?" *This* man, Jim McCullough, is no longer alive, yet he still holds power over Tyrone's fate—all too common of white people.

When the judge dismisses us for a break, a tall, thin jurist pulls a cigarette and lighter from her purse and hustles to the door for her nicotine fill.

"How are *you* doing with all this?" Rikki asks me, as we leave the courtroom. It's funny she would ask, because up until now, I've been fine, but now I'm feeling light-headed and a bit queasy. "I miss the simple life on campus." I wink at her. No sooner do I say it than I realize I *can escape*, but Rikki doesn't have that luxury. I pull myself together, ask her how she's doing.

Connelly comes out, pulls Rikki aside and whispers a few things to her. Rikki nods her head, slides her thumb nail along her teeth, listens. She nods her head again, and then Connolly shakes her hand. She comes over to me and whispers, "Connelly will be calling his first witness. C'mon—let's go get a pop, then get back in the courtroom." Down the hall Rikki stops to lean over the water fountain, for a long drink. Images flash in my mind from photographs of the sixties when girls like Rikki had to drink from separate fountains. I take my sip, get water all over my mouth, and try to stop it from dripping onto my shirt. Rikki's light-hearted, challenging me to dash with her down the hall to the vending machine. We grab our pops, then Rikki stops at the restroom to freshen her make-up.

I walk down the empty corridor, my heels echoing on the shiny flooring, until I get to one of the hall's beautiful benches with ornate wood carvings. I close my eyes, asking to be filled with love and kindness, to be free of suffering, to be peaceful, at ease and happy. I ask that for Rikki—and for Tyrone. I do my best to release the ideas and fears that float through my mind...why did I come here? What are there more of: fathers like Tyrone who have not been allowed to raise their children, like Clarence and Eddie with high standards for achievement and raising children, or fathers like mine? Where did Rikki learn to be so disciplined— from her real parents or the Coopers? Then I consider again the likelihood of Clarence even being present at this trial. It's an act of grace if there ever was one.

Then the enigma of my own father's death floods me. Did he deliberately stop on the tracks? My mother will never believe this. She'd rather I didn't talk about it. What if there were a court case to decide, where everyone who knew my father was allowed to share their facts? "Yes, Mr. Fitzgerald was hospitalized for depression. Yes, it was the first time he was out driving without his meds," or "Yes, he loved his wife and daughter very much and would never have ended his life." Finally, I think of Chuck, the pain of missing him and dismissing his insistence that I take spring break with *him,* not Rikki.

Thankfully, Rikki returns from the bathroom before I can go any deeper with my thoughts. Not long after we make our way back to our courtroom seats, Connelly calls Jim McCullough's daughter, Maryl, to the witness stand. From a distance, she has a youthful look, tall, svelte and there's the flip cut Geneva described. When she takes the stand and swears in, with light shining directly on her face, you can see that her make-up is camouflaging deep lines from aging on her fair skin.

"Tell me," begins Connelly, "what you know about your father's relationship to the defendant, Mr. Tyrone Daniels."

"He was a tenant in the apartment above our bar," Maryl replies.

"How old were you at the time?" Connelly asks.

"I was sixteen."

"Tell me about your relationship with your father," Connelly continues.

"I put up with my father until I could leave home, Mr. Connelly. My father didn't like me, and he was a violent man. He yelled at me and hit me if I didn't agree with him. He'd do the same to my mother, and I kept my distance from him. He was an abuser, Mr. Connelly. He was not cut out to be a father. To him, I was just a nuisance, until I was old enough that he could put me to work. I wasn't the son he wanted—I must have heard that a hundred times. And he threatened me on more than a few occasions to stay away from the Daniels."

"Ms. McCullough, did you know that your father testified that Mr. Daniels pushed his wife down the stairs?"

"I do, Sir. He knew I witnessed the fall, too, and he told me he'd beat the hell out of me if I mentioned it to anyone."

"Tell me what you saw on June 21, 1968."

"Our office above the bar shared the same staircase to the Daniels' apartment. Our offices had a tinted window with a view into the hallway and the landing at the top of the stairs. The night of the *accident,* I was in the office to grab supplies and could hear Mr. Daniels begging Mrs. Daniels to stay home. I watched them through the window and saw he'd just come up the stairs. Joveda was carrying a bag on her arm, preparing to leave. Rikki was right behind Mrs. Daniels, waiting for her father to get home. When they had the money, Mrs. Daniels would have me watch Rikki so she could run errands before Tyrone got home. I cared about the little girl." Maryl looks over at Rikki and then back at the judge. "I'd play with her, often outside. We'd draw with sidewalk chalk, play hopscotch…I'd let her style my hair." I look over at Rikki and she's leaning her face on her two hands clasped in prayer.

"Mr. Daniels kissed Mrs. Daniels on the cheek," Maryl continues. "I could tell Mrs. Daniels wanted to get to the store—and they didn't have the means to have me babysit. She was nine months pregnant, and they were saving for the baby. She traded places with Tyrone and moved by the top of the stairs. She turned to check on little Rikki, and as she faced Tyrone, he reached out to pull her toward him. She stepped back and lost her balance. Then Tyrone and the little girl were screaming. I ran to our separate staircase as fast as I could, down to the restaurant and out the door. By the time I got outside, someone had called an ambulance. But it was already too late. Mrs. Daniels was gone. She'd broken her neck in the fall."

"When there was a question of Tyrone's guilt, I told my mother exactly what I saw, and she tried to convince my father. But he wanted to believe, no matter how I described the series of events, that Tyrone pushed Joveda and killed her. When I said it wasn't true, my father hit me in the face and slammed me into the wall, in front of my mom. He was angrier that I witnessed the fall than he was that I talked back to him. He told me never to mention it or contradict him, and he hit me again. We never talked about the fall after that. We carried that secret between us, but I knew that any mention of it would bring him to rage, because he beat me for things much less. I can't stay quiet about it anymore!" She hesitates, looks down at her lap, but then looks at the jurists.

"You seemed to have let it go. What's prompted you, Ms. McCullough, to take this up again?" Connelly asks.

Maryl closes her eyes and takes a deep breath, then looks right at Connelly. "I've been thinking about this, Mr. Connelly, all my life."

She tucks her hair behind her ear, then looks for the first time at the prosecutor, Mr. Olson. "When I was 21, my mom wrote a letter to me, which she had notarized—recording exactly what I described to her on the day of the tragedy."

"Sirs and Ma'am, I have this note, marked as Exhibit 1."

"My mother never showed it to me. She kept it hidden in a safety deposit box at her bank. When my father died a few years ago, Mom pulled it out for me to read. That did it. I had to take action!"

"Any other evidence, Ms. McCullough," says Connelly.

"The other note, Exhibit 2, I found in my father's coat pocket after he died. Mom had kept it in the safety deposit box too. It was written to one of Dad's white supremacist cohorts on the Michigan City Chamber of Commerce." From her bag, she pulls a small piece of paper that's so old and wrinkled that it hangs like a piece of fabric.

Connelly asks Maryl to read it, so she begins.

183

"*Hey, Doc, why'd the City Council vote to give all the development money to the [n-word] center on E. Michigan? Why not set that damn place on fire? They'll think some poor bastard from the center did it anyway. Why the hell do we need a place where all these idiots will hang out and cause trouble? I don't want any more problems in this town than what we already have. Jim*"

Olson is clearly taken off guard, as am I. *It's our Community Center we're talking about here.* Rikki's scribbling notes furiously on a note pad she brought. My heart's in my throat. I've seen images of the Ku Klux Klan and the fires they've set to crosses. I knew these things happened, especially because of the death threats, but I thought we could put some of this behind us. But no, it's insidious and persistent to this day.

Olson's been like a steady machine this whole time, but now he's malfunctioning, noticeably agitated.

Connelly then asks, "Ms. McCullough, do you believe that Mr. Daniels is a dangerous man?"

Maryl turns her gaze to Connelly, points her index finger in the air as if to teach a lesson. "No, Mr. Connelly, Mr. Daniels is not a dangerous man! I'm here to testify that Mr. Daniels is an innocent man. And to apologize to him, Rikki, and all others for taking so long to come forward. Tyrone worked hard. I've always felt bad that my father took little Rikki's father away from her. Mr. Daniels was his employee. My father should have supported him. But he couldn't even treat Mr. Daniels like a human being. Mr. Daniels was heartbroken when his wife and child died—I saw it in his eyes. And Joveda was as kind and genuine as she could be. Ever since that day, I have felt awful that Mr. Daniels was blamed for her death. And I played into it—because I was afraid that my father would hurt me and my mom and maybe even Rikki."

Connelly thanks Maryl, and Olson stands to cross-examine her. Tyrone keeps his head bowed, so that I can't make out his expression, while others speak of him as though he's not present. Good Lord, what must he be feeling at this moment?

Olson adjusts his tie. "Before the incident occurred," begins Olson again, "what kind of interactions did you have with Mr. or Mrs. Daniels, or Rikki?"

"Since their apartment was in our office building, I would see Mrs. Daniels' math students come and leave. Mr. and Mrs. Daniels didn't like little Rikki to play outside our building—it was a bar and some of the customers were mean—taunting Rikki as she passed by. They called her the baby n-word."

I look at Rikki for her reaction. She's glaring into the distance, looking at no one in particular. I want to comfort her, but giving her space is the best thing I can do. I imagine her surrounded with light and warmth.

"Ms. McCullough, wasn't your father one of the first business leaders to hire disabled workers in Michigan City?"

"My father knew that hiring disabled workers allowed him government subsidies. He did it because there was something in it for him, not out of the kindness of his heart."

"Ms. McCullough, did your father not provide inexpensive housing to the Daniels for over five years?"

"Mr. Olson, the Daniels' apartment was neglected and needed a lot of work. My father didn't maintain it and refused to put money into it. And the apartment was above his noisy, smoky bar—with a steep stairway entrance I might add. He needed the money, and the Daniels were willing to live there. They actually painted and upgraded the place. My father could have cared less about Mr. Daniels, but he paid attention to Mrs. Daniels because she was a beautiful woman. He called her a 'looker,' then made cruel, racist comments."

Rikki gives me a wounded glare. A tear spills from her eye, as she sits in quiet agitation. Maryl's testimony, and the poise with which she delivers it, is convincing despite how hard it is to hear the truth.

Feeling himself losing ground, Olson says, "In the first trial, a witness claimed that Daniels had a reputation for harassing the restaurant patrons. Did you see any of this behavior?"

Maryl interjects fervently, "My father had a bar, not a restaurant! And never once did I see Mr. Daniels treat a patron disrespectfully! He was kind, a hard worker, a good father and husband, so far as I knew. He was a human being like the rest of us and THIS I know for certain. Mr. Daniels did NOT kill his wife. I'm here today to affirm and convince the jury and judge and all gathered that this is true." She looks at Tyrone, then Rikki. "Mr. Daniels, Rikki and all impacted, I am so sorry. I can never give you back the years you've lost together. I beg your forgiveness." She says that *her father, not Tyrone,* is the type of man who would push his wife down the stairs. She tells us again that she could not live with herself until she came forward to free Mr. Daniels.

There's a deep silence in the room as Olson stares at his papers. "No further questions, your Honor."

I turn my head to look back at Liza who's casting a concerned eye on us. I nod to her. I've never been in a situation where the future of someone's life hangs so delicately on the words of a few people. Even though we're not awaiting Tyrone's death sentence, it feels as though a guilty verdict could easily drain what little life is left within him. And the spark of hope in Rikki's heart right with it.

Before my own father died—as he, too, was feeling his own life force recede as I've just learned—he worked a bit with youth in the criminal justice system. I first heard the word "delinquent" from the movie "West Side Story." I thought of the teenage boys as interesting, even funny, because of the Officer Krupke song. Dad told me that lots of the boys were innocent, that he believed they'd done what many would do in their circumstances. "Sometimes young boys tell the truth, and no one believes them. I was there to finally believe them," my father said.

Rikki's hand is shaking. I'm flooded with love for her,

love for us all. I look over at Tyrone, who has lived in isolation and disgrace he hasn't deserved. How has he held on, I wonder.

Tyrone turns to look back at Rikki, but she doesn't notice. She's staring at the seat in front of her as a focal point to buy herself sanity. Tyrone then looks straight at me. "*Tyrone hates whites," Rikki's told me. "He told me I'm out of my mind to go to a school full of them.*" I nod to him with a half-smile of understanding. I think he understands I've got Rikki's back. Rikki's intensity is in his face, too, but I see something else—something lighter and more appealing. Could it actually be hope?

It's a powerful thing to look in someone's eyes. When you do, you peer into that vulnerable place where our primal innocence resides—the place where we're each an extension of the other.

The truth hits me, and with it a small wave of vertigo. I rest my head on my arms. When I feel my composure enough to lift my head, I breathe in deeply, inhaling the fullness of Rikki's patchouli. When court is recessed for the day, Liza and Eddie come over to us and hold Rikki in a tight embrace. Clarence comes over, too, as much for me as for Rikki. Seeing Clarence allows me a fleeting memory of my father's face. Mostly, I recall Dad's piercing blue eyes, and I can almost feel them on me in this moment. "You OK, honey?" Clarence asks me, placing his strong hand on my right shoulder. His attention to me takes me by surprise.

"I'm alright," I whisper. And I really mean it. Though we're all tired, and the weight of the trial gnaws at our collective strength, I understand some things now. I know Rikki does too. What we're learning will change our lives forever.

☻ *A Nobility of Spirit*

The next day in court as I sit quietly waiting for Rikki, Eddie is pulling Clarence into a discussion. When Rikki joins me in the courtroom, she's freshened up her appearance and tried to camouflage her puffy eyes. No matter what the outcome of her time here, Rikki will keep command of her life. I've never joined anyone with as much strength as Rikki has—in any effort.

I ask her how she's doing. She whispers to me she's relieved that her testimony is over, that she did her best. She plays with two silver rings on her ring finger, then looks me straight in the eye. "How could I ever have thought he might be guilty?" she asks.

I shake my head, and I'm silent. I put my hand on her arm and give it a squeeze. "You didn't have all the information," I say. "Sometimes, ya just don't have all the information." I've been feeling guilty myself about having my own questions.

"But how could I believe such horrible things...?" Her comment echoes my thoughts exactly. "I thought that by this time in my life, I could sort the truth from the lies," Rikki whispers.

"I wish it were that clear," I quietly say back. "But it's not. We start with the path of least resistance." And I wonder in this moment how much Tyrone himself has internalized the shame bound around his life and reputation—or learned to be angry and hate—from his jail experience.

Judge Tan calls the court to order once again, and we all fall quiet.

Connelly calls Clarence to the witness stand in Tyrone's defense. As Clarence steps up to take the witness stand, goose bumps rise on my arms. It feels as if he was sent by my father, so I give him my full attention. In fact, I listen to Clarence as if he alone could turn this thing around.

There on the stand, surrounded by the fluorescent lighting of the courtroom, even Clarence, who is usually the example of wisdom and light-heartedness, seems stripped of his dignity.

Connelly asks Clarence how he knew Jim McCullough.

"I knew Jim McCullough from city meetings," Clarence says. "He attended civic gatherings, primarily to argue against programs that would benefit the poor or Blacks in our community."

Olson interrupts. "What relevance does this have to the case, your Honor?"

"Continue, Mr. Connelly," Judge Tan responds. "You've both seen Mr. McCullough's letter to a friend of his at the Chamber of Commerce."

Connelly asks Clarence, "Did Mr. McCullough take a specific action against you or your community?" He holds his fingertips from each hand tightly together as he awaits Clarence's answer.

"Yes, when I first attempted to open a neighborhood center in 1960 to provide effective support programs for minority children and parents, McCullough sent mailings and made phone calls to stop the construction of the center. On one occasion, he personally threatened that he would cut my throat if I tried to bring any more—*niggers* was his term—if I tried to bring any more Black people into our town."

Tyrone is watching me again. It's as if he can read my thoughts. I sense his strength—the same determination in Rikki—but it's hidden beneath the role he must play as the character in this play. You've seen the movies, the ones that grow dark in dreaded suspense when a group of white boys chase after a Black man caught defenseless and unaware. In one account I've read, a Black man gets beaten just for visiting his own wife at a home where she's working as a maid. In my heart, I'm pinning my hopes for humanity on Tyrone's release. When it's Olson's turn to cross-examine Clarence, he asks him if Tyrone sought help for behavioral problems from a referral to the Community Center.

"Mr. Daniels," Clarence begins, "sought work through our center, beginning in the summer of 1966, because he could not find other work. He did *not* seek help for behavioral problems. He never exhibited such. He helped clean the place and even started coaching a little basketball. The young basketball players were fond of him…they trusted him. The center offered employment support, which did allow him to work with one of our counselors."

189

Clarence looks over at Tyrone and acknowledges him.

"Mr. Sage, did Mr. Daniels have behavioral challenges that kept him from finding work?" Olson asks more pointedly.

Clarence clears his voice and looks Mr. Olson right in the eye. "Sir, our center recognizes the housing, health care, and employment barriers faced by Black men. That's why we provided work for men like Mr. Daniels and support to go with it. Mr. Daniels did not have any behavioral challenges that stood out. He was a good role model for the young boys."

I see the color and spirit draining from Clarence's face, but he continues. "Tyrone's main problem was that he did not know how to write well. He had to care for a dying parent at a young age, which made it hard for him to focus in school and to finish high school. Primarily, he needed help with the work application process. When we spent time with him, he was a quick study. Mr. Daniels was a quiet, respectful man, who had a good influence on the boys at the center."

"Thank you, Mr. Sage," says Olson, and then he tells Judge Tan that he has completed his questioning.

Connelly and Judge Tan have an exchange of quiet words and gestures, after which Connelly stands up, pulls his belt and pants up over his stomach and looks over at Tyrone. Then he says something I don't expect. "I would like to call to the stand the defendant, Mr. Tyrone Daniels. Mr. Daniels," he says, looking directly at Tyrone, "please come to the witness stand."

When Tyrone stands up while everyone else is seated, I see that he has a sturdy natural build like his daughter's. It's dispiriting to think of the time that he's spent wrongly accused and incarcerated, when there's virtually no evidence that he's guilty in this retrial.

The spark of vitality Rikki summons in competition has been siphoned away by the stress of the trial, but she gives her father her full attention.

When Tyrone approaches the witness stand, he sits tall

190

and confident—leaving little evidence that he's spent his last dozen years in prison. His hand is large and strong as he stretches it out to smooth down his hair in back. His handsome features resemble Rikki's, though his nose is wider and flatter, and his eyes a little farther apart. He's wearing wire-rimmed glasses, which give him a scholarly look.

Connelly stands up, tugs his belt up with both hands, clears his throat. He then asks Tyrone to tell him what happened on June 21, 1968.

As he begins to speak, Tyrone's voice is quiet at first. He stares far off into the courtroom as if he's looking for someone else to walk in the room. I glimpse something else in his eyes beyond the defenses—sincerity.

"The night of the acci...the tragedy, I was tryin' to get Joveda to stay home. She was nine months pregnant, and I didn't want her goin' out. We were standin' together at the top of the stairs, and I was tryin' to convince her to stay home. It was late— and dark. I wanted her to stay safe at home. It was a hectic day— and hot. I was in constant anxiety knowin' that I needed to make more money to support Mrs. Daniels, Rikki, and our baby. I tried to talk Mrs. Daniels into stayin' home with me and little Rikki. I grabbed her arm to keep her home, and she pulled from me, then lost her balance. Had I known there was so little space behind her and the stairs, I'd have grabbed her again! I honestly thought she had more room."

His voice is shaking, but the more he speaks his truth, the stronger his voice becomes. "Fact was, I didn't see as clearly as I should 'ave. I was havin' ma own problems with dizziness and everything, just bein' tired, makin' it day to day with a young child. I thought it was because I was just tired. But also, I wasn't seeing well because I needed glasses. And I couldn't get help to buy 'em either—I didn't know where I could go to afford 'em. In some respects, the whole thing might not 'ave happened had I just got myself a pair of glasses," Tyrone adds.

191

Tyrone stops there, and Connelly tells him it's OK and he can take the time he needs.

I expect some type of emotional release from Tyrone, for him to break down in tears, but instead he asks Connelly to please excuse him for a moment, repeating that it'll just be a moment. Then he rests his elbows on the desk, folds his hands in prayer and rests his head on his thumbs. I read once that faith is like courage, that it shows itself most purely through our fear.

When Tyrone lifts his head from his reflection, Connelly asks him if there's anything more he would like to say.

"No, thank you," Tyrone says calmly. His voice is no longer shaking. It has a resonance and command I didn't hear earlier.

Judge Tan asks Olson if he has questions for Tyrone. Olson immediately digs in. "Mr. Daniels, we heard in trial in August 1968 that you pushed your wife down the stairs. A jury found you guilty of pushing your pregnant wife to her death in August of 1968. There is little evidence that much has changed. Did you push your wife down those stairs?"

Tyrone rises up in his seat, leans forward, musters all his strength and looks directly at Olson. He keeps his hands together, as if they're forced into prayer. "I did NOT push my wife, Sir... I grabbed her to keep her from fallin'." He pauses, and we all pause. Tyrone looks at the jury, "I did not push ma wife."

Tyrone leans back and looks at Rikki. "I have a good relationship with ma daughter. We write to each other, and there's a real respect between us. Ma daughter understands that I did not push her mother."

Rikki's weeping next to me, and I press a Kleenex into her hand, which she just clutches. She lets the tears flow freely down her cheeks, doesn't even cover her face.

"Mr. Daniels, when your daughter was interviewed before the first trial, she was unsure that you *did not* push your wife. Why would she have thought that?"

"Well, it was actually ma pullin' Mrs. Daniels, not pushin' her, that made her lose her balance. I did touch her, but it was to pull her toward us—and when she pulled away, she fell back. Rikki was behind me. She must 'ave seen me reach for ma wife—and by then, she was fallin'.'"

"Also, there were others who didn't have her best interests at heart and may have tried to convince her that I was to blame. Little Rikki was understandably upset with me that I didn't save her mother. But, I also believe ma baby, Rikki, over there, she's known all along I'm innocent. She knew I loved her mother—and her—more than life itself. I was caught in ma own grief. Killin' my wife is not something I could ever do." Tyrone unfolds his hands and rests them on his stomach.

"And I didn't just lose Mrs. Daniels. I lost both ma girls, including ma unborn baby daughter." He wipes away a tear but keeps going. "My error was to not reach out far enough and fast enough to catch Joveda when she fell back. As little Rikki and the landlord's daughter started screamin,' I ran down the stairs to Joveda, but I could tell by her neck and her empty stare that she was gone. Gone. It settled in me right quick that all I had was just ripped away. Then the storm began. First came the arrest, then the accusations that it was my fault, that I killed Joveda. Then the storm of hatred and lies—until they landed me in jail for all these 14 years. Who was gonna believe *me*, a poor black man jus' doin' all he could to pay rent to a hateful tyrant who hit his daughter and wife. His own daughter would come to see us to get away from him when she could!"

"Ma'am and Jury, mark my words: I, Tyrone Daniels, am innocent. I stand by this truth with everything in me—forever!" He looks at Rikki.

Olson is stunned and has nothing left to say. He utters, "That's enough, Mr. Daniels. Thank you." Deafening silence takes over the room like a fog, so that the only thing you can hear is the ticking of the clock. Time—the unsettling and rectifying force that pulled us all together in this courtroom.

I look at Rikki. She looks at me and just says, "Wow. I didn't know my dad had that in him." The tears in her eyes are glistening with a spark of hope.

I nod. "He knows the Truth of this whole thing with a capital T." Rikki shakes her head yes.

There's been enough pain and fatigue with this trial, but something else palpable is in the room. It's as if the heaviness has flowed through and a larger force, a nobility of spirit, is taking its place. None of us know what to do with it, except perhaps Connelly who's rushed to Tyrone's side. His cheeks are flushed, and he's nervously clearing his throat. He whispers something to Tyrone and Tyrone nods in agreement. Tyrone no longer looks like Connelly's downtrodden client. He's beginning to look more like a strategic partner.

Judge Tan announces to the court that the session has ended for the day and the closing comments will resume in the morning.

Rikki and I gather our papers and pens, tuck them into our bags. I grab a dime from my coin purse and give Rikki the heads up that I'm gonna call Mom. She says she's going to the restroom. When I ask the receptionist where I can find a pay phone, she invites me to use her phone. I dial Mom's number and get her on the first try.

"We're done for the day," I tell her. "You can come get me."

"How'd it go today?" Mom asks.

"It was pretty intense, Mom. We heard from Clarence—and even Rikki's dad. The evidence is not holding up that Tyrone is guilty. It's quite a long story, but Tyrone was framed by his landlord, and…"

She interrupts me to say she'd better get on her way. "I made meatloaf and baked potatoes, and they're in the oven, Chris. I don't have time to waste. I'll get in the car and come over." I

194

realize that the story, in all its complexity, is a long one. One I'll be telling all my life. At least for that, we have plenty of time.

● *Passing Through the Crucible*

Sleep feels short and fitful, wondering what the outcome will be. The morning comes quickly and before we know it, we're in the courtroom and Olson's preparing his closing comments. Olson is every bit the victim of obligation, unlike Connelly, who seems to get into more flow with his work. If Connelly's a moving picture, Olson's a slide projector that clicks from one appointment to the next, by reflex and on command.

"I'm ready for my closing comments, your Honor," Olson says to Judge Tan. Then he pulls himself up to look taller, takes a few steps, nods at the jurors and then at the Judge.

"Ladies and Gentlemen of the Jury," he begins, "Mr. Daniels was convicted of murdering his wife in August 1968. He was charged with shoving his wife down a staircase after a domestic argument. Mr. Daniels' own daughter told authorities in 1968 that she thought her father pushed her mother down the stairs."

Olson drones on, until I can no longer hear his words. Heat is rising within me, making my cheeks burn. I block out the intrusions, Olson's senseless rhetoric. It floats through my mind in pieces: "McCullough...track...record...of...giving...strong commitment...clothes for the poor...murdered...dangerous..." I hear the words, but don't allow them into my consciousness.

When Judge Tan invites Connelly to give his closing argument, I listen and listen hard. Despite his unpolished appearance, he's focused and energetic. He cares—and you can see that in every move and gesture, even as he takes time to tuck a stray shirt flap back into his trousers. All of us shift nervously, wondering if the storm Tyrone spoke about is gaining force—and if we're about to be blown by a strong, but arbitrary, wind.

"Ladies and gentlemen," Connelly says, "pushing his

eyeglasses up his nose, "Mr. Jim McCullough's own daughter Maryl has come forth as a witness in support of Tyrone Daniels. Ms. McCullough was sixteen years old when she witnessed Joveda Daniels' death. She had a relationship with Rikki Daniels as a child and feels a responsibility to that now. Ms. Maryl McCullough's father is no longer alive, and she has no reason to lie about what she saw. Her father's violence is no longer a threat. On her own, she—herself—came forward to re-open this trial and urge Mr. Daniels' release. As the Daniels' neighbor and friend, she did not find Mr. Daniels to be dangerous or guilty. She witnessed Mr. Daniels reaching out to pull Mrs. Daniels to him— and saw Mrs. Daniels lose her balance and fall. When Ms. McCullough told her father what she saw, he refused to believe her and swore her to secrecy. In fact, he punished her physically and psychologically. He threatened to disown her and cut off contact with her. That is an unnatural and abusive response for a father to have towards his daughter. We have no evidence whatsoever that Mr. Daniels abused his wife. The Daniels' daughter, Rikki, has testified as a grown adult that she believes her father is innocent."

"New facts and accounts show another side to Jim McCullough other than that of civic leader. A note he wrote, found in his coat pocket by his daughter Maryl McCullough, contains racist, derogatory language. Jim McCullough wrote he would have gone so far as arson to jeopardize the Community Center in Michigan City. It also demonstrates that he would not have treated the incident between Mr. and Mrs. Daniels with any objectivity."

"I ask you, respected jurors, to honor the testimonies that you have heard in this trial and to consider what Mr. Tyrone Daniels has been through. Not only has he had to absorb the shock and grief of losing his wife, but he also lost his unborn child—and custody of his daughter. He has been set up as a criminal by our system—which ladies and gentlemen, is designed to be a system of justice. Maryl McCullough had the courage to come forward to re-open this case so that Mr. Daniels can be a free man. She has shared evidence that was missing at the first trial, due to significant threats from a father who would regularly hit both her and her mother. With this newly disclosed evidence, I ask that you find Tyrone Daniel's not-guilty and release him now to his rightful freedom."

Judge Tan nods to Connelly, thanks him and dismisses the court for jury deliberation.

The jury leaves the courtroom, and the rest of us are free to move around though most of us remain still. The grief of my own father loss quickens in me, as if my heart's wrapped in strings that are tightening. I put my hand to my chest to stop the feeling. I know it well—the choking, gripping ache of deep sorrow. Holding my heart, I realize that Rikki and I have a primal understanding of each other. Our father loss is essential to who we are. It's deeply woven into our choices and the way we approach our lives.

Tyrone lost his life in a different way. Rikki looks at me. Her eyes hold fear and pain, but they soften as I look in her eyes. We have no words for each other, but she knows I understand the truth. Her people—and her father—have borne the weight of human cruelty. As slaves, they were beaten for learning to read and write, while we still wonder why they've struggled to pass on social capital and wealth through the generations. Yet, each day we ask them to forgive the sin of white supremacy and to move on in this world they did not create for themselves.

A tear slips out of Rikki's eye as she studies her father. Rikki waves over to him, and he waves back. Even if Tyrone is released, it can't bring Joveda back. Yet, his face is more relaxed now, too, his eyes shining as he sees his daughter is here caring about him.

I have a recurring dream that my father never really died. Rikki's grown up without Tyrone at her side, but he's alive and standing in this room. Not even Rikki's fighting spirit can change

197

the minds of the jurists now. The outcome depends not on what's right or wrong, but on the stories people have told over these few days. It depends on what the jury has internalized—and what they will decide when the narratives pass through the crucible of their own beliefs and inclinations.

Rikki finally nudges me to go with her to her father. I pick up my things and follow her, hearing the whoosh of my shoes' rubber soles. When she gets to him, all she says is "Daddy," and they embrace. "Hey, Rikki girl," he says, and I see the gray in his hair, the lines in his face. They squeeze each other tight, and I want to disappear. I think of Annie and all my friends who have their fathers and take them for granted. I want to fill them with this moment—stop the laws, the demanding bosses and social fears that keep fathers from their children. There's no doubt in my mind that Tyrone loved Joveda as much as Clarence loves his wife Callie, or Eddie loves Liza.

Rikki introduces me to her father, and I shake his hand, making a special effort to hold it tight so he can feel the strength I've learned from his daughter. "We're friends from college," Rikki says. "Chris is one of my *best* friends." There's a pause and lightness in the air. *Best Friends.* It's the first time I've heard Rikki say this, and I hold it in my heart in this profound moment while her father smiles and nods his head in approval.

"Thanks for comin' and bein' here with Rikki and Me, Chris," Tyrone says. His voice is low and deliberate, forming words with what energy he has left.

"It's great to meet you, too, Mr. Daniels..."

"Tyrone," Rikki interrupts. "You can call my dad Tyrone. Right, Dad? Doesn't that sound better?" This is huge, I know, letting me relax the "Mr.," the prefix of respect. The prefix that Black men were once required to use when they spoke to any white person.

"Tyrone. That's right," he says.

This feels like talking to someone whose language of

origin is different than my own, as we allow apologetic smiles to say what we don't yet have words for.

Rikki says that she needs to go to the bathroom. I'm relievedf—not because I don't enjoy getting to know Tyrone, but because I'm fatigued from interpreting all the quiet and weighted cues.

Rikki and I make our way to the restroom and this time we're silent. I fuss with my hair in the mirror, but Rikki doesn't. She just looks down and lets warm water flow over her hands. Water is Rikki's elixir—it's something she can trust.

"Where do you want to go?" I finally ask. "We've got some time."

"Let's just walk a little around this building," Rikki says. "Just walk with me."

"Rikki," I say, "can we just go sit on that bench in the hall for a second? I have something I want to give you."

"Sure," she says and we both slt down. While I reach into my bag, Rikki flicks her pointer fingers over her thumbnail. Rikki's nails are so beautiful that she could be a hand model.

I pull out a brown paper bag and hand it to Rikki. "I didn't have time to wrap it, Girl. Hope you don't mind."

She reaches in the bag without looking. She feels it..."A keychain!" she says.

"It is," I say. "I've been wanting to give you this for a long time."

She pulls it away from the paper. It's a little stuffed Batman on a chain. He's not as big as my Batman doll was as a little girl, but this gives me a second chance to give the doll away with love.

"Batman?" Rikki says, laughing at the small stuffed action figure. "What's up with Batman?" she asks.

"When I was little," I say, "I had a Batman doll. I adored Batman because he'd always make every bad episode end with

199

justice. Plus, he protected me from my fear of bats. I thought you needed a Batman to make you feel strong—to remind you there's justice and beauty in the world when it's not readily apparent."

"You're a funny Girl, Chris Bliss," Rikki says to me. I act like it's normal, that she would be the only person other than my father to call me "Chris Bliss." She knows the power that his term of endearment has for me.

"That I am," I say calmly. "Rikki, I just want to say...well, whatever happens... I mean..."

"I know what you're gonna say, Girl," Rikki interrupts, "that even if Tyrone—Dad—isn't freed, we'll know he's..."

"We know he's innocent, Rikki!" I finish. "Whether or not the jury's persuaded, we know the truth. Your relationship with your Dad is solid no matter what." Oh, what I'd give to have that again—to be able to talk to my father. Part of me wants a relationship with Tyrone too. Look at the two of us. We're looking for any blessings at all that we can count.

"Chris, there's something I have to tell you."

"What's that?" I ask.

"I care about you," she says. She looks straight in my eyes and sits completely still, a new version of herself. "Whatever happens, I really care about you. Thanks for being here."

"You're welcome," I say. It means so much for Rikki to tell me that out loud. I know it means that whatever the outcome of this trial, we have a new understanding between us. What we're living will imprint itself like graduation day—when you stand next to people with whom you've learned deep lessons, absorbing the mystery of how to apply them moving forward.

● *Deep into the Unknown*

The next morning brings a gentle rain. Rikki and I are both drawn to walking in the rain, especially if it's just a light sprinkle. Even so, when Rikki proposes that we walk near the courthouse, it's as though she's reading my mind. The bright green of the virgin leaves brightens the day, even with the cloud cover. It's also much cooler out, which I find refreshing, even as I pull my sweater tight around me.

"By the end of this day, we should know about Tyrone," Rikki says. "We'll know if he can be free again."

"I'm not even you," I say, "and I feel like I'm hanging on the edge." It feels like waiting for the biopsy of a tumor and hoping it's benign so that we can have a new lease on life. Even if Tyrone is exonerated, breaking free will have its own set of challenges. "Any sense of how your dad's doing?" The thought gives me a cold sweat, and when I wipe the rain from my brow, I can't tell which is which.

"I got to talk to him a little bit last night after you went home," Rikki tells me. "He's kept his expectations very low, which doesn't seem good, but in this case it is. If he's acquitted, it'll just be a welcome surprise. He won't let himself think beyond today. He's prepared for just about anything. He feels more alive just having people care for him and defend his rights." Rikki looks at me, blinking the misting rain from her eyes. I don't expect her to smile, but she does. Perhaps anything Tyrone experiences from here on will be a step up. Mostly, he's much less alone in this fight.

"I'm sure that's how he's made it this far," I say. "Not thinking beyond the minute he's in."

"I respect my father," she says. "From the letters we've exchanged, I know that whatever happens, he's resigned to starting over. He used to believe my mama's fall was somehow his fault, but he knows better now. And so do I. If that's what we get out of this, that's *a lot*." Rikki's voice trembles, but in a brave way, as though she's not saying this just to me, but to a whole audience.

"Rikki, I'm so sorry this is happening to you and your dad," I say. "This has been awful. I've been changed, too, by all of this. I've never been so close to all the things that go wrong in

201

our justice system. I can only hope that today something will go right for a change." I touch her arm, both to lend support and to guide us both back to the building. The rain's picking up and I don't want us both drenched before we sit in the courtroom for a few hours.

Rikki doesn't say anything more as we make our way back inside. She shakes the rain from her hair and wipes it off her face with her sleeve. We move forward, not a word, like two tired sisters, heading to where we know we need to be, too many thoughts in our heads to try to speak them.

As we get to the door, Clarence opens it for us. "Ladies," he says, "It's time to get back in the courtroom. The jury's reached a verdict." Our thoughts are locked within our heads, and the verdict seems the only key that can release them. The three of us move swiftly and silently together.

We enter the room. We see the faces. There's Tyrone. It's painful now to see any look of hope in his eyes which risks being dashed in an instant. Tyrone's the brave one here. Clarence, Rikki, and I do not look or feel at ease—or even hopeful. We're just here. Waiting.

Judge Tan calls everyone to order. "Ladies and gentlemen, jurors and family members of the defendant," she begins, looking directly at Rikki, "A verdict has been reached. This has been an emotional case. I must remind you before I announce today's verdict that we must have order in the court following the verdict—no outbursts of any kind, including shouts or clapping."

Judge Tan pauses, then announces the verdict. At first, we aren't able to absorb it. "*The jury has declared Tyrone Daniels not guilty.*" We look at each other to make sure we heard it correctly.

The words begin to register when the Judge orders Tyrone's release and dismisses Tyrone. Activists in the courtroom on Tyrone's behalf smile, shake hands and high-five. Several offer up a *Praise the Lord.* Some, including Callie and Clarence, hug one another. Rikki holds her face within her palms, as though she's not quite sure how to express her relief. It's a moment of shared humanity. With Mr. McCullough's hatred no longer in play, Olson was literally the only person in the room who fought this outcome.

Tyrone looks as though he's been switched on. He looks around him, as if to make sure that he has what he needs to leave the courtroom. He also gives a slight wave to Rikki, nodding to her and to Clarence. He mouths, "I'll be back," then leaves with the court security to finalize his release.

The rest of us remain still for a moment, including Rikki who closes her eyes and takes a few deep breaths. As if coming out of meditation, people begin to stand up and move. Rikki turns to me and the two of us hug one another and hold on a little while. Our tight squeeze gives our contracted hearts permission to open.

"The worst is over," I whisper to Rikki, still trying to convince myself.

Rikki exhales a sigh, then says, "Let's go see Liza and Eddie." Once she decides to go to them, she walks swiftly, until Liza scoops her in a deep embrace and Eddie wraps his long, strong arms around them both.

Connelly gathers his papers nearby, holds them under his arm while he rubs his palms in excitement and steps close to the three of them to congratulate them and say that Tyrone will be back any minute. He's too much of a servant leader to understand that he deserves any congratulations himself.

Liza, ever modeling inclusivity, notices that I'm standing alone and reaches towards me, inviting me to be part of the embrace. Her hand is beautiful, and what I notice is that despite her silken, dark skin, our palms are the exact same pale pink as we join them together. "Honey, you've been a godsend to our Rikki. You've been just a godsend," she whispers in my ear.

"You've all been a godsend to me," I whisper back.

"Now what?" Rikki asks. "Where will Tyrone live? Where will he go?"

"You let me take care of that, honey," Eddie says. There's just nothing like a big, strong man like Eddie, a man of few words, but a man with conviction and the connections to act on them. "We'll get Tyrone back on track. For now, he can stay with us."

Then I remember Clarence, who has joined with Connelly in an animated discussion, the two of them grinning, nodding their heads in agreement with intermittent hearty laughs.

This is the Clarence I remember as a little girl. My father wanted to be an attorney. He'd started law school and had to quit when he needed to support our family. Had he followed a career in law, he could have easily been assigned to defend Tyrone.

Clarence sees me watching him and his jolly expression softens. Between Liza and Clarence, I feel I have a new set of parents, and it's taken me by surprise. I haven't been able to explain to my own mother why I've become so absorbed in Rikki's world. My mother is a people lover and a lover of life, but her choices have kept her in small, Midwest towns with little exposure to real challenges faced by African Americans. On two occasions, she's told me that growing up in Chicago, she was careful not to walk through Black neighborhoods because she was assaulted once by an African American man. My father's work—and now my friendship with Rikki—have demanded that she stay the course. She's always loved Clarence and Callie, the first family to invite us to dinner after Dad died. She'll be relieved to hear the verdict.

As if Clarence can read what's on my mind, he finishes with Connelly, shakes his hand and puts his arm around my shoulder. "D'you expect this?" he asks me.

"I didn't know *what to expect,*" I say, "but I'm surprised you didn't tell me about the arson threat when we had breakfast together. Why not?"

"Because, my young friend," Clarence says, "we had a lot of other important stuff to talk about. And sometimes you just

204

need a critical mass. I knew Tyrone was innocent. I couldn't bear to think of him in prison for something that broke his own heart...that he didn't do..."

"I know," I say, "I've been thinking about that. And I've been thinking of my own father too. He's innocent too, right?" I ask it as if he's still here, and there's yet another important trial to attend.

Clarence clears his throat, loosens his tie slightly. "My girl, you're not thinkin' your Daddy did something wrong..."

"No, but his depression..." My eyes well up with tears, and I look down at the shiny flooring in shame. I look at Rikki, who for the moment is occupied with Liza & Eddie. I adjust my bangs with my hand to discreetly hide my pain. "You said," I say slowly, "you said he was depressed, that he tried..."

"My dear girl," Clarence says, "the Lord brought us together again for me to tell you something. Your Dad was a shining star. That was his problem, you see. He saw things way ahead of everyone else. Now if I had that gift, I might find myself a little depressed too. Your daddy's only mistake was not to understand how gifted he was. Now I imagine you have that same problem a bit—do you, Young Lady?"

"There's *no one* like my father," I say. "But we're still learning from him, aren't we?"

"That's for sure. Whatever you do, you stay in touch, all right?" he asks, "I don't want to lose touch. Seeing you is like seeing Ryan all over again. You got his eyes, his nose...you bring him alive again."

Clarence Sage is the only person, besides my uncles, who could bring Dad back to life. "It's unreal, Clarence, unreal...that's all I can say, but yes...I'll keep in touch. How about you give me your address?" I pull out a receipt from my purse and hand it to him with a pen. "I'll write first," I promise.

As he's scratching down his address, Tyrone enters the room and joins Rikki, Liza and Eddie. "I'm a free man," he says,

"I'm free!" He tries out the words, sees how they sound. Clarence stops writing, and we all focus entirely on Tyrone, as though he's a young warrior who's emerging from a rite of initiation.

"Congratulations," I'm the first to say, as if people are released from prison every day.

Rikki moves over to her father. I expect him to hug her, but it's Rikki who wraps her strong, invincible arms around her father. At first, he pulls away, and then he lets her. They both have tears streaming down their faces, and I start to cry too. As Rikki holds her father, he rubs his hand up and down her arm as if he's done it all these years. "It's over, Daddy," she says. "All the nightmares, the worries, the mistruths…Daddy…"

"I don't know what to do with myself," Tyrone says, holding tight to Rikki, his eyes squeezed tight. I can relate. Not getting our wish is often the familiar territory. Getting our wish throws us deep into the unknown.

And what will Rikki and I wish for now—now that this part of our lives is over? Not unlike Tyrone, we'll soon be looking for summer work and places to live.

"Got so used to having nothing, I did," Tyrone says. "Gotta get out and see the light of day."

"You do, Daddy. You do. Mr. Sage said he can help you find a place to live."

"Great! No more apartments above restaurants." His smile, the first I've seen, is lopsided and endearing, and now I see a space between his two front teeth.

"No, not that for you, Daddy." I'm surprised to hear Rikki say Daddy so many times. She says it like she's practicing it, which of course she is. At one time, she avoided him, was confused by what he symbolized to her, blamed him for the painful memories they shared. She had to learn that she was reacting to the trauma they shared. This is a new Tyrone. He's given us a glimpse of resurrection—and even though he did nothing wrong and could easily harbor hatred, he acts with a courage and grace I've never seen.

Connelly, standing by and waiting for the right moment, shakes Tyrone's hand and welcomes him to the world. Connelly greets me and Rikki again. Rikki hugs Connelly and thanks him, as if she's known him all her life.

"What will you do tonight?" Rikki asks her father and I realize this won't be easy for either of them. Now that Tyrone's free, he won't want to sit in Michigan City, far from his daughter, nor will she want to stay in Minnesota. We're headed back to Gary, then back to school, and Tyrone will begin his new life on his own, no family members close by. Now, when Rikki has breaks from school, she'll have two families to visit, Tyrone *and* Liza and Eddie. With a youthful look of freedom in his eyes, Tyrone looks more like Rikki's brother than he does her father. Still, the prison time has aged him, and his step is slowed by a slight, but humbling limp.

"Come eat with us all, Daddy," Rikki says.

Tyrone looks at Connelly for permission, still internalizing the parameters of his freedom and what it will mean for him. "Is this acceptable?" he asks.

"You're a free man!" Connelly says, his face red and his eyes twinkling. "I'll check in with you later." Connelly doesn't take himself seriously. His joy is not derived from ego—it comes from a genuine place, from what he's co-created with Tyrone. I like that about him.

Eddie and Liza come over to our group and shake Tyrone's hand. Liza tells him she's overjoyed with his release. Liza and Eddie offer to take us to a family-owned restaurant specializing in linguini. Clarence hugs us all good-bye, promises Rikki and me that he'll be in touch with Tyrone every day until he has a place to live and work.

We all settle into the back of the Coopers' Chevy Caprice. Eddie has Tyrone sit up in the front passenger seat, and Liza joins us girls in the back, with Rikki in the middle. As I stare out the windows of the Coopers' car, I dream of getting my own father back. I would want him to sit right next to me here in the back, and maybe I'd hold his hand the whole way. We probably wouldn't say much. It would be like the increasingly rare dreams where my father appears. I can't remember his looks so clearly now—it's been ten years since I've seen him. But he would sit near me, my own father, whose mere presence would keep me at my best, a little kinder, a bit more intelligent.

We all need some loving presence like that—to calm us, to bring out our noble spirit and impart to us the sense that we're being prepared for something greater—that we'll have everything it takes to get there. I was blessed that, for a short time, that figure was my father.

Tyrone is explaining to Eddie that the last time he had linguini, he had it with fried red tomatoes, not green. He's speaking about it as though it's the most normal thing in the world, not something you'd dream about from prison. He looks over at Rikki and says, "I want to make that for you—fried *red* tomatoes."

Rikki says, "Daddy, I can't wait."

"All right! I'm gonna fry 'em in butter and use the crispy bits left in the pan to make a delicious cream sauce. You'll love it!"

It may still take time for Rikki and her father to know each other better. But he's already dreaming of ways to demonstrate his love with food. As we dream together about the ordinary act of preparing food, I realize that we're all being that loving presence for one another. Rikki and I sit quietly listening, hearing very carefully each word Tyrone has to say.

● *A Sense of Conviction*

By the time I leave for school, Mom, too, has a much deeper understanding of how important this week has been for us all. She hates good-byes as much as she hates apologies, and as she sits with me in Michigan City, waiting for the South Shore

Line headed to Gary, she takes my hand and says how much she loves me. I know that she loves me in all the ways she possibly can.

I stay at Liza and Eddie's the night before I leave for the airport. This time, I'll travel alone, while Rikki stays with her family a week longer. Rikki's stayed closer to me than ever through this trip, and we're really getting to know each other. The court case and the spending time with the Coopers have magnified my need to make something of my life—to influence young people through my teaching. I've been thinking about Chuck, about Annie, my teaching, how Rikki and my friendship will evolve from here. This trip's cemented something about us: we've become friends because on a deep level, we *care what happens to one another*. There are things about me that only Rikki knows and things about her she's told no one but me. Because we've been friends, each of us will go out in the world and be able to do so much more.

As I get ready for bed, I hear Rikki's characteristic ratta-tat-tat at my door. When she comes in, her face is glum, puffy and sallow. I didn't anticipate this at all—this is supposed to be a time of celebration. I open my arms to her, and she starts sobbing. All the emotions of the week well up within me, too, and my head throbs as I try to hold them back. "I'm so sorry, Rikki. This has been so hard for you."

"You don't even know what I'm so upset about," she says.

"Well, I know how much you wanted Tyrone to be..."

"This isn't about Tyrone. Chris," she says, and she gives me her look. "This is about *you*!" A wave of dread flows through me. What'd I do now?!

"About me?" I ask. "What'd I do?" I suddenly feel as though I've eaten a pepper and the spicy hot has spread from my mouth to my whole body.

"You got under my skin. That's what you did!" *Oh, Rikki,*

I think to myself, this is really upsetting you.

"You're upset at *me*?" I'm surprised, as if I'd expected a compliment and was being told instead that I made a grave, inexcusable error.

"I am, but not for the reason you'd think," she starts. "Number one, I'm upset you're leaving tomorrow. You've really been there for me. Much as I believe in God, I've learned how I needed someone next to me so I didn't have to work it alone. I never expected you to come with me." Her feelings are strong, and she's being brave about them.

"I don't get it. So, I stood with you, and you're happy about that, but that's also what's so hard?"

"Chris," she says, comparing the length of her nails to one another, and then looking up at me sadly. "I'm transferring."

"You're what?" I ask. I feel my body start to tremble.

"I've been accepted to the University of Michigan on a swim scholarship. I won't be returning to Minnesota."

OUCH.

"But all your belongings are at school. You *have to* go back. You only have a few more years...."

"I know all that. Look, I didn't expect to get a scholarship for the U of Michigan. It's just better for me all the way around...except for you and me..."

"Why haven't you mentioned this?" I figure that if I protest enough, she'll change her mind. But then I feel my own strong feelings. "You didn't even tell me you were thinking about this!" Then I think, *God, our friendship has been a lot of work. Maybe this is for the best.*

"I didn't expect to get the scholarship. I just thought I'd try. I didn't tell anybody. There was a good chance it wouldn't work out."

I'm silent. Through my head, I'm running a few protests and the responses I expect from Rikki. Then the wiring in my brain

210

short-circuits, and I can't hold a thought. I cross my arms over my heart and study the clean, white line of the ceiling molding as a distraction. I look back at her, resigned that my thoughts are what they are, imperfect like the nicks and gouges in the wall.

Rikki continues and I do my best to follow her words. "Look, my life hasn't been easy, but it's taught me to think for myself. The University of Michigan's an easier drive for visiting my father—and not as far from Liza and Eddie. This has nothing to do with you. If anything, that's what makes it hard for me. Maybe you're the whole reason I went to school in Minnesota."

"Rikki, you're doing so well. And you know how the swim team relies on you. You're really important to our school. We can drive back together when I visit Mom..."

"We can make arrangements to see each other when you visit your Mom. I need to set something straight. Minnesota swim teams cater to affluent white swimmers. I've been around them all my life. Except at the Y when I was young, every pool and meet I've swam in, I was consistently the only Black girl in the pool. I want something different for myself. The coach at Michigan assured me I won't be the only minority swimmer on the team."

I can't argue that, much as I want to. I have no idea what it must feel like for Rikki, so she tells me. "I don't want to be in such a small school where everyone pays so much attention to every little thing I do—every choice, anything I say, *just because I'm Black.*"

"That'll be an issue, wherever you go. You have a way of getting people's attention, Rikki. It's just that—what if it's not all that much better in Michigan—and could even be worse?"

"Chris, I have to give it a try, especially when I can start over. Do I look like a girl who runs away from her problems?" Rikki checks my expression.

"Sometimes," I say calmly. "Sometimes you do. We all do."

Rikki does the most amazing thing, something I thought she'd never do. She listens to me, doesn't fight back and looks down at her toes. Then she says, "I guess I have. But this time I'm not. I'm thinking of myself. When I become a medical doctor, I'll be spending the rest of my life thinking of others. I better get my relationship with myself right first."

The more she says, the more I understand this really is the right choice, and the less I can argue. Like a child who's fallen and doesn't want the bloody wound on my knee, I turn the *if only's* in my mind. But I know, from the look in her eyes, that she means it and nothing I say will stop her. I've never been able to stop Rikki, but then I've never had a reason to. Her sense of conviction infuses me with hope. I want to adopt it.

"I just can't believe you're not coming back," I say.

"There's something I want you to know," Rikki says. "I've kept this quiet because I didn't want you to talk me out of it. I knew you would. I had to get through this trial before I made a decision for obvious reasons. But, I've wanted to live closer to my dad."

I couldn't argue with that either. Maybe it hurts so much because part of me wants to go back to Indiana, or to Michigan, to be closer to my own mother. I want to jump right back into the familiarity of my childhood. But it no longer fits me. Much as I can feel like I've abandoned Mom, she's never expected me to stay close by. She's never stopped expecting me to make something of my life beyond what our small town can offer.

"I'm sorry," I finally say. "I'm thinking too much of *my* loss. You've caught me completely off guard. I didn't even think of you transferring as a possibility."

"Girl," Rikki says back, "one thing I've liked about us is the independence we afford each other. You'll be just fine. Besides, Chuck will be happy to have your attention focused back on him."

Chuck. The last few months, I've prioritized being the

best friend I could be to Rikki. I've trusted Mom, Chuck and even Annie to give me room for my emotional journey with her. Certainly, *she* hasn't been basing her life on what I need. She's perfectly happy to go where she needs to. She's been clear about her swimming and pre-med aspirations all along. And me? I've gone the extra mile to be supportive—because my father would have, and because I have few role models besides him of other white people who do. Now, through Rikki's example—and permission—I'm reminded that it's time for my own teaching goals and relationships to have their time in the sun.

"Chris, you OK?" Rikki asks. "You're still mad at me, aren't you?" She's sitting close to me, saddled on her chair, her hands clasped tight. "I'm so sorry," Rikki says. "I should have told you."

"Rikki," I say, under my breath, reluctant to use my full voice. "I wish you would have trusted me."

"I do trust you," says Rikki. "I trust you more than I trust most people. That's why I couldn't tell you. I trusted you'd talk me out of it. I had to make this decision on my own."

Part Four: Release from Room 322

☻ *The Turning Point*

That's the last time Rikki and I were alone together before she left Minnesota. Our college time together was brief, but intense, and I still remember how dejected I was when she decided to move to Michigan. I tried to make sense of those sad feelings on my flight back to Minnesota, but I was seated next to a born-again Christian holding a book with a Bible quotation for anything I said, so I couldn't exactly delve into my sorrow. When I told him I was studying to become a teacher, the topic of discipline came up pronto. My seatmate hastened to tell me the problem with kids today is that their parents don't give them a big swat on the bottom now and again to show them who's boss. After telling him that the world holds enough of its own punishments, I told him I'm learning that the children who struggle the most are the ones whose parents do swat them. He tried to argue with me, but I excused myself to read—all the while thinking that clearly, his God was not the vision of a loving, compassionate Creator that my father modeled for me. I often remember that moment as the turning point when I promised myself to be the face of a deeply caring God for my students. No matter what their cultural or faith traditions, I wanted to be the example of someone that gave them faith in *life*.

Now, as I wait for release from the hospital, I reflect on *who* in my life embodied that for me—and I think of Rikki. She's always been one of my best teachers. While most of my friends at school were concerned with getting good grades, finishing term papers, who was dating whom and partying, Rikki and I understood on some level that our friendship was born of trying to understand why we grew up without our fathers. Rikki transcended every pre-ordained barrier put before her to become an accomplished athlete and a trusted medical doctor. I've become a teacher and a mother, doing my all to stay present to the needs of my own children and other little ones in our community who need caring adults in their lives. Chuck and I have deepened our own bond, while our children give our lives an air of enchantment even on the bad days, those days of tummy ills—and spills—that jolt us from any illusion that we're in control.

Clarence's miraculous look-alike, Marcus, enters my room, striding boldly with those white clogs. As he takes my blood, I'm flooded with nostalgia for my babies, our pets and our chaotic life at home. "You got some really marvelous flowers there, Darlin'," he says, and I'm glad he's distracting me. Still, a tear slips out of my eye.

"Yes, my mom likes to send me carnations," I tell him. "They're simple, but elegant, and they'll last a while. That's Mom in a nutshell."

"Simple, elegant and will last a while," Marcus repeats. "What a great description—wish more people came like that! That describes you, too, especially now that you're on a solid path to healing!" Marcus' enthusiasm is contagious—as Clarence's was. He's the type of person who gets you thinking about springtime birdsongs and sunlight so warm you don't need a jacket.

"I hate blood tests, Marcus," I say. "But they're quickly over with when you give 'em."

"Oh Darlin,' we take good care of you here," he says. "There are plenty of life trials to get through on your own—driver's tests, work deadlines, public embarrassment—but at least when you get a shot, you've got one of us standing right with you." He winks at me and buzzes out of the room. The welcome dose of pluck and warmth he leaves in the room call to life memories that are truly lovely, like the wonder of a newborn baby crossing her eyes as she tries to focus on a toy or face.

As Rikki guessed, I've been diagnosed with glomerulonephritis, brought on by exhaustion, dehydration, and undiagnosed strep. The bacterial infection inflamed my body's waste filtration system. Thankfully, I've gotten medical support in the nick of time, and I'll make it without permanent renal damage. Going through the tests, including a biopsy of my kidney, has helped me realize that my illness isn't limited to nephritis. I might have avoided all this if I'd listened better to the intelligence of my body, my sore throat and thirst.

Instead I'd been living in my head, caught up in pursuing the same idealism my father prized so dearly: believing that the awareness and contributions of good people will counter greed and violence; that we can acknowledge the inter-generational pain in our country's history and find our place in the healing; that we can learn from those still hurting from injustice; that young people are valued as society's most precious resource—and that we will be intelligent about investing in them. I still believe such things, but now I temper my hope with work of the heart. To mature, we must learn to fight—yet continually forgive—the human failings that make our social contracts inhospitable to children. I will forever work on that forgiveness.

My father rarely cried in front of me, only toward the end of his depressive illness—or rather the end of his life. Sometimes I wonder if he'd lived longer if he'd taken more time for things, or if he'd learned to just sit quietly with his thoughts and feelings. If he'd walked more in nature instead of attending so many civic meetings. Or just indulged more often in tickling me on the floor!

I thought that my father was not alone in bringing me to different churches to witness the congregants living their beliefs; or by researching schools so carefully so I could have the best education available to me. I thought that visiting prisons was something that fathers did—to make sure those inside had social security and plans for what they'd do upon release. I know now that my father was uncommon—a challenge that he paid for with his own life. That factors into my illness. Perhaps I'm paying for his courage too.

Sweet Burden of Crossing

Get Well Card from Rikki, Ann Arbor, Michigan, 2004
● *Rikki's Get-Well Letter*

Dear Chris,

Girl, it felt good to hear your voice, even if your health's stirring things up. Been thinking of you–and even how we met. When you first called me in college and asked me if I wanted a ride to Indiana, I didn't know what to think of you! I didn't even know you. I was really fine with taking the Greyhound!

And I thought, "I've gotta ride for hours with this strange white girl with her own car and I won't be saying a damn thing." So awkward. At the same time, I knew there was something about you that made you call me. Not every day a white girl reaches out. What did you want, besides gas money?

And Lord, some of those faces you made at me! You probably didn't realize how you stared at me. I know you didn't mean to, but it's as if you were studying me, I felt so judged by you, like you were gonna run back and report to all your friends what traveling with me was like.

And it was sizzling hot! Even the damn Greyhound would have had air conditioning. But you know at some point, I just put my concerns about you to rest. I knew you weren't mean. A little caretaking maybe. But not mean. I just thought that you'd be like all the other white folks I'd met, naïve about history. Wanting me and anyone with brown skin to get over ourselves, wanting to ignore our whole ugly history.

But you kept being yourself. Then we decided to stay in Madison with the storm and all. There we were. You were different from the rest. I could see that. But I didn't want to get my hopes up.

I'd misread you. You weren't judging me. You actually did want to learn from me. I think that's why I invited you in to meet Liza. Until you, I'd never had that feeling before. Every other white person I'd met had something they thought they should

217

teach me. Some way they wanted to fix me. You just wanted to know me better. To this day, I remember that about you. It blew my mind, Chris. That a white person just wanted to know me. Didn't want my vote. Didn't want to recruit me to some church or group. Didn't treat me like they knew it all. Didn't use me to get over their bad feelings about history. You just liked me the way I was.

I'm sorry you're hurting, Chris. It won't last forever. You're awesome, Girl. Keep the Faith. I'm excited to see you soon!

Love you.
Sis' Rikki

☻ *The Pink Box*

Along with the gift of unconditional acceptance, my beloved Rikki has given me another gift—that of allowing me to reinterpret history—even my father's death—with new information. His death was more within his own grasp than perhaps he even realized. I take some odd comfort in that.

My mom's moved her photography business to Eau Claire, Wisconsin to be closer to me, our children, and one of her favorite cousins. Now, a visit to us is a comfortable drive, and she's come to spend the day with us. As Mom's gotten older, she's dropped the severe black and white clothing that have been her hallmark, and to my great surprise, she's experimenting with bright colors.

Being a grandmother suits my mother well. She was always dignified and trim, but now she's more relaxed in her style and in her gait. She's wearing beige slacks, a coral sweater set and multi-colored mosaic earrings. Her lipstick is not her trademark red any longer—that, too, is a shade of coral, and the lines on her face aren't haggard and drawn. They're soft and well-placed as any facial lines befitting those who age gracefully. Sunlight shining behind her reveals the soft hairs on her face, giving her a subtle glow.

My children reflect that glow, too, and when they see their Nana coming, they skip to her and wrap their strong little arms around her long and sturdy legs. "Nana!" they yell, and she strides onto our porch and opens the door as if she owns the place. Before I know it, she's unpacking gifts for Gracie and Max—and even pulls out a box wrapped in pink with a silver bow for me. My mom, bless her heart, even in her deepest grieving, has been a maven of enchantment. She's always prided herself on her gift selections, and she is one who, not having seen a friend in a month or so, will come bearing some little delight for them. The delight's usually personal, too—like a tube of lipstick or a silk scarf, but always just the right color and treasured forever. The other thing about Mom: it's never about price. What matters is how much the recipient will enjoy the gift. She'd hate for anyone to think that she's hostage to a price range. It reminds me of making my first friend in France, Genevieve, and having her slip me the new Yves Rocher fragrance I'd secretly longed for but couldn't afford. This is the one thing that's always surprised me about Mom. I used to think that she needed to have friends and family members associate her with gifts in order to like her. But in her smile today, I see that she can't quite help herself. It's a sport for her, the whole hunt of finding the exact thing that will bring joy to those she loves. She can barely contain herself as she watches Gracie tear through the wrapping tissue to find a miniature fairy doll with sparkly wings and a box of addition flash cards, then prompts little Max to open a sticker book of big red fire trucks. I resign myself to the fact that I have to steer Mom from gender-specific toys.

Then, it's my turn. I take the pink box, shake it as by tradition, and gently remove the bow and set it aside. Mom likes it that I recycle bows and paper, even as she doesn't give a care to the children's spontaneous ripping. Savoring the wrap is a rite of passage. I pull the cardboard box out and pull out the bundle of tissue inside. I see my gift in spurts—first the little black boots, then the gray stockings and finally the trademark yellow belt of

Batman. My God, a Batman doll. How did she know? How could she have remembered? Before I can even react, Max pulls the doll out of my hand, and says, "That's not for Mama! That's for Max!!" I bundle him in my arms, hold him tight and tell him, "No, Honey, it's for Mama. Mama loves Batman too," and I quickly add, "Let's share him but you can play with him now." He runs off with the doll before I can even give it another look, and before I know it, Batman is saving Gracie's fairy from being attacked by a wicked aircraft. I sit in disbelief, as though I'm a child again at Christmas mass, trying to sit still with the high of receiving a gift that couldn't be more meaningful, not having known prior it was just what I needed. I remember the feeling now…looking just like any other little girl in the church, but cupping my own joy, as if it were a baby bird, in my heart. Now, I need only look at a few strings of holiday lights to be reminded of how longing can sometimes, in rare instances, be quelled by the spirit of giving. Amazingly, Mom had held a memory when I thought it had only belonged to me and my father.

I have spent so much of life trying to understand my father's death and my brief, ten-year life with him, that I've thought much less about my mother's sacrifices and the steady, selfless care she's given me. Where my father taught me to respect those who were different from me, it's truly been with my mother where I've learned the fine dance of realistic expectations, negotiation, and forgiveness.

As Max and Gracie whirl around in excitement, over the dramas between the two new dolls, I ask Mom what she remembers about me and Batman. She checks to see that my little ones are occupied. Then she moves over to our living room couch, slides the picture books into a crisp, tidy pile, and pats the seat beside her to motion me over.

"I'm not ignoring your question," she says. "I just don't want to say anything mean about your father in front of my grandchildren." She smiles slyly with her mouth closed. She waits as I settle myself onto the couch, which I rarely do, unless we're going to watch a movie as a family. Then she says, "I thought your father was awfully harsh to make you give away that doll. Can you imagine taking it away from Max now?" she began. I see—this is something she's wanted to correct for a long time.

"Well, that's one way to look at it," I say. "I felt so ashamed, so terrible."

"You weren't terrible, honey. You were a shy child, wanting to get attention like any other child. And you were absolutely smitten by the other little girl…"

"Cece!" I say, interrupting.

"Yes, Cece," Mom says with a far-off look, trying to recall the details. "You were absolutely taken with her. You liked her so much you wanted to see if she could help you get over your fear of bats."

"But the more I told her, the more I frightened *her*."

"You were being a seven-year-old," Mom says, squeezing my arm as if I'm still her baby. "You wanted her to like you. But you didn't need to be shamed for it."

Still, I hated to disappoint my father. With his work and civic commitments, I didn't get as much time with him as I wanted. His presence was always evanescent, as if from the beginning his spirit filled my life more than his physical body. I had no idea that my memories of our fleeting time together would have to sustain me for a lifetime.

Yet, Mom has always been there for me, as she is right now. It was Mom who cooked for me, brought me places, tucked me in bed, sang to me. It was Mom who made me drink my orange juice before I hopped on the school bus. Who saw to it that I learned my math facts.

Gracie and Max buzz in, Gracie galloping on her stick horse holding Batman high up in the air to fly. Max is on the chase, alternating between the sounds of a race car engine and a rescue vehicle. My own guilt is setting in for not observing them more closely; in my mind, I'm begging them to fly and zoom to one of their bedrooms so that I can indulge myself in my mother's uncommon transparency. I fear losing this moment.

Max comes by to give me and his Nana a hug. I'm surprised at how well he and his sister are playing. They gallop to Gracie's room, taking their giggles and *vrooms* with them and leaving me and Mom awestruck by their flurry of play.

Mom looks at me as if she should continue, and I lean in a little closer to her as if she's a teenage friend about to reveal her new crush. "Go on, Mom," I say. "Tell me more about Dad." Her eyes widen with excitement, as though talking about Dad can bring him alive again.

"Your father was a brilliant man, an inspiration for the community...," she repeats. "So many people loved him. When he wasn't stewing about some injustice, he was very endearing—and powerful in the ways he could influence people. His doctor had clinical observations, and I should have paid more attention to them. I knew he was suffering, and I knew that his illness was being exacerbated at work. I really should have talked him into finding new work." We both know he loved his job, as witnessed in Mom's scrapbook of ways he broke all kinds of barriers for people through his work.

"I love hearing you talk about Dad, Mom. But I always thought he really loved his work."

She holds her wedding ring up to the light, and I know she's remembering how Dad paid dearly for it with the little money he had.

"He was a perfect fit for his job, but he hated the politics. The straw that broke the camel's back was when he placed a call to George Wallace, an Alabama governor who was very supportive of his Social Security initiatives. Wallace was dead set on racial segregation."

"Are you kidding me? Are we talking about *the* George Wallace?

"Yes, your father actually reached out to him to persuade him to change his agenda. He told him about all the good work at the Community Center, the way the children were thriving not only because they were getting the resources they needed, but because their field trips with children from area schools—white children—were introducing them to new and enriching experiences."

"How'd Wallace react?"

"He was not impressed. He was solidly against Brown vs. The Board of Education and the Civil Rights Act that had just passed. He told your father that ending segregation would only cause a host of problems in the workplace and schools, for people on both sides of the racial divide. Your father argued with him, telling him segregation would never survive, because it was wrong. 'You're a good man, Ryan Fitzgerald,' Wallace told him. 'But you're wrong when it comes to segregation. You just wait and see. No matter what people do, there will always be more harmony when the races are separated. They want it too.'"

"Wow, Mom, that's just awful," I say. And yet even now, I see how entrenched the divide is. Sadly, I don't know very many people like me who have a friend like Rikki. My heart sinks, as if it's been pulled down to the pit of my stomach.

"Here's what was awful, Chris. Your dad could not be honest with Wallace about the racial tension in his own office. The fight for civil rights was half the battle. Then there was the practical reality of building relationships with African Americans who had fought hard against discrimination. There were two African American women who inherited your dad as their supervisor but wanted little to do with him. They clearly had their own suspicions that they could ever trust the new law—or a white man like your father. Your dad was new at being a boss too—he

223

had his own hang-ups about *his* supervisors. The boss relationship, by nature, is tricky, and Dad used to say 'Boss spelled backwards is S.O.B.' After all his efforts to work for civil rights, here he was—in what felt to him a role that still enslaved people in a different way." She takes a sip of her tea. She's watching me closely.

"But it was *Dad*," I tell her. "He always found a way with people."

Mom breaks a cookie in half, places a half on my plate and takes a small bite of her own half. "Chris, what I'm trying to tell you is that your father did not find a way with people *this* time."

"But it was what he wanted!" I protest. "To work *with* African Americans to change the laws. Couldn't he just tell that to the people he supervised? Maybe he was trying *too* hard," I say, imagining my father torn between meeting his own impossible standards, then tripping over himself to impress the women. I still do it with Rikki. Though I'm her friend, I still symbolize a whole people who didn't have her best interests in mind. Rikki certainly wouldn't like being thrown into working for a white man—it wouldn't matter who he was.

Mom, the survivor who isn't easily stumped herself, wrinkles her forehead and closes her eyes. She folds her hands together as if in prayer, then with her elbows on the table, she props her chin on them. She's collecting herself, but I see that tears are slipping from her eyes. I'm moved to do what *she* taught me— to talk her out of her pain. But for a change, I disobey that old pattern. Rikki's taught me more recently to honor someone's pain when it surfaces. So I stay quiet, put my hand on her arm for comfort.

Mom opens her eyes, moves her folded hands back down to the table. She looks me in the eye as though she means business. "You don't understand, Christine. He knew he *needed* to go the extra mile. That's what he was doing. Some of us know we *have* to do that."

Mom's right about going the extra mile, but not right about me not understanding. "So, what *did* Dad say that offended them?" I ask.

"It wasn't what he said, Chris. It was that he wasn't the one who hired them and didn't yet have a relationship, then had to delegate assignments." Mom begins to stack our empty dishes as though she's through with the conversation. Then she stops abruptly and crosses her arms across her stomach as if for protection.

"One of the women filed a complaint against your father—that he was giving her more work than others because she was black. That is true, in a way. Dad would try to check in with her and see what she needed, but she didn't want to listen to him. He would role-play with me on what he might say. He knew there was a noble side to her. She was warm and engaging with her friend. He would hear them talking and laughing as he approached the door, then become dead silent as he walked in. They would make the clients laugh and relax. Ironically, the very manager the one woman kept in touch with was the one who most cursed the demands of the Civil Rights Act. He scapegoated your father so *he* wouldn't be at fault. Anyway, Chris, we really need to get on with our day." She stands up with our cups and dishes, carries them to the sink and begins rinsing them.

I stay still. Questions volley through my mind and if I get up, I'll lose Mom's rare willingness to tell this story. "Couldn't he win them over with his humor, Mom?" It's an innocent question.

"He tried, Honey," Mom responds. "The misunderstanding only grew. Dad told the woman that he knew they got off to a rough start, but he wanted to do all he could to make things work. She simply stared at him and said, 'I work with you because I have to.' He even told her that he worked his radio show and speeches to support the Civil Rights Movement. She looked at him with disinterest and said, 'This is not *your* Movement, Mr. Fitzgerald.' She had made up her mind. Your

225

father was not a man to her, but a symbol of what was wrong." Mom gets up to clear and wash the dishes, so I stand up too. My role's to dry them, then stack the cups and saucers in our cupboard. We don't say a word. She tidies around the sink. I grab the sponge and wipe the table with the figure-eight movements she taught me to get all the crumbs.

It's a vivid image. Dad, working in his suit and tie (the suit he was married in with holes in the jacket's inner lining, because his work as a civil servant didn't pay him enough to replace it), impassioned to uplift the marginalized and suffering as taught by the Catholic nuns. Yet, the woman working with him, impatient for justice long overdue to her people, could only see the power and role of the oppressor in my precious Daddy. How would she know he'd served heroically in the Korean War, was responsible for having social security documents translated into Spanish, served as the Board President for the Community Center, and was consistently honored for his civil rights efforts and radio program? He spent his life breaking such barriers. But he couldn't break this one. And it broke his heart.

As if she's suddenly much older, Mom shuffles to the living room and sits down. She stares off at the next children's program about a little boy who starts to see how some of his daydreams come alive to support his village. I listen to the story but watch my mom. In spite of her beauty and unflappable demeanor (she's very much a woman of her generation), I see the shiny tautness of her aging skin, the lines on her face, and tears in her eyes.

"Max and Gracie are watching too much TV," she says. She's reached her limit with our conversation. She tucks her wavy dark hair behind her ear, as if to show off all the class that's captured in her medium-sized pearl earrings. There's an actress in my mother. There's a woman with nerves of steel. I've often wondered how she's done it over the years when there were only two of us. She looks at me with her luminous blue eyes and she

226

doesn't blink: "Christine, don't give this all too much thought. Your father triumphed in the end because he made his decisions out of love."

● *The Ones Right Around You*

It's Easter and Rikki's arrival is just a week away. It's a glorious spring day. We've just had a cleansing rain, and everything's shining: the puddles, the tree leaves, the automobile chrome. My heart is twinkling, too—I'm excited that I'll be seeing Rikki after all this time.

I pop into my white OOOToyota Camry, with a steaming cup of Columbian coffee and one of our favorite songs—the Doobie Brothers' "Takin' It to the Streets." I roll down the window and sing at the top of my lungs. I'm at one with the world and feel good in my skin today. It's as though my body is still twenty, lithe, and strong as it was when Rikki and I became friends. My good friend Rikki, bless her heart, she's like an elixir. She's bringing me back to a part of myself I thought I'd never know again. And somehow, it feels even more powerful now, as I integrate it with who I've become with Chuck, Gracie and Max.

It's early afternoon as I drive to pick her up. The sun's balmy warmth has me feeling a happiness that's rare to me. The mere thought of Rikki animates me. While Chuck has given me the safety and steadiness to nurture my instincts and gifts, Rikki brought my fighting spirit to life. I've learned a whole new stamina from the hurdles she's climbed in her life—and the poise with which she's done it. Rikki's taught me that you've got to take a gamble and speak your mind—and from time to time, she's shown me how *not* to do it. I'm feeling on top of the world in my car. It feels like I'm running away, though without anger or sense of revenge. It's anticipation mixed with deep love for my fellow human beings, all of whom seem to have puzzled and tense looks on their faces. Because I'm fiddling with the CD player, I neglect to give another driver the right-of-way at a four-way stop sign. I stop and motion for him to go ahead, while he—a senior man with gray hair and glasses—shames me by shaking his pointer finger at me. My instinct is to let him upset me, but I decide not to give him any power. After all, I'm going to pick up my friend. Usually it's hard to find parking at the airport, but not today. I zoom into the ramp and a minivan pulls out as if to give me an instant parking spot. Rikki's plane is on time—and I've got fifteen minutes to spare. Because of heightened security after September 11th, she and I have planned that I'll meet her at her baggage claim. As I approach the circular conveyor of Claim Area 9 where the luggage for Rikki's flight will come in, I see a sizable woman of African descent, her hair wrapped in vibrant African fabric. I comment to her about the rather large suitcase on the conveyor. "The baggage claim goes fast. Takes some muscle to get at that luggage," I say to her.

She looks at me, gives me a blank stare, doesn't say a word. Can she hear me? I watch her, choose not to talk again, wait to see if I can get eye contact. Why does it matter? I want to win her over but give her space instead. A friend comes over to her, and I hear her say something about an affectionate gay couple across the way. "Wish they'd keep their hands to themselves!" she says. "I just don't agree with this gay movement." I sit quietly, look at my knees, feel my humility come back. To me, choosing to be gay is no different than any other right to be respected in this culture. We so easily become divided in our views even when we share the same cultural heritage.

A little boy Max's age pretends to shoot people with his fingers as they ride down the escalator. His mother is a beauty, short but slim, with gorgeous red hair. She's reading a "Time" magazine article on Islamic fundamentalism. When the boy's abrupt gun sounds, the "pkooooo, pkoooo's" get louder and louder, she looks up and says, "Quiet, Tommy." Then she motions him to come to her and whispers in his ear. He's quiet and forlorn for a second, but he doesn't keep his eyes off the folks riding the escalator down into baggage claims. Tommy's not far from the lady with the head wrap. A couple times I see him look at her and squint his eyes as he sizes her up. He doesn't see me watching, pulls his finger out of his pocket like it's a real weapon and takes a couple shots at her. His mom doesn't notice because he doesn't make the sounds.

How do I tell Max or any other little boy that I see nothing good about guns? I only see them as a symbol of killing, the single weapon responsible for taking down the fathers of a whole generation—Mahatma Gandhi, Martin Luther King, the Kennedy's. Dignified men who built their movements patiently over time.

As we step off the escalator, then move toward our carousel, little Tommy pulls me out of my daydream as he aims a "Pykooooo" right at me.

"Now you got me," I say to him. I put my head back, close my eyes. Then I straighten back up and tell him I'm dead.

His mother's embarrassed that he's gotten me to talk. "Tommy, please mind your manners," she says.

He looks at me, completely unsure of what to do with himself. He didn't expect a victim who would talk back. And I, for one, am happy that he chose me and not someone else who would shame him and give him a *real* reason to want to shoot someone.

"Hand it over," I say to him, jokingly, acting like a police officer. "Hand over your weapon."

He gives me a puzzled look. "I can't," he says. "It's not a weapon. It's my finger."

"You mean you shot me with just your finger…well then, maybe I'm alive after all."

"Glad he didn't get you!" comes a full-bodied, husky voice somewhere beside me. I turn and look and there she is— Rikki. She's taller than I remember, sleek as always, but as I look into her eyes, I see a deep warmth. To Tommy's dismay, we fully embrace one another, just as he decides to shoot us both.

"Welcome back to Minnesota," I say. I tell Tommy that it's been fun playing with him, but now I need to be with my friend. No sooner than I tell him, his Mom already has her hand around his and is leading him back to his chair. He's pulling away from her, and I hear her saying something about his promise to not shoot people. I wink at him and hope, as I always do, that his Mom will hit the sweet spot with the teachable moment.

Rikki watches him and me, sizes me up. "Look at you, Christine," she says. "Can't believe you're the Mama of two children. Where are they all?" Rikki's hair is cropped tight to her head with small curls, and her black eyeliner gives her eyes an almond shape. She's still wearing silver hoops, but they're smaller and doubled, with tiny pearls wedged between them.

"Chuck took 'em out to get their Easter haircuts. I thought it'd be nice to pick you up on my own."

"Well, it's sure good to see you, Chris. You feelin' better? You look *good*!" She reaches her hands out and touches the scarf I put on for the occasion—it's gray with black Chinese characters.

I tell her that I'm doing much better, that in fact, my health's stabilized. The luggage conveyor starts with a grinding sound at that point, and we both look over to see fat suitcases easing down from the luggage shoot towards the circular conveyor for pick-up. It doesn't take long for Rikki's suitcase to drop down onto the belt. It's a modest-sized, black roll-along that means business, nothing like the casual and worn duffel bag that Rikki took on our first road trip.

"So, how long's it been since we were together?" Rikki asks as she grabs her luggage, and I remind her that I was slightly pregnant with Grace the last time she visited. She says she couldn't forget that but couldn't recall the year. Of course, I'll never forget it because I spent the whole time with first trimester nausea that I was trying to hide. Since the babies have been born, I seem to clock every event, moment and year by their births.

230

"That was almost five years ago," I say out loud. "The times gone fast."

"It just flies by for me," Rikki says. "Funny cause I spent my youth racing the clock in that swimming pool, and what I've taken from it is to beat the clock in every facet of my life."

"We all do," I say. "But I never beat the clock like you did, Rikki." Raising and teaching children, I have to go at their pace.

I look up and see Tommy's mom lift his little pull-along from the pick-up. He sidles beside her and rolls his case up and back in front of him as though it's a push-and-pop toy. He looks over at me, and I wave good-bye.

"So, tell me, Girl, "Rikki says. "Are you really getting into being a mom?" She manages to walk briskly and keep an eye on my reaction at the same time.

Her question gives me pause, but I love my babies. "I am," I say thoughtfully. "I can't imagine life without Gracie and Max. They're little sweeties. Wait till you meet them. Gracie absolutely loves the water. For such a little squirt—she's only five, she jumps off the side of the pool deep into the water and even dives for toys at the bottom. Maybe she'll be a swimmer like you."

"She's a swimmer, is she? Lucky Girl." As Rikki says it, she has her own thoughtful look.

"You still swim, Rikki? It's part of your calling, right?"

"Of course I do," she answers right away. "Swimmin' will always be a part of me. Except now I have to go in the early morning, before work. I go about 6:00 in the morning, so I just jump in, swim, jump out, you know. And then I work, and every now and again, I find my way to the pool in the evenings on those days I don't have meetings and such." I look carefully at Rikki, imagining her rising at the break of dawn, by herself, then navigating all her appointments, then going home to an empty house. Does she?

We're ready to pop on an elevator with a young couple and a senior couple with what appears to be their teenage grandson. Rikki nods at me, and we wait while the others get on. In such close quarters, I scan everyone's faces and Rikki winks at me when I catch her eye. Rikki's awareness of all that's around her has always kept her a step ahead of everyone else. She has a poise about her now, a patience with others as they get up to speed with her brilliance. In her slim, gray pants and high-heeled boots, Rikki could have been a model, top executive or news reporter. She still has an equanimity, a quiet confidence that allows her to move through most situations with ease, just as she swam through the water as a competitive swimmer.

When we reach our floor, we make our way through the cold, dank parking garage that smells of auto exhaust. The temperature's in the high 50's, but it's chilly without the sunlight. I'm quiet and so is Rikki as we make our way to my Camry. I use my fob to flip open the trunk.

"This reminds me of our first trip together when I barely knew who you were," Rikki says, as she throws in her roll-along.

"I think about that, too," as we hop in. Unlike *that* trip, it's only about a twenty-minute drive to my house.

"We've come a long way, huh? You were one of those white girls who wanted to save everybody, but didn't know how to save yourself," she says. She checks my reaction, and I shake my head and laugh. Rikki's told me this before, and I didn't like hearing it. But now I understand exactly what she means.

"I was—and still am sometimes," I admit. "And I'm still working on saving myself, but I have made progress. I remember seeing you on campus and thinking of how admired you were. You weren't approachable to me, especially that day we were in the laundry room together."

"The laundry room?"

"Your coins kept jamming in the machine—you couldn't get it to work. Since you were swearing and kicking at it, I tried to help but ended up flipping a paper clip in your face."

"Oh my God. That was *you!* Are you serious?!"

"That was me. I always assumed you knew that." We pull off the Crosstown towards Hiawatha Avenue which will take us into Minneapolis.

"How funny. When I first got to the Twin Cities, a lot of the white girls looked the same to me. You're right—I didn't really pay attention to you in that laundry room. Can you forgive me?" I shake my head.

"What is that—is that a yes?" Rikki reaches over and lightly pats my right shoulder. At a stoplight, Rikki points at the grain elevators behind the McDonalds. "Wow. There's a mural painted on that building. Look at the moon and the night sky."

Rikki pays attention to detail and still makes ordinary things that I miss come to life. "Amazing. I wonder how long it's been there, and I haven't really looked at it."

"Kinda like me with you in the laundry room."

I laugh, as I turn right on 42nd Street. "I did finally figure out a way to get to know you, didn't I?"

"You sure worked hard for that. Why did you?"

I'm so absorbed in what to answer that a car in my blind spot honks at me as I go to switch lanes. *Pay attention,* I say silently to myself. "I guess I was intrigued, because of my dad's relationship with Clarence. And I think, too, it's because other students talked about you as someone to watch and evaluate as a swimmer, but not necessarily as a real person to *care* about. The Black students on campus were largely invisible, but you weren't."

Rikki pulls out a tin of mints and offers me one. "I hope you understand better now. That's why I had to transfer."

"I get it," I say. "I just felt horrible that you made plans to go without telling me." I sometimes wonder what would have happened if she'd stayed—if we'd been able to be friends together at college. Rikki functions at a whole different energy level than me. If I'm a beta, she's an alpha. If I'm a contemplative, she's a dynamo. If I'm smart, she's brilliant. "I never had to prove myself like you did, as a woman and a Black person. Which is why we both supported Carol for President."

"At least that got us both to be delegates to the DFL National Convention in July, so we'll get to hang out together in Boston! And there are a lot of strong political organizers coming out of the South Side of Chicago," she says, "including an Illinois State Senator Barack Obama, who just won the primary for U.S. Senate. We just have to stay at it, Chris." I turn onto the lovely West River Road near the Lake Street Bridge which always gives me comfort that I'm close to home. As we reach our 1920's bungalow in south Minneapolis, Rikki says, "It's good to be here. I've missed this place, and I've really missed you, Chris. You're a gem."

We hug each other in the car before getting out to greet Chuck, outside with little Max, my pride and joy, splashing in a mud puddle. My family has become my world—and my gift that consumes most my time. Being with Rikki, though, always excites and challenges me to do more—to be a better friend, to stay politically engaged, to fight injustice and to follow in my father's footsteps. Chuck, on the other hand, grounds me. He reminds me that being a good person is not just about making life better for a whole lot of people. In the end, it's about how you treat the ones right around you. I'm ever looking for the balance.

☻ *Hearts Beating Together*
Chuck's been taking down storm windows and putting up screens. When he does anything, he's thorough and meticulous. There he is wiping out each streak from the storm windows while little Max thoroughly bathes himself in the mud.

Rikki gets out of the Camry, holds her nails out for inspection, and makes her way to Chuck and Max. "Hello, there,"

234

she says heartily, and to Chuck, "Hey Chuck, how's life treatin' you?"

Before he can answer, my own dear little Max takes one look at Rikki and says, "Hey, you got brown skin!" Even as we've been mindful to keep his play groups diverse, he's no less sensitive than the rest of us to the difference of skin color. You can spend your life trying to overlook racial differences and dance around them, and still our children get right to the heart of the issue without wasting time.

"You got brown skin too," Rikki says right back to him, and indeed he does. The rich brown mud is sparkling in the sunlight.

"I can wash mine off. Can you?" Max says.

"'Fraid I can't," Rikki says, "nor would I want to. How about you—you want to wash it off?"

"No way!" says Max. "I like it!"

"You're my kind of man." She stoops down to his level with a big smile and shake his hand, with no concern about a little mud on her manicured hands.

"Good to have you here, Rikki," Chuck says. "S'pose we'd better clean up."

"Take your time," I say. "I'll get Rikki settled in upstairs." Our bungalow has an upstairs expansion that runs the length of the house that we turn over to guests. Now, being so little, Gracie and Max are sharing a space. Before long, Gracie will take over the upstairs room. I'm happy it hasn't happened yet. The room is where I go for solitude to write and plan my school lessons.

Rikki pulls her suitcase out of the trunk, carries it up our stairs into the house and sets it on the kitchen floor. "Girl, let me just look around your place. I love your house. It's…cozy. That's what it is—it's cozy," she says. "It's great to be here."

"Thanks," I say. "We like it." And I do, but today I wish I'd picked up more of the toys.

As we head upstairs, Rikki eyes my photo gallery that lines the wall. Admittedly, most of the beautiful photographs were taken by Mom, whose sense of composition is great and who often shoots in black and white because of the classy look it gives the subjects. "You have one handsome family," Rikki comments. As she says it, Gracie emerges from her room, carrying her rag bunny, "Beenut," who is supposed to be "Peanut," but Gracie likes "b's" better than "p's."

"Hi Gracie Bo-Basie," I say. "This is my good friend, Rikki." "Rikki, this is Gracie Joan. Ms. Gracie just turned five."

"How about a high-five?" Rikki asks, holding her hand up for Gracie to slap it. She looks at Rikki like she's absolutely crazy, till Rikki puts it together that Gracie hasn't high-fived much. "Watch me and your Mom, Gracie Girl. Give me five, Chris," she says to me. And I slap my hand on the sweet spot of Rikki's palm. Gracie looks at us both amazed and we all laugh.

"But what's it mean?" Gracie asks.

"It means you're really cool. That's what it means," says Rikki. "Now you gonna take me up your stairs and give me the tour?"

Rikki mesmerizes Gracie, who stands tall and says, "Alright, let me show the way," squeezing ahead of us. Gracie proceeds to tell her all about our house, about the time we had it blessed by our priest in the storm, the time all the lights went out and we had a picnic by candlelight, about how she stayed with her Nana (my mom) while Max was being born and she couldn't, for the life of her, imagine where Max would fit.

Rikki absolutely loves Gracie. Of course, how could she not? Gracie's a charmer and has a natural sense for what animates people. She also knows who she can trust. "Mommy said maybe you'll be here to hunt Easter eggs with us. Will you be?"

"Oh Honey, I promised your Mommy an Easter visit, but I'm only staying a few days. I won't be here on Easter itself, but that doesn't mean we can't have our own hunt."

236

"Can we, Mommy?" Gracie implores. "Can we have our own hunt with your friend and Max?"

"This is Rikki," I tell her. "My friend's name is Rikki."

"Wicky?" Gracie asks.

"Yes, we can with *Rikki,*" I answer. As Rikki situates her suitcase on the queen-size bed, and the light beams in on her through an upstairs window, we begin to scheme. Rikki and I make a pact through winking at each other that we'll do a little private Easter shopping when we can get the chance.

Once Rikki and the children are all in bed, and it's after 11:00pm, Chuck and I finish unloading the dishwasher, drying and shelving the big salad bowl and the wine glasses. Max wanted shrimp, which he knows we have on special occasions, and Chuck and I realized after going through all our options that we'd save money and stress to eat here at home. With Max and Gracie in their familiar environment, we didn't have to watch their every move. We've learned we only have so much attention to give and that Rikki would have a better chance of adult dialogue if we didn't have to keep the kids from crawling under restaurant tables.

I remember our college days when I used to obsess about Chuck, wondered if he'd call me, if we'd ever get married, if he'd find it in him to put his love for me before his loyalties to his mother. Now, he's wiping off the stove with even and steady circles, very focused on what he's doing, as if it's a form of meditation. I tap him on the shoulder, and as he turns to me, I kiss him on the lips once and then again, pulling his full body toward me and forcing his mouth open with my tongue. We kiss for the longest time and then we hug. Two people couldn't fit together better than we do. I nestle my neck into Chuck's and stay there, and we rock gently together. I fend off the undercurrent of my worries about the politics of Chuck's work, my own career, our aging parents, a budget that grows with our children even as our income seems to decline. I excuse myself to get ready for bed.

Clearing my clothes from our bed gives me déja vu. Chuck

and I began our relationship at exactly the same time Rikki and I did. I don't know how to explain that, except that Chuck filled me up for the times I stretched my limits with Rikki. And true to form, just that passionate kiss with him set the world straight again.

I squeeze my face into a knot, as though it's a washcloth I'm wringing, to release my tears. I feel a deep love within me for all of us. Everyone bears some heart-wrenching truth on the way to adulthood. For Rikki and me, the early loss of our fathers taught us early on that the world wasn't safe, that we had to be on our guard. I want Gracie and Max to feel a safety I didn't have—to explore their world as though every day is a new adventure. It makes me want to teach again, which I know I'll do once I've healed.

Chuck brings me a glass of wine, nuzzles my neck from behind. Without even seeing my face, he senses the sadness in me. "What's got you, Babe?" he asks.

"I didn't expect life to be so complicated," I tell him.

"Oh, neither did I," he says.

A deep yearning laces through me and I tilt my head back to kiss him. He reaches down and holds my chin back to him, then strokes my neck until he's reaching down to stroke my breasts too. My whole body aches with a ripeness knowing that I will open to Chuck as a blooming plant opens to light.

I grab him and tug at him, stroking the soft fur beneath his shirt with my fingers. He prolongs my desire and we gently touch each other beneath our clothing. With children, and now a guest, there's a silent agreement between us to leave them on. Chuck whispers to me to go to our room, so we dutifully set our wine glasses on the kitchen counter, close our door and quietly resume our gentle exploration of each other's bodies. We use every part of ourselves to touch the other until the full release, after which we lay in gratitude in each other's arms. After a few moments, Chuck and I find our pajamas. He throws on his boxers and an old T, and I throw on a cami and cotton drawstring bottoms.

238

I admit to Chuck that it feels a bit elicit to make love with a guest in the house, but the passion's come back like an unexpected breeze on a hot day. Chuck tells me he's glad to see me happy again—that the illness has had me in its clutches, and he's missed me this way. I know exactly what he means. I've missed him this way too.

When we finally settle into our spoon position, Chuck asks me how it feels to have Rikki back. "It's really great," I say. "In some ways, she hasn't changed much. In others, I like her even better. How is it for you?"

But he's not answering. He's already dozed off. He's been bucking for a raise on top of everything else. He's so tired he's dozing off in spite of himself, then pretending to hear me out.

So, I let him slide off to sleep and no longer attempt to awake him. I let him go and settle my thoughts, along with my body, beside my beloved. Chuck and I joke with each other that we are like batteries, and that as we lie beside one another, we both restore the energy and charge we need to survive. So, I settle in to be re-charged.

Scientists are just now starting to understand the anatomy of love. When couples like me and Chuck are separated (and Chuck goes on an extended business trip), then the major stress hormone, cortisol, begins to rise. If this continues for any length of time, as with separation or death, the bodily rhythms are deeply disrupted: a low heart rate, abnormal heart beats, lighter sleep with less REM dreaming, and challenged circadian rhythms. As much as I enjoy my independence, I know now that I'm stronger with Chuck. Our hearts are beating together, and that makes it seem like anything's possible.

● *Patient, Soulful Work*

Chuck surprises us in the morning with the aroma of buckwheat pancakes, the breakfast entree he's mastered—browned just right, with a thick, soft center and crisp edges. I'm usually up before Chuck, but our house being the modest home it is, we've no master bedroom, only a main bathroom that Rikki must come downstairs to use.

I take advantage of the children still sleeping and lie in bed while Rikki—ever the athlete and a very early riser—comes down to use the shower. Once I hear her leave the bathroom and make her way up the stairs, it really hits me that Rikki's with us and I'd better get ready. I get up, slip into the bathroom, and greet myself in the mirror. I imagine myself better than what I see in the mirror—especially in the morning. Today, I look closely at my furrowed brow and rub the thing as though I can make the crease go away.

But Rikki doesn't care. She's always considered intelligence and kindness to matter more than appearances, even as she always looks her best. When our looks do factor in, it's ironically more about our bridging the races to remain friends than it is about beauty standards. Our friendship's taught us how, in many ways, the Civil Rights Movement has only just begun. There's so much left to do—even though so many around us want it to be in the past. Others love being carried by the adrenaline of the fight but turn away when they learn that true liberation requires patient, soulful work. My father held both tensions, but I wish he hadn't burned out so young. His example is imprinted deeply within me, so I have to be careful and approach these dynamics more steadily. Yet, is balance even an option to those most vulnerable to the changes needed?

Like Rikki, I jump into the shower to cleanse this out of me, but for entirely different reasons. In my pretty bathroom with peach paint and bright white tiles, I have vanilla almond shampoo, mimosa shower gel and a lavender-colored massage brush to banish cellulite. When I use them, I can usually go into my own happy trance. Not this day—having Rikki under our roof reminds me that I have a choice in whether or not I think about our racial differences. Even with the advantages she's been given, it's not a choice for Rikki. The more successful she is, the more she's expected to bring resources to her home community. My own upward mobility has been assumed by nearly everyone in my life, and only my mother and Chuck hope for something back from me.

I wrap myself in a towel and hustle to my room, where I have the space I need to put lotion on my legs and arms and dress myself. Though I'm a 60's child, I was too young when the Boomers wore headbands, traveled to Woodstock and dressed in tie-dye. My Catholic upbringing made me care about people and global issues, but we tend toward the missionary approach— coming in as people who know better, rather than with reverence and humility. Only now do I realize the full impact of the times in which I was born. I throw on a pair of used designer jeans and pull out a few shirts until I settle on a purple scoop neck tee that fits my mood. I settle on yin yang earrings I bought at an outdoor market in France and go out to meet Chuck and Rikki.

Max has gotten up and is holding onto Chuck's pant leg for dear life. Rikki's at the table, with a steaming cup of coffee, no small stack of pancakes and bowl of fresh strawberries. She sees me come in, says good morning and asks right away if we always eat this well. "Only when we have a guest or have just gone shopping." I laugh.

"You're stylish today," she tells me, after giving me the once-over.

"You think?" I ask, knowing she means it.

Gracie comes in with her little French doll, Marie, who wears a black beret, black and white striped skirt and says, "I like to shop for clothes" in French. Rikki loves it, and has Gracie squeeze the doll until she, Rikki, has the phrase down: *J'adore acheter des vêtements.*

Max comes out of the kitchen to see what's going on. "Her play with dolls?" he asks me. I nod yes, and ask him if he'd like to show Rikki *his* doll. He gives me a big nod back and runs to his room, comes back with a plush flying monkey and hands it to

241

Rikki.

"My Lord, what's this thing? Oooh, this is not a nice little dolly." She raises her voice and makes her eyes all wide, and Max steps back as though she's the Wizard herself.

"Is a monkey," Max says, careful to talk like a big person.

"But flying monkeys are naughty," Rikki says. "They work for the witch, don't they? Where's the witch in this house?" Now Max really looks confused, and Gracie answers for him, "There's no witch in this house. That's just Lawrence. He's a *nice* flying monkey."

"How do you know there's such a thing?" Rikki quizzes Gracie.

"Because there is and my brother has him. It's what we decided." She puts her hands on her hips, pulls Marie off the table, and goes to ask her father if her buckwheats are ready.

Rikki looks at me, raises her eyebrows and says, "She ain't gonna let nobody mess with *her*."

"That's my Gracie," I say as I prepare plates for me, Chuck and the kids and motion everyone to the table.

As we sit and eat, I say very little. Once at the table, Chuck designs a face on Max's pancake with banana eyes, chocolate chip pupils, an upside-down strawberry nose and a bacon-strip mouth. Chuck adds more chocolate chips for the hair. The face looks like Ernie from Sesame Street.

"He's made of chips, Daddy!" Max, says pointing at the hair. "I'm gonna name him Chip." And rather than enticing Max to eat, the little face has the opposite impact. When Chuck tells Max to take a bite, he looks very sad. "I can't, Daddy! I'll kill Chip!"

"That's just for fun," Rikki says to Max. "That's not *really* a boy named Chip."

"That is *absolutely* a boy named Chip, Wicky." Gracie puts her hands on her hips and looks in Rikki's eyes. "And I need a Chip too."

"Your pancake would have another name, wouldn't it?" Rikki asks.

Chuck tells Gracie he'll make her a pancake *if* she'll eat it once it has a name. Then he realizes how crazy that sounds and takes his glasses off to rub his eyes. To his surprise, Gracie says she'll eat the pancake and he gets to work on the design.

It's such a joy to have Rikki share this family time with me, Chuck, Max and Gracie.

"Now Max and Gracie, Mom needs to see how Rikki's doing, OK?"

"That's your first problem, right there," says Chuck. "Asking permission!" We all laugh, while I take that as my in.

"Rikki, I've been thinking so much about your dad. How is he?"

Everyone's watching her intently as though she'll be disclosing the wisdom of the ages. "Daddy's doing well," she says, winking at the children. "He's gray, you know. And he won't easily talk about his misfortune…or Mama. He lives like it never happened. But he's got a girlfriend—Jeanine. She's a real sweetie, 'cept for she spoils Papa and he gets real lazy round the house. She does keep him workin' though, so he can buy her fancies." Gracie hears Rikki say "buy" and suddenly Marie's repeating that she loves to shop.

"How's his work going?" I ask. As one who misses my work and looks forward to returning, I know the paradox of how work can—all at once—fill us with a sense of purpose and be the source of our deepest angst.

"He's got himself a car wash now," Rikki says, "Started out there wiping windows and stayed there for years. Over time, he took over management of the place, and the owner left half of it to him in his will. Tyrone's made out pretty good, over time, when you consider how this got started. He still suffers, but he knows he's one of the lucky ones."

"How about Liza and Eddie—they doin' alright?" I ask.

243

Gracie tells me that I'm starting to talk funny. Rikki and I look at each other and smile. I've inadvertently adopted Rikki's casual, rhythmic style. In French, I work on matching my intonation, rhythm and words to the person I'm speaking with, but with Rikki—or other English speakers—I have to appeal, not steal.

"Your mama's just showing off," Rikki explains to Gracie with a wink. To me, she says that Liza and Eddie are a blessing and that they've been the epitome of grace while Rikki navigates having two places to go on holidays.

When we're finished eating, I tell Chuck, Gracie and Max that Rikki and I are going on a mission, something that we have to do on our own. I wink at Rikki and we rely on silent gestures to get out the door. The children resist and Chuck has to literally hold them from following us, but Rikki and I manage to get back in my white Camry, which I've named Dovey, and zip away.

☺ *UBUNTU*

I'm driving us to yet a new adventure, but this time around, it gives a freeing sensation, as though we've been given license to run through ocean spray on a coastal beach. When I was first getting to know Rikki, I experienced her more like a tide that was pulling me out against my will. But now I'm grateful and refreshed.

The weather's funny this time of year, as mercurial as our emotions in college—when we shared the lessons and uncertainty before Tyrone's release. It's bright, and the budding trees lay their webbed shadows over the street. It's breezy, too, and if you're not in a pocket of sunlight, you can easily be chilled. Still, Rikki and I decide between us to open the sun roof and let the sunlight pour in.

"Where we off to?" Rikki asks and I shrug. I've thrown her into one of my patterns with Chuck. We get so intent on getting time to ourselves, that we arrange for the sitter and leave our home, only to realize that we haven't made specific plans.

"What about the Como Zoo and Conservatory?" I ask. It's open now and there's a new rainforest exhibit.

"Fine by me," Rikki says.

We're silent for a little bit, a sign that our relationships evolved to the point where neither of us have to fill in the quiet spaces.

"So how YOU doin?" Rikki finally asks. The question feels good, and I can tell that Rikki's becoming a doctor has made her keep her focus on the health of those around her.

"Well, I'm healing, Rikki. It's been a tough time for me. I've had to admit to Chuck, to the kids, to *myself* that I can't do it all. I move at a different pace than a lot of people anyway, and to have kids has really slowed me down."

"Oh, so you mean you're human?!" Rikki laughs.

"Guess that is what I mean. Being human isn't always a walk in the park—or even in the zoo!" We make our way there through residential streets and see no small number of people out raking winter's dead leaves out of their gardens.

"No, it's really not. No one tells us how rough it'll be. Our parents launch us like a pinball, and we bump against all kinds of obstacles until we fall and get hit again!"

"You said that right. Maybe we should try to be the flipper and not the ball."

"That's good to have in mind, Chris. But it just seems you bump against a few more obstacles when you're Black."

I listen closely. We stop at a stoplight and the man next to us in his red Honda civic has rap music booming. Rikki points out his bumper sticker with the African American flag, with a map of Africa super-imposed over its stripes of red, black and green.

"Rikki," I say. "I have a confession to make."

"You what?" she asks me, as she traces her slim, long fingers over the leather zipper of her purse. As always, Rikki's style is simple, elegant. She's still toned, still the athlete, but her almond-shaped eyes and ability to rock any kind of hairstyle give

245

her sophistication. Like her father, she's gotten over any instinct to playact and has found what works for her in this crazy world where the gap between haves and have-nots widens ever more each day.

"Sometimes I feel ashamed of being white," I say to Rikki, as the last thought escapes me. "Had I been born to wealthy parents rather than to a civil rights activist, I'd be a whole different person. But from the time I first had memory, I was taught about the Civil Rights Act and Nelson Mandela being imprisoned in South Africa for opposing apartheid. Being white, I can choose to ignore these struggles, but I can't because of how I was raised. From the moment I saw you swearing at your laundry in our dorm, I wanted to know more about you. So, maybe I was overly curious about our differences, but I wanted to make an extra effort to be friends with you."

"Well, I sure didn't make friends with you because you're white. If anything, that was a turnoff." Rikki laughs. "I couldn't explain it. I just felt like you were a little crazy or something."

"Well, I'm sure I was. But if people like me don't pay attention, who will? Some of us have to bring feelings of hope about the change we can create together. And do our best to understand what we don't experience."

"Well, I started to see you'd be willing to learn some things."

"When did you?" I ask as I turn into the packed zoo parking lot. A free community space, it's a mingling of folks, with young children walking alongside elders using walkers, echoes of different languages like Hindi and Spanish, some youth talking sweetly to the animals, others mocking them and telling their peers that's what they look like.

"On the airplane," Rikki says calmly.

"On the airplane?" I ask. "But you brought me to your home to meet Liza and Eddie—and you…."

"I didn't trust you fully until the airplane. Until then, I

246

thought you had your own agenda. Besides, on the airplane, I had to trust you. I was scared as hell—maybe the most scared I'd been since my mother died. I don't know why, but that's when I got it. That the main reason you'd come with me was because you cared."

We finally find a parking spot, I put on a baseball cap, and tuck my purse under the driver's seat. I lock the car and we start walking to the new zoo entrance, following dozens of families. We walk for a bit in silence, watching all the preschoolers skip and jump, as their younger siblings watch from their strollers, wiggling.

We follow a little boy and his family to the primate building, where we see the spider monkeys with their penetrating, knowing look and the sloth, all but its fur hidden so it looks like a wig hanging on a tree, and I imagine it can't be an easy partnership. Yet, they manage—all they have, besides their custodians, is each other.

It hits me then: real friends don't just tolerate each other or humor each other to get dolled up for the dance—no. They obey a relational pull in the same way that primordial dust formed whole planets. Even as Rikki has driven me crazy with her fast thinking, her answers to everything and her necessary focus on what's not working, her big heart and whip-smart intelligence save lives beyond mine. She allows a window to a world I only thought I could understand. Even as I've promised myself I'd carry on my father's passion for civil rights, I've had to learn the hard way the depth of distrust between whites and nonwhites. Each day, I either disarm it or fuel it—staying poised to go the extra mile. No matter the cause we're fighting for, the language we speak, or the source of our morality, a friendship is not a friendship without the reciprocal caring and initiative Rikki and I give to one another. And reciprocal can be a funny word in a society that defaults to giving me every advantage Rikki hasn't had.

A mother and baby baboon romp close by the exhibit glass and Rikki squeals as the baby holds on for dear life. "A miracle, those two," she says. "They're just like humans. They can only pass on what they've been exposed to." We watch the mother groom her baby, then chase him.

Rikki invites me to follow her out into the sun and to go over to some shade trees. We watch a muster of peacocks from a quiet area. One of my favorite gifts from Rikki was a peacock feather. She's taught me the feathers are symbols of good luck.

Rikki takes her head wrap off and lays it lengthwise on the dewy ground. It's made of a thick and hearty muslin. "Let's sit down."

I look at her twice. "Sure you want us to sit on your head wrap?"

"It's fine!" She sits down and pats the ground next to her.

"I'm so glad you've come to visit, Rikki! Ever since I knew you were coming, I've had a miraculous turnaround with my health. I've been thinking a lot about how grateful I am to have you in my life."

We're sitting on the ground with our legs bent in front of us. Rikki straightens her back, shakes her head, then holds her head between the palms of her hands. "It's amazing we've been able to trust each other with everything stacked against us. But I love you, Girl. You understand me!" She fiddles with a stick and uses it to draw designs in a small patch of dirt. "Heh I brought you something." She reaches in her bag and pulls out a copy of the Michigan City News Dispatch. "A young man won the high school essay contest. Check it out."

The paper's folded precisely so that all I see is the article. The young man's name is Spencer, and the article is called "Crossing the Divide." I scan the piece quickly as I sit with Rikki. Spencer, a junior at Michigan City Senior High, wrote about how one organization turned the tide for him after he lost his father to gang violence—a place where he was accepted just as he was and

248

where he had his first positive exposure to playing with white children. At summer camp, the children would run, swim, hike and canoe together. But it was more than learning practical outdoor skills. They were also learning together how to plan, laugh, play and explore. They would take field trips to Washington Park, the Dunes, and Chicago's Museum of Science and Industry. Spencer wrote how the culture of the Center was one of *Ubuntu,* a term used in South Africa to describe a philosophy of *shared humanity,* that each one of us is who we are because of the community in which we're raised. Since the Center's community was founded on caring and love, the children served within it learned to embody a spirit of strength that they could bring into their families and schools.

"Ubuntu," I say out loud. "Yes, I learned a bit about that in my college prep for teaching. I've always been drawn to the idea that we're shaped greatly by the spirit of our times. But the reverse is true. We can shape our times by who we choose to be." I run my fingers through the wet clovers and do a quick search for one with four leaves.

"Chris! Did you see the name of the Center that Spencer was writing about?"

I look back down at the article and look more carefully for the name of the Center. And there it is: "Oh my God," I say. *"The Sage Community Center! Not only is the Community Center still serving youth and families—it's finally been named after Clarence as it should be."*

"How about that, Chris? Look at the gift your father left you —and the community."

"Rikki, thank you," I say. "Thank you—really. It means so much for you to share this face to face. You didn't have to come all this way to tell me all this."

"Oh yes, I did, Girl. I most certainly did. Because we only get so many moments like this in a lifetime. You know that."

In that moment, there is something that Rikki has in

common with my father, the one who magnified and brightened everything in my world, if only for ten years—the birds, the trees, even the sidewalk cracks. Even when it stormed, I knew that I was safe with him. Because of him, I knew what it was like to really feel loved. I knew we were making history, just the two of us in our quiet way. I've thought he's left me forever. But he hasn't. He's been working through Rikki all along. I know that now.

I reach over and give Rikki's forearm a squeeze. She pulls her arm up, slips her hand into mine. We walk to the car that way, quiet and resolute. Then we help each other figure out the best way to depart from the zoo and get home through traffic.

Epilogue

Despite COVID-19, Rikki's come here for the weekend to join me for a visit to the memorial site of George Floyd at 38th Street and Chicago Avenue in Minneapolis. His Houston funeral took place last Tuesday, and I take her past some of the sites that were vandalized and burned on our way to view the area where he took his last breath—including the shopping area my children frequented after school.

As we approach the site, Rikki holds her hand to her heart. I stay quiet as we absorb the power of this one humble man who died so visibly and viscerally, sparking protests and revolution in all 50 United States and the whole world. The artist who organized the painters for the world-famous mural of George Floyd worked with Gracie at her high school to paint a mural depicting the Preamble to the Constitution that included a graphic image of a lynching as we make our way to a better democracy. This time, George Floyd has a halo with the names of Black victims of police brutality—artwork that has become a worldwide symbol of solidarity against oppression, reproduced in Manchester, England; Nairobi, Kenya; Belfast, Northern Ireland; Idlib, Syria; and even what remains of the Berlin Wall.

I watch Rikki bow her head at the outdoor shrine to George Floyd, where you can even see an outline of his body on the street where he was killed, and it's as if we're again at Tyrone's retrial. I can't see her expression under the mask, but I watch her wipe her tears with her forearm. Around us are the aromas of expensive flowers being sold as offerings and the smoke from Bratwursts and burgers on grills. People of all ages and ethnicities are drawing tributes to George Floyd with chalk, and a small band is playing rhythm and blues.

I'm thinking how powerful and heartbreaking it is, at once, for people of all ethnicities from all over the country to come here to pay their respects. Just as I walk past the Black Lives Matter signs being sold for $25 a pop, Rikki puts her hands on her hips and says, "Chris, I feel like Jesus in the temple. I want to get all these items being sold out of here—and the white people with them! This is a SACRED SPACE to pay tribute to George Floyd, and people are making it a marketplace—a tourist destination! Come see where the latest Black person was murdered! Bring your dog and take your family photo near the spot where he was lynched! This is sick, Chris. It's SICK!"

"My God, it is, Rikki," I say. "My people have so much work to do. We're dumping our work where it doesn't belong—and perpetuating the violence. I see that. I'm so sorry." It's true—for too long, we've expected our Black and Brown friends to carry a great weight that we haven't been willing to carry too.

"If there's no video, there's no consequence. It's like cops in uniform have been sanctioned to hunt us down and kill us, while life goes on for them. How are we supposed to function at all when it's like this? I can't even eat! Why are white people so afraid of us?!"

"It's a good question," I say. "As white people, we are reacting to our projections of fear and shame. This is not coming from people who love ourselves. If we did, more of us would learn from the strength and resilience of Black friends. We have to detox from patterns that allow us to enjoy what friends like you can't benefit from too. About time some of us get it right, not white."

"Indeed it is," she says. "We're all a work in progress, and our country is too."

Just two months ago, COVID-19 took Tyrone's life. In the end, with all that he battled, even his release from prison could not undo the profound impact that discrimination and unjust incarceration had on his health. At one time, Rikki and I thought we found a happy ending. Now we understand that it was never about just achieving Martin Luther King's dream. Rather, it is

252

about lifting ourselves up, treating others the way we want to be treated and building the stamina and grace we learned from Rikki's father. As Rikki's friend, I've been called to do more heavy lifting—and not just physically. It's time for me to build my emotional and spiritual muscles too.

The End—or just the beginning.

Chris and Rikki's Playlist

"All I Do" by Stevie Wonder (1980)

"Back Stabbers" by the O'Jays (1972)

"Could It Be I'm Falling in Love" by the Spinners (1977)

"Ghetto Child" by the Spinners (1973)

"Going Back to Indiana" by the Jackson 5 (1971)

"Got to Get You Into My Life" by Earth, Wind & Fire (1978)

"The Hustle" by Van McCoy & The Soul City Symphony (1975)

Jesus Christ Superstar, the rock opera with music by Andrew Lloyd Webber and lyrics by Tim Rice (1970)

"Linus and Lucy" by the Vince Guaraldi Trio (1964)

"Lovely Day" by Bill Withers (1977)

Off the Wall, the album by Michael Jackson (1979)

"Takin' It to the Streets" by the Doobie Brothers (1976)

"Until You Come Back to Me" by Aretha Franklin (1973)

"Upside Down" by Diana Ross (1980)

"What's Going On" by Marvin Gaye (1971)

"You're My Best Friend" by Queen (1976)

Sweet Burden of Crossing™ Discussion Guide

Prologue:

1. Why does Chris perceive her city being burned and her stores being vandalized as a sacred moment in time?

2. Chris identifies herself as a first responder to the work of reparations—and to relieving friends of color from their fatigue. What does she mean by that?

3. Chris' neighbors don't believe her when she tells them she found a threatening note on her front door. What do you think it would take for them to believe her?

4. Have you ever felt terror in a public setting from protestors or demonstrators? If so, what about the circumstance crossed the line for you?

Part One: Abbott Hospital, Minneapolis

5. The book begins with Chris realizing she has crossed a threshold. What kind of thresholds do you see her crossing?

6. As a young girl, Chris was aware of threats to her family because of her father's work. In her current life, she once again sees racial unrest leading to violence in her community. How do you think she internalizes this?

7. As a nine-year old, Chris is referred to as white trash by a woman at the Community Center her father founded with his Black friend. Describe your reaction.

8. Chris feels an instinct to scare her first Black playmate, Cece. Where do you think that came from? How do you feel about her father's response?

9. The book capitalizes the "B" in Black, but does not capitalize the "w" in white? Also, at times the "b" for black is in small letters. Why do you think the author made that choice?

Part Two: Leon College, September 1980

10. When Chris sees Rikki's frustration in their college laundry room, she catches herself wanting to help and observe Rikki just because she is Black? How do you feel about that?

11. Chris is ambivalent to give Rikki a ride home. What made her go for it?

12. When Chris pulls up to Umoja House to pick up Rikki, Rikki's friends don't greet her. What if the situation was reversed, with a Black friend picking Chris up and her white friends holding back? Would Rikki be inclined to introduce herself? Would this feel any different?

13. Rikki is sharing her observations about a book she's reading with Chris. What threshold does Rikki reference, and why is it important?

14. How are your friendships with your same race friends like that of Rikki and Chris'? How are they different?

15. When Chris is scared and uncomfortable driving in a storm, why doesn't she let Rikki know?

16. Our exposure to racial, ethnic, and cultural differences impacts our comfort level with the experiential reality of race. How does Chris hold her awareness that she and Rikki are experiencing two different realities?

17. What do you see happening between Chris and Rikki that makes them care for one another?

18. What is the book telling us about fatherhood and its influence on daughters?

19. What do you think about Chris' reaction to dressing in front of Rikki? How might you feel similarly—or different?

20. When the storm hits, Chris stays in the hotel anxiously, but Rikki throws caution to the wind, jogs outside and shrugs it off. What does that tell you about the two women?

21. What does Chris' discomfort with being white have to do with learning another language?

22. Chris has felt compelled to follow her father's example to respect and care about Black people. What are ways in which her being white feels uncomfortable to her?

23. If Chris' father were still alive, what might he say about his friendship with Clarence?

24. What prompts Chris to say that Rikki's adoptive sister Regina's reaction to her is unexpected, but to be respected?

25. In what ways has Chris' mother prepared her for greater cultural sensitivity? In what ways might she have held Chris back?

26. What *sweet burden* does Chris' mother hold? What other *sweet burdens* are in the story? What *sweet burdens* do you hold in your life?

27. The author makes use of the themes of black and white throughout the book. What are other ways, besides race, that she has us think about the contrast between light and dark?

28. Chris' father believed that he could work within government systems to make them better? Would he be likely to believe that now?

29. White women are conditioned to being nurtured and to having Black people nurture, care and protect them. How does the story make that apparent?

30. Chris and Rikki did not have cell phones and social media to distract them during their time together—or to give them opinions on anti-racism and how to organize in real time. How would their college experience and friendship be impacted by today's technology?

31. Chris' father was committed to the Civil Rights Movement—and he was proud of our American flag and

the Navy Anthem. If he were alive today, how do you think he would hold his patriotism?

32. What are historical events that took place when Chris and Rikki were in college—and how do you look at them now?

33. What world does Chris see as she works closely with learners in an urban school?

34. What's it like for you when you sit in a cafeteria and notice people of color sitting apart?

35. Did your parents talk about race? How often and in what context?

36. What were your family's values around discussing politics and religion?

37. Does a Black man marrying a white woman upset you? Or does it not make any difference? Why or why not?

38. Chris wonders why white people who are open to what Black people experience don't get more credit. How do you feel about that?

39. How are the dynamics of a platonic relationship different from that of an intimate, sexual relationship?

40. How are your friends different from one another, and what do they teach you about life?

41. Is it possible to have reciprocity in an interracial friendship when the white person has been given every

advantage, including a history that may include being served by Black people?

42. What is it that makes some people go against the grain and make time for people that others ignore, as Chris' father did? How much influence comes from a parent's example? What people ignored by others do you welcome into your life?

43. What does it take to understand the legacy of individual and historical trauma? How does being in a friendship like Chris and Rikki's help us contextualize how trauma is lived and inherited?

44. When Rikki first tells Chris about her father being in prison, she cries with her, showing her vulnerability for the first time. Yet when Chris tries to comfort her, she backs away in anger. What happened?

45. Chris talks about being "born white" as part of the problem, which includes her cultural heritage. What does she mean by this?

Part Three: Tyrone's Retrial, May 1982

46. What kind of friend would you want with you if one of your family members were facing harsh circumstances?

47. When visited by Maryl McCullough, Rikki blames herself for not being more aware that her father may have been falsely accused. Have you ever lost objectivity and trust with someone you love?

48. Chris compares the purpose of a church with that of a courtroom as community spaces. What similarities and differences do you see between the two spaces?

49. After Clarence and Chris leave the diner for breakfast, he says, "there will be justice that we haven't had in a long time." What do you think he means by this?

50. Chris wonders how Tyrone has handled being in prison all these years. What would your feelings be if you were in Tyrone's shoes?

51. What do you think happened to Chris' father?

52. Chris says that the day of the verdict is like waiting for the biopsy of a tumor—hoping it's benign. Have you had a situation in life where you felt that a decision by others would have a profound impact on your life?

Part Four: Release from Room 322

53. Chris is energized by Rikki's Easter visit to her. Do you have friends from different backgrounds that affect you this way?

54. Why did Rikki not remember first meeting Chris in their college laundry room? Why is this an important aspect of the story?

55. Chris talks about the Civil Rights Movement as just beginning. Do you agree and what does this mean to you?

56. Chris naturally changes the cadence and rhythm of her speaking to match Rikki's. What do you think that communicates to Rikki?

57. Rikki says she didn't trust Chris until their shared airplane ride. What emotional dynamics were present to make this so?

Epilogue

58. Rikki asks at the George Floyd memorial, "Why are white people so afraid of us?" Why do you suppose this is? How has this trend been continued in our society?

Acknowledgments

My soulmate, Jeff Towle, told me that I was meant to write a novel, and I would not have taken on this work without his nudging. This story gained clarity as I supported my children in the Minneapolis Public Schools and took action to address racial disparities in education. Thanks to my daughter, Freesia Towle, and my son, Loren Towle, who embrace with me the rich beauty of Black culture and talk with their friends, family and community about race.

Thank you to my brother, Michael Joseph Beiser, who taught me to value books over television, and my sister Margie Beiser Lapanja, who urged me to boldly pursue my dreams while practicing self-care. This book is about them too, though they have a strength and power of their own beyond the scope of this story.

I have been blessed with dear Black friends who have allowed me to learn and grow with them in their sacred spaces: to elders Katie Sample and Mahmoud el-Kati, who schooled me in the grace and creative genius of Black people; to Rose McGee, who taught me the power of sweet potato pie as a practice for racial healing and action; to Titilayo Bediako, who invited our family to We Win's annual Kwanzaa celebrations; and to Ben Mchie for grounding us in Black history. Thanks to our Sweet Potato Comfort Pie® team for tending our community with caring and connection. Thank you to the Emmett D. Wise Community Center in Michigan City, Indiana for the community-building you've been doing since 1966. This story exists because of your work.

I have deep gratitude for all my dear BIPOC friends, models of resilience and courage; and for my white friends, who stand with me on the learning curve. I'm thankful for Linda Lucero, for teaching me to be a Kuwanyauma Woman. My spiritual directors,

Barbara Leonard and Latriste Graham, help me find what's sacred in everything.

Thank you to s.t.a.r.t. (students together as allies for racial trust) leaders and the YES! (Youth Equity Solutions) leaders. Your work has never been more important! Thank you to Cecilia Saddler and Teresa Taylor for taking educational risks with me.

To Phil Lund, Jackie Mosio, Burt Berlowe, and others at the Loft Peace & Social Justice Writers group, the early audience for my book. All early readers have kept the dream alive! Dee Sweeney and Bill Smith, your help with my court scene was invaluable. I'm grateful to Dr. Larry Mulhern for the information about nephritis. Thank you to Fran Pascal and Michael Stewart who hosted me in Golfe Juan, France so that I could write about race with James Baldwin close by in St. Paul de Vence. Thanks to Tamara Root, Walter Blue and Cynthia Cone for teaching me the cultural depths of language acquisition and understanding.

I am so grateful to Julie Landsman for polishing an early draft of the story and to Nancy Barton, whose editing brilliance lifted my work. Every step of the way, I puzzled through the themes of this book with my dear friend Lori Gleason. Thank you, Lori! A special thank you to my friend Jay and his pup Fletcher who have kept me humored throughout this lengthy process. I've also been blessed to explore the *literacy* of peace in our uncommon times with Paul K. Chappell, Shari Clough, Caren Stelson and Walter Enloe. A special thank you to Rebecca Janke, a master at putting peace literacy into practice.

Jo Ann Deck and Char Howard have been champions of my work, putting in extra hours to tend my book baby. You have both helped me transform this web of dark dreams into a bright and whole story.

To my friends who have triumphed from incarceration, including my dear friend Dorsey Howard: your faith and strength inspire me to put in my time. To Fr. Harry Bury and friends at Twin Cities Nonviolent for believing we can get to the root of this crisis.

I am who I am because of my parents: my dear father, Joseph Ryan Beiser, whose exemplary battle for friendship and justice took his life too soon; and to my mother, Alma Denyse Hughes, whose wonder for life is immeasurable. Thank you to my step-father Paul Hughes, whose steady love makes the world turn.

Finally, Angie Barrera, I am so deeply grateful for your lovely interpretation of the beauty that rises through the cracks.

265

Author's Note

A 2020 report by the Kapor Center for Social Impact on workforce barriers states that "75% of whites don't have any non-white friends in their social network."[i] In a Public Religion Research Institute Report from 2016, only 5% of whites have friends of color, while 8% of Blacks have white friends (Cox et. al., 2016)[ii].

While there are many great books that can enlighten white people like me on being a better ally, I risked asking myself the question, "What does it look like to be a better friend, to know deep in my heart that our joy and suffering (our sweet burden) are bound together?" What I found missing are narratives for white people that allow us to see ourselves living day to day with the humility and grace required to internalize the lived experiences and struggles of our friends of color. When we care deeply for one another—and know that we are threads together in the web of life—we will find our way to love and to a just world.

---

[i] "Tech Workforce Barriers." *The Leaky Tech Pipeline*, leakytechpipeline.com/barrier/tech-workforce-barriers/.

[ii] Cox, Daniel, Ph.D., Juhem Navarro-Rivera, and Robert P. Jones, Ph.D. "Race, Religion, and Political Affiliation of Americans' Core Social Networks." PRRI. Public Religion Research Institute, 3 Aug. 2016. Web. 03 Apr. 2017.

.

Made in the USA
Middletown, DE
20 April 2021